THE SCOTTISH THREADS

To Merville.
With Regards.
Lilian Comey

25/10/98.

THE Scottish Threads

Lilian Comer

The Book Guild Ltd
Sussex, England

My thanks to the Maritime Information Centre and W Laird Clowes' *The Royal Navy Volumes IV & V* (London: Jas. Murray, 1899 & 1900) for providing details of the Battles of the Nile and Trafalgar. These details form the basis of pages 254-262 in my book.

This book is a work of fiction. The characters and situations in this story are imaginary. No resemblance is intended between these characters and any real persons, either living or dead.

This book is sold subject to the condition that it shall not, by way of trade or otherwise, be lent, re-sold, hired out, photocopied or held in any retrieval system or otherwise circulated without the publisher's prior consent in any form of binding or cover other than that in which this is published and without a similar condition including this condition being imposed on the subsequent purchaser.

The Book Guild Ltd
25 High Street,
Lewes, Sussex

First published 1996
© Lilian Comer 1996
Set in Baskerville
Typesetting by Southern Reproductions (Sussex)
Crowborough, Sussex
Printed in England by
Antony Rowe Ltd.
Chippenham, Wiltshire

A catalogue record for this book is
available from the British Library

ISBN 1 85776 048 4

They say life is a tapestry,
Its threads both dark and light.
The threads may form our destiny,
Some seen; some out of sight.
Some threads so fine, yet others stout
They travel to and fro.
These bonds that bind us to our home
No matter where we go.

1

In the autumn of 1786, not far from the city of Glasgow, a sweet manufacturer, William McCall by name, nervously held his first-born, a son. His wife, Alice, lay on pillows wet with perspiration, her lovely face drawn with pain. The doctor departed, saying that he would return later, and left the local midwife with them.

'He is a bonnie laddie, but should he be as wrinkled as this?' William asked.

His wife sighed. A descendant of the Macdonald clan, she firmly believed that she had married beneath her.

In the year 1691 her ancestor, Macdonald of Glencoe, on a point of honour, he thinking it wrong to take an oath of allegiance to the English, delayed signing it until the last moment, then purposely went to the wrong place to sign. The following year, troops commanded by Campbell of Glenyon, the hereditary enemy of the Macdonalds, were sent to Glencoe and entertained there by them for two weeks. They suddenly attacked their hosts, brutally murdering the chief with 37 of his clan, and lifted their cattle, impoverishing them. This, Alice believed, was why she had had no dowry to speak of, and so had married a middle class tradesman. She groaned loudly.

The midwife took the child from his father, placing him in a crib at the foot of the bed, then pushed William out of the room. He longed to stay, but the door was firmly closed against him.

William McCall's family had not always been traders. His mother's family were an ancient and noble line of seamen who owned their own vessels, sailing with such men as Drake and Sir Walter Raleigh. Wives and mothers left on shore brought up their families alone, their menfolk absent for years sailing the high seas, risking life and fortune. It was little wonder women encouraged their children to lead less adventurous lives, but domesticity had scant appeal for the imagination of these young men.

Alice proved unable to feed her baby, and a wet nurse was found for him. The new mother developed a fever and her breasts became swollen and discoloured. The doctor applied a pump in an attempt to remove the congealed milk, seeming to delight in the loud screams of his patient. This failed. He then applied scalding poultices followed by hand-pressure to squeeze out the offending fluid. This, the medic insisted, was solely his duty, as his hands were stronger than the midwife's.

William, unable to endure his wife's screams, decided to seek the advice of Fiona Brown, who was renowned for her herbal cures among the poor, and the workers at William's factory.

A mysterious woman of indiscernible age, she had iron-grey hair, strange piercing, flecked eyes and a gaze which was unnerving in its steadiness.

No one knew where she hailed from, only that she was not local. It was Fiona Brown who provided William with the oils and flavouring for the medicinal pastilles he made.

Alice objected to the foul taste of the concoction that she had to take, and complained bitterly of Fiona, saying that she smelt and was dirty. However, within twenty four hours the new mother was sitting up in bed taking nourishment, her breasts back to their normal size and colour.

William spoiled his wife as he thought her to be delicate, and Alice wallowed in the pampering bestowed on her. She was soon entertaining visitors whilst languishing in her 'boudoir', as she now called her bedroom, or her 'salon', which had been William's bedroom until, to please her, he had relinquished it and converted it at her request. Alice thought it fashionable to speak a few words of French she had picked up from her émigré visitors. William disapproved of most, of these callers. The ladies 'la-la-la-ed', and males of questionable gender sported powdered wigs and grotesque paint. William hated the way they squinted through eye glasses at him as if he were a strange specimen. He found it offensive as they appeared to have forgotten the peculiar horror of the guillotine in the homeland they had fled.

William became concerned about the lack of interest shown by his wife in their child. The baby was slow developing and sickly. William asked Fiona Brown to look at the child, and within two weeks the improvement in the infant was remarkable. Fiona was persuaded to move into the household permanently.

Alice thought that Fiona should leave, however, and that the baby should have a proper nursemaid. Many nursemaids came and went, never staying long. The mistress took up most of their time by demanding that they should act as her lady's maids, and fetch and carry for her guests. Some of the men behaved very badly, making amorous advances to the young maids.

Despite Alice's objections, Fiona stayed. She had fierce scenes with the girls for she had to do most of their work and would frighten them with menacing looks, convincing the poor creatures she was putting 'hex' on them. It became impossible to find replacements as the nursemaids left, which greatly annoyed Alice. Fiona, however, had come to adore the baby, and as she attended mostly to him, was glad to have him to herself without interference.

She grew very possessive of Phillip John Thomas, as he was named, and he blossomed in her care. Most of the day the child spent in the warm, cheerful kitchen. When the weather was fine, Fiona wrapped him warmly and, using a shawl to strap him to her back, like a North-American Indian mother with her papoose, she would take him out to forage for herbs and plants.

By the time Phillip was two years old, he was watched over constantly by his beloved 'Yonna', as he called Fiona, and by the scullery maid, Florrie. Portly Mrs Read, the cook, would often pick him up and cuddle him as he toddled around, and bake him special biscuits in the shape of little men.

Florrie had been in the house just four months. She had been brought there by Fiona who, in the market place one day, had seen the little waif steal a loaf of bread and secrete it in the rags she was wearing. Fiona had followed the emaciated creature making her way through the dirty, mean alleys, until a burly fellow leapt from the shadows. The ruffian had started beating the girl with a cudgel, yelling that she had eaten his bread, for a piece of the crust was missing. Fiona had leapt at him, the shock causing him to drop his weapon. Picking it up, she had rained blows on his head and shoulders, screaming wildly that she would knock his brains out. Terrified, he broke away and ran for his life.

Fiona persuaded Florrie to accompany her home, where she and the kindly Mrs Read bathed her skinny, bruised body and gave her food. For three days, Florrie cowered in a corner of the scullery like a whipped hound. She hid the food given to her, eating it only when she thought no one was watching. On the fourth day, Phillip toddled over to where she crouched. Reaching up he started to feed her with his biscuit, then, placing his small hand in hers, he drew her to the fireplace. The child looked up at Mrs Read, 'She be told,' he said, meaning that Florrie was cold.

When Monday morning came, Fiona asked Florrie if she would help fold some sheets. Soon she was turning the handle of the big mangle, then she offered to clean vegetables. When illness beset the old woman who came to the house to do rough work and help out on wash-days, there was no need to replace her. Florrie was a godsend, Mrs Read told William. He gave his permission for her to stay on.

Now there were no nursemaids, and Alice thought Florrie far too rough and uncouth to serve her. Mrs McCall became frustrated, and felt desperately in need of a lady's maid. She had discovered that Fiona manufactured creams, lotions and oils for use as beauty preparations, and persuaded her to provide some for herself. Then she wanted some for her growing circle of visitors, who eventually came only for these and the free food. As demand grew and grew, Fiona provided less and less.

Alice was still determined to obtain a lady's maid, and planned to be extra charming to her husband. Again William was allowed to share her bed, having slept on his own since their son Phillip's birth. However, all her cajoling, pleading and making up, did not persuade him that a lady's maid was needed. William argued that his finances did not run to an extra servant at that time. Indeed, all her entertaining was already putting a strain on their resources.

Alice would not admit it, but she had grown fond of sleeping with her husband, and had come to admire the gentle manliness which made him so different from the stale-smelling, effeminate males who came to visit her. They rarely removed their face-powder from one month to the next, whereas William bathed often. He did this, he said, to remove the odour of the syrups and the smell of his factory. As his office was on a floor above and to the side of the workplace, he had a bird's-eye view, but was also a target for the fumes and heat that rose from the vats.

One September night in 1789, thunder rumbled, Alice snuggled against William, and their daughter Aimee was conceived. As soon as the pregnancy was confirmed, William asked Fiona's advice.

'Ye leave mistress tae us. Jes' tell she tae do my bidding, an' she be as right as rain. So wi' the little bairn.'

Alice objected to the doses of oil and herbal tea brought to her by a silent Florrie, who was in awe of the mistress. She stood her ground, however, making sure they were all consumed, for Fiona had said they must be taken with no argument. At first, Alice was embarrassed when Fiona instructed William how to massage his wife, and particularly her breasts, with aromatic oils, but it became an immense pleasure for them both.

When her time came, and Alice went into labour, William wanted to fetch the doctor, but Fiona would have none of it. Leaving William, she went down to the kitchen and brought Florrie back with her. Giving Alice a draught, Fiona then asked William to go and get Tug Wilson. Tug was a night watchman at William's factory who could turn his hand to anything. He often did odd jobs for the family. Fiona thought it best to send William for Tug, as he could look after little Phillip instead of Mrs Read, whose help she might need. Tug was also asked to find a way of keeping the master out of the way until he was needed.

In less than two hours William was sent for. He was thrilled to see his wife propped up in bed, a look of calm amazement on her face as she gazed down at the bonny infant suckling at her breast. Later, the new mother told her husband that when he had left she had felt as if she were in a dream. There was Fiona's voice telling her to push, the slightest of discomfort, and then their little girl was born.

Alice was soon entertaining again, thrilled at being complimented on how brave she was, and how enlightened to breast-feed her new offspring. The torture she had endured with her first-born she had made known to all, so revealing the unconscious reason for her lack of affection for her son.

Pretty little Aimee was over-indulged by her mother. No nursery for this little one; her cradle was brought into her parents' bedroom.

Phillip preferred to stay in the kitchen. A place was always cleared for him on the table where he could sort and draw the flowers that he had picked when rambling with Fiona. She, Mrs Read and Florrie, the scullery maid, loved the quiet, serious, little boy. His father never failed to come to him each day, when he would stop and take his son on to his knee, and look through his drawings. There was not a great deal of conversation between them, but William hugged Phillip often, enjoying the shared moments and the freshly-baked biscuits.

Alice was now more the partner he desired, but still very demanding. She insisted that while he was at home, he should spend most of his time with her, leaving never enough to share with his son in the kitchen. So William took Phillip fishing at a very early age, in order to spend more time with him, and was thrilled to find his offspring shared his love of the sea and ships. Tug Wilson, the watchman at the factory, often accompanied them. Tug was an ex-seaman and worked for Mr McCall as no one else would employ him because of his odd appearance. An unsightly scar from a sabre gash ran down the left side of his face, obscuring Tug's left eye. His right eye, many folks believed, was the 'evil eye', for this scar pulled the skin and eye socket to one side. But to people who really knew him, Tug was a most honourable and gentle person. When he worked as a night watchman he would share his fire and food with anyone, and never tire of listening to people's troubles, or of telling them exciting tales of his sea-going adventures. Of late, Tug had spent less time working at night and more as an odd job man, acting as coachman and taking young Phillip out in a boat. Phillip was an apt pupil. Tug taught him general seamanship, how to tie knots, and to read signs of the weather.

Fiona objected strongly to these boat trips, for she had less time with 'her boy', but was quick to notice how Phillip developed an appetite on returning home. She was also thrilled when he would allow no one to see the drawings he had done, before she had examined them. Thus Phillip spent the early part of his life in the company of servants, including the three who loved him.

Alice entertained her guests, hardly noticing her son, but her little golden girl, Aimee, she spoiled and over-indulged. Aimee grew quite fat, and when she stooped or bent over, she would pass wind noisily. Often, the child took food from the plates of guests, returning half-eaten morsels, then wiped her sticky fingers on their garments. Some visitors found this far from amusing. Even Alice grew tired of Aimee's antics, but never blamed herself for spoiling the child. Nor would she admit that Aimee was partly why visitors stayed away, but instead blamed Fiona for stopping her supply of potions for them. Fiona responded with sharp words and Alice threatened to dismiss her. Fiona just ignored her, however, and returned to the kitchen muttering under her breath.

Alice was convinced this muttering was a curse, and told William as much. He replied that she was being silly; Fiona was far too fond of them to wish them harm.

'She might be fond of you and Phillip, but to me and my friends she is rude and insulting,' Alice sobbed.

Later, William asked Fiona why she had stopped supplying the lotions to Mrs McCall and her friends. Fiona said she was getting too old to hunt for herbs, for 'folderols for such as they to titivate, especially stuck-up ninnies that know no difference 'tween fish and flesh.' William hid a smile. ''Sides, maester, it takes all my time fetching stuff for thy lozenges and things.' Fiona's sayings caused much laughter in the kitchen. William knew she meant the different treatment the children received from their mother and some of her guests.

William was very fond of Fiona; he knew of her love for Phillip. And soon Alice, too, discovered Fiona's worth and loyalty. Alice became depressed, becoming very impatient and cross with Aimee, very often slapping her sharply for merely touching her mother, or even her mother's belongings. The child sought solace and company in the kitchen.

2

Monday morning was busy in the kitchen of the McCall household. Boilers in the scullery filled the air with steam. A ridged rubbing-board stood in a bath of soapy water. One tub was placed under the pump to rinse out the suds, and another deep, barrel-shaped tub held a washing dolly. This dolly was made of wood, the base like a small stool with three thick legs. It had a long handle at the centre and was used for washing the large items like bed linen.

Wash-day was special for Aimee. She loved the creaking of the large mangle, the swish of was washing dolly, and most of all the bubbles.

One Monday, standing on a stool at the side of the deep dolly-tub, Aimee was having a grand time scooping out suds and blowing bubbles. Florrie went for more soiled sheets and did not see the child reach over, toppling head-first into the tub. Fiona saw it. The shock robbed her of speech, but she hurled herself across the kitchen. She was only able to pull the child partially out of the tub for, being so plump, she was wedged between the tub's side and handle. Mrs Read, dropping her tray of bread, shouted for Florrie to come quickly, frightening the girl. Florrie became hysterical, throwing her apron over her head. Mrs Read held the dolly one side, as Fiona, holding the child around her legs and waist, with great effort managed to withdraw Aimee, handing her to Mrs Read. She then took the little sodden body and laid it on the hearth.

Fiona collapsed into a fireside chair and found her voice, asking for something to wrap Aimee in as she lifted her, face down, across her knees. Turning Aimee's face towards her, Fiona forced two gnarled fingers into her mouth, shouting to Florrie, 'Ye stop skrieking!' She thumped Aimee's back, working her arms until the child spluttered and cried back to life.

Alice felt great remorse for neglecting Aimee, and weeping, she asked that the child be carried to her own bedroom. Fiona was again made welcome in Alice's room, after being completely ignored and forbidden access to her mistress's private quarters.

Mrs McCall now begged her to stay with her, and said how extremely grateful she was that Fiona was there, for she herself became quite ill when Aimee vomited and had diarrhoea, having to leave the room. Each time Fiona cleaned up the mess. Laughing, she confided to Alice that diarrhoea was to be expected. 'Don' ye tell a livin' soul now, but in cases of long bind, I do roll soap in a sugar-covered pill, and it always does the trick.'

After a few days of watching her, Fiona thought the much thinner Aimee was well enough to be left for a short time, so that she could go out to replenish her herbs. When Fiona returned she found the house in turmoil. Aimee was having problems breathing, and a doctor had been brought in to attend the child. Fiona rushed up to the landing.

The doctor ignored her as he addressed William coldly. 'There is nothing more to be done here until she reaches the crisis.' He was about to leave when Alice, seeing Fiona, dropped to her knees.

Clutching at Fiona's muddy skirts, she wailed, 'If my darling little girl dies, it is all my fault. You saved her once, cannot you do it again?'

'Ye will do nay gaied carryin' on like this,' Fiona chided.

Alice turned to William, sobbing and pulling at his clothes. Haughtily, the doctor suggested she should be removed from the sick room. William carried Alice into the room that had been her salon, which he had now converted back to a bedroom and study for himself. The doctor, dismissing Fiona with a wave of his hand, mixed a sleeping draught in water and forced it roughly between Alice's quivering lips. Then, without saying farewell or 'by your leave' he left abruptly.

Staying with Alice only until she fell asleep, William returned to the room where Fiona was attending little Aimee as she struggled for breath. The faithful servant was bathing the small fevered brow, cooing softly.

'Maester, we had best do something for the little wain if we don't want to lose her,' she said softly.

'We must send after the doctor for him to return,' cried William.

'Nay, maester, ye trust I' dinna ye?'

William nodded silently.

'Will ye bide wi' little lass till my return, doing that I ask of you, and tell others to do my bidding, wi'out question?'

'Yes, yes, if it will help our little one,' he sobbed.

Fiona left him stroking the tiny hand. Time and time again William checked his pocket watch, as it seemed that Aimee's breathing was becoming more laboured. Where was Fiona? It seemed a lifetime since she had left the room.

In fact it was less than 30 minutes later when Fiona came back, bringing Tug Wilson. Once again she had sent for him to attend to young Phillips's needs, and assist generally. Tug asked William to move to one side as he tucked bed-clothes around Aimee in order to lift her out of bed.

'I'll do that,' William insisted, lifting the child bundled in bed-clothes. He followed the pair, wondering if he were doing the right thing, for the little girl seemed to be suffocating.

In the kitchen, William saw bed-sheets draped on a clothes line fastened to the ceiling beams to form a cubicle. In the opening of the cubicle, a brazier with a kettle, its spout facing in towards the interior, sent out strong-smelling steam vapour. Fiona's truckle-bed had been wheeled in, and she asked William to lay Aimee upon it.

The damp sheets brushed William's face. He could not help thinking that this must be sheer folly, but in the past Fiona and Tug had proved their worth, and he had to place his trust in them.

It was then that he noticed Fiona had changed her clothing.

She now wore a long, white, cotton gown, very like a nightshift, and completely covering her hair was a white puddingcloth. Fiona asked him to discard the quilt and the bedding Aimee had been wrapped in, then placed her on a clean, linen sheet. She covered the child with another sheet, piling several woollen blankets on top. Fiona asked for Florrie and Tug only to be left to attend her, firmly telling William to keep everyone else away, including himself, unless sent for. Lastly, giving him a powder, she told him to be sure to administer it to the mistress before she completely regained her senses.

William felt weary, crestfallen and useless. Once again he was being shut out, as he had been when his son was born. All he could do now was pray that his little daughter would be spared.

During that night, the only people to sleep in the house were young Phillip and his mother. Mrs Read was dozing, sitting in a chair at the bedside of the mistress, but she was immediately awake when William tiptoed into the room.

Forbidden access to the kitchen, William had spent most of the night listening at the small serving hatch of the morning room next to the kitchen, where different odours of pungent herbs came drifting through. He tried to identify them. 'Was that camphor or oil of eucalyptus? That was certainly creosote.'

Straining to hear the breathing of his child, all he heard was Fiona issuing orders, demanding more water on the sheets and more fuel for the fire. It was almost dawn when Mrs Read came to him saying that Alice was stirring. William, remembering Fiona's instructions, asked her to go and see about some hot chocolate, giving her the powder given him by Fiona to put in it.

William fought off the weariness threatening to engulf him. Mrs Read brought in the chocolate and left. William poured out a cup and held it to Alice's lips. She drank it thirstily, and was soon back in a deep sleep.

Looking at his wife, so pretty in slumber, William felt a sudden dread at the thought of losing their little girl, or any of his family. He felt thirsty, too. Forgetting about the powder

Fiona had given him, he poured a cup of chocolate into the cup his wife had drained. Later, when Mrs Read came to bring him refreshments, she tried not to disturb him as she removed the cup hanging in his limp hand as he slept.

William awoke with a start. 'What was that noise?' He felt guilty at having slept, and realized it was someone knocking at the bedroom door. Stiffly and slowly he rose. Looking at Alice, he saw that the was still in a deep sleep.

The knocking became insistent. William snatched open the door, revealing the red-faced doctor, and a very angry Tug Wilson who protested loudly, 'He were not sent for. I did tell him maester, but no odds, he would come causing upset int' kitchen too.'

'Alright, Tug, you go back down, I will see to the doctor.' Ushering the irate man outside, William closed the door behind him and guided the medical man downstairs.

'In all my professional life, sir, I have never experienced anything like today, being ordered away from my patient by a woman no better than a fishwife. And to be told this was on your orders! What kind of household do you keep here?'

William apologized. As the hall clock struck three he realized, feeling woolly-headed, that it was now afternoon. He held open the sitting-room door and invited the doctor inside. The irate man refused a seat.

'Sir, witchcraft is being performed under your roof,' declared the doctor. 'You will receive my account, and I shall certainly be reporting the matter to the authorities.'

William felt a surge of anger. 'You dare to accuse my servants of witchcraft, these loyal folk who go without sleep and toil to save a child's life, when you would leave, saying there is no more to be done except wait for the crisis.' William tossed some coins on the table. 'Take your fee from that, sir, and a very good day to you.' Turning his back on the man, he summoned Tug from the hall to show him off the premises.

William climbed the stairs, his tall frame bent wearily. He returned to sit with Alice, who, mercifully, was still sleeping. There was a gentle tapping on the door and, tiptoeing to open it, he found Tug, begging his pardon and asking, could he come down to the kitchen. Thinking the worse, William blanched. Tug, seeing this, said quickly, 'Don' go 'specting miracles, sir, the wee lassie be a mite better.'

Breathless, William bounded down the stairs. Cautiously entering the kitchen, he thought to himself that it was no wonder the doctor believed witchcraft was being practised. The air was filled with fumes from the brazier, mixed with many herbal odours. In the dense cloud of steam hanging under the ceiling, Fiona's head appeared from behind the steaming sheets, damp tendrils of hair escaping from the pudding cloth, her wet clothes clinging to her boney frame.

'The fever's broke. The bairn is not out of the woods yet, but the Lord has seed fit to spare her.' She gave him a weak, tired grin.

William sank to his knees, not seeming to notice the puddles of water on the stone floor. The tears in his eyes could have been caused by the acrid air, but Fiona and Tug did not think so.

William, happy that Aimee was improving, was persuaded to eat something before returning to sit and doze at Alice's side. She remained unconscious for quite some time. On waking, she did not seem to fully understand what was being said to her, but by the time she was fully conscious, Aimee's condition had improved yet again. The child was then sleeping peacefully.

Alice insisted on getting out of bed to go and see for herself. Unsteadily she tried to stand, and would have fallen had William not caught her. He held her in his arms for quite some time before he sat her on a chair.

'Dearest, you had best get back into bed, and I will bring you news of any further developments.'

'No, Willie,' she said. He blushed with pleasure, for she had not called him by that name in a long time, but Alice was determined she should go herself to see how her child was. William brought a robe, helping her to descend the stairs.

The atmosphere in the kitchen had changed completely, for

here was a place bustling with life. It was still such an early hour, barely 7 a.m., just 16 hours since the doctor had left. The aroma of toasting bread made William feel hungry. Aimee sat on Fiona's lap, as she told her a tale of fairy creatures, whilst she swallowed spoonfuls of milk-bread sop popped into her open mouth.

Alice sobbed with pleasure to see their child almost well again. The whole household shared hot buttered toast. Aimee now sat on her mother's lap, whilst Phillip proudly showed his father his latest drawings.

3

There was a change in the months that followed. Aimee was still allowed to play in the kichen, but forbidden there on Mondays. Phillip would share his drawing materials with her. They often squabbled, but Phillip was always first to give in, much to Fiona's annoyance. Sometimes when Aimee was really naughty, she gave her a gentle slap. Aimee would then run to her brother for him to comfort her, then give her his best pencil or crayon. Fiona scolded him saying, 'Ye're not helpin' the bairn that way, frae aw she thinks her has tae to tae get her ain road, is skriek.' Aimee loved all this attention.

When Mrs Read was baking, she would give Aimee a piece of dough to play with. Aimee would roll this out with a small rolling pin Tug had made for her until it was as black as coal, insisting her 'cake', as she called it, should go into the oven to be baked. Mrs Read always contrived to have a piece of dough the same size and shape to exchange and replace this, diverting the child for a second while her original cake was thrown into the fire. Aimee would wait impatiently for it to cook and cool, then she would devour the bun as if she were starving. While this went on, Phillip had a respite from his sister's demands.

One day, Mrs McCall arrived during a baking session, and was horrified to see her little girl smothered in flour, her hands stained with dirt, crayon and goodness knows what.

She grabbed the child, attempting to carry her out, but Aimee kicked and screamed so loudly Alice had to release her, and ran out of the kitchen with her hands over her ears.

The scene in the kitchen when she had tried to remove

Aimee after a baking session, convinced Alice that the children were in need of someone to look after them, such as a nanny, especially when she heard that a distant relative of hers, a girl named Noani Burns, was looking for such a position. The girl had recently terminated her employment at a very grand establishment north of Glasgow.

In the following weeks, Alice and William had many heated arguments before he finally agreed to let her engage Noani Burns as the children's nanny.

The new nanny, because of her relationship to the mistress, thought she was far superior to the rest of the staff, and they took a great deal of offence to her attitude, falling out with her for her rough and indifferent ways towards the children, who appeared to be afraid of her.

Alice became bored now that few visitors called, and she believed that their absence was due to Fiona refusing to provide lotions and creams for them. She pleaded with William to beg Fiona to supply her friends again with beauty preparations.

Quite sharply, he told her that almost every day and many nights, people came to look for Fiona to attend their illnesses or to one of their family; besides supplying the oils and the flavours for most of his sweets. It was she who saw to all the medical needs of his employees and their families, and a lot of the fish and fowl they ate was given to Fiona as payment for her services.

William was also pleased that their home was no longer a haven for folk who often treated him like a usurper, and he welcomed the money saved on the refreshments that had constantly been served to them.

William, to cheer her up, told Alice he was thinking of taking her on a trip to London soon. She became very excited, saying that while they were there, she must have some stylish clothes made. William said they would only be staying a few days, therefore there would not be enough time for shopping for clothes, but he did not mind if the French seamstress who copied the very latest styles made up some new garments before they went.

Alice was a little disappointed, but soon cheered up when the seamstress brought brightly-coloured brocades and silks which made choosing very difficult. But everyone agreed that the pale green brocade with deep pink ribbons, for the dinner-come-evening gown she chose, was the perfect choice for Alice's fair skin and hazel eyes. When William said she could have the cloak of velvet, trimmed with Russian sable, and a matching muff that were illustrated in an elegant magazine, Alice declared she was in heaven.

A few weeks later, merrily they set off on their trip. Five wonderful days were spent going to theatres, enjoying all the sights and sounds, comparing the fresh country surroundings of their home to the dirt and squalor of parts of London they considered were even worse than the worst areas of Glasgow. Alice enjoyed the parks and the rotunda on the river. William paid two shillings and sixpence entry for each of them, but it was well worth the expense, he said, if only to walk and show off his beautiful wife, for she looked as regal and royal as any princess.

Noani started giving orders to the others when their employers were but a hundred yards from the house. She screamed at Florrie, calling her useless and stupid. Fiona glared at her, and told her to mind her manners. Noani then called Fiona a scruffy old cow, telling her to shut her blasted mouth.

Fiona retaliated, 'Don' ye dare talk tae I in that manner, and 'tis ye that wants tae shut thy mouth usin' language like that in front o' babes.'

Noani crossed the room, and snatched off Fiona's cap, twisting Fiona's thick, grey hair in the fingers of both hands. Holding on to it, she pulled her off the chair, down to the ground, then with her knee she thumped into the small of Fiona's back.

The children vainly tried to pull her away, screaming in terror. Poor Florrie was paralysed with fright. In the outer pantry, Mrs Read was cutting a joint of meat from a carcass of lamb when, hearing the racket, she rushed into the kitchen brandishing a cleaver, and forced Noani's fingers, one by one, to release their hold. The fingers came away with tufts of hair pulled out by the roots. Mrs Read, menacing Noani with the cleaver, shouted at Florrie to help Fiona, and pushed the snarling wench out of the kitchen. The cook warned the creature, on fear of her life, never to come in there again.

Now that Noani was not allowed in the kitchen, the children spent most of their time there. At first, this annoyed Noani, but not being too keen on work, she spent her time in the master bedroom, trying on Alice's clothes, jewellery and toiletries.

Quite a way off, Noani saw the coach returning with Alice and William, for she sat in the window of their bedroom, where she had been idling most of the day. Hurriedly removing the mistress's finery, she tidied the room before rushing down to greet them.

William was surprised that the children stayed in the kitchen and were not there to meet them. Mrs Read came. William sensed the strain between the Irish girl, Noani, and the usually robust and jolly Mrs Read.

'Where are the children, Mrs Read?' he asked.

'They be in the kitchen with Fiona and Florrie, sir. When ye and the mistress have settled, I will bring them to the sitting-room wi' refreshments that are all ready.'

Later Aimee, bubbling over with excitement, ripped away the wrappings from the beautiful doll brought her. Phillip, on the other hand, carefully undid the string and paper around the books brought for him. Alice sat on a high-backed chair on one side of the cheerful fire, with Aimee prattling merrily at her knee. Phillip, squatting at his father's feet, turned the pages with pictures of ships in his new book.

Bursting into the room, her face flushed, Noani declared that she had unpacked for Alice, not telling what she had mainly been doing: making a thorough check that no evidence was left of her use of their bedroom, and the mistress's belongings. William, feeling Phillip's body stiffen, was sure that was a look of fear on little Aimee's face when the nanny came into the room.

Alice came back from the trip to London feeling wonderful.

She thought Noani a treasure, for the Irish girl could not do enough to ingratiate herself. She massaged her mistress, dressed her hair and gossiped, agreeing with everything Alice said.

William was not fond of Noani, for she crept up on you when least expected, catching you unawares, and forever hovered in corners and behind doors.

Alice began feeling unwell in the morning, so William suggested she should see the doctor. Alice would not hear of it, remembering his rudeness on his last visit.

'Let Fiona mix me a tonic, she is better than any doctor.'

Noani was sent to fetch Fiona, returning indignant and alone. Venomously she told them, 'The dirty old crone refuses to come.' William scolded her, telling her not to refer to Mrs Brown in that way. But he could not understand why Fiona had not come when sent for, so he went himself to see her.

'Why didn't that uppity piece say it were ye wanted me, Maester, fer I would come aflying as ye knowed.'

William smiled, 'It is the mistress, Fiona, she is not feeling well.'

'Ah, too much cooped in her room she be. That be no good at all.'

William led the way to his wife and entered the room, but Fiona, seeing Noani there, hung back, causing William to think there was something wrong. Then he realized Fiona would not come into the room because Noani was there, and asked her to leave. As Noani left, Fiona stood well away from the doorway to let her pass before entering herself, carefully closing the bedroom door behind her.

After scrutinizing Alice's face Fiona grinned. 'Has tha been sick in the morning?'

Alice nodded.

Fiona asked William if she could have a glass tumbler. Opening the bedroom door suddenly, he almost fell over Noani crouching on the landing. Guiltily she rose and hurried to her room.

With the glass pressed up against Alice's tummy to listen, gently feeling the slight swelling, Fiona chuckled. 'I be almost sure ye are again wi' chil' lass.'

William beamed with delight. 'You must let Fiona look after you, dearest. And when the weather is warm, you must spend plenty of time out of doors.'

There was a faint tap on the door. Without waiting to be asked, Noani entered and crossed the room. Pushing Fiona to one side, she plumped Alice's pillow as she lay on the bed. Smirking, she said, 'We will have to take good care of you now that there is another little one on the way.'

William fumed. This girl had the cheek to creep back after he had caught her eavesdropping, and was stupid enough to give herself away. 'Where are the children, Fiona?' he asked.

'They be in the kitchen, maester.'

'Thank you, Fiona, would you please leave us for a little while. I will send for you later.'

When Fiona had left the room, he turned on Noani. 'I thought you were engaged as governess to my children, but they are seldom in your care or even in the nursery. I would be pleased if you would execute the duties you are supposed to. Now go and ask Mrs Brown to come back, and politely tell that lady it is I who requires her services.' William placed great emphasis on the words 'lady' and 'I' to make his feelings absolutely clear.

Tossing her head haughtily, Noani swept out of the room. A few minutes later Fiona arrived and agreed to stay with Alice while William, regretfully, left on an errand of great importance.

Noani did not come near, for she would not dare share the same room as Fiona.

It was almost lunch-time when William returned. While he was away, Fiona had persuaded Alice to get out of bed and sit at her dressing table to sample a skin preparation she had brought for her. As soon as William came back Fiona excused herself, leaving them alone together.

William placed a blue leather case on the table in front of Alice.

'What is it?' she asked.

'Open it and see.'

Pushing back the gilt clasp of the case, she cried out, 'Oh! William, they are beautiful.' On a satin lining, a string of pearls shimmered.

'These were to be your birthday present,' he explained, 'but we have to celebrate this occasion. I thought you should have them now.'

Later, over lunch, William asked Alice to try to discourage Noani from spending so much time in the bedroom.

'Oh, she is so clever at dressing my hair,' Alice wailed. 'You know we have had such difficulties in the past getting anyone to look after the children, mainly because Fiona frightened them away.'

'I know, but that was because Fiona thought Phillip was her special charge. But what of Aimee? She has become subdued and very quiet of late, and is never in the nursery or with that Irish woman, but in the kitchen with Mrs Read and Florrie.'

The next day being Sunday, William and Alice were having a late breakfast in the salon when Noani entered. If she had knocked on the door, the couple did not hear it.

William snapped at her. 'It is customary to knock and wait to be asked in before entering a room. What is it you require?'

Noani raised her eyebrows. 'I thought the mistress would like help with her toilet, or her hair dressed.'

'Why do you not attend to the duties you are employed for, and look after the children?' cried William. 'During the early hours of this morning, our daughter, Aimee, cried out. Fiona and Florrie rose to comfort the child, but I saw no sign of you.'

'The children prefer that idiot, Florrie, to put them to bed rather than myself. And in the daytime it is impossible for me to attend them, when they are in a place where I am forbidden to enter, being encouraged by peasants to ignore my every request and instruction.'

'Explain what you mean,' demanded William.

'It's that Fiona, she has undermined my authority,' Noani snapped.

William asked Alice if she knew anything of this.

She admitted she did. 'There was trouble in the kitchen while we were away. To avoid further friction, cook forbade Noani access there.'

William ordered Noani to follow him to the cheery nursery, where a fire crackled merrily, but there was no sign of life. Going down to the kitchen, they found Phillip quietly drawing at the table and Aimee lying on an old rug spread on the stone floor beneath the table, happily playing with her dolls. When the children saw Noani, Phillip jumped from his chair and Aimee crawled hurriedly from beneath the table. Both ran to hide behind Mrs Read's ample skirts.

William suggested to the children that they would be far more comfortable in the nursery. Phillip, peeping from behind Mrs Read, begged to be allowed to stay in the kitchen.

'But son, it is far better to play in the nursery. Why don't you and Aimee go there with Mistress Burns? I'm sure cook does not want you children underfoot.'

Mrs Read firmly denied this. 'They are no trouble at all, sir, 'tis a joy having them here.'

Fiona was not in sight. Noani made as if to pull Phillip from his hiding place. Florrie, washing up at the sink, speedily dried her hands on her apron and put her arm around Phillip's shoulder, as if to protect him.

'What is going on here?' demanded William.

'I told you, didn't I, that these children prefer the company of dirty, stupid, half-wits like that one.' Noani pointed at Florrie.

William, seeing the children were upset, grabbed Noani by the shoulder and steered her from the kitchen into his study. 'It appears, Miss, that our children sit on kitchen floors, preferring indeed, the company of menial staff whom you refer to as "stupid". I will, in future, keep my eyes on you, and you will learn to get on better with the staff here. My children's happiness and welfare are paramount, but as you are a very distant relative of my wife's, and I do not wish to upset her in her delicate condition, I shall not dismiss you. So, kindly mend your manners and ways.'

Chastened, Noani kept away from the kitchen staff and tried in vain to win the children's affection. Peace reigned for a time.

4

It was decided that Phillip should start his academic tuition at a boarding school on the banks of the River Clyde. The fees were 30 guineas a year for board and tuition and it was reputed to be very good. Phillip at first missed the friendliness and warmth of the kitchen and home, and even his sister Aimee.

His father came to visit him as often as his business allowed. When William was unable to come, Tug Wilson deputized for him. Sometimes, all three went out together. William loved spending these times with his son, enjoying the walks by the river. Together they indulged their passion for boats.

When Tug Wilson came, they would go out in a small boat and Tug would teach Phillip seamanship and how to tie knots. Tug would fish while Phillip sketched large ships at anchor, and asked about the family.

'They be fine,' Tug would say.

'How is Fiona, does she miss me?'

'Surely, Maester Phillip, they do all miss you, 'specially your sister. The wee lassie, alus do kiss I, tae bring tae ye. I tell her tae save her kisses till ye are hame, but I be pleased she do kiss an ugly auld cuss like I.'

It was nearing the end of term. Phillip had a feeling of excitement, longing for the warmth of the kitchen and Mrs Read's cooking. Most of all he wanted to see his beloved Fiona.

His father came to take him home in a phaeton. Quite a distance from home, Phillip thought he could smell the special dishes cook prepared. He rushed into Fiona's outstretched arms. Florrie giggled nervously. Mrs Read was beaming, and his sister, Aimee, demanded his attention. He was home once again.

William's aunt Agnes came to visit them as William, through pressure of work at the factory, and getting Phillip settled into school, had not been able to make his monthly visit to her. Alice was now in her third month of pregnancy.

The stately old lady commented that one could hardly tell Alice was pregnant, she was so thin, and asked her if she were eating enough. 'If this child should be another lass, her name, no doubt, will begin with the letter "A", for our family seem to favour that initial for females.' Alice said she hadn't thought of this before. She liked Aunt Agnes who, in age, was still beautiful. She had been much loved by her diplomat husband, their only unhappiness being that no children had survived to bless their union. They had travelled extensively, and then he had died in the prime of his life, leaving her a small income and many wonderful memories.

'Where are that young niece and nephew of mine?' she asked now.

Alice apologized for Phillip's absence, for he, not knowing Aunt Agnes was coming to visit, had gone out with Fiona. Alice sent Noani to bring Aimee. The child at first wept and struggled, but soon settled down when Noani was sent from the room by the aunt.

The old lady sat Aimee on her knee. 'Alice, I am not at all enamoured of that young person. She has an air of slyness about her.' Cuddling Aimee, the aunt whispered, 'You're not fond of that wench either, are you pet?'

Aimee fingered a diamond-and-emerald brooch that was pinned to the lace fichu around her aunt's shoulders.

'Oh, you like this bauble, do you?' Aimee nodded her head. 'Stand down for a moment, sweetling.' Agnes moved Aimee off her lap to stand in front of her, and unfastened the brooch, pinning it on the child's white pinafore. 'You might as well have it now as have it when I'm gone.'

Alice objected, saying it was far too valuable for a child.

'Let it be. If it gives the little one pleasure to wear it, that is all I ask, for it will not suit the shroud I shall soon be wearing.'

Alice told her that she hoped she would have many more years yet.

'Nay, my love, I have grown very tired of late, and have waited o'er long to be again with my beloved husband.'

Less than three weeks had passed when Agnes had her wish.

William and his young brother, John, settled their aunt's estate. The taxes took most of the money from the sale of her house, and what was left William arranged to be placed as an annuity for his younger brother, who was studying to be a doctor at the university of Edinburgh.

William and his brother were the only survivors of their branch of the family. The annuity helped to ease William's financial burden a little, as for more than four years he had maintained his brother, believing it was John's due as his share of the business left to William by their father.

Before their mother died, she had asked her elder son to look after and care for his brother, as he had looked after them both since his father had died. William kept his promise. Although the brothers were rarely in each other's company, they had great affection for each other.

At half-term, Phillip went to visit his father's factory. He gaggled at the sweet, sickly odours in the steamy air; the smell of sweating, unwashed bodies made him feel sick. Young children worked there. One swept sugar to the side of a table then into a sack. Another used a large scoop to shovel sugar onto the other end of the table where a woman, scantily dressed in rags, scattered it on the putty-like toffee before feeding it through a large set of wooden rollers. The child scooping up the sugar then stood on a stool, throwing ground sugar at the rollers to stop the toffee from sticking to them.

Men, stripped to the waist, stirred large cauldrons filled with steaming, amber liquid. In spite of the stained rags tied around their heads, moisture ran into their eyes, and streams of sweat running down their bodies lent their skin a striped appearance. Older children shovelled coal into the fires beneath the cauldrons. They stopped only momentarily when their employer passed them, men touching their forelocks, the women curtseying. Some young children hid their faces behind a woman's skirts, puzzling Phillip until Tug explained that maybe this was their mother, for whole families worked in the same place.

Word had spread throughout the factory about who Phillip was. Towards the end of the tour he was bravely managing to control the rumbling in his stomach, when he was approached by a little girl no bigger than his sister, Aimee, who had retrieved a much-stepped-on jujube sweet from the floor. She rubbed it on her rags and proferred it to him.

Phillip felt deeply ashamed as the vomit spurted from his mouth, not because of the grime sticking to the confectionery, or the grubby little hand that held it. It was seeing the child pop it quickly into her small, pinched mouth with such relish. He could not help comparing the difference between this little mite, himself and his plump little sister.

After the visit Phillip was a little distant with his father, wondering how a man so kind to him could treat other children in this way. He put the question to Tug when boating with him soon after. 'Why is Papa so cruel to other children, when he is so good to me?'

'Your papa cruel? I've never heard the like, for your faether, laddie, is the kindest man in the whole of Scotland, nay the whole world, that I know. What makes ye say such things, Maester Phillip?'

'Those children working in that horrible sweet factory that belongs to Papa. It was so terrible!'

'Terrible is it? Nay, yon place be heaven to some places. Why, there are bairns working underground that ne'er see the light of day, 'cept Sundays. Even then they hae nay time to see it, frae they are out on the refuse tips, picking fuel frae their ain fires, or else slaving for some farmer frae a few tatties. Folk that work frae Mr McCall & Son are indeed fortunate.'

They fell silent, each to his own thoughts. Phillip stared at the dull waters of the Clyde. Tug contemplated his fishing, sucking on an empty pipe.

There was panic in the house. Aimee had lost the brooch that Aunt Agnes had given her. Everyone searched, but to no avail. It was nowhere to be found.

A few days later, the adults were taking an afternoon rest, and Aimee went wandering. The door to Noani's room was open, and the governess was not there. Unable to resist it, Aimee entered, and first looked under the bed. Then she dragged a chair to a set of drawers. Standing on the chair she loosened the cap of a bottle of toilet-water, not liking the smell as it reminded her of Noani, and tugged a drawer open containing hose and kerchiefs. The bottle with the loose cap toppled over, and Aimee reached in the drawer for something to mop up the spilt liquid. Something sharp stuck to her hand, causing her pain.

Withdrawing her hand she cried out, as she was roughly grabbed at the back of her gown. It almost strangled her, and she wriggled so much the heavy chair fell over, landing with a thud on Noani's foot. The nanny released her hold of Aimee for a split second.

Like a frightened rabbit Aimee ran out of the room down to the sanctuary of the kitchen. In the passage just outside the kitchen door, Noani again caught hold of the screaming child. Florrie rushed to the rescue but failed to release Noani's hold, until joined by Mrs Read who pushed her burly form in between the governess and her captive. Glaring at Noani, she silently pointed the way back upstairs.

Florrie removed the brooch. The pin had dug deep into Aimee's palm and must have caused great pain for the little one who had held on to it so tightly. Florrie bathed and bound the wound, then she and Mrs Read both kissed it better.

During this time Fiona was attending to a birthing, as she called it. Mrs Read, and poor Florrie who seldom had much to say, were worried. They were faced with a bit of a problem when Aimee told them what had occurred with Noani, and where she had found the brooch. It would be most awkward accusing a relative of the mistress, especially as they had been heard so often expressing wishes the girl would leave. They were both convinced that their employers would think it was a plot they had hatched to get rid of the nanny.

Florrie wished Fiona were there, she would know what to do. And that Noani was afeared of Fiona, she thought. 'Mrs Read, that nanny, she doesna come nigh the kitchen, and she wonna dare gae in tae Fiona's things, would she?'

'What are ye thinking o' lassie?' asked Mrs Read.

'Weel, ifen we hide the bauble in Fiona's things, nobody would go nigh it, 'specially that woman, and bein' everybody do think it be lost, let it be stayed lost for a little while more!'

'Lassie, ye may look like a cabbage, but ye are nay green,' smiled Mrs Read.

The experience had tired Aimee. As she sat on Florrie's lap, Mrs Read asked her could they take the brooch and hide it away in a safe, secret place only they knew about. Aimee, loving secrets, readily agreed.

Next day, Aimee seemed to have forgotten about the incident. The bandage had come off while she slept, and she seemed hardly even to notice her sore hand.

A month after Aunt Agnes's funeral, Alice, although saddened by losing a favourite relative, had recovered quite well. But she was shocked when William suggested they should accept an invitation to an engagement party soon to be held at Greenock Manor. She said it was impossible; they were still in mourning for Aunt Agnes.

'Aunt Aggie would say that life is for the living, not the dead, my love. The French seamstress will have plenty of time to make you a gown, black if you want. You can carry it off better than anyone I know.'

'Oh! William, a ball gown in black, indeed! There has never been such a thing!'

On the night of the ball, Alice had to admit that the velvet gown suited her admirably. Her condition not at all visible, was hidden by the pleated apron on the skirt front, which became the back bustle. Her skin was translucent and clear.

Thinking she ought to wear some jewellery, she looked for

the ruby necklet and the diamond pendant and matching earrings Aunt Agnes had bequeathed to her. She searched and was unable to find them, so she put on the pearls William had bought her. Noani dressed her hair up in coils, entwined with seed pearls.

When he saw her, William gasped, 'Darling, you look magnificent, and you're wearing the pearls. You look –. You look –. Words fail me!'

Alice glowed with his praise. She refused the more strenuous dances because of her condition, but she was still the belle of the ball.

Removing her pearls later, she reminded herself that she must search thoroughly, first thing in the morning, for the jewels she had been unable to find.

Alice, helped by Noani, searched and searched to no avail. The missing gems were not to be found. Alice became flustered and quite cross, and was positive that Noani had confused her by looking in the same place more than once.

As the missing jewels were definitely not in her room, Noani said, 'We had better go and question that simpleton Florrie, for it is she who cleans the rooms. And she would not know the value of anything. She was a known thief before she came here.' Noani had somehow found out about the loaf of bread, no doubt by eavesdropping. 'And,' she went on, 'she, being little better than a senseless animal, should be kept outside with the horses and dogs!'

Poor little Florrie was happier than she had ever been, with food to eat, a corner of the scullery floor near the wash boiler, clean straw to sleep on, and the added luxury of some old blankets to pull over her. She was dumbfounded when accused by Noani, who kicked her bedding-straw apart, shaking the blankets.

Fiona was blazing with fury and flew to defend Florrie, who was being hit about the head by Noani. 'Ye wicked bog Irish, keep yer honds tae yersel'. This poor lass has nowt but the rags she wears, and the bed ye have defiled, and if ye dare tae, why not search my belongings?' Fiona dragged out her truckle bed.

Noani roughly pulled off the blankets and shook them one by one, then turned over the straw mattress to reveal Aimee's emerald brooch, as Fiona looked on, more amazed than anyone.

Noani insisted that Fiona's other belonging were searched, and tipped out bags containing herbs onto the table, where she spread them out, sifting them with her fingers. She found only dried herbs.

With a look of disgust, Fiona swept them up and threw them all into the fire as if they were tainted.

Alice complained she felt sick and became unsteady. She asked Noani to help her back to her room.

When they had left, Fiona gathered up all her belongings and said goodbye to Mrs Read and Florrie who wept bitterly, begging to be allowed to go with her. But Fiona told her she must stay to look after little Aimee and Master Phillip, in case the Irish woman should ill-treat them. Fiona asked them to be sure and tell 'her boy' that she loved him, and to entreat him not to think ill of her.

Mrs Read puffed up her rosy cheeks, 'Whilst I be around, no one will say ill of ye, Fiona Brown. Florrie and me do know who the thief be, an' we should ha' told ye afore of the bairn's bauble, but we forgot.'

It was only then that Fiona learnt how Aimee's brooch had come to be under her mattress. Both women pleaded with her to stay, but their pleas were in vain.

'I had best gae, for I'll not stay here being thought of as a thief, and ifen thet wench comes nigh me, upsetting I or the bairns agin, it will not be thievin' I'll be accused o', but murder.'

'Where will ye go, old friend?' asked the friendly cook.

'Awa' up tae Perth an' see my ain lass.' Fiona hurried to leave behind the two people who had become her friends, the one mystified, the other sobbing bitterly.

When William arrived home, Alice told him what had transpired. He was furious. Not for a second would he believe that Fiona was a thief. He rushed down to the kitchen.

'Where is Fiona, Mrs Read? I must apologize to her for her

gross humiliation.'

'She be gone some hours since, sir.'

'Gone? Gone where?'

'She said to Perth, sir, to her daughter, but I never heard talk o' any daughter afore. She said she could not bide where she was thought to be a thief, which I know that she b'ain't.' She wiped away her tears with the corner of her apron.

William consoled her and said he knew Fiona was not a thief, when a sound, like the howling of a dog, came from the scullery.

'It be Florrie, sir, she's been like that since Fiona left.'

Taking a light to the unlit scullery, William saw, in one corner, the huddled form of Florrie, fingers of both hands in her mouth, her face bathed in tears.

'Now, now, lass, don't fret. I will go after Fiona and bring her back.' William spoke softly.

''Twer my doing, sir,' Florrie sobbed bitterly.

'Your doing? Did you steal the jewels?'

'Nay, sir, it were I told the babe to put the bauble for safeness in Fiona's cot, for the Irish woman be afeared of Fiona.' Even speaking of Noani, Florrie's eyes took on the look of a scared rabbit.

William assured Florrie that no one was going to harm or chastise her, and persuaded her to come into the warmth of the kitchen and take a hot drink. There he asked Mrs Read to enlarge on what Florrie had said.

Mrs Read told how Aimee had found the brooch in Noani's drawer, and how the governess had given chase. 'Ye would have been proud o' the little wain, how she held on to that bauble like grim death. And young Florrie there, although she were in mortal terror o' that woman, she protected the babe wi' her own body, didn't ye lass?'

Florrie's sallow complexion coloured.

'But,' went on Mrs Read, 'that there Irish banshee be no match for me. No, sir, I soon saw her off.'

'But why should Florrie take the blame for taking Aimee's brooch?'

'Well, it was she who had the idea to hide it under Fiona's

mattress, thinkin' it were the safest place, for that nanny be afeared of Fiona, she thinkin' Fiona has the evil power. Them that are evil think evil o' others.'

William decided to go after Fiona immediately. Taking a lantern, he crossed the yard to call Tug, who now lived in the ostler's quarters above the stables, where he was on hand if Alice or the staff should need help. He was also more convenient when he deputized for William, when he was unable to visit Phillip.

Acting as coachman and handyman, Tug also tended the fruit, vegetables and herbs in the kitchen garden. Mrs Read thought he was a wonder, for no job was too menial for him. Once a week he took her into town to purchase provisions which were cheaper and fresher than when delivered to the house. She reckoned, even with supplying Tug's food, that housekeeping bills were down to less than half.

Out in the yard, William called to Tug who, hastily getting dressed, soon appeared at the top of the stairs.

'What be it, sir, be someone ill?'

'Saddle Blue Boy for me! Fiona has gone, and I am going after her to bring her back.'

'It would be better if I hitch the shay, sir, I could come across wi' ye. Two heads be better na one.'

'Stay, you may be needed. She'll not have gone far on foot and I can travel faster alone.' William was unaware that Fiona had been picked up quite near to home, by a tinker who was returning to his own home on the outskirts of Glasgow.

Riding through the night, William overtook the cart festooned with pots and pans, unaware that Fiona was huddled inside. He did not think of hailing the driver to ask if he had seen Fiona, for the driver slept on his seat, secure in the knowledge that the mule, plodding the familiar road, would take him safely home.

William was weary after working all day and being at the ball the previous evening. He decided to spend the rest of that night at an inn.

He rose very early the next morning to go to the factory, where he found Tug waiting for him. Excited, he asked if

Fiona had returned home, and was bitterly disappointed when told that she had not.

Tug explained that he thought it best if he came into town as he knew quite a few of Fiona's friends and acquaintances. 'I ha' often ta'en her tae certain parts, tae apothecaries and the such. If she be in this town and can be found, I shall find her.'

'Please let me come with you,' William begged.

'Nay, beggin' pardon, sir, it be best ye gae hame tae rest. It looks as there be no wind left in thy sails for journeyin' abroad.'

'No, I will not go home, but stay here and wait until you return, and pray to God that you will return with Fiona.'

Tug knocked loudly on the apothecary's door. A head appeared at the first floor window wearing a tasselled nightcap.

'What be ye a-wantin' at this early hour when folk are abed?'

'It be eight of the clock. Most folk have been about for hours. Ha' ye seen Mistress Fiona Brown this day or yesternight?'

'Nay, I've not see Mistress Brown for nigh on two weeks. What's amiss?'

'Nowt that should worry ye, but if ye see Mistress Brown, tell her tae get tae Master McCall's sweetie factory, 'tis of great importance.'

All day Tug searched, asking at all the places he knew Fiona visited, but she seemed to have vanished.

Fiona had friends Tug knew nothing about; friends who would lie and cheat for her, to repay her for the many times she had doctored for them and theirs, and they had had no means of paying in cash or kind. Many owed their lives to Mistress Fiona Brown.

She kept well away from places known to Tug and William, her stubborn pride forbidding her to stand and defend herself. Feeling deeply hurt, she went to ground like a wounded animal.

William and Tug were silent on their journey home, where a

very angry Mrs Read tried to comfort the weeping Florrie upon seeing no Fiona with them. Tug sadly shook his head.

Neither man could eat the food that was placed in front of him.

William asked that his food be served on the kitchen table. Tug felt great embarrassment at being asked to sit at the same table as the master, but William said they had a great deal to discuss. 'I know that Fiona is not a thief, but there is a thief in the house, and suspicions are not enough. We have to have proof.'

'I wish Fiona had not run off like that. She should know I would not think she could steal.'

'We know it be that governess, she has the smell of evil around her,' declared Mrs Read with passion. 'All along I did think there were sommat wrong about she.'

'What do you mean, Mrs Read?' asked William.

'Well, there was the washing, sir.'

'What washing?'

'Very grand hose and kerchiefs the mistress said did not belong to she. Then that wench came alooking for they, saying they be hers.' Mrs Read bristled. 'She did snatch them away from I, and make off wi' them pretty sharp. We ha' seen no hide or hair on, since. Those things were far too fine an' good for likes o' she, sir. I would gi' a bright shillin' to find out where she did get them from.'

William admitted to himself he did not like the girl, thinking she was secretive and sly. A plan had to be devised to prove Fiona's innocence. They must have proof. They must concentrate on finding Fiona.

'Could the Burns woman's belongings be searched, Mrs Read?' William asked.

'I be difficult, sir, fer each time Florrie gies tae see ta fire, and clean her room, she do stand o'er her and watch every move, so she must hae sommat she doesna want others tae find or see.'

'You might be right, Mrs Read,' said William thoughtfully.

5

William had many people search the area for Fiona, but to no avail. No one had ever heard her mention Perth before, or any living relative. They assumed she had invented the daughter in Perth out of bravado, to make them think she had somewhere and someone to go to.

The whole family, with the exception of Noani, were greatly upset Fiona could not be found. It was thought best not to inform Phillip that Fiona was missing, so as not to upset him. William delayed visiting him at school until the visit could be put off no longer.

Alice was unusually concerned when her husband returned from the visit, asking if he were ill.

'No, dearest, I am very worried about not finding Fiona, for we have not an inkling or a whisper of her whereabouts.'

'I, too, am worried about her, and miss her,' said Alice, for she again suffered a great deal of flatulence and discomfort. In the past a similar indisposition had disappeared after one dose of medication and a back massage from Fiona.

Wearily slumped in a chair, William asked Alice where Noani was, as he had not seen very much of her lately. Not that he had spent a great deal of time at the house!

'I have asked her not to spend too much of her time with me, and spend more looking after our daughter, but I fear the child does not like my cousin, and I have altered my opinion of the girl. I have discovered she can be hard, and has such a quick temper. I now wish she had never come to our home, and we could find a way to make her leave.'

William's face relaxed a little. 'Oh my dear, you have solved one problem for me.'

'What have I done?' asked Alice.

William crossed to the door to check there was no one in the hallway to hear them. Satisfied, he spoke quietly. He had spent, he said, a terrible day evading questions from their son. 'Your saying that you wish your cousin would leave has made it easier for me to speak, for I did not want to malign a relative, and someone I thought you were fond of.' He related the tale of the fine linen in the laundry, and Alice said she had some vague recollection of certain mysterious items of finery turning up in her washing.

William then told her how Aimee's brooch had come to be placed under Fiona's bed.

'Aimee told me,' said Alice. 'I thought the child disliked Noani and so had placed the blame on her, not for a moment thinking Fiona would steal from us, for I am sure that she would not.'

William was pleased to hear this, and asked if Alice had suspicions of anyone else.

'It once crossed my mind, for, as Noani pointed out, she was once a thief, that it might have been that poor creature Florrie. But you can see she adores the children, and I'm positive she might steal *for* them, but never, no never, would she steal *from* them.'

Both voiced their trust in Mrs Read, for she had been in their service many years and was seldom above stairs. The only time Tug Wilson had visited their private quarters was when Aimee was ill. Having heard of no other robberies in the district, the couple hatched a plot to uncover the culprit.

Early one morning Alice told Noani she had planned to go into town that day to purchase linen for the expected infant. But, as she felt unwell, would Noani please go in her place?

Noani hurriedly dressed in her Sunday best, the chaise awaiting her with Tug on the driving seat.

Arriving in the town, Noani demanded to be taken around the same streets twice, saying she was looking for a certain trader.

Tug pretended to be annoyed but, as he had been asked to keep the governess out of the way for as long as possible, and to try not to arouse her suspicions, he secretly took his time.

Alice had given the girl a list, with extra money for her to buy lunch. Noani was determined not to rush back, it being wash-day. With Fiona not there, she might be asked to help.

Tug waited patiently whilst Noani tried on millinery and other clothing. It was almost noon when she came back with parcels for him to stow away. Standing waiting for Tug to assist her into the carriage, she lifted her skirts, exposing a great deal of her leg. But Tug took no heed as he busied himself placing the items of shopping in the box of the driving seat.

With a wave of her hand, Noani ordered him to drive on.

In a mocking voice, Tug asked her, 'We'er to, me liddy?'

'That way.' She pointed forward. 'I will direct you.'

They stopped at a tavern. Tug knew it to be the hang-out of the worst type of villain, and asked Noani if she had made a mistake bringing them there.

'You mind your business,' she retorted, 'and I'll mind mine. Why don't you come and eat? 'Tis the best food in this rotten town.'

Shaking his head, Tug told her he had brought his own food, and would stay with the carriage and purchases to guard them. Driving away, he called that he would come back in a couple of hours to collect her.

William's factory on the outskirts of Glasgow was less than a mile away. Tug went to inform his master what time he and the girl would be starting for home.

As arranged, William left work thirty minutes after Tug had left him to return to Noani, then caught up with them a short distance from home. Pleasantly, William called to them that he would ride ahead.

Unwrapping the parcels, Alice complimented Noani, and asked if she would go to the kitchen to make them a cup of chocolate. Noani went reluctantly.

Tug, his eyes closed, sat on one side of the kitchen range. Noani thought he'd been quick doing his stable work. Mrs Read was shelling peas into a bowl on her lap. Florrie was doing some mending.

Noani ladled just enough milk for two cups from the large earthenware pot in the pantry, crossly throwing the ladle into the pot instead of replacing it on the rim by its hooked handle. Roughly, she pushed Tug's feet away with her own foot, sneering, 'A drink for her ladyship!'

William, who had not been in sight before, suddenly appeared, 'How nice, chocolate. Would there be a cup for me?'

Startled, Noani fished out the ladle she'd thrown to the bottom of the pan. Was it anger, the heat of the fire, or something else that caused the deep flush that spread over the Irish girl's face as Mrs Read told Florrie to fetch down that pillow that needed seeing to?

'Bring a sheet and tip those lumpy feathers oot, an' be sure yon stitchin' be better than those are sewn there the noo.'

Florrie almost fell over in haste as she spread the sheet on the floor and unpicked the poor stitching at the end. Holding the pillow bottom, she shook out the feathers. A leather pouch fell out, too. Gingerly she picked up the pouch, and handed it to William, who emptied the contents onto the table.

The jewels glistened in the lamplight. Alice's ruby necklet, her diamond pendant and earrings lay among gold shirt studs and a gold locket holding a portrait of a boy not unlike Phillip when a little younger.

Noani spilled the milk all over the hearth as she fled.

Tug chased after her and brought her back. William asked Florrie to go and bring the mistress down. When they returned, Florrie was carrying Aimee, and said the baby should not be left alone upstairs.

Alice said the locket and studs did not belong to them. Noani vehemently denied knowledge of the pouch. Mrs Read, looking as if she would pulverize the girl, angrily shouted that it was *her* pillow, and no one else but she had used it. William had to restrain Mrs Read as she threatened to beat the living daylights out of the wretch.

William asked Noani whom the locket and studs belonged to, but she remained sullenly silent until Mrs Read, armed with a fire-iron, threatened her. 'They come from a place called Bearsden, and I'll tell you no more.'

William suggested she should remain there until morning, under the watchful eye of Mrs Read.

'If you let me go now I'll never come nigh again. Please don't let me be with that old besom, she will surely kill me by morning,' Noani pleaded.

Noani was determined they should release her immediately. It was obvious the headstrong girl would divulge no more information, but William was concerned that the hour was late and, being alone, she would fall foul of footpads and cut-throats. If she insisted on leaving, he said, he would accompany her to the place she said she could go to. Tug said he would go with her instead, as William should stay with the family and rest.

As they were leaving, much to Tug's disgust, surreptitiously William slipped Noani some coins.

When Tug returned in the early hours, Mrs Read was waiting for him. While she was making a hot drink he declared, 'That wench would be match for any footpad or villain wi' misfortune tae meet up wi' her!'

'Where did ye take her, Master Wilson?' asked Mrs Read.

'Tae that rough Glasgae tavern where she were at earlier. The scurvy landlord greeted the little thief as if she were close kin.'

Alice, sure that the locket was of great sentimental value to someone, begged William to trace the owner. She was almost sure that 'Bearsden' was the name of the hall where Noani had previously been employed.

As it was the only clue they had, William said he would start there. Tug, who insisted on accompanying his master, thought he looked far from well.

There were only a few scattered bothies when they came to Bearsden, homes of shabby, grey men scratching a living with a few scrawny hens and sheep. William asked if there was a hall nearby, but they either didn't know or were too nervous to speak with strangers, and hurried indoors.

It was afternoon when they came to an old house shrouded in mist.

The pitted arched doorway held the remnants of an oak door which hung drunkenly from its rusting iron hinges. Where once a grand hall had stood, chickens scratched, and a pig routed in the rubbish.

Calling loudly and getting no reply, Tug banged on the broken door panels with the handle of his whip.

An old man poked his head through a hole in the wall at the side of the doorway. His headgear was a piece of old blanket worn as a turban. He shouted loudly, asking their business, and held a tin trumpet to his ear.

William could hardly understand the old man, but the place-name he repeated to Tug was not the one they sought.

The evening sky, the kind of sky the ancients had called a 'mackerel sky' because of its grey and orange marbling, suddenly darkened as they left for home.

Early next day, again they went to Bearsden and, by chance, met a man leading a cow on the roadway. They inquired if he knew of Bearsden Hall, and couldn't believe their luck when he told them there was such a place. It belonged to sassenachs, he said, and gave them directions.

The house was on a hillside, its stone façade appearing pale gold in the weak sunshine. Drawing nearer, they saw the colour was from the lichen clinging to the walls.

A footman showed William into a drawing-room. Its walls held panels of pale damask that matched the faded curtains. They were drawn, and the only light in the room came from the flames of the bright fire.

A lady of about Alice's age sat on a high-backed chair near the fire. There was an aura of sadness around her. She beckoned and asked William to be seated, her voice soft and musical.

William, sitting opposite her, was stunned by the fragile

beauty of her face, the extraordinary clarity of her huge eyes. Suddenly he felt uncomfortable in the over-heated room. He paused to collect himself before asking if Noani had been employed there.

'Yes, a very strange girl the priest brought to me, you see I am of the Catholic faith.'

William had noticed she was constantly fingering the crucifix around her neck.

She continued, 'I believe there was some trouble in the servants' quarters.' She sighed heavily before adding, her voice faltering, 'There was no longer any need of her services.' Some minutes elapsed whilst she stared sadly into the fire.

Leaning forward, the locket in his hand, William asked if it was her property, or belonged to her family.'

Lady Folland caught her breath. Her eyes filled with tears as she held out her shaking hand to receive the trinket. She tugged on a bell-pull to summon a servant, and whispered to the footman who came.

He left the room, returning within minutes holding a miniature of the child pictured in the locket.

Lady Folland clutched the two items to her bosom. Choking with emotion she excused herself, instructing her servant to give the guests anything they desired. With tears rolling down her finely-chiselled cheeks, she stumbled from the room.

The manservant provided William and Tug with refreshments, and what they wanted most; information. The miniature was of Sir Henry Darnley, a brilliant naval officer killed in battle, the exact likeness in the locket, a portrait of his only son. It was less than a year since the tragic death of four-year-old Henry Charles, the footman told them. It had almost sent his mother insane. All the staff said the death of the Darnleys' only child was due to the gross neglect of his nanny. The servant went on to explain that young Charles had developed a very heavy cold, and awoke frequently in the night, crying out for his absent father away at the wars.

Noani Burns, the nanny, had been left in sole charge of the child at night, his mother staying by his side throughout the day.

By the third day, the cold seemed better and the boy wanted to get out of bed. He was promised that, if he were good, he would be allowed up for a few hours on the following day.

Next morning, the nanny appeared in a panic, saying her charge was very ill. The child died of pneumonia later that day.

A manservant was convinced that, in the early hours of that morning, he had heard the child crying very close to his room. But he had thought he was dreaming, never having heard the child crying at night-time before. His quarters were in a different wing on the other side of the house, well away from the nursery.

A groom swore on oath that, just before dawn on that same morning, he had seen the nanny steal away from the stables, her clothing in disarray, followed soon after by the second footman, Jimmy.

All the staff heard the quarrel between Jean, the maid, who was betrothed to Jimmy, and Noani, and most witnessed the fight between the two women, who fought like dogs. Jean screamed that Noani had stolen the bracelet that Jimmy had given her as a betrothal gift.

There was no proof, just suspicions, until Jimmy, feeling remorse at the death of the child, confessed he had spent the whole of that night in the stable with the nanny. He wanted to end the affair and tried to avoid Noani, but he was asked to play along with her for a little while.

Jean, his betrothed, forgave him, and was agreeable to this plan for she wanted revenge, and was sure Noani had stolen her bracelet.

Other things, too, had gone missing. As nothing was found, the coachman told of the day he had taken the nanny to get medicine for the child in Glasgow, and she had made him take her to a tavern where the landlord was a well-known fence for stolen goods. He was also in league with the press-gang, among other evil practices. The nanny had gone in with a bag, the coachman remembered, but had come out without it. She was seen later, thinking she was unobserved, counting money.

Jean and Jimmy kept up the pretence that they had broken off their engagement. The staff were disgusted with the nanny's brazen behaviour, flaunting herself with Jimmy and taunting Jean, without a scrap of remorse or sign of sorrow at the death of her little charge.

The keeping of the betrothal bracelet was Noani's undoing. At every opportunity the nanny, especially when there was someone watching, would throw her arms around Jimmy until one day, pulling her arms away and telling her he had work to do, he felt the bangle under her sleeve, and held on to her, calling for the butler.

The staff held a private tribunal. All voiced the opinion that she was a thief and a murderess, and forced her to leave the house.

After hearing the story, Tug said that he'd known she was a bad 'un. William was grateful that the things stolen from them could be replaced, and that *they* still had both of their children, one thanks only to the skill and love of the wronged Fiona.

He made a vow that, no matter how long it took, or what it cost, he would find Fiona and bring her home.

William and Tug thanked the servant and expressed their wish to bid his mistress farewell. He led them to a tiny chapel where, with head bowed, Lady Folland knelt at the altar clutching the locket, the miniature and the rosary. They asked the manservant to pass on their respects and crept out, leaving her to her devotions.

On arriving home, William told Alice all they had found out about Noani Burns. It was imperative that they should find Fiona, he told her. He would set off once more to look as soon as arrangements could be made.

Tug again begged to accompany him. 'Fiona's been a friend to I. It would be an honour coming we' ye, sir.'

Alice told William she would prefer it if Tug went with him. She would pray they found Fiona quickly, for she could not bear the thought of confinement without Fiona there to see her through.

Arranging for his cousin, Robbie, to take charge of the factory, and a young man called Stephan to take over Tug's duties, William prepared to start his journey.

Mrs Read packed enough provisions to feed an army, swearing that if she got her hands on the 'Irish varmint', as she called Noani, she would beat her within an inch of her life.

Florrie wept with joy that there might be a chance Fiona would be coming home. She and little Aimee missed her sorely.

The two men set off in the direction of the town of Perth.

6

Arriving at Perth, they asked for an apothecary, thinking Fiona might be doing some doctoring, and need to replenish her stock of herbs.

Their hopes rose when he told them he knew of such a person who had lately become a customer of his. They were soon dashed, however, when they found the person whom he had directed them to. She was a dirty, old gypsy woman who spat at them for not giving her money, screaming curses after them until Tug went back and said something to her that made her retreat into the wagon, clutching her rags about her head and screaming.

They spent nights at inns, where William questioned the locals. One evening, an old man claimed to remember Fiona. 'Man, she be deed mony a year, she bein' older than I.'

'That cannot be the Fiona Brown we seek, she was alive a short while ago,' said Tug.

'Fiona Brown, nay, that were not her name, 'twere McCready. Didna the daft auld besom hae a small chil' wi' her, and kept a-searchin' for another Fiona? She were off her heed!'

Ordering supper, William paid the landlord for a dram for the old fellow, and went to sit near the fire.

Tug stayed to talk with the old man, then went to join William at the fireside, telling him he had not wasted his money buying a dram for the old man, for he had something interesting to tell that might be of use to them.

Next morning Tug led William through mean, narrow streets where the stench was sickening. Rats scuttled in open sewers as they dodged slops thrown from above, and the clutching hands of ragged urchins.

Turning into an alley littered with rubbish they stopped at a shabby, dirt-ingrained door. Tug knocked a few times. Receiving no reply he called out, 'Helen McCready, be ye there?'

A head of matted, unkempt hair appeared at the window above the door, the face beneath the hair showing the ravages of the life she had chosen.

'Who be calling at this ungodly hour?' This was Helen, or Nellie McCready as she was now called.

Tug, standing close to the door, was obscured from her view by the deep window sill. She could hardly see William.

'What can I do for ye, me fine laddie, a bit o' fun, eh?' She touched the side of her nose with a badly stained finger, winking her eye.

William shuddered when she opened the door and they were invited to enter the hovel. He felt physically ill as the unclean smell wafted towards him. A pile of empty gin bottles and rotting food had been thrown under, and lay on top of, the filthy table, and half-burned rubbish smouldered in the hearth.

The woman leered at him, her stale breath forcing him to turn away.

Steeling himself, William asked if she knew Fiona.

'Know her!' she almost spat. 'I know the evil faggot, she be me mother.'

This crude creature could not be Fiona's daughter, thought William. Fiona had an odd turn of phrase, but crude she never was. The smells made William retch as he rushed to the open door.

'Ye leave this, ah, *lady* tae I,' Tug told him.

'Weel I suppose ye be better than nought, me little Toby jug,' said the woman as she sidled up to Tug in a familiar way.

'Now, we will hae nothin' o' that,' countered Tug, 'what I seek is information. If Mistress Brown be thy mother, where be she the noo?'

'We'er be she tha noo, I no ken, and no care, for it was she who deserted I, leavin' me with a daffty woman when I was a babby. She called I a dirty whore, expected tae feed and house she, frae nothin'.'

Tug thought Fiona was right about, 'dirty'. 'Filthy' would be more like it.

The woman went on, 'I dinna care if she be deed in some gutter, forget her, and call in yer friend tae share a dram and a little company wi' me.'

Disgusted, Tug threw coins on the cluttered table and left to join William.

Outside, William was being propositioned by a woman younger than the doxy they had just left. She was gripping his arm, telling him it was foolish and unwise to wait for Nellie, for she was believed to have the French disease, and born of murderous kin.

Tug spun her round, releasing her hold of William. He demanded to know what she knew of Nellie NcCready.

'What do I get out of it, little gargoyle, if I tell thae? Come awa tae my lodgin's, 'tis not far.'

'Ye can see my friend here is far from well. We were told we would find a woman who could supply some medicine for him, that lived here,' said Tug.

'Ah, ye mean Fiona! But she be gone, chucked out by that evil bitch, Nellie.'

'Do ye know where she be, or who might know where she be?'

'Nay, but there be my friend who do know the history of Nellie, and her mother, for she says her mother, Annie, were best friend to Fiona Brown.'

Although excited, William, not wanting to go to any premises vaguely like the ones they had just left, asked if a meeting could be arranged in more pleasant surroundings.

The Three Keys coffee house at noon was agreed. At 1.30 p.m. Moll Green and another of her kind sauntered in.

Moll Green introduced her friend as Mistress Betty Floyd, and suggested, as both were hungry, that they should have a small repast. Between them the two devoured an enormous dish of roast beef and potatoes, washed down with two large tankards of porter.

The room was crowded, the air thick with smoke, so William chose a table near the open door. Moll Green called for more drink, hailing men passing outside to come and join them.

'Ye will ha' nae maer, until we get some information,' said Tug, testily.

Moll Green rose unsteadily, 'Come awa, Bett, seems these fellows don' know how to treat a lady.' She staggered out alone.

Elizabeth, commonly known as Betty, stayed. Her thin, wistful face had the look of someone lost.

'Ye were askin' o' Mistress Fiona Brown, mother to Nellie McCready. I know a deal o' Nellie for she lived along o' us like my sister, but little o' her mother. My mother once told me Fiona Brown had had a tragic life.'

William begged her to tell them what she knew.

'When I was little, afore me mother died, Nellie and her granny came tae live wi' us. Nellie was very bitter, she thinkin' her mother, Fiona, had deserted her, but my mother said this was not true. Fiona loved her family, and must ha' be dead or deranged for her not tae come back tae them.'

Betty told them how her mother, Annie, had met Fiona when she was a young girl, when they were all fleeing after a terrible battle, and how Fiona had worked with her mother, and fallen in love and married a wounded lad they had saved from death. When Nellie was a young babe, Fiona and her husband, with Fiona's simple-minded mother, had brought a dwelling from Annie, which she had inherited.

Tug asked her could she take them to this dwelling.

''Tis not there anymore, 'twas burned tae the ground by a madman, they say, the same demon did killed Fiona's husband and stole away her feeble-minded mother, along wi' the bairn, Nellie.'

When asked if she would accompany them to this place she said she was not well, and much fatigued. Tug felt a wave of pity for this frail creature, and was glad that at least she had partaken of a good meal that day. Going as far as the edge of town she pointed to the hills, and a place called Scone.

Before parting, William insisted on giving her some money. A few weeks later, some of this money paid a doctor for closing the sad eyes of Elizabeth Floyd, who had died of consumption.

Travelling for a few miles away from the town they turned off as instructed, and came to a valley and the moss-covered shell of a building.

Tug was telling William not to build up his hopes, when they saw the figure stooping near a pile of stones. Jumping down, William raced towards her, with Tug following him.

She appeared unaware of them until William gently touched her shoulder. William and Tug went down on their knees beside her, at what appeared to be a cairn, where fresh wild flowers had been placed.

'Fiona, dear friend, we have been lucky finding you and have come to take you home. You have been misused, misjudged, and sorely missed.'

'Maester, ye'll no want the likes o' me in the house. Leave me here, where once I was happy and loved.'

'You must come home with us, to folk who need you, grieve for you and, indeed, love you very much.'

William and Tug, each taking an arm, helped Fiona to her feet, for she was very unsteady. Both men thought she looked so frail, and seemed to have aged. She asked them to help her to the ruins so she could collect her meagre belongings, which were in the rough shelter of bracken and branches against an inner wall.

Tug drove the chaise slowly, occasionally glancing back at her. Evening was approaching when William suggested they should stop at an inn. Fiona whispered not to stop at Perth: the place held nothing but shame for her.

At Dunblane, outside Stirling they stopped, asking for rooms at a tavern. Fiona said she did not need a room, only to sit on the settle near the cheerful fire. Tug said he did not want a room, either, and would sit keeping her company. Fiona just stared into the flames without looking away to accept the food offered her. Tug told William to go up to his bed and he would look after Fiona.

Next morning, she refused breakfast of hock of ham and eggs. William begged her to eat a little bread and honey with a dish of milk, and join them at the table, but she remained where she had spent the night and ate alone.

On the homeward journey, William and Tug did not question her, but as William wrapped a warm rug around her, as if flood gates had opened, she poured out the story of her early tragic life.

Their arrival home was met with much jubilation. Mrs Read held the corner of her apron to her wet eyes. Florrie cried out with joy at having Fiona back, eagerly showing her the new clothes provided by the mistress. Aimee hung tightly to her ragged skirts.

It was all too much for Fiona. Her knees buckled under her. William caught her just before she fell, and carefully carried her up to the room Noani had vacated, which Alice, Mrs Read and Florrie had prepared for her.

Alice was ashamed she had not made more of an effort to prevent Fiona from leaving, and bitterly blamed herself for bringing Noani into the house.

Fiona sorely needed the garments Alice had provided, as the ones she wore were threadbare. New ones had been made with great care by Florrie under Mrs Read's tuition. Florrie had swelled with pride when the mistress complimented her, saying the sewing and garments were fine enough for any lady in the land.

William had lain Fiona on the clean coverlet of the bed, and asked Mrs Read and Florrie to do all they could to make her comfortable. No expense was to be spared, he said, before he and Alice left the room, taking Annie with them.

When William returned later with the doctor, Fiona had been carefully sponged down with warm water perfumed with rose-water, then her thin torso had been dusted with the expensive talcum powder Alice had given them.

The young doctor was quite concerned, for she lay still, a death-like pallor on her countenance above the lace-trimmed night shift. Florrie kept vigil at the bedside all through the night, smoothing back the grey hair, constantly changing kerchiefs damped with cologne water, and wetting the dry lips with lime juice-water.

The day after Fiona had been brought home, Alice relieved Florrie at her bedside. Mrs Read and Tug between them looked after Aimee and also shared Florrie's household chores so she could be constantly at Fiona's bedside. There she stayed, refusing to take a rest.

William went to visit Phillip, dreading the very thought of it. He told the boy briefly what had transpired. Phillip pleaded with his father to allow him to come to be with Fiona. William thought if Fiona should die, Phillip would be inconsolable, and would never forgive him, so he decided the boy must come home.

For three days, father and son kept vigil by Fiona's bedside, picking at the food that Alice and Mrs Read insisted they eat. They only left the room under pressure, for Mrs Read and Florrie to change the bed linen and see to the invalid's toilet.

Mrs Read firmly ordered them to go and attend to their own ablutions, but Phillip was soon back, holding the blue-veined hand and pleading with Fiona to open her eyes.

It was noon when Mrs Read came with a tray of sandwiches and hot soup. William and Phillip sat on chairs facing each other, with the tray balancing on their knees, when a weak voice was heard begging for a drink. In the excitement the tray crashed to the floor.

William called for more soup and was surprised how quickly Florrie came into the room. Florrie had never been far away from the bedroom door. Mrs Read swore their staircase and landing must be the most polished in the land!

'Please let me feed Fiona, Father,' Phillip begged. Florrie craned to see as she mopped up the spilled food from the tray.

William, knowing Florrie's devotion to Fiona, told her that as soon as she had finished, she could take over from Phillip. His son, he said, was in sore need of a wash to restore his unkempt appearance.

The mopping-up was done in record time, as was Phillip's freshening-up.

William eagerly went to tell Alice and Aimee that Fiona had regained consciousness, and was taking a little soup. They had both been in the drawing-room when the tray fell and, fearing the worst, had been afraid to come out.

Mother and daughter wanted to rush up to see Fiona, but William asked them to leave it for just a little while so Florrie and Phillip could be alone with her.

After two weeks of careful nursing, Fiona wanted to get out of the bed she said was too grand for her.

Phillip, deeply proud of his parents' actions, protested loudly that it was nothing of the kind, for she was part of the family, and if there was anything more she required, all she had to do was ask.

'Begging pardon, there do be summat. This room be large and grand, and I be sure Florrie be cold and lonely in the scullery.' Florrie still slept on straw with tattered blankets for covering.

'What a good idea, why didn't we think of that before!' said Alice. 'I really don't know how we could have managed without the girl while you were away, with that Noani gone. It is she who has looked after Aimee, seeing to all her needs as if born to it. Our little Aimee adores her.'

Fiona's truckle-bed was brought. Florrie thought she was in Heaven, for never before had she had such luxury and fine clothing, with even a drawer and cupboard of her own to keep them in.

Florrie's moving in with Fiona pleased young Aimee, as the nursery was next door. When the wind howled, when it thundered, or even when she had nightmares, Aimee would climb into Florrie's bed until Florrie rose in the early hours to go about her daily chores.

Minutes after Florrie had left the room, Aimee crept over to Fiona's bed to climb up and snuggle in the crook of the old woman's arm, until Florrie came back to wash and prepare both of them for the day.

Alice suggested another nursemaid should be engaged now that a new baby was on the way, but all the staff protested loudly, saying that they would work twice as hard, and twice as long, rather than have another such as Noani in the house.

Fiona wanted to resume all her duties and go out foraging for herbs for the factory and her medicines, now that she was allowed to do a few light kitchen duties.

William would not hear of it, arranging with the apothecary to provide the herbs she required. She accepted this on condition that when the chemist could not supply the roots and plants she required, and the weather was suitable, she would be allowed out.

William eventually agreed, but only if she were accompanied by someone. Phillip insisted it should be he who went with her, but became quite cross when Aimee wanted to accompany them. William scolded him for being selfish with his little sister, and upsetting Fiona.

Phillip had been home from school for more than five weeks, and William was concerned he would fall behind with his studies, to he told the boy his being at home was putting an extra strain on the already overworked staff, and unwillingly, Phillip returned to college.

7

Phillip was very slow settling in at the college. On his next visit, William was called in to see the headmaster, who said the lad was academically far behind students of the same age. The only subject he was good at was Art, and many times he had missed lessons and meals, especially breakfast.

Phillip would get up very early to go down to the river with his sketch-pad, wandering oblivious of time, and was often seen with rough seamen. This was thought dangerous, for the boy always had coins in his pockets, and murder had been committed for a few pennies, or even a pair of boots.

Like most boys of his age, Phillip's imagination was fired by tales of battles with the French, and his excuse was that he needed to study ships, and talk to seamen to learn about them, for his intention was to join the Navy.

His father told him if this was his wish, it would be far better to study to become an officer, for there were many ordinary seamen, but there was a great need of good officers. Phillip tried hard to catch up with his studies but Mathematics foxed him.

The Art master, Mr Bruce Peel, also taught Geography. All the boys liked this young master for he made lessons interesting. Mr Peel had an absorbing hobby, Astronomy, and sometimes invited a few boys to study heavenly bodies through a home-made telescope. Phillip was one of these boys, and he soon became fascinated.

Battling with extra studies and viewing stars at night, the boy had little sleep. During an Art class Mr Peel caught Phillip napping and determined to find out why he was so fatigued.

On discovering the reason, he started coaching him privately in Mathematics.

Phillip did not have much time for wandering abroad on his own, but as Mr Peel loved being in the open air as well, when it was fine, he and Phillip would study out of doors, and sometimes sketched.

Bruce Peel encouraged Phillip, thinking he had great talent for drawing. The caricature sketches he made of old sea dogs, and people hanging around the waterfront taverns, were excellent.

Tug Wilson came to visit Phillip in place of his father, and immediately took a liking to Mr Peel. William had told Tug about the concern for Phillip's welfare, so Tug went to old 'salts' who knew and had served with him, and asked them to keep an eye-out for the lad. Bruce Peel became very friendly with these old salts and grew to respect them.

Phillip's caricatures and the improving of his Mathematics were to alter the rest of his life. Life at the McCall home was almost back to normality.

It was Sunday, and Alice had great discomfort. William decided to stay with her, so Tug went on his own to visit Phillip.

By mid-morning, Alice was in pain, so William went down to ask Florrie to stay with her while he went for the doctor.

Fiona was coming in from the garden where she had been picking herbs Tug had grown for her. 'It not be time for the mistress yet, for another six weeks or so. Let me look at her first, maester, afor ye bring any doctor,' said Fiona.

William argued he thought she was not yet fit to look after anyone, but Fiona was on the staircase and in the bedroom before him. On receiving Alice's permission, she gently pressed her extended abdomen.

Florrie, following them upstairs, hovered in the doorway. Fiona told her to go and look to the bairn, Aimee.

'Maester, will ye bring a wine glass wi' nae foot?'

William brought her a tumbler which she placed on Alice's belly.

Chuckling, Fiona told Alice, 'It be a bad case of colic. Hast a dram o' brandy or whisky in the hoose, maester?'

William said he had whisky.

'Ask cook tae make a toddy, and if she would please fill stone warming-bottle with hot water!'

Alice pulled a face drinking the toddy, holding the comforting bottle to her as she lay on her side. Fiona rubbed her back, telling William he looked as if he could do with a dram himself, and be best away to get it. He was pleased to have Fiona back even if she ordered him about.

Alice blushed deeply as she passed wind. 'Oh! Fiona, what must you think of me?'

'There be more room out tha' in,' laughed Fiona. 'Passing wind be natural gas tha' canna get awa', and causes pain.'

William's brother, John, came visiting. He was four years younger than William and in his final year at the Royal College of Medicine in Edinburgh. He was fully aware his bother longed for a maritime career but had given up his dream to take over the family business when their father died. In less than a year their mother had died also making her elder son promise to look after his brother.

John admired William immensely, knowing it was more than dreams his brother had sacrificed, so that he could become a doctor.

Alice told her brother-in-law of her ailments, and Fiona's treatment. He was impressed and advised Alice to take plenty of rest and the advice of her resident physician, Fiona.

It was late September. Blood pressure and swollen feet made Alice take her brother-in-law's advice and she rested, but suffered bouts of extreme boredom.

Fiona taught Florrie how to massage Alice when she had stiffness or flatulence, as Fiona soon got out of breath with the least exertion. At first, Alice complained that Florrie's hands were too rough, so Fiona made a mixture of coarse salt and oil, which Florrie rubbed into her work-stained hands each morning after her work. This smoothed the roughness away, and also removed the worst of the stains.

Fiona sat and talked to the mistress during the massage, telling how lately she had had very little need to go foraging, for Tug had brought the roots, seeds of the herbs, and plants that she needed for her flavourings and medicines. She had no need to go far from the house, as most grew in a patch he tended for her.

If she needed anything that grew further afield, such as the bark of certain trees, Fiona would show Tug a sample, or do a drawing of the leaves of the tree. As she did not know the correct names of plants, only what they were called in their own locality, drawings were much less confusing.

Not normally a great conversationalist, Fiona tried to distract Alice by describing how the trees had changed their colours to many shades of gold, red and green, and were beautiful to behold in the gentle autumn sunshine.

Alice begged William to be allowed outside, and Fiona told him she could see no harm if the weather were fine, and the mistress wrapped up warmly. Alice was helped downstairs, and she and Fiona took walks to where Tug burned dead leaves and garden refuse. Aimee, attended by Florrie, accompanied them.

Florrie would hastily pull 'her babby' away as Aimee threw twigs on the flames. Fiona stood well away from the fire, a strange look on her face.

Alice, noticing this, asked, 'Are you afraid of being burned, dear friend?'

Visibly shuddering, Fiona said that fires out-of-doors held bad memories for her.

As weeks progressed the weather deteriorated. Indoors, Alice again became fractious. She questioned William often about the journey he and Tug had taken in search of Fiona, repeatedly asking what he had found out of Fiona's history. She became very upset when William told her sharply that was Fiona's business, and if Fiona wanted her to know, she would tell her herself.

Alice was sure there was a mystery, and was determined to discover what it was. Pleading constantly that she would surely go 'mad with boredom', she asked Fiona to tell her about her youth, where she was born, and where she grew up.

Florrie did most of the housework now. Mrs Read and the

mistress thought the girl a treasure who improved daily. Florrie, benefiting from good food, and encouraged by Fiona and Mrs Read, took time to groom her hair and appearance, and blushed readily at their praises.

William had given strict instructions Fiona was not to exert herself in any way and she confided in William that she felt guilty about being so useless. He told her she was far from useless in view of all she did for the mistress.

'She be asking I tae tell the tale o' my youth and I be ashamed, maester.'

'Old friend, your past is your affair, and from what I have learnt, any harm done then was not your fault.'

Fiona decided she would tell her life story to Alice.

8

Born in the Highlands, Fiona was the youngest of three children. She did not know how many babies her gentle mother, Fiona, had borne and lost. Her father, Angus McCready, married her mother only to get the dowry her aged father had scraped together. The old man had consented to their marriage for fear that the only child of his old age should be left alone and unprotected.

Fiona Sheedy was thought to be backward. Her mother was well past thirty when she gave birth to her first girl and the poor creature died in agony as the babe Fiona Mary was born.

Angus McCready, a violent man, soon spent the dowry on drink and philandering, and was abusive to his family. His wife bore the brunt of his anger when trying to shield her children.

Angus was ever ready to do battle, insisting his two sons should be like himself, and always ready to fight their enemies. When the father went on skirmishes with the English, he forced his sons to accompany him, causing their young lives to be wasted.

The only child left to them, the girl, Fiona, named after her mother, had reached her twelfth birthday by the year 1745. Her father again went to war.

The Battle of Culloden in 1746 was bloody, the Duke of Cumberland employing troops he himself had drilled. The rear ranks were to fire volleys, while front ranks knelt with fixed bayonet thrusting at the Highlander on his right front, that being the enemy's unprotected side. It was a triumphant

English victory. The Duke gained the name 'Butcher' for his gross cruelty, and the many executions after the rebellion.

It was the custom for troops to take their womenfolk with them to provide their creature comforts. After each battle, the camp followers always went *picking,* looking for loved ones, and collecting things, especially weapons, for these were scarce among the Scots.

The child, Fiona, hated picking, loathing the smell of carbon and rotting flesh. Refusal meant severe beatings for both herself and her frail mother, however.

Among the followers was an old woman named Annie Floyd who had a large hump on her back, giving her a crippled and deformed appearance. Annie never washed, her filthy clothing a mixture of both male and female apparel.

Most folk were afraid of Annie, but she feared nothing. When Angus McCready was beating his wife and daughter, Annie set about him, driving him off nursing his head. The child had never seen her father back away from anyone, or anything, before. The dirty old cripple became her only friend.

Annie, wise in the ways of foraging, taught young Fiona which roots were edible, and how to chew leaves into a paste for small wounds, and use cobwebs for larger gashes.

After the battle, Annie told the girl to hide among rocks and bushes while she went to look for her mother, whom they had left down among the women pickers wearing their skirts tucked up to their thighs to keep them out of mire and gore.

The stench and smoke choked Annie as she asked had they seen the McCready woman. They pointed to where a figure crouched beside a body. The blood-soaked head of red hair had been severed from its torso.

'Help me, 'tis my ain Angus!' the demented creature, Fiona's mother, cried.

In the distance, screams could be heard. The English soldiers were dragging off women, and spearing men not

---

* scavenging among bodies

quite dead.

   Annie dragged the struggling, wailing creature, telling her to come away before death, or even worse, should overtake them. Annie did not fear death, but she knew from personal experience that it was common practice for men of their own nationality to rape and defile even women of their own clan.

   The damp evening air, or it might have been her nervousness, caused Fiona's thin frame to shiver. She drew her skimpy shawl tightly about her, to hide the first signs of her budding womanhood.

   Drawing back into the undergrowth, she yelped with fear as her hand was grasped in a steel-like grip, pulling her down. She attempted to prise the bloodied fingers from her wrist, crying for her mother. Just then Annie appeared, dragging the wild-eyed Fiona.

   Annie released the fingers on Fiona's wrist, then, shielding the flickering lantern, wiped away the gore from the still, pale, face of a youth; a young face that seemed so like the faces of the sons Annie herself had lost.

   Travelling at night was very dangerous, so they lay hidden until dawn. The youth was barely alive when the woman lifted his limp body onto a cart they had fashioned, covering his broken body with rags and rubbish. They left behind the stench of death and war, and journeyed towards Annie's home. The child, when she was asked, was ignorant of her birthplace, and her mother was far too confused to remember where home was.

   The travellers dressed in dirty rags laboured to push the cart along rough, little-used pathways, sleeping where and when they could. The nights were cold, so Annie wore a jacket she had picked from the battle-field. The elder Fiona did not object to wearing blood-stained clothing, but her daughter refused to put on any of the garments offered, saying they were dirty.

   They were sheltering in a sacked church. The lad's wounds had started to bleed afresh, and he had a raging fever.

   Annie went to forage for something to eat, and check the

snares and traps she had set. A band of Highlanders came upon her.

They pushed and pulled at her. Searching her bag and finding only a few roots and leaves, they decided she was better than nothing to satisfy their carnal desires. They were about to tear away her rags when a lad in his early teens said to leave her be.

'She be one o' our own breed, auld enough tae be ma granny and the poor auld biddy is a cripple as well!'

The young man stood his ground, with sabre in hand, while Annie crept away.

Returning to the church, Annie could see the youth's condition was bad. She tried removing his tatters but he cried out so much she had to cut them away. She heated a dirk in the fire, then cauterized the gaping wound in his neck. He gurgled and, mercifully, passed out.

She then straightened and tightly bound his leg, using rags to hold pieces of wood as splints. He was coming round by the time she pulled at his arm, trying to straighten the shattered bone into place. He lapsed into unconsciousness as white-hot metal again touched his flesh.

Annie asked young Fiona to bring water from a nearby stream, being careful to keep out of sight, as there were many dangers lurking.

Young Fiona caught sight of herself in a still pool, running her hands over her budding breasts. Then she dashed water onto her burning cheeks, stooping low to wash her body.

She heard a rustle. Remembering Annie's warning, she lay stock still in the undergrowth, frightened to breathe.

When she returned, Annie scolded her for taking so long. Fiona explained how she had had to hide, almost scared out of her wits.

Annie told her she must wear the male clothing she had offered her before. Unwittingly, Fiona put on the tattered trews and jacket, and tucked her hair into a cap, finally daubing earth, mixed with water, on the cheeks she had washed earlier.

Next morning, Annie rose to place more kindling on the

fire. She looked across at young Fiona, bathed in the rosy glow of dawn. She had crept close to the youth, for warmth maybe; who is to say? His uninjured arm lay across the body of the maid like an embrace.

As if Annie's gaze had been a shout, Fiona suddenly awoke and wriggled sheepishly from his hold.

Folk kept their distance from the smelly, dirty group, especially as the one was thought to be a witch, another a mad woman. In their ignorance they feared madness was contagious, and there was enough pestilence abroad as it was.

Annie was shocked at the evidence of uncaring cruelty, to see bodies unburied and left where they had fallen.

She had been away from home for more than two years, unaware of anything going on around her for many months of that time. Arriving at a street of terraced houses, Annie banged on a door. It was opened a crack by a woman who looked about the same age as herself. 'Who is there?' she squeaked.

'Open the door, ye daft besom, 'tis myself, Annie Floyd.'

The old woman fell back, amazed at the face in the light of the door. 'Annie, me poor Annie, thy grief and tribulations have aged thee tremendous, come awa' in.'

They were given a thin gruel which they hungrily devoured, and Annie asked if water could be heated, as she sorely needed to bathe. Fiona asked if she also could wash, for the top of her legs gave her pain and she could hardly move them.

Annie washed Fiona's hair, then washed her own stiff, grey locks. Mud ran down her face in scrolls and, withdrawing her head from the bowl, she asked Fiona to throw clear water from the pail over her. Fiona cried out seeing the head with lustrous hair emerging from the water. The head and face were younger than those of her mother.

With clean water they bathed, Annie giving Fiona some balm to ease the soreness caused by caked blood from her first periods, which ignorance had prevented her from asking, or telling, anyone about.

Fiona the mother, her mind in another world, submitted to bathing like a child would.

All wounds attended to, they lay down on clean straw to sleep.

Next day, Fiona, looking at Annie, was unable to recognize the old, hunchbacked hag who had been travelling with them, and she was curious to know why she wore such a disguise.

Annie started telling her story to the young Fiona, which she, in her turn, related to Alice McCall.

9

Annie was an orphan, hidden away and brought up by her cousin, Willie Haig, a butcher by trade. Willie was a few years her senior and had no affiliation to any chieftain.

Annie's father and mother had been killed by a borrowed executioner, for their laird had no executioner of his own, as did some lairds. The squirearchy of the period held lives in their hands and dealt out death sentences for the most trivial offences.

No woman they took fancy to was safe. When such a woman was done with, the poor soul and her children were taken away and sold as slaves for the colonies. This was the fate planned for young Annie before she was rescued by her clansmen and their women.

Thamas Floyd was a young stockman to Laird Malcolm McGregor, known far and wide as 'Black' Malcolm McGregor. One day Thamas was arranging the sale of animals for slaughter to Willie Haig, and saw Annie. He fell deeply in love with her, and she with him. This did not please Willie greatly, for he loved Annie, too, but he was a widower older than Annie, and she a blood relative.

Tam was an honourable man, and did not expect a dowry, so Willie could not object. The young couple toiled hard and long, Tam with his flock, Annie in the fields, and caring for their three children.

The eldest son, Tammy, named after his father, was a mirror image of him, and his brother one year younger, was named James after Annie's father. Young Tammy was tall for his age, but his younger brother, Jamie, was taller, and had the look of his beautiful mother.

Baby Jean arrived when her brother, Jamie, was eleven years old.

Annie was working in the fields near the stockman's cottage where she lived with her family. Baby Jean was in a cradle hung in the lower branches of a tree. Malcolm McGregor and a henchman rode by, the henchman passing a remark as to what a fine figure of womanhood Annie was.

Shortly after the laird sent for Tam, telling him he was to select 30 sheep and herd them down to Dundee to sell them there.

Tam journeyed to Dundee, and mysteriously disappeared.

The laird came to Annie, telling her that after extensive inquiries and searching, Tam's whereabouts were unknown. And as the money from the sale of the sheep sold was missing, there was no other course but for her husband to be branded a thief.

The two boys were in the hills attending the flocks. When they returned home, they found their mother squatting on the earthen floor, crying hysterically. In her arms she held the body of their baby sister wrapped in her torn, bloodied skirts.

When they had buried the shattered little form, the boys questioned their mother, but she was in deep shock and it was days before they discovered from her quivering lips what had occurred.

The laird had promised that if she would submit to his desires, and she and her children became his unpaid slaves, he would allow them to stay in the cottage. She, holding her baby close to her, had refused.

Malcom McGregor wrenched the babe away from her mother, throwing her roughly towards the bed. The poor mite crashed her head against the stone wall, her skull crushing like an eggshell.

Annie was then violently raped on the bed where the body of her dead baby lay.

Annie was packing their few belongings prior to leaving the cottage, determined to go in search of her husband. They were on the point of leaving when the laird came, ordering the two boys, Tammy and Jamie, to join him and the group of men he was taking to fight the enemy. This was his feudal right. To refuse meant immediate death.

Annie's sons comforted her as she wept bitterly, saying they would be near the man who had killed their sister and dishonoured *her,* beside branding their father a thief. In battle it would be far easier to take his life, and this they vowed to do as soon as the opportunity arose.

Their belongings were tied in a bundle with a harness of leather straps around its middle. Annie held this while Tammy put his arms through, and carried it like a back-pack. Jamie had a large bag over his left shoulder with the other things they possessed. Annie carried her pots and pans.

Striding along, with her sons on either side of her, Annie was so proud. She thought how tall they had grown, and how broad their shoulders. Tammy, the eldest, was so like his father. Jamie had her looks, too fine for a man, but his size and strength deterred anyone from mentioning his girlish features.

They travelled with a motley group carrying an assortment of weapons, staves, hay forks and scythes. Some even had muskets with daggers they called 'bayonets' fitted to them.

Annie, seeing these, thought they were evil, and as if she had had a premonition, shuddered at the very sight of them.

The fourth evening was wet, the fine drizzle turning the ground into a quagmire. Annie's sons erected a shelter of a blanket stretched on branches to keep off some of the rain.

Leaving their mother while she prepared food they, having no weapons of their own, went to see if they could barter among a party of compatriots who had joined them that day. They hoped for a sword or, if they were lucky, even a musket.

Annie was stooping over the fire when she felt arms grab her and drag her backwards through the mud.

The mature Annie, relating her story to young Fiona,

choked with emotion as she reached this part. She halted until Fiona, with the impatience of youth, pressed her to carry on.

Reluctantly, Annie carried on with her tale; how she had been dragged through the mud by her legs, one held by Malcolm McGregor, the other by one of the two henchmen accompanying him.

They tied both her hands above her head. She was held down by Black Malcolm's leering cronies as he stood astride her.

Bending over her, he reached for her throat with his huge hands, tearing at her garmets, ripping them from her writhing body.

He unbuckled his kilt and exposed the lower part of his bare torso, forcing her kicking legs apart. He held them apart with his feet. His cruel saliva-flecked mouth gaping, he stared at her with wild eyes for what seemed an eternity.

His massive body fell on her as he bellowed to his cronies to go about their own business. Then his rotten teeth sank deeply again and again into the soft flesh of her breasts.

Annie's eyes rolled back in their sockets. She was unable to cry out for they had gagged her with a dirty rag. Black Malcolm thrust into her savagely, plunging, penetrating her brutally, until she was choking on her own vomit.

Blinded by tears, she did not see the two enraged figures come out of the mist.

One swirled a claymore above his head and roared. The other, grasping a dirk, was silent as both weapons were plunged into Black Malcolm McGregor's hairy buttocks.

He screamed like the struck swine he was.

Annie felt warm liquid trickle down the inside of her thigh as Black Malcolm screamed once more as the claymore, withdrawn from his backside, came swirling down. Narrowly missing his head, it cut deeply into his shoulder.

The laird's screams brought his henchmen just as Tammy was striking this blow. Both lunged at his back with their bayonets. His young body slumped to the ground, joining the twisted form of his brother who, although dying, was still being hacked by Malcolm's bully boys.

As her beloved sons' blood mingled with the rivulets of rain, Annie screamed soundless screams. The badly wounded laird was carried away bellowing for revenge.

Women, having no love for their lord or his henchmen, for many had suffered at their hands, bound Annie as she struggled fiercely to remain with her sons.

They buried her in the mud near their own camp, squatting near her grave and constantly on watch to replace the hollow reed they had put in her mouth to enable her to breathe. This she spat out, wishing to die of suffocation and join her loved ones.

McGregor's men failed to find Annie and moved on. Two women stayed behind. They complained of ague, saying they were unable to travel further and desired to return home.

When all was clear they dug Annie out. She lay so still, it was thought she had died, but as they cleaned soil from her face, her eyelids fluttered.

The demented look in her eyes caused the women to weep.

In vain they tried to feed and clean her. She struggled so much that, not wanting to hurt her as she had already suffered so much, they gave up.

The two women made a makeshift shelter and stayed with her one more day. They and others had retrieved some of her possessions, replacing them in a bundle which she sat cradling like a baby. She winced with pain as it came into contact with her chest. Gently, they led the still stunned woman to the place where they had buried her sons, glad that she had not witnessed the barbaric spectacle of their poor bodies being used for bayonet practice.

Mercifully, Annie was out of her mind, unable to communicate or be communicated with. She refused the food offered her, and would not allow them to attend to her wounds. The gouging of her breasts was plainly visible, as her clothing hung in shreds.

Feeling able to help her no further, her rescuers draped some clothes around her shoulders, and went on their way.

One, looking back to see Annie still cradling her bundle, prayed that her suffering would not be over-long, and a peaceful death would come soon to the poor, demented soul.

No one noticed the filthy, spidery hunchback who was forever searching for people called Tammy and Jamie. Annie had somehow survived, and managed to catch up with the party of 300 on their way south to join their prince.

One party had been greatly delayed on their journey, for their chieftain, Malcolm McGregor, complained at every bump in the road. As he lay on his belly inside a wagon he demanded many halts to attend to his wounds and needs.

Annie had not washed away the mud or the grime that lay on her skin in deep ridges. She had eaten very little and was just skin and bone. Her precious bundle was strapped to her shoulders next to her skin. The rags she wore, being too large for her, completely covered the pack, giving the impression she was humpbacked.

Young Jamie's dagger had sunk deep into McGregor's flank, and the wound was festering. As there was no surgeon with the party, it was women who doctored the sick and injured. They declared the chieftain's wound must be cauterized.

A goodly measure of liquor was poured down Black Malcolm McGregor's throat. The women delighted in hearing him scream as he had made others scream.

When the task was completed it was mentioned that the skin scorched appeared to be a much greater area than the original wounds.

For some strange reason, Annie kept close to Malcolm McGregor's wagon until she was seen by a woman who had helped to bury Annie on the night of her sons' death.

Dorothy Allen at first only recognized the clothes Annie wore, for it was she who had given them to her. Dorothy, afraid someone else would recognize Annie, held her hands and pulled her well away into the rear.

Dorothy took Annie to the edge of the camp, where the sick and wounded were being cared for. Most of these were young men, ill-prepared for the privations of travelling.

Many suffered wounds received from their own kind during combat training, as their drunken instructors yelled for blood, goading and taunting them all-too-often to fight to the death. This was one of the main entertainments beside gambling and molesting women.

No one went after Annie for they believed she suffered from a wasting disease and was mad. Not that Annie's unclean state was unusual, for many of the company were unwashed and were only bathed when they entered the world and if they were lucky enough, when they left it.

Dorothy Allen kept Annie well away from the wagon of Malcolm McGregor, and the women forced to attend to him, for they were often flogged as he believed they made him suffer unnecessarily.

His closest companions grew tired of his tantrums, eventually persuading him he had best return home to the care of his long-suffering wife, Lady Ruth McGregor, for his injuries would only worsen as they travelled. The laird made the return journey with four retainers.

Dorothy's husband and their son, Patrick, had been forced into military service by their chieftain. Her husband had died of his wounds, whilst the son sustained a leg wound in combat-practice. His mother bound up this minor wound to look as if the leg had been amputated.

Dorothy was sick of being a camp follower, forever in fear of being attacked by drunken lechers lusting after females. She kept a very low profile, dreaming of escape to start a new life for herself and her son. Tending the sick and wounded, she also tried to bring Annie back to the land of the living.

She was attending a youth of about 14 who had a deep wound in his side. This lad developed a fever and called for his mother. Annie had now become Dorothy's shadow, and squatted near her as she bathed the boy's forehead. Dorothy placed the damp cloth in Annie's hand guiding it to the bowl of water. After doing this a few times she could feel Annie's resistance, so she let her carry on alone.

The group had little in the way of transport. Some manually

dragged litters made from branches, and some of the officers had horses or mules, but most people were on foot, and the lame helped the feeble.

Many deserted, not caring for battle against the mad foreigners in the enemy's army. Those not knowing what else to do, or where to go, carried on.

Annie unconsciously mopped the brow of the lad throughout the day as he had now become her sole charge. She was unaware that he had slipped into his last sleep. By nightfall some of the sick and wounded had fallen behind the main party. This group included Dorothy, her son, Annie and the dead youth.

Dorothy wrapped up the body prior to burial, and Annie let out a cry from her soul, 'Tammy, my ain sweet boy.'

Annie, in her confused state, believed this was her own son.

Dorothy Allen asked to be alone with Annie and the dead boy. Hiding Annie from prying eyes, she helped her remove the bundle from beneath her rags. Annie took out sweet-smelling herbs and sprinkled them into a bowl of fresh water. She removed the boy's bandages. With tears streaming down her cheeks, making grooves in the thick grime on her face, she bathed the lad's body.

With linen she dried him. Kneeling beside him she kissed a cross of brass hung on a string of black bog-wood beads, a gift from her beloved husband, and prayed as he was placed in a hole dug for him.

This was the beginning of Annie coming back to the reality of a harsh world.

Dorothy stopped her from washing her tear-stained face, for she would have washed away the disguise that had kept, and was keeping her safe. Strapping the bundle back onto Annie, Dorothy replaced it as before.

Putting a marker of two branches tied as a cross at the head of the lad they had no name for, they continued on their way.

Many more died, and were not given a Christian burial, but left where they had fallen. For it was the women who performed burial services, often a huge task requiring great effort, and as they were frightened of being left behind by the main party, frequently they hurried the work. Many times the task of burial was completely abandoned and the bodies left to rot, or for the ravens, foxes and other beasts to pick the bones clean.

It was little wonder that disease and pestilence became rife.

Annie was still very confused. Until now she had not attended to her wounds, or permitted anyone else to attend to them and she suffered pain from the wounds on her breasts.

She stayed close to the friendly Dorothy Allen, and together they found shelter and food where they could, attending to the sick with herbs and what was to be had.

Annie struggled to attend to herself without attracting attention, which proved very difficult. Her friend helped by putting poultices on her festering bite marks. The gentle Dorothy cursed Malcolm McGregor.

They suffered many privations, but in the main they were not molested, for they attended to the sick and dying, their patients either relatives of, or of the same clan as, men who did the molesting.

Dorothy knew there were many men with ties of loyalty to Malcolm McGregor, who would not give up the search for Annie and would gladly kill her if she were recognized. Annie stayed disguised.

Away from others, the three took refuge in an old barn outside the town they had refrained from entering. In towns there were inns and alcohol, which led to trouble.

During the night they were greatly disturbed by the hooting of owls, the scuttling of many rats. Dorothy's son, Patrick, had a fear of rats, letting out a terrible scream as a rat ran across his face. As he swept it away, the rodent bit him. Blood spurted. Within seconds, more rats attacked the youth, who lost his balance as one leg was bound up.

Annie helped the mother beat off the squealing attackers.

As it was August, they felt it best to sleep in the open.

Patrick developed a fever, an evil-smelling growth appearing in his groin. His mother helped him to lie against the wall of a ruined thatched cottage whilst she sought the advice of a woman who had much experience of fevers.

The woman cautiously came near to the boy, then turned and ran, loudly screaming, 'Plague.'

Annie refused to leave them, but Dorothy told her she had to go away from them, or she would become affected. This sweet woman knew what had to be done.

Annie, sitting under a tree a little distance from them, watched for two days and nights as Dorothy tried to feed and comfort her son, collecting all the tinder available and piling it around them. Her movements were slow and laboured. She called to Annie, begging her to leave, and go with God's blessing.

Annie saw her bend over to kiss her son then place a torch to the funeral pyre she had built for them.

Screaming, Annie ran towards the smoke and flames, sinking to her knees, stupefied.

It was thus that a dirty hunchback crone came to meet the two Fionas, for Annie had attached herself to the party travelling to war at the Battle of Culloden.

It was the body of Duncan McCready, cousin to Angus McCready, (they as like as two peas in a pod, but for one being a little taller than the other) that was mistaken for young Angus, the husband of Fiona's mother.

Angus McCready had gone, leaving behind him the wife who thought she was a widow, and their daughter, who fled with Annie from the morass of dead and dying. The prince they supported was also fleeing, with a huge bounty of £30,000 on his bonny head.

Thus it was, Annie explained, how she came to wear the disguise that had saved her many times from molestation. In her future Fiona remembered this and used the same disguises effectively.

Annie, the two Fionas and the wounded youth started a new life at the home of Morag, who was kin to Annie, and had helped Willie Haig, the butcher, hide and raise Annie when she was a child.

Annie's cousin, Willie, was broad and brawny and, like many large men as gentle as a lamb until roused. It was said Willie Haig could hurl a cleaver splitting a sparrow in two at a hundred paces. Those who really knew him, knew that he might tackle a mad bull, but never would he harm a tiny bird.

Old Morag's father had been a weaver who had taught his daughter the trade. But now she had difficulty working the foot pedals because of the rheumatics in her legs.

With Morag's tuition, Annie took over the job of weaving. Money was very short, so they went gleaning wool from the brambles.

Fiona's mother, who still had not recovered from the shock of finding the decapitated body she thought was her husband, accompanied them. The simple soul gathered thistledown and flowers, presenting them to her daughter with a sweet smile. So lost was the elder Fiona in a world of her own, that her daughter had now taken on the role of mother, and appeared to be the only person for her mother in the whole universe. For when she was out of her mother's sight, the poor soul became most distressed.

The youth's wounds slowly healed, leaving a scar across his throat. The fingers of his left hand were so stiff they were almost useless and he painfully dragged his right leg. The loss of speech troubled him greatly.

Annie and Morag taught young Fiona all they knew of herbs and their uses.

Willie Haig called with meat he said was unsaleable, or which he was not able to cook himself, he being a widower, and, as Annie always invited him to share their meals, it was she who did him a service.

He would come in the evening, doing his utmost to hide the affection he had for Annie. It was painful to see him suffer. Annie admired and liked him, but could not return his love.

After the meal, he would sit watching Annie and Morag

carding the wool they had gleaned. Fiona sat at the table sorting herbs and tying heather in little posies.

Four days in the week, her mother following her like a little dog, Fiona would take a basket of herbs and posies, and a few lengths of cloth Annie had woven, and try to sell them in the busy market place.

It was Morag who was first to notice young Fiona and the youth were attracted to each other. They had decided for want of a name, to call him Andy, for he had not yet been able to tell them his real name. The youngsters were getting on well together, sitting close, and with the use of signs Fiona seemed to understand a great deal of what he wanted to say.

One night Morag discovered them embracing and told Annie that if it was what they wanted, it would be best if they were wed.

Asked if this was their wish, both nodded their heads.

The preacher was brought. Fiona wore a shawl Annie had woven, and flowers in her hair. Andy wore a jacket and trews washed, made-over and repaired by old Morag.

'Before I begin,' said the minister, 'what be the names?'

There was utter confusion when Annie said his name was Andy.

The boy became agitated, and repeatedly tapped himself on his head then pointed to a sword hanging on the wall.

'What is this lad trying to do, has he lost his senses?' demanded the minister.

'Nay,' said Willie, who had been invited to the ceremony. 'He be tappin' his head and pointin' to your sword, head and sword, headsword. Be thy name Edward, lad?'

The youth nodded joyfully.

'Ye are sharp, sir. Now, see if ye are sharp enough to find out the surname of this young person?' snapped the cleric.

Edward pointed to the minister's brown boots and leather belt.

'Are ye called Boots, laddie?

'No, then is it Leather?

'No, it canna be ye are called Belt?'

'Ye daffty, 'tis Brown!' chuckled Morag.

Edward nodded, smiling.

Thus young Fiona became Mrs Brown, and married the father of the child she unknowingly carried.

10

Events over the next few months prevented Fiona from continuing with her story for Alice, who was getting very near the time of her confinement.

Fiona had told her how she had married her Edward, and how very much in love they had been, although their prospects for the future had been poor.

Alice's water broke, and she had a short, easy labour. Fiona, with the help of Mrs Read and Florrie, delivered her nine pound son. The child had a head of thick, dark hair which, Fiona told Alice, was the cause of all the painful flatulence she had suffered while carrying him.

William was delighted with his new son, declaring he was the bonniest of children. Young William Robert had a fat, pink face, and a hand which reached out for his father's finger, holding it, according to the proud parent, with an amazing grip.

William was fascinated watching his wife breast-feed for the very first time, not ushered out as he had been in the past. The infant was a hungry little chap, who only stopped feeding for one short time, screwing up his face and burping unaided.

Fiona praised him for doing this, and they all laughed merrily. How much had changed in the past months! Here was Fiona being treated almost like an equal, Alice not wanting her out of sight.

Little Aimee was a changed child. Of late, she had become disciplined and quiet, more like her brother, Phillip. She adored her Papa, who never missed a visit to the nursery as soon as he arrived home, with sweetmeats for her and Florrie.

Aimee also loved Tug, and he spoiled the child outrageously.

Tug had bought a St Bernard dog they named Shaggy, and Shaggy pulled a little carriage which had been beautifully made by Tug. The carriage interior and seat, which was large enough for two children, had red leather upholstery to match the reins. Aimee would ride around the garden under the watchful eye of Florrie.

Alice became so besotted by the baby in his early months that she did not pursue Fiona to carry on with her story.

Master Phillip was again home from school, and William invited Mr Peel, the Art master, to visit. The grateful father was profuse in his thanks to the master for his extra tutoring of Phillip, begging that he might be allowed to make a small retribution, for he knew a schoolmaster's stipend was extremely small.

Mr Peel declared it was a pleasure to be of service, for Phillip was a very pleasant and intelligent person to work with. William decided he would think of some way to repay this good man.

Baby William was four months old and thriving. Tug made a wicker hanging-cradle which they suspended from the lower branches of an oak tree. As soon as the babe was fastened safely inside this cradle, he would go to sleep, to be heard only when it was time for his feed.

Phillip was reluctant to return to school as home was such a nice place to be now. Even his mother's attitude had changed a little towards him. His father praised him so highly for his progress, however, stressing he would be letting not only himself down, but Mr Peel also, that he returned to college.

Fiona and her husband settled down to wedded bliss in Morag's shabby little home. Edward, not having much use in his left arm and hand, became adept at holding things by pressing them between his elbow and chest. Although he was unable to speak, he and his wife, Fiona, had no trouble communicating with each other. When she was at home, their heads were forever close together, and they were constantly touching.

Shortly after they were married, Edward was waiting at home for the women to return, Fiona from her peddling, Annie and Morag from the miles they walked in search of wool to glean.

Annie flopped down removing her ancient boots, the soles of which had worn right through, and she rubbed her sore feet.

Edward, with a very sharp dirk, was cutting up string ready for Fiona to tie up her bundles, when he took hold of Annie's boots and started hacking at them with the dirk. From an old leaking leather pail he cut and fashioned soles, and mimed hammering onto the uppers.

'Well, I be damned!' cried Morag, 'He be wantin' a hammer an' last to repair yorn boots.'

The last was borrowed, nails and hammer procured, and the boots were repaired so well it was obvious Edward had done this work before.

He managed to convey to his wife that boot-making had been his father's trade, and Edward his apprentice. When his father died, the business was taken over by their landlord, and Edward was commandeered for the army. He managed to tell her something that she kept a secret from the others; her Edward was not a Scot, but a Sassenach from a place called London.

The months went by. Edward built up quite a business with his boot repairing, through the advertising of the generous Willie Haig. Willie assisted him to make a work-bench with clamps, and other features to help with his disability, and as a butcher, bargained with the local tanner to get good quality leather and skins at reasonable prices. Edward started making boots of excellent quality, besides repairing saddlery and leather goods.

The house was overcrowded, for the weaving-loom took up a large floor space. Edward's bench was near the window, with more and more work coming in. When they were all at home there was barely room for them to sit. Daytime was not too bad, for Willie had found a stall for Fiona in the market place.

This stall was directly opposite his shop, where he had full view of it through his window and door. Young Fiona, with her mother, sat selling herbs and cloth and shawls Annie and Morag had woven, collecting payment for shoe repairs. She also took the orders for new boots and slippers, which were in great demand.

She arranged for Edward to be at the stall at certain times so the clients could have their feet measured, the sizes then given to a cabinet-maker who made the corresponding shoe moulds.

Many people paid on the barter system, but Willie Haig was always on hand to see the young couple had the better of the deal. They bartered for skins and wool, saving Annie and Morag from going gleaning. This meant more time for weaving, and less room in the house during the day, with three people working there full-time.

When Fiona's baby was born they named her Helen, but alas, this became Nellie later on. Annie raised the necessity of finding larger accommodation.

Most places they had seen were unsuitable. On Sunday, that being the only day when they were all together, they were about to go out to view another place when they had a very important visitor.

The wife of Malcolm McGregor, Lady Ruth McGregor, was the last of her ancient line. She had married the clan chieftain, Malcolm McGregor, to retrieve the promissory notes said to have been given to him by her dead father. Chieftain McGregor was constantly harassing her dying mother for payment of these debts, but said he would cancel them if their only daughter would marry him.

He had long coveted their estate which adjoined his, and would not, therefore, become entailed but would pass to the heirs of his union with Ruth.

They had been married less than one month when she overheard her husband boasting to his drunken friends, that his stupid, dead father-in-law owed him no debt whatsoever.

Cautiously, Annie invited her in. Whispering, she asked

Fiona to run and bring Willie Haig. The Lady graciously refused the offered refreshments. Annie became very nervous when she said she had been searching for many weeks as she needed to make retribution.

Annie blanched and shook so much, Edward came to her side and made her sit down, glaring with extreme anger at the visitor.

'Oh, please,' she cried, 'you have misunderstood me. I have come here not to demand retribution, God forbid, but to make retribution to you, for all that you have suffered.'

She told them her husband had died of his wounds.

Black Malcolm had died in great fear of damnation. He had called loudly for a priest who failed to arrive, so he confessed all his sins to the wife who hated him.

Annie wept with Lady McGregor when she spoke of the great wrong done to her, and sobbed bitterly when told the Laird himself had arranged for her husband, Tam, to be taken by the press gang and branded a thief, for her to be alone and raped.

Disgusted, Lady Ruth told how he had pleaded the baby girl's murder was an accident.

They both wept for the children lost, and the children one had not been blessed with. Placing a leather pouch and a parchment on the table, Lady Ruth asked Annie to examine the latter.

Gingerly, Annie unfolded the legal-looking document.

'I'm feared I dinna ken what this is, ma'am, not able to do the reading.'

'It is a legal document, a deed, giving you the freehold of the stockman's cottage, together with two acres of ground. It is legal and binding, for it bears not only the seal of two dignitaries, but that of Malcolm McGregor himself, made over to you before he died. And this,' she said, pointing to the pouch, 'is a sum for stock, grain and pay for assistance to clear the land that has lain fallow for more than two years.'

'I canna take this, my lady, it will no bring back my bairns, or my man.'

'No, but it will provide a home and living, or do with it what ye will.' Not wanting to raise hopes, she did not speak of the man she had engaged to find Tam Floyd, Annie's husband. Reports sent to her were encouraging. It was a frequent occurrence for men to disappear at seaports, shanghaied and taken on board as slaves, often to die in their manacles.

Remembering caused Annie great grief. She cried that she could never return to a place which held so many bad memories.

Arriving with Fiona, Willie told her to accept the gift, for it was little compensation for the harm done to her. He suggested she could sell or rent it if she did not live there herself.

Edward grunted and made excited movements as Fiona translated what she believed was the gist of what he said.

'Edward says there be twa many folk livin' here. Ifen Annie doesna want the cottage, could he, mother an' me have it? We could pay rent and sich now that the business be doin' well.'

There were no objections except that Fiona would not be able to run the stall, for the cottage was some distance from the town.

Willie solved this, saying he would look out for a little donkey and cart, and there was no need for Fiona to be at her stall every day of the week.

In just over a month, Fiona and her family moved into the stockman's cottage. Annie and Willie had found men to do minor repairs to the roof and the buildings, as well as painting inside and out with lime-wash, which was the custom in those days to deter creeping and crawling things.

Fiona bartered with one of her customers for a dozen good laying hens and a proud, strutting rooster. Another paid his bill with a fine sow which was soon to increase the family by six pink piglets.

Edward was too busy with his work, and too proud to ask for help to build a proper sty for the family of pigs, so they wandered freely in and out of doors, but mainly resided inside the house to the great amusement of the baby.

Baby Helen thrived under the watchful eye of her father,

and the tender attention of her gentle, simple-minded grandmother.

The grandmother had had no inclination to accompany her daughter to market since they had moved, but stayed near the baby and crooned to her, decking her in garlands of flowers. This affection for her grand-daughter warmed Edward, but he would not allow them out of his sight, fearing his mother-in-law's inability to see danger.

Working from dawn until dusk, he stopped only occasionally to pick up his child to kiss and cuddle her, with her grandmother smiling happily.

Fiona came home with fresh work, and the payment for work done. She loved playing their favourite game of holding her daughter as unsuccessfully she tried to chase the pigs out of the living room.

Edward made baby Helen slippers of the softest kid.

Lady Ruth McGregor, a frequent caller, seeing the baby's slippers admired them greatly, and asked Edward if he could make her a similar pair. She was thrilled with them, vowing no other shoes had their comfort, and telling him that henceforth he should make all her shoes.

While Fiona was preparing goods for the market, she would try to help Edward to regain his speech, until at last, Edward managed to say, 'Nay' and 'Yea', 'Lellen' for Helen and 'Nona' for Fiona.

The pride Fiona had in her young husband was immense, and no words were needed to express how he felt for his wife. The look of adoration on his face when he looked at her spoke volumes.

At first Annie would not visit them, but Willie brought Morag who, watching the grandmother play with the babe, said, 'If that soul be daft, there ought tae be maer dafty folk i' the world.'

The laird's widow revelled in the welcome she received at the Brown house, and her greatest joy was when she was allowed to hold and cuddle baby Helen. She took delight at feeding the child from a silver spoon she had brought as a gift for her.

This spoon was a family heirloom which was to have been given to her first-born at the child's christening, the first-born she had lost in the eighth month of pregnancy, when her drunken husband had demanded the use of her body. In the face of her reluctance he had forced himself upon her, then beaten her viciously because he was unable to perform. She had miscarried, never to conceive again.

Lady Ruth never became cross or upset when the child blew bubbles of food over her clothes, and objected to Fiona scolding her telling her, 'Do not scold the little darling, this is a favourite game. Clothes can be washed, but it is most difficult to wash away a hurt.'

It was evening when an excited Lady Ruth came to the cottage. Edward was helping Fiona with the donkey and cart.

Lady Ruth asked the driver of her carriage to assist them. for she had something of importance to tell them. Refusing the pannikin of milk offered, she rushed through her information.

'For months I have been making inquiries as to the whereabouts of Thamas Floyd, husband of your friend, Annie. At last, I have a communication of his possible whereabouts, but it is not one hundred per cent sure and I do not want to raise Mistress Floyd's hopes unnecessarily.

'But I am almost bursting with excitement, and I need to share this news with someone.'

Two anxious weeks passed before Lady Ruth came to the market place to see Fiona at her stall. As a mark of respect, Fiona hurriedly drew down the hem of her top skirt, which was tucked up into the waist-band, thus covering her money satchel. She slipped her bare feet into the shoes Edward had made for her, which she only wore when walking to save them from wearing out.

Willie Haig came hurrying across, and greeted Lady Ruth with deference. He had discovered this lady was generous to a fault, impoverishing herself in an attempt to right the wrongs committed by her evil husband.

Willie, seeing that there was something afoot, told the two

women to go into his shop and close the door, that they might converse in private. For he had few customers that late in the morning, and the ones which came to Fiona's stall he would ask to come back a little later.

Lady Ruth said excitedly, 'Thank you for your offer, Master Haig, but I do not mind you hearing my news.' She told them that the men looking for Annie's husband had at last traced him.

Willie's heart sank at first, at the thought that his Annie's world, which he had tried to put back on an even keel, would be upset again. But then he thought, the worry of not knowing what had happened to Tam would be with Annie and haunt her for the rest of her days.

Lady Ruth spoke of what had been discovered. Tam Floyd had been waylaid in the town of Dundee when completing the sale of the cattle. He had been drugged and thrown onto a British vessel with many other unfortunates suffering the same fate.

As they fought the French their ship was destroyed. Tam survived and was thrown into a prison in the French town of Fortenay.

An Irish officer, a prisoner in the same dungeon, was not in as bad a state as most there, for he had means to bribe the warders for extra comforts.

An assailant intent on robbery and murder, had stood with knife poised over him, about to strike, when Tam sprang between them, receiving a serious injury.

The French government, realizing money was to be had from ransoms, thus saving the expense of keeping prisoners not fit for work, accepted the ransom the Irish nobleman's family sent for his release, with enough also for the man who had saved their son's life.

Thamas Floyd was at present recuperating, being nursed back to health at the home of Sir Connal Flannahagan.

Contact had been made with this gentleman who, though loath to part with his friend, agreed that as soon as Tam was strong enough to take the journey, he should be sent home to his wife.

That morning Lady Ruth had received notice that Thamas Floyd had been placed on a vessel bound for the port of Ayr.

'When will Annie's husband be coming home here, m'lady?' asked Fiona.

'Maybe in two or three days, but I will come here with him.'

Willie looked after the stall for Fiona while she and Lady Ruth hurried to Annie with the news.

The interior of the house was dusty and gloomy. Morag was busy keeping an eye on the intricate pattern Annie was weaving on the loom. With the noise of Annie's foot pedals and their deep concentration on what they were doing, it took a few minutes to attract their attention.

When first told the news, Annie was stunned into silence. She then jumped up, grabbing Fiona and jigging madly round with her, laughing and crying at the same time. Suddenly she loosened her hold on Fiona, and sank to her knees beside Lady Ruth, clasping both the lady's hands to her lips and kissing them as they all wept together.

Some days later, Annie held out her arms to her husband being helped from Her Ladyship's carriage. Tears streamed down her face as she felt his wasted frame through his clothes. Closing her eyes she remembered how bonny he had looked as he waved her goodbye the day he had left for Dundee.

Fiona and her family had been told he was arriving, and were brought to be introduced to him.

Lady Ruth McGregor he knew already, but Tam at first had difficulty speaking to her, because he now knew her lord was the instigator of his misery. It was later when he discovered the laird was now deceased, and the vast energy and expense of this wonderful woman had brought him back home, that his feelings softened towards her.

Tam wept bitterly when told his three children had died. Annie, not wishing to dwell on the way they had died, only said that the two sons had died when soldiering. He did not inquire how his baby daughter had died, thinking that it was a children's disease that had been the cause. Annie did not enlighten him.

They spent two weeks, glad to be reunited, gently lying in each other's arms.

Tam desired to go and see the grave of his daughter, and this was when Annie first went back to the cottage.

The first time Tam tried to make love to her, Annie cringed and drew away from him. He felt hurt and rejected. Before he had gone away, that side of their relationship had been nigh perfect. Becoming aggressive, he demanded to know why she had changed, saying she had found another man, or even men.

Tam found out the cottage had been bequeathed to Annie, and accused her of being a whore who sold herself for money. Taking what money he could find, he stormed out of the house, returning the next day smelling of strong drink and demanding more money.

Annie gave him all the money they had, and he left, screaming curses at her.

Days passed with Willie Haig going in search of him, finding him at last in the street outside a tavern he had been thrown out of.

Willie, taking him first to his own house to try to clean and sober him, found it a great strain to stop himself from crushing Tam's emaciated body with is bare hands, for Tam kept cursing Annie, calling her vile names.

Semi-conscious, Tam lay on Willie's bed, and Willie went for Annie. She asked him to help her take Tam back to Morag's.

Willie wanted to know what has caused the change in Tam, but Annie could not tell him. Morag did, however, relating what Annie had reluctantly told her; how she had been raped by Black Malcolm McGregor, who had killed her baby girl, and how her two sons had been slaughtered.

Willie's rage was terrible. He had thought that the compensation paid to Annie was for the abduction and branding of Tam as a thief, but never did he think that she had suffered such abominations. His heart bled for her and he told her she must tell her husband all. Secretly she wished she were his, so that he could protect her.

When Willie had gone, Annie told Morag how ashamed and tarnished she felt. 'Perhaps it was my own fault that that evil man abused me and killed my bairns. If I had been more careful, and not flaunted the good fortune and pride in my beautiful family, he would not have noticed me.'

'Ye talk a load o' rubbish, lassie, 'twere nay fault o' yorn that lecherous creature, may he burn i' hell, did tae ye, and yor bairns. Morag said that Willie was right, if she told Tam the truth he would understand and return to his old self.

Annie went up to the room where her husband lay awkwardly, having slipped sideways. She gently lifted his head onto a pillow, his haggard face so unfamiliar to her. Sitting on a chair watching him, she cried, longing to hold him and have him hold her.

She must have fallen asleep. Morag had crept in and was shaking her. 'I've brought up a bowl o' water for ye tae freshen thasen.'

Annie stripped to the waist as was her daily custom, for cool water eased the scars on her chest. With her back to the bed she felt there were eyes glaring at her, and burning through her spine. As she half-turned, the morning light streaming through the window fell on the terrible bite marks on her breasts.

Leaping off the bed, Tam snatched away the towel she held up to herself as she tried to hide the marks left by McGregor's teeth.

'What in the name of God be those marks?' demanded Tam.

Annie sank to her knees and somehow found the strength and courage to tell her husband the whole tragic tale.

Tam begged her forgiveness, saying he must have been mad to treat her so badly, but he had been jealous and angry for she was so beautiful.

Morag, having excellent hearing, heard the murmurings and sensed a reconciliation. She called out that she was going out to visit a sick friend and would lock the door so no one would disturb them.

On the bed they lay, side by side. At first she was shy when he kissed the scars, but his tenderness and caresses aroused her. He whispered that he loved her above life itself, and she melted, the warmth flooding through her body. Once more she was alive. Her man was home.

The exertion of loving brought on a fit of coughing for Tam, bringing blood to his lips.

Annie was frightened. At last she had her beloved back with her, when she had thought him to be dead, and now this sickness he had might rob her of him again.

Tam reassured her it was not serious. He thought that if he could get away from the smoke and dirt of the town, to get where he could breathe air that was pure, he would be well again. It was then that he expressed a wish to return to his birthplace, the Shetland Islands.

Annie told him she would go to the end of the world with him if he desired it, for now she had found him again, he was not being let out of her sight.

Morag and Fiona pleaded with them to stay, for Annie had no kin or friends in that far place. Tam, a young orphan, had left his home to seek his fortune and he was not sure whether he had any kin left there either.

Arguments about where they would live or earn a living did nothing to deter them. It would be impossible for them to collect the rent of the cottage from Fiona and Edward when so far away. Lady Ruth McGregor suggested that the couple should buy the cottage from Annie, and she would advance the complete purchase price of 20 guineas to Annie to give them a good start in their new lives. The couple would then pay the sum back to her at the same rate as the rent they now paid quarterly, until the full sum was repaid.

This was agreed by all, only Annie said 20 guineas was too much. Lady Ruth explained, however, that this was the true value of the house and land.

Early on Sunday morning Tam and Annie wished everyone goodbye, Annie tearfully telling them nothing short of death would ever part her and Tam again.

All had gathered outside the cottage, with the exception of

Willie Haig, who had bashfully murmured goodbye and made the excuse that he had to be away to see someone about stock, but would return to take his Aunt Morag home.

Edward presented Tam with a pair of sturdy boots, and Annie, shoes of fine kid. Morag and Fiona both said they were always welcome at their homes should they return.

Annie asked to hold the baby before climbing beside Tam on the seat of the cart.

Lady Ruth had presented them with a chaise, drawn by a dainty little mare, but Tam would not accept it and chose instead a strong cart for the mare to pull, insisting he would only take it if he paid full price for them both. Lady Ruth's servant lifted a huge hamper into the cart as they pulled away.

Willie returned not long after Annie and Tam had left, his face a picture of abject misery. He did not speak a word to Morag on their journey home.

Fiona had invited Lady Ruth inside to partake of breakfast, and she had accepted, telling her coachman to return for her in a few hours.

Ruth's face was a picture of contentment as she spooned the milky oatmeal into Helen's mouth. Her sad eyes lit up with merriment as the baby blew bubbles and chuckled whenever food splashed onto the gown of the one who fed her.

Ruth wiped down the front of the little girl's gown with a fine kerchief trimmed with lace. The lace caught on a pin that fastened a small pouch to the child's garment.

Fiona crossed the room, almost falling over one of the piglets, and Edward guffawed. Fiona raised the cloth she held, pretending to strike him with it.

Freeing the kerchief with puzzled expression, Fiona examined the pouch, trying to remember where she had seen it before. She undid the string and shook out the contents. Five gold coins fell onto the table.

'Annie!' Lady Ruth and Fiona spoke in unison.

'How did you know it were Annie, my lady?'

'For she complained too much was paid for this cottage, by a good third, and she had no need for all that money. You have a good friend who will be missed.'

'But what shall I do with the money? Annie has already done so much for me.'

'Save it for this little one, she might have need of it one day. I see my carriage has returned and I have stayed over-long.'

Lady Ruth said her goodbyes, thanking them profusely and asking could she come again. Edward nodded his head in consent as Fiona said she could come visiting any time. Edward fashioned a much smaller pouch of soft leather, just big enough for the coins and a small cross Fiona stitched into the hem of Helen's petticoats.

Spring turned to summer and the child was mischievous while Fiona was away at market, and Edward, with ever-increasing work, found it hard to look after her.

Lady Ruth was in financial difficulty for she, on a point of law, had now become landlord of the cottage, as rent was paid to her. The government demanded more tax from this gentle lady, who had to ask her groom and gardener to leave her employ. But they chose to continue to work for her for no wages.

Edward, through Fiona, let it be known that he wanted someone who would not overcharge to build a pigsty. The gardener and groom offered, and did an excellent job. Alas, the pigs refused to use their new home, and spent days and nights commuting between out-of-doors and the living room.

The sty was not a waste of money, however, for the brick building became an excellent playpen for Helen and her grandmother.

Edward had no need to go into town to fit people for new shoes anymore, having to work hard to fulfil all the orders for the clients he already had. Their shoe moulds and sizes, all with their own personal marks, were near to hand. The family prospered, and did so well they were able to pay half the purchase price of the house and land by the second quarter.

Fiona bloomed for she was again pregnant.

11

Fiona had a respite from telling her tale, for Alice's attention was diverted for a time in another direction.

Amos Ogilvy, Alice's father, was still alive and lived in a large house on the banks of the Firth of Forth. He and his daughter did not get on well together, for he disliked her high-and-haughty ways which were the same as her mother's. From the early days of their marriage, Alice's mother had failed to curb her husband's lewd behaviour.

Amos was never cruel to his family, but the only one he truly cared for was his son, Thomas, who was a year younger than Alice. The boy Thomas was 14 years old when his father bought him a beautiful stallion, and by then he had taken his son many times to houses of ill-repute. Thomas was never refused anything by his father, who seemed to enjoy taunting his wife when she chided him about the over-indulgence of their son. He made a point of giving more money to the boy when he had spent his allowance, while she was present. He was not so generous to her, or their daughter.

Having no money left after an evening spent wenching, gambling and drinking, young Thomas, racing his horse, misjudged a bend, and both horse and rider crashed to their death over a cliff.

The mother blamed her husband. Refusing to forgive him for the loss of their son, she took no food and lay in her bed for two months before she joined the boy.

Alice, on leaving her mother's funeral, went to live with her maternal grandmother, and it was there she met William McCall, who fell in love with her.

Alice was unaware that William had been maintaining his father-in-law, who had become a recluse.

Margaret Darnley Macdonald, Alice's grandmother, was a very understanding woman, and had told William before she died that, although she did not condone her son-in-law's way of life, in a way she could understand it.

Her daughter, his wife, had run from his bed the night of their wedding, and returned to her mother saying she loathed his touch and loved another man, but she had no dowry and he could not support her extravagant ways.

The widow Margaret had made the girl return to her new husband, telling her that she had no money to keep her. But the girl had gone instead to the man she loved, only to find him in the arms of another. Her husband had forgiven her, but had less affection for her than at first. He was expecting his first-born to be a son, and was sorely disappointed with the girl-child, the image of the mother he was not allowed even to hold.

When a son was born, he made a god of the child. Completely rejected by his wife, he went and found solace elsewhere.

William, out of curiosity, went to see the old man, but could not gain access to the house that had, through years of neglect, fallen into disrepair.

Making inquiries at a nearby cottage, he introduced himself to an old lady there, who told him she had once been a servant to the Ogilvies. Even now, she and her daughter left a few provisions on the doorstep without seeing the owner, only knowing the old master was alright because the goods were taken in by him, as her grandson, Simon, watched from the shrubbery.

William asked old Martha, for that was her name, to keep supplying the provisions, and he would pay a sum of money each month for anything they thought the old man might need. He asked if someone could come to his factory to collect the money.

Martha said her grandson would do this. 'But sir, be advised, keep this quiet for the auld master hae mony creditors after money, tha' be why he do lock hisself away.'

Each month for more than a year, young Simon Toomey came for the remittance, until he came a full two weeks before his regular time, to tell William the goods for the past two days had not been collected from the doorstep.

William drove the boy home, and was shown the food on the step being watched by the grandmother, who said she had been calling out until she was hoarse but had heard nothing.

Simon's father, Alex, on William's bidding, smashed down the door.

The old man, Amos, lay prostrate on the littered kitchen floor. In one corner of the room, a pile of old hay contributed to the smell of decay that prevailed.

Alex sent Simon to fetch his mother. Rosy cheeked and cheerful she came, and was soon taking control. Ordering the men to lift the body onto a threadbare sofa, which had first been thoroughly beaten with the broom, to scare any creatures out of it, Bess told them to lay the old master down.

She asked them to go upstairs to see if they could find bedding and a mattress. Her mother, old Martha, said she would show them as she knew where these could be found.

Old Martha tutted at the state of the fine, old house, muttering that the mistress was turning in her grave at the sight of it.

The sheets in the linen closet were rotten and mouldy, as were all the beds and bedding in the large chambers, for the tiles missing from the roof had allowed the elements through.

The mattress in one room was not too bad, for the bed and furniture had been covered with yellowed dust-sheets, and the room was under a part of the ceiling not stained by damp.

This was the boy's room, which had remained undisturbed for many, many years.

They carried down the mattress that Bess had instructed them to take to the kitchen, where she had thrown open the doors and windows to allow a cloud of dust to escape. For Bess had swept up the accumulation of rubbish on the table and floor.

William and Alex brought down the bedstead and erected it in a corner near the kitchen range, where Bess was attempting to light a fire. Martha informed her the bedding was unuseable and, with Simon, brought sheets and blankets from their home.

Amos was installed in the bed and conscious when the doctor Alex had brought diagnosed the old man had had a seizure, and was suffering from malnutrition.

He told William the old man might live a week, but doubted he would last a month. William left some money with the Toomeys, telling them he would do his best to return on the morrow.

He did his best to persuade Alice to come with him to see her father, but she categorically refused.

It was two days before William could return to see his father-in-law, but when he did he was surprised how the place had changed in such a short time.

Amos was propped up in bed wearing a clean, albeit much-patched, nightshirt, and the funniest bobble-bonnet on his head that William had ever seen.

The cobwebs and dead cockroaches had been swept away, and the kitchen floor was still damp and clean-smelling after the vigorous scouring it had received.

A fire burned in the grate and William was invited to partake of the aromatic barley-and-vegetable broth that was being ladled out, as it was approaching lunch time.

Bess Toomey apologized for there being no meat in the broth, and for her whole family being there.

William told her, 'Dear lady, why should I mind? The difference you and yours have made in this house, is nothing short of a miracle.'

Coming up the driveway, which had been almost cleared of weeds, he had seen her husband, Alex, and her son, Simon, clearing the undergrowth from around the entrance to the front door. This now stood open, letting in the fresh sea air to drive away the musty, dank odour that had pervaded the house on his first visit.

Bess called to her husband, son, and someone named Kate. The man and the boy came quickly and washed their hands. Martha went to the back door and shouted, 'Kate, come this minute, else ifen ye hae tae be fetched ye will get a tannin'.'

A child of four or thereabouts came running, clutching a bunch of weeds. Breathlessly she announced, 'These be for me Grandee.'

'I hope ye will take no offence at me little bairn, sir. She has longed for a grandad, not having known one, and has taken so much to the old master, and I am sure he to her,' said Bess. 'He watches for her, seeming to listen to her childish prattle. She put that silly bonnet on his head, and he will not part wi' it.'

William said he did not mind at all, and thought his children must be brought to see their only grandparent.

They finished the meal of homemade rye bread and broth, which William said was delicious.

The child, Kate, climbed up onto Amos's bed and mopped at his mouth with a piece of cloth which she unfastened from the bib of her overall to use as a kerchief.

The old man's face twisted into what might have been a smile as she scolded him for being a terrible dribbler.

William asked would it be best if Amos could be moved to another room.

'That be no problem, sir, if ye will come and choose a suitable room,' said Alex Toomey.

Going through the ground-floor rooms, they chose a small study with a French door overlooking the garden. Through the branches of the neglected trees there was a glint of water.

William asked was it possible the room could be prepared soon; he would pay for extra help to do the work. He had noticed the clothes Alex wore were those of a mill-worker, and felt it was not fair for him to be kept from his normal employment.

Alex told him there was no need to get workmen, for he would be glad to do the work. He was now unemployed, having lost his job at the ironworks after being away sick for a few days when his foot was crushed by an ingot that had slipped from its chain-sling.

William went to his factory before returning home. He had not confided to anyone the strain he was under, financial and otherwise. There had been a run on the banks, and they were foreclosing on mortgages.

He had ventured into another side of the business, that of jam-making and preserves, borrowing money for new machinery and keeping both his son and brother at college while away from his work searching for Fiona. And now the strain of looking after his father-in-law was beginning to show.

William collected his books. He felt weary, and wanted to be with his family.

Alice was quite cross at the late hour he came home, for she knew that he had been to see her father. She was very unreasonable when William tried to explain he had been most of the time at the factory, having spent less than two hours at her old home.

When William told her she should feel more Christian charity towards her dying father, she became quite hysterical, screaming, 'You do not know a fraction of what that devil did to my mother and myself!'

William told her to calm down, the disturbance would upset the whole household.

She quietened down a little, but her temper erupted again when William said he thought the children ought to be told of their only surviving grandparent, and should at least be taken to see him before he died. There was no stopping the abuse that Alice screamed about her father.

William, for the first time in their marriage, shouted at her, 'It always takes two to argue and there are two sides to each coin!' He repeated what her grandmother had told him, then stormed from the room.

Two days later, Tug drove the carriage as William with Florrie carrying baby William, rode inside with a very excited Aimee. They were going to pick up Phillip from school, then on to see the grandfather they had never known existed.

The baby slept through the whole journey. Aimee was first to approach the old man staring out of the open French window, for she had been led to his bedside by chatterbox Kate, who introduced Amos as her grandee. But she told Aimee, who hit it off with her straight away, that this was *her* grandee also, so she had been told.

William stopped her parent from ushering the child out of the room, saying that it would please him if Kate could stay.

Amos did not divert his gaze from the window, not even when baby William was held up to him. Phillip hung back nervously. Florrie begged William's pardon, but she thought the baby was due for a feed, for now he had been weaned and was bottle-fed.

Florrie left, carrying the babe into the kitchen, closely followed by Kate and Aimee hand-in-hand. Kate called over her shoulder, 'Don' ye go upsettin' my grandee the noo, for there be enough work wi' him as 'tis.'

Her mother scolded her, saying she must mind her manners to her betters.

William thought, what betters could anyone meet than these kindly people? He coaxed Phillip to come nearer to the bed. Slowly he approached, and a change came over the old man's face. He lifted his hands as if to hold the boy, and murmured a sound like the name, 'Thomas.'

William believed that Amos thought his grandson was the son he had lost many years before.

It was at the children's request that William next took them to see their grandfather. Where Aimee was concerned, it was to play with her new friend, Kate, and Simon, her brother, took time off his strenuous work alongside his father, to take Phillip to see the ships and dockside.

Amos had improved very slightly after their last visit, but

had become quite agitated. He, not having the power of speech, could not convey what he wanted.

'It were Kate who found out, sir. She were playin' near the master wi' her box o' toys, and he kep' beckonin' her, pointin' first to the box, then to himself, but when she did give the box to him he pushed it away. Then young Kate told us 'twere his own box he wanted.'

Bess hoped he did not mind their imposition, searching and bringing every box, including the heavy clothes chests from the bedrooms, until at last an old box was found by chance as Alex was setting a rat-trap in the cupboard under the stairs.

'This were the box that were wanted, sir, and Alex understood by the master's actions he wanted the box opened. The documents in the box ha' ne'er left him since. He keeps them close by him as they be now.'

William sat with Amos, who appeared to be asleep. He was amazed at the change in the once-beautiful house. Everything possible had been cleaned, old drapes washed, repaired and replaced, all in a matter of two short weeks. He wondered where he could find extra money to increase the small amount he had given these wonderful people. William fell asleep.

Bess shook him gently, asking if he would take Sunday lunch with them.

The large scrubbed table had been laid for only three people. William asked had they had their lunch and, being told that they would take it later, refused to sit unless all there were to join him. He would not hear their protests that servants did not eat at the same table as their masters.

William explained that this was not so. As far as he was concerned, this was their table, and he had been invited as a guest. And if there were enough food to spare, he would be obliged if they would also invite his coachman, Tug, inside for a bite to eat.

William had never seen Phillip eat so much; the rabbit stew, a succulent goose and fresh vegetables made a feast equal to Mrs Read's excellent fare.

Florrie ate very little, and kept looking at William cooing in a large laundry basket.

Straight after lunch William took the children into see their grandfather before the journey home. As soon as Phillip neared the bed, Amos became animated and reached out for him. William told the boy not to be afraid, the old man would not harm him.

Struggling and writhing, Amos drew from the bedclothes a bundle of yellowing documents and pressed them into Phillip's hands.

'What must I do with these, father?' he asked.

William asked Amos if he could see the papers. Eyes streaming, Amos nodded.

The papers were the deeds to the house and surrounding lands. Retying the ribbon, William placed them back in Amos's shaking hand. He pushed them away, pointing in turn to Phillip and William, then sank back exhausted.

They were saying goodbyes when Kate ran out, screaming her grandee was not talking to her.

Alighting from the carriage, William returned to the bedside of his father-in-law. The old man's face was peaceful.

William closed the eyes that were still damp.

He asked Tug to return home with Florrie and the children, and inform the mistress that her father had passed away.

Alice was persuaded to attend the funeral, and was surprised at so many people being there. She later discovered the larger number of these were creditors, who hoped to pass the debts of her father on to his heir.

Also there was a friend of William's brother, John, who had shared the same lodgings while they were studying, the one Medicine, the other Law. Both had passed out with honours, John going to London to become a hospital intern there, and Andrew Savage to a Law office in the city of Glasgow.

Andrew came with condolences and, sensing there was something wrong for William looked so worried, offered his assistance.

William confided his financial worries, about not having sufficient cash to cover old Amos's debts.

Andrew told him he would make inquiries about selling the

property that was now Alice's, she being the nearest and only blood relative of the late Mr Ogilivy.

A week later Andrew returned, saying the property had been so neglected it was worthless, and the land was worth a sum not nearly enough to pay half the creditors.

He asked William if he could obtain a sample of Amos Ogilvy's signature.

William was not sure Amos had been able to write, until he asked Alice and she was indignant he should think one of her parents, even one she disliked, was illiterate. She produced a book signed on the inside cover by her father.

Taking the book to Andrew Savage, William asked why he required the signature.

'You see, Mr McCall, I shall only accept bills to be settled that are signed by the departed, for times being what they are, many creditors try claiming sums that are not owing.'

William was still downcast, for he had the unpleasant task of facing old Martha and the Toomeys. They were still looking after the house and grounds, and he had hoped that if it were sold, the new owners might, on his recommendation, give work to at least one of them.

The welcome William received from the Toomey family made him feel worse. Then he told them what the valuers had said, that the property was unsaleable.

Alex declared he wished he had some money so that he could buy the old gatehouse.

'But, my dear fellow, why? It is practically in ruins,' said William.

'Aye, sir, but the roof be not that bad, just needs repair. Me and my boy could do that, and more, ourselves, and it be far better na no place at all.'

William asked why they could not stay where they were. He knew that it was very small, but it was neat and tidy.

Alex explained that the cottage was, and had been, leased to Martha and her husband for many years. Alex and his family lived in a company house owned by his employers, who deducted the rent from his wages. But with no job, he had no house.

Alex went on to say they would all have to move out of Martha's house soon, for they had fallen behind with the increased rent, and broken their agreement by moving in with her.

William had heard of company house, and stores, abhorring the very idea of folk working most of their lives, duty-bound to buy provisions at exorbitant prices from the store, ever kept in debt, even when dying. Their families had to keep paying.

He put down some money, apologizing that it was not enough to repay them for all they had done. But he promised to have words with Mr Savage, his legal adviser, to see if he could come up with a solution.

A few weeks later, Andrew Savage had news for William; only a third of Amos's debts were genuine, and some of those might already have been settled.

He explained that Amos Ogilvy had been a partner in a small shipping firm, busy following his other pursuits when his son was alive, then after his death taking no active part in running the business. He engaged an agent named Samuel Macavoy to do this for him. This agent falsified the accounts to show the firm was bankrupt, and told the sole surviving partner, Amos Ogilvy, that he had found someone to take over the business who was willing to pay a nominal sum to cover Amos's expenses only.

Amos, with his poor eyesight, signed a paper giving Power of Attorney to this Samuel Macavoy. Luckily the deed and contracts were in the box Amos kept. The agent, hearing of Mr Ogilivy's death, and frightened greedy creditors in league with him might spill the beans, fled leaving evidence of his treachery behind.

With the documents from Amos's box, very important information came to light.

Old Martha's house stood in the grounds of the Ogilvy property and had therefore been owned by Amos Ogilvy. In grander days it had been the head gamekeeper's cottage.

Martha and her husband had been Amos's servants, as had Martha's parents before them, to his parents. When Amos became a recluse, he told the agent that as long as she lived, Martha was to live in the house rent-free provided that she did not bother him, and left him some food outside.

Martha had always provided bread she had baked herself, eggs from her hens, milk from her goat and fresh vegetables, but the agent told her she had to pay the new owners a low rent, and when her daughter and family moved in with her, the rent had to be increased.

Amos locked himself away, not speaking to anyone. This enabled the scoundrel to take over, plotting with tradesmen of his acquaintance to present claims that, as Amos's agent, he should have paid. He urged them to go to the house for payment.

These unscrupulous traders soon confessed, withdrawing their false claims when threatened with punishment for Fraud.

William was thrilled, and conveyed the news to Martha and the Toomeys that there was no need to move, or pay rent, if Alex and his family became caretakers of the property until such time as it was decided what to do with it. If Alex desired, he could move into the gatehouse as well.

Alex asked permission to use materials such as slates and timbers from the many old adjoining buildings. The whole Toomey family and Martha blessed William, saying they would never let him down.

Alex and his son, Simon, managed to get part-time work on the dockside, and felt that, at last, their fortunes had changed for the better.

Although some of the worries had been settled for William, alas he was far from being out of the mire of financial worries.

He had a large sum of government taxes to pay, and on top of these, a demand came for the taxes that had not been paid for many years by his father-in-law.

Andrew Savage had been untiring in his efforts to find a buyer for Amos's estate. The only one who had shown the slightest interest was a high-ranking British army officer who was retiring from his post.

Prior to going to view the property, he and his wife stayed overnight with William and Alice at their home. After the viewing they went back to William with a substantial offer, not for Amos's property but for their own home, the wife declaring that to her it was like a gem in a perfect setting.

Tug had been working really hard. The gardens were extremely beautiful, and he had replaced the badly-soiled gravel, blackened by many carriage wheels of visitors who came during and after the funeral, with fresh, white stones.

Andrew Savage, who had accompanied the prospective buyers, told William he should go and see what was being done by Alex Toomey.

At the weekend, William drew up to the driveway, and was amazed at the transformation in the old gatehouse. The roof had been retiled, and the windows and doors had been repaired and were freshly painted. There was no sign of life.

Arriving at the main house, William saw Martha and Bess hacking at the overgrown undergrowth. Even little Kate was down on her knees, pulling at weeds. There was a shout from the roof of the house where Alex and Simon were busy replacing tiles on the gabled rooftop.

Alex came down from the roof to greet William, and invited him to partake of the food and drink from a big basket on the now-cleared terrace, where already shoots of petunias and plants were showing in the large, ornate pots.

Bess and Martha came from the back of the house where they had rushed young Kate into the kitchen to have a quick wash and clean-up. William was deeply embarrassed by their royal treatment, but eating a sandwich of fresh bread and cheese in their company, he felt quite at home.

He thanked them all for their labours, asking Alex where the money had come from to do the many repairs that were so evident.

'All the roof tiles and most of the timber came from the old buildings at the back, sir. Come, I will show ye!' He turned to Simon and told him to carry on cleaning more tiles but to mind that he did not go aloft until he returned.

He led William through a side garden, then through quite a large walled garden, where bees buzzed around in the overgrown foliage and old, cleaned and repaired hives.

'In a month there will be a few more o' they hives, sir, but first we must see that the houses will be finished afore bad weather sets in.'

They arrived at the site of what had once been a very large building, which William had not noticed before. The remains of the glass from the dome that had been in the roof were neatly stacked near the slates from the same roof and a large pile of cleaned bricks. Tubs of water containing decorated floor tiles soaked off the grime.

William wondered how Alex found the time to do the part-time work he said paid for the materials that had to be bought.

He was even more amazed when Bess apologized, asking if he minded that she and her mother had been 'tidying up the house,' as she put it.

'Ye see, sir, there were strangers coming, and we did not want them to think badly on it.'

He asked to be shown what had been done. Silently he followed her through the large reception and hallway, where all cobwebs and filth had been swept away. The floor tiles had been washed and, where they had been broken, there was evidence that someone was in the process of repairing them.

It was the bedrooms that really shook William, for they, too, had been cleared of rotting drapes and mattresses, the furniture and floors cleaned, and the windows opened wide to let in fresh air.

Again he had the greatest difficulty getting them to accept the money he had on his person. It occurred to him that these sterling folk were doing all this work with never a thought that if the place were to be sold they might be depriving themselves of their own home.

Next day William contacted Andrew Savage and commissioned him to draw up a deed stating that the Toomey family and Martha were not on any account to be evicted.

Mr Savage told William the officer, Major Henry Folland, had been in touch with him again, and was prepared to increase his already excellent offer for William's home.

William spoke to Alice, saying that he had never realized in what a beautiful place she had spent her youth, begging her to come and visit it with him and their children.

William had touched Alice's pride, and at last she consented to go with him.

The weather must have been smiling upon William and his family when they went down to Wychwood House. The lawn had been cut, and some of the beds planted with small but already flowering plants. Terrace statues had been scrubbed, and stood white in the sunshine.

Strangely, Alice did not seem to recall the gardens looking quite like this.

The two older children were soon running around with Kate, who had taken over, showing them all manner of things; nests in the trimmed hedges, the holes of slow worms.

Alice was not indifferent to Bess Toomey, and she had a vague recollection of Martha, who fussed over her, declaring her Ladyship had grown most beautiful, just like her sainted mother.

Going through the bedrooms, Alice started to remember, and told William which room had been whose. She lingered quite some time in a large room with a window opening onto a balcony, with a view of the Firth. She told William this had been her mother's room.

After they had partaken of the massive hamper Mrs Read had packed for them, Phillip wanted desperately for his father to come to see the water-front that Simon had shown him.

Alice said she would like to wander in the grounds, as Bess had promised to keep a sharp eye on Aimee and Kate, and Martha was cooing and cuddling young William.

On the journey home, the children asked how soon they could pay another visit, thinking it a great place. Alice was silent until she suddenly said, 'I'm glad the terrible old Orangery has been demolished.'

She did not disclose this was where she had by chance come

upon her father in a compromising situation with one of his lady-friends.

One week later, Aimee was again pleading to visit her new friend, Kate. Her mother told her she must wait, and when she turned to plead with her father, he told her that he had a great deal of work to do over the weekend, trying to balance the books.

William had told Alice of the Major's increased offer remarking that this money would solve most of his problems.

'But if we sold this house, where would we live?' asked Alice.

'I was just making a comment, dearest, but there could be one solution. Would you consider moving and residing in your old home?'

Alice was silent.

'We would have money to pay for it to be restored to even better than its former splendour, and the children love it there. The house and grounds are much larger than these.'

Alice thought for a while, then agreed.

Mrs and Major Folland were thrilled, and complimented Alice on the excellent meal that Mrs Read had prepared for them, expressing a wish that they could have such a cook in their kitchen.

Mrs Read, when told the family was moving, was a little put out, for she was used to the kitchen where she had reigned for many years. Also, the master had mentioned a Mrs Toomey, who would be employed as her help. She did not mind Florrie, as she had been trained to her ways, but a stranger might be different.

When she aired views to the master, he asked would she stay on at the old house as head-cook if it could be arranged. Mrs Read had already warmed to Mrs Folland, her being so profuse in praise of her cooking, and when told by her that she, and she alone, was to be in charge of the kitchen, and at an increased salary, she accepted the offer to become their cook.

12

The two older children were thrilled with their new home and Alice was quite pleased to have more staff. Florrie was at first a little put out, for Fiona got on so well with Martha, and Aimee spent most of her day with Kate. But Florrie was kept very busy in her new position as upstairs maid and, as she had become experienced in massaging and dressing the mistress's hair, she also acted as the lady's maid Alice desired.

Martha and Tug got on so well that Fiona intimated there could be the start of a romance there, whilst Phillip was so delighted with the dockside, and the sights and sounds of the ironworks, especially when furnaces were being tapped, that he was loath to return to school.

Mr Peel, the Art master, visited often, and each time he and Phillip spent a great deal of time together.

William told Mr Peel how difficult it had become getting Phillip to go back to school, or even yet to study, and that he was afraid that, academically, the boy would fall behind again.

Mr Peel said he would have a word with the boy, for he and Phillip had become very good friends.

The young master thought broaching the subject direct with Phillip would be of no use, knowing of Phillip's dream of going to sea. Each time he had visited, Phillip had been very keen to hear any news of the battle with the French, so Mr Peel made a point of finding out as many details as possible, especially of naval warfare and the exploits of brave officers.

With the help of Tug, who had many sea adventures to

relate, he thus encouraged Phillip back to his studies, determined to become at least an Admiral.

The McCall's settled down very well in their new home, where Alice played the grandam beautifully. Some of her old so-called friends sought her out once again, much to the annoyance of William, and the hidden disgust of the staff.

They flounced and minced through the house and garden, speaking in French. Alice appeared not to take any notice of their rudeness until, one day, seeing one of them roughly push little Aimee and young Kate out of their path, jabbering at them in French, Fiona, like a fighting cock, flew at them, shouting in their own tongue. Alice was flabbergasted, for Fiona had never let it be known she spoke the language.

The French people soon left, not to return, for they were sure they had been overheard in their criticisms of their hostess. For they thought all, except themselves, were low-life, new-rich peasants, to be used and made sport of.

Alice asked Fiona where she had learnt French, and why she had become so angry.

'Well, mistress, now I be on a different footin' than I were afore, and ye and the maester have made me feel like part o' the family. When they Frenchies came afore, I felt no right to speak out agin they, so I stopped makin' potions and creams, not wantin' tae be o' service to they who maligned folk who were good tae them. But no one on the face o' this earth is a going tae call our bairns bad names.'

'What did they say? What names did they call the children?' asked Alice.

'Ne'er ye mind, ye dinna need tae know, but I told them fair and square what I thought o' they from the beginnin'.'

Alice told the tale to William when he came home, and he said that nothing Fiona did or said surprised him for, in his opinion, she was a wonderful, truly learned person.

He hoped that they had seen the last of the French contingent. Now that his finances were improving, he did not want the expense of buying the fancy foods Alice had brought in for them. Not that he minded providing refreshments for guests, but these people were refugees who should know about want and waste, and they wasted far more than they consumed.

Alice said she would dearly love to find out where Fiona had learnt French, but William told her not to bother the woman.

The French people did not return, but Alice had lost other friends, too, as they had disliked the shallowness of her French guests, and stayed away.

Alice had no visitors, and begged Fiona to sit with her and talk, for she was lonely.

Fiona was pleased to be asked, for she now had time on her hands. While doing some mending, or sorting out herbs, she sat with the mistress.

Alice asked her how she came to speak French.

'Well, that be a long, sad story mistress.'

'We have the time, and now that we are such good friends, nay, you are like part of our family, I should like to know more about you, for you have had such a varied and interesting life.'

Of late, Fiona had felt more comfortable with Alice, as she had lost some of her airs and graces, and now treated all her children with equal affection and love, showing interest in Phillip's progress and always praising his schoolwork and artistry. Fiona's esteem of her had increased tremendously.

Although it pained her greatly to remember the tragedy in her life, once more Fiona agreed to tell Alice all about it.

13

Fiona had told how they bought the cottage from Annie, who had gone north with her husband, Tam. Fiona shed tears for Annie's suffering, and although she would have preferred to forget this part of her life, she steeled herself to speak of it.

Fiona was happy, expecting her second child and travelling to market each day. Her only worry was old Morag. She being a market trader, at the end of the morning's trading would barter with the other traders for bruised fruit and damaged cakes, which often she would get for next to nothing.

Twice a week Fiona would go around to Morag to share with the old woman who had been so kind to them, and began to notice a change in both Morag and her house.

The loom had gone, which Morag explained was because she was no longer able to work on it.

As Fiona arrived, a woman was leaving carrying the thick blankets Annie had left. Entering, Fiona found Morag on the floor, where she said she had fallen.

Fiona went to Willie Haig, asking his advice, for he was kin to Morag. It was a Friday, and Fiona should have been on her way home.

Willie promised he would go with Fiona early Monday morning to see Morag, and she told him she was going to ask Edward if Morag could come to live at their home with them. Willie blessed her.

Edward was anxiously waiting for her, holding baby Helen. While having supper, Fiona broached the subject of Morag. Edward willingly agreed that she should come to live with them, and was eager to go that night for her, but Fiona told him to leave it until morning, as she would be at home to look after the baby.

Edward returned home alone, agitated and upset. Fiona understood that he had found Morag's house empty. Unable to ask where she had gone, as he could not get people to understand him, he had been followed by a group of rowdies intent on mischief. Catching up with him in the square, they had formed a circle around him, pushing him from one to the other, chanting, 'Stupid Dummy'.

A group of dark-skinned people had recently arrived in town; two men, one older than the other, two women, again one older than the other, a youth, and two dark-eyed children.

It was the two men and the youth who went to Edward's assistance.

A crowd gathered. Some men who had been drinking at the inn joined with the rowdies against the 'Gyppos', as they called the foreigners. They were winning the battle, as there were more of them, until reinforcements in the shape of Willie Haig came to sort out the fray, putting a quick end to it.

Willie helped Edward up and apologized to the street performers, for the older woman had a small cart from which she made and sold pastries which she called *churros.* These were made from soft dough cooked in a large pan of oil until golden brown, then rolled in fine sugar. Three drunks had overturned her cart, and were dancing around her as she tried to put out the fire the oil and coals had ignited, which was burning her wooden cart.

Willie caught two, one in each hand, and crashed their heads together. Dropping their lifeless bodies, he pole-axed a third with his elbow. One by one he held them by their feet, shaking every coin out of their pockets. He gave the money to the old woman.

On the Monday morning before setting up her stall, Fiona put the donkey and cart in Willie's yard. Locking it up, Willie asked how Edward was, and gave her a brief account of Saturday's fracas, telling her she should be proud of her man, for although he was disabled he had given a good account of himself. He also spoke of the street performers and how they had pitched in to help Edward.

Fiona had seen them admiring the dark beauty of the younger woman with her colourful costume, and her grace of movement as she danced with her tambourine, while her husband juggled and the children tumbled to the fiddle-playing of the old man.

Fiona had thrown a farthing into her tambourine more than once, for the husband had been kind to her before.

She had been overloaded with fruit and goods she had bought and been given. Two oranges had rolled off her 'carrying-shelf', as she laughingly called the bulge of her pregnancy. The man had been juggling at the time, and had deftly collected them, mingling them with the balls in the air. Then one by one he had placed them back on the pile whence they came.

The crowd had applauded as he removed his hat, bowing with a courtly flourish.

'Manuel Fernandez Mendosa at your serveez, senora. As you have too much to carry, I weel assist you.'

So saying, he had gathered up all her purchases, taken hold of her elbow, and guided her back to her pitch.

The door of Morag's house was not quite closed. Willie knocked, pushing it open further. A woman was poking up the chimney with a broom, peering up at the same time. A cloud of soot fell upon her head, clinging to the sores on her face, making her look even more grotesque.

'What ye be doin', mistress?' asked Fiona.

'What business is it o' yorn?' asked the hag.

'We came for Morag to take her from here.'

'Morag be wi' us now, for that Annie Floyd left her tae starve.'

'Don' ye dare say that of Annie,' fumed Fiona.

Willie stood between them, holding the woman's arm as she raised it to strike Fiona.

A weasel-faced individual stuck his head over a board-platform which formed the sleeping quarters.

'There be not a farthin' here, and ye do look a sight,' he snorted.

The woman danced with rage, shaking the fire-iron which had replaced the broom in her hand. She was having difficulty trying to prise bricks up from the hearth, and shouted to weasel-face to come and try.

Finding nothing but ash and a dead cockroach, he cursed loudly, 'I'll have no profanity in my presence. You know I have the religion,' the woman snarled.

Fiona smiled, thinking that with her looks, witchcraft would be more suitable than religion.

'When can we see Morag?' Fiona asked the woman, recalling that this was the one she had seen taking away the thick blankets.

Instead of answering, the hag pulled a face at her.

Willie told her that he would be around to see Morag, and she had better be all right, for she was his kin as well.

He steered Fiona into the street, as she wanted the woman to take off the boots she was wearing, saying they belonged to Morag. Willie said to leave it, that she did not want to contaminate herself with Poxy Meg and Foxy, a bad pair who ran a bawdy house near the river. And who would want boots Meg had worn? She was diseased, and at one time had thought she was dying and so had turned to religion.

'But I fear it be too late to save her black soul,' said Willie.

Early afternoon the next day, Willie and Fiona made their way along back-streets where children in rags squabbled and beat off mangy cats and skinny dogs for the refuse thrown out by the inns and taverns. They came to a street with high stone walls and a large door containing a small door.

Willie turned the ring-handle, pushing the small door inwards. He helped Fiona over the step, and felt her trembling as he held her arm. The yard was in shadow, and she felt this place had never known the sun.

What had once been the entrance hall and ground floor of a big house was now the yard. All that remained of the original building were stone steps leading up to the part of the first floor where beam-ends stuck out like the cross-bars of gallows, and four doors that looked down like two pairs of eyes.

'Show yerselves!' bellowed Willie.

Half-a-dozen girls no more than children, came out of the doors above, and leant on the rail of the narrow balcony before them. They were scantily dressed.

'Tell Morag McIntyre, Willie Haig be here to see her,' he shouted.

'Ye dinna want that auld biddy. I will serve ye much better,' said one mocking young voice.

'Or me! Or me!' went up a chorus.

'I said "Morag McIntyre", or do I have tae pull this heathen place apart tae find her?'

Something moved out of the deep shadow, where the large fireplace and over-mantel were still recognizable. Morag hobbled towards them using a cleft stick as a crutch.

Seeing Morag's obvious decline upset Fiona. In the poor light, she was almost sure there were bruises on Morag's face as well as dirt. Almost in tears, Fiona went to touch her old friend, saying, 'We have come here to take you home with us.'

Morag backed away into the shadows, saying, 'Ye dinna want anither burden on ye, lassie, ye have enough wi' another bairn on the way, and that sweet mother of yours. 'Tis nay so bad here, an' when my leg heals, I will gae upstairs wi' the lasses. They be good, do bring I food and such. I earn my keep by answering the door tae the gentlemen, callin' for the maid they want.

'Ye get on wi' yer life and be happy, an dinna worry about I, for I mun get ready for the night's work.'

They failed to persuade her to leave with them, and came away feeling downhearted.

Willie and Fiona arrived back at the market square to find men fighting amid broken glass from flying bottles, upturned stalls and the scattered debris of crushed fruit and vegetables everywhere.

From where they stood they saw that the old gypsy woman's stall had been overturned and was burning yet again. The two women were pinioned against the wall of the inn as five or six men fought with their menfolk.

The landlord of the inn, bleeding from a gaping wound in his head, was trying to comfort the two little children averting their eyes from the punishment their parents and grandparents were being subjected to.

Willie quickly opened the door of his shop and pushed Fiona inside, telling her to lock the door and crouch behind the counter, opening the door only to him.

Watching through the window, Fiona saw Willie grab the throats of the two men holding Pillar, the younger of the two women. Lifting them bodily, he tossed them over his shoulders as if they were bags of straw.

Pillar, once released, picked up a piece of wood, bringing it down on the head of one man who held her mother, whilst Willie sent the other in the wake of his mates.

Willie, with Pillar wielding her club, and Teresa, her mother, finding one similar, set about the men who, with fists and boots, were attacking *their* men. Willie hurled bodies every way, and Manuel, cartwheeling and somersaulting, struck out with his feet. The fight soon came to an end.

Bully-boys able to stagger, dragged away the ones who could not even stand.

Pillar collected her children and thanked the friendly landlord who had been wounded protecting them.

Willie asked them to wait at the inn for him and he would fetch Fiona to them. When he returned with Fiona, they were provided with refreshments.

Jesus, the older man, was shaken up, and put to lie on a settle while his wife, Teresa, bathed his head.

The skirt of Pillar's spangled dress was torn to her waist, so a serving girl kindly brought her a large apron to tie around her to cover her scratched legs.

Willie asked their host what had started the fight, and was told that a red-haired man drinking heavily there had been asking if anyone knew a Fiona McCready. Two ruffians had said they might know her, so he had bought them drinks.

Fiona's face drained of colour as she slumped to the floor in a dead faint.

Willie lifted Fiona'a limp body and lay her on another

settle, facing the one where Jesus lay. Pillar smoothed her cheeks and murmured she should not have to be upset in her condition.

Burned feathers were held under Fiona's nose, and the innkeeper went on with the story.

He told how this stranger had become aggressive the more he drank, and how a scuffle had developed into a battle, with bottles flying and furniture being overturned and thrown about.

Some of the market traders had assisted the landlord to evict the rabble into the street. The inn door being closed to them, they had been joined by others with a taste for a fight, and with the possibility of looting from someone they thought better off than themselves, they had turned on the traders, who had hurriedly closed shop, making their escape.

It was then that someone had suggested having a little bit of fun with the foreigners. But that had got out of hand, for the children trying to help their parents had been thrown to the ground.

The inn landlord had brought out a musket which was wrenched from his hand, and turned on him, but it was unloaded, so used as a club.

Although wounded, he had managed to drag the two children to safety, and had been attempting to help the women being molested when he was struck again, and called 'Dago lover'.

Willie asked what was the name the red-headed man had been looking after, for he had a vague feeling he had heard it before.

'Fiona McCready,' said the serving wench.

Like a flash, Willie remembered where he had heard that name before; it was at the wedding of the young woman who was just coming out of her fainting attack, and being told to lie still.

Manual said it was time for them to move on to a different place.

Willie asked if, first, he could accompany him as he took Fiona back home. He had a strange feeling there would be more trouble, and also felt there was need of haste.

Manuel said he would be honoured to go with him.

Willie asked if he could borrow the loaded musket from the landlord, as Teresa and Pillar helped Fiona to her feet. The street was quiet as she was helped up the steps of the caravan and laid on a bed.

Teresa stayed with her as Manuel drove it. Willie rode his horse, holding the small girl up in front of him, and Pillar's father, Jesus, took the reins of Fiona's cart. The youth, with his mother, Pillar, beside him, drove a cart carrying the remains of the *churro* stand, and other equipment.

Although they were travelling as fast as was possible with the carts and caravan, Willie leading them, arrived at the scene first.

Placing the child at a safe distance, he joined the shadowy figures trying vainly to put out the flames consuming the cottage.

Pillar and Teresa tried to hold on to Fiona, who was struggling to get out through the narrow caravan doorway, but she escaped their hold to stumble down the steps.

A series of small explosions threw her to the ground, and forced the fire-fighters back, just before a larger explosion of spirit dye blew out the main walls.

A man-servant of Lady McGregor's appeared and asked Pillar to accompany them as he carried Fiona to her Ladyship's carriage.

Fiona struggled as a blazing beam crashed down, lighting up the scene enough for her to see the body of her husband, propped against a tree, with a gaping wound across his throat.

Fiona struggled and kicked so much the man-servant had to release her. She fell to her knees in front of Edward's body.

The open wound was like an extra mouth mocking her as Fiona, gently rocking, held Edward's head close to her breast.

A man came to her bearing the charred remains of a petticoat, with the scorched leather pouch containing five gold coins and a small crucifix.

Sobbing, Fiona brought the burnt remnants to her lips and fell, moaning, to the ground, on her face.

Teresa, Pillar's mother, rushed to her, seeing the fresh blood on Fiona's skirt, and called Ruth's attention to the still-spreading stain.

Teresa pointed silently to the caravan. Ruth asked Willie to carry Fiona inside. He lifted her as if she were a feather, and solemnly followed the woman up the steps.

Inside she lit oil-lamps. Their light reflected in many ornate crystal mirrors, almost blinded him as he squinted around. He was motioned to lay the limp figure on the bed, and backed out of the van.

By torchlight they searched the smouldering remains, where the sickly smell of burnt flesh hung in the air. Voices in the distance called for Fiona's mother, then gave up their search until it was daylight.

Teresa emerged, carrying a tiny bundle wrapped in a cloth. Going to Manuel she crossed herself. Then she said something to Manuel, who had his arm around Pillar's shoulders as they held their two children close to them.

Lady Ruth asked what Teresa had said, so Manuel told her.

'The old mother said that the little one came too soon and, as he has not breathed, he is now one of God's cherubs.'

Fiona became greatly upset relating this part of her history to Alice, and had to be helped by Florrie to her room.

When William came home he was very annoyed with Alice and told her she was on no account to badger Fiona further.

'But dearest, Fiona volunteered to tell me her tragic story without any force on my part,' Alice argued.

William did not quite believe her. Later, when he went to see Fiona, he told her that there was no need for her to continue if it was going to upset her.

'But Maester, I did tell Mistress of my own choosin', and the telling of it, besides bringing back the loss and sorrow, refreshed the feeling of love I still have for my dear husband,

and the remembrance of the many folk who were kind to me.'

'If it hurts you in any way, you must stop. Your past is your own, and I will not have you upset,' William declared. He bade her 'Goodnight and God bless'.

William left the room, shaking his head.

Within two days Fiona told how the search for her mother revealed nothing except signs that someone, or something, had been dragged through the undergrowth.

At dawn men searched the cinders, discovering the bones of a small creature.

Fiona was kept sedated with potions given by Teresa.

Because they were strangers to him, the minister refused to bury Edward, the unchristened stillborn, and the small, charred remains, in the kirk cemetery.

Lady Ruth was furious and sent for a bishop who was kin to her, and he blessed the land where the three resting-places were dug.

Fiona awoke with no memory. She was barely aware of Teresa feeding her. When Willie and Lady Ruth came to see her, she did not recognize them. Turning her head away, she would cling to Teresa, her mind in some far-off place.

Some hens had returned, as had a scorched cow, and a very angry sow, minus one of her litter. A week had passed since the funerals. Fiona had not spoken or shown a spark of life.

Willie came each evening. Lady Ruth spent half her day talking softly to her, but neither received a response. The only reaction or show of emotion from Fiona was distress when old Teresa moved out of her sight.

Manuel told Willie they would have to leave soon for they needed to be on their way to find a warmer climate before winter set in, when travelling would be too hazardous. The problem was, what was going to happen to Fiona?

It was decided, as she would not leave Teresa's side, that she should travel with them.

Lady Ruth paid generously for the stock, giving the money to Teresa to help provide for Fiona. But the foreigners refused the donkey and cart for, already having two vehicles of their own, a cart and the caravan, travelling by ship would become too costly for them.

Sadly, Lady Ruth and Willie Haig waved these gentle wanderers goodbye.

'Oh, you went abroad with these Spanish people. How interesting!' said Alice.

'They were no Spanish, but Portuguese. Manuel told me a great deal of his history.'

It was there the tale was interrupted yet again, as a man from William's factory came to ask Fiona to accompany him, and to bring her medicines.

14

Private coaching given to Phillip by Bruce Peel soon advanced his Mathematics even further than his classmates'.

The master of Mathematics at the college, Mr George Skulley, a man of volcanic temper, took pleasure in inflicting punishment, caning the bare backsides of his pupils. Mr Skulley suspected Phillip of cheating. The sprog who had been a duffer now sailed through lessons with ease.

Skulley hated most people, including this boy's father for having the money to buy a telescope for the school, so that Astronomy was added to the school curriculum as an optional course. Pupils and masters alike had become interested in this new toy, increasing the popularity of the already well-liked Mr Bruce Peel, whom Mr Skulley also hated.

William had found a way to repay Bruce Peel for his coaching and interest in Phillip. Now solvent after the sale of the house, William had asked his brother, John, to purchase a very fine telescope in London for him.

Mr Skulley was waiting like an animal for an opportunity to catch Phillip out and have an excuse to punish him. That day arrived, bringing the event that was to change Phillip's future.

The lesson on Algebra that day Phillip soon finished. With time to spare before the hour-session was over, he kept his head down, and was putting the finishing touches to a cartoon of Mr Skulley, accentuating the hooked beak-like nose above his thin, drooling lips. Mr Skulley was indulging in his favourite sport of flaying the bare backside of a howling victim.

A boy named Peter Shaw shared Phillip's desk. They also shared the same dormitory. Peter liked Phillip, a quiet lad who always offered around the abundance of sweetmeats provided by his father.

Nudging Phillip, Peter indicated he would like to see his drawing. Surreptitiously, Phillip slipped the sketch-pad over, and within minutes it had been seen by half the class, and was causing a ripple.

Mr Skulley swooped. He brought the cane he held by the thin, straight end in his left hand and, using the curved handle, hooked the neck of the boy furthest away from him. His right arm pushed the boys' faces down to the desk, and with his grubby, ink-stained claw, he grasped them by their fashionably long hair, dragging their heads back.

Seeing the cartoon, Mr Skulley drew in breath through his rotting teeth like a hiss of steam. He demanded to know who the artist was. Pulling viciously at the boys' hair, he repeated his demand.

Sending their heads crashing down to the desk-top started the boys' noses bleeding. They winced as, again, their heads were jerked back, and the cane came down on the desk, sending the sketch-pad to the floor.

Looking as if he were examining something containing all the diseases known to man, Mr Skulley flicked through with his cane and came to the cover. The name was Phillip T J McCall.

With silent rage, holding the pad aloft he tore the pages to shreds, throwing them like confetti over the heads of the white-faced boys. Snarling through saliva-flecked lips, he pointed his wavering cane at Phillip.

'Come tae the front, laddie, for me tae show these little horrors the genuine article, instead of a very poor attempt at the describing of it.' Phillip reluctantly went to the front of the class. The master pointed to a three-legged stool, indicating to Phillip to bring it forward.

The boy, refusing to remove his breeches, was told, 'That is alright, me laddo, the way I use my weapon makes no difference tae pain when I perform.'

Phillip bent over the stool. The master spat on his hands.

It seemed like an eternity before the first blow struck. Mr Skulley liked his victim to wait and contemplate, whilst he savoured the pleasure he was going to feel, basking in the terror that his performance was creating.

Phillip heard the swish, biting into his lip as the first blow fell. The fifth stroke parted the fibres of the cloth, the sixth brought blood, which seemed to goad the man to use more force and quicken the pace.

Foaming spittle dribbled down his pointed chin, and he jumped up and down. Without mercy, he continued flaying the unconscious form. The bloodied cane rose and fell again and again.

A pupil stamped his feet, and the rest of the class joined him, chanting, 'Beastie! Beastie!' This only infuriated the teacher more, for now he had completely lost control, and was screaming obscenities.

The classroom door burst open. The dean entered, accompanied by the horrified Mr Peel, who tried in vain to pull the torturer away.

The burly Sports master came, and gave the madman a blow to the back of the head with his fist, stunning him so that he could be dragged from the room.

When Mr Peel asked for help to carry Phillip to the sick-bay, the whole class rose as one. Four of the biggest lads carried Phillip, face down, out into the hallway, and the care of the plump matron.

The boys slowly and carefully carried their classmate out into the wide hallway. The other boys were going to follow them, when Mr Peel begged them to return to their seats, promising he would report back to them on Phillip's condition.

At one end of the corridor, the men holding Mr Skulley had arrived at closed double doors. One released his hold to open them and Mr Skulley, with demonic strength, escaped. Screaming, he raced back to the boys carrying Phillip.

He arrived level with the open gymnasium door, where a

senior student, holding an Indian club across the aperture, stood keeping other athletes inside, out of the way.

As the maniac passed them, this student brought the club crashing down. All the others rushed from the gym to fall on top of the stunned man, only moving from him enough to allow him to be securely bound with climbing ropes.

The blow would have kept a normal man senseless for hours or days, but this man was gaining his senses, hurling curses at everyone.

A gag was called for, and a dirty rag used to clean the blackboard was brought by a lad with a bloodied nose.

Hog-tied, Mr Skulley was manhandled into the gymnasium, and with more rope secured to the wall-bars.

A groundsman was sent post-haste to the asylum to fetch people to incarcerate the man, who was obviously out of his mind. They pushed the shrieking master, who had bitten through his gag, into the wagon.

Upstairs, matron had difficulty seeing through her tears, and wondered what ever she could do for the terrible wounds inflicted on the poor lad's rear and back.

William had been sent for and told Phillip was badly hurt, but he had not been told in what way.

In his own carriage he sent a workman with a message for Tug, asking him to bring Fiona to meet him at the college, and to ask Fiona to bring her medicines with her. Fiona had often been sent for in this way to treat accidents at the factory, so Alice suspected nothing.

Driving his horse, Blueboy, hard, William soon arrived at the college, where the dean tried to explain what had happened, but was too upset. It was Mr Peel who told William, speedily taking him to Phillip's bedside.

The matron, helped by the dean's wife, was cutting away torn material, and trying unsuccessfully to remove the shreds of cloth from the criss-crossed bleeding gashes. They were hardly able to see through their tears.

Fiona arrived and took over, calling for plenty of bowls of hot water, in which she put a few drops of the oil of a herb named by the Romans 'Satureia', but later renamed 'Savory'.

Fiona had learnt about its uses from her Portuguese friends during her wanderings abroad.

Strips of linen were immersed in this, and constantly changed by the matron and the dean's wife, who were much impressed by Fiona's patience and skill. They had stopped crying and were carrying out all her orders like well-trained soldiers.

Fiona gently laid these swabs over the wounds, each time, when they were lifted, plucking bits of shredded cloth from where they had stuck to the torn flesh.

Once when the boy uttered a weak moan, Fiona, lifting his head, dribbled a liquid from a phial between his lips that his teeth had bitten deeply into.

Phillip's clothes and the sheets underneath him were now very wet. Fiona asked for help to move the boy.

Mr Peel, with the Sports master, lifted his lifeless form very carefully, and placed him on another bed.

For days Fiona sat with Phillip. She dozed, and rose at his every sound. A few times she put the phial she had told his father contained a mild sleeping draught to his lips, and constantly changed the dressings on his back.

The matron and the dean's wife came to relieve her, but she would take time only to refresh herself, with a wash and a change of apron.

There was concern that the beating Phillip had received would affect and damage his mind, as well as his body. Fiona, whilst attending to him, spoke softly, telling him to rest, and that no one was ever going to harm him again.

The master, Mr Skulley, was declared a lunatic, to be locked up for the rest of his life, which was but a few months. For he was pacing around in bedlam, whipping invisible pupils, when by chance he struck a patient who had committed many murders by snapping the necks of his victims with his powerful hands. He had added Mr Skulley to his list.

Fiona asked if there were some method of administering liquid to her patient, for he needed a constant supply of fluids.

The Science master constructed a frame holding a funnel

with a tube connected to it. The liquid in the funnel was contained by a peg pinching the tube. When the peg was removed, the tube, held between two fingers, was squeezed, allowing a small amount into the mouth. At the same time the throat was stroked to help swallowing. This worked well, and on the fourth day Phillip coughed, and weakly asked to be allowed to go to the toilet.

Fiona almost shouted, 'God be praised!', and restrained Phillip as he attempted to rise.

'Ye lay there, my bonny love, dinna fret!'

She placed a huge goose-down pillow to support his back as he lay on his side, while she held a jug for him to urinate into. Again, Fiona thanked the Lord when, on examining the fluid, she found no blood, for she had feared she might.

Phillip's schoolfriends all wanted to visit him. The dean forbade them to do this, until Fiona said it might be beneficial to stimulate Phillip, if they came two at a time, and did not stay too long.

They trooped in with gifts, and talked boys' talk.

Festering abscesses erupted, which were poulticed until they burst, revealing shreds of cloth.

Everyone marvelled at the wonder of Fiona and her knowledge, while she marvelled at the miracle of the human body.

Now that Phillip was out of bed, he sat for very short periods in a chair Tug had made for him from soft sheep skins, fleece-side up, fastened to a frame, very like a sloping canvas cot on board ships of the day.

Fiona completely refused rest. William begged to take her home, afraid she would collapse, but she refused.

Saying he would be honoured if Mrs Brown would take a room in his quarters, the dean assured Fiona that she would receive the best of attention, which a person of her ability and knowledge deserved.

Fiona agreed, and was given the best room they had. She fought off sleep for many nights, but the dean acquired her phial of sleeping draught.

Fiona accepted and relished the dish of soup, not knowing a

few drops of her own medicine had been added to it by her new admirer, the dean.

Fiona slept around the clock, watched over by the matron and the dean's wife in turn. Within minutes of her waking an elegant tray bearing her breakfast was brought to her bedside.

She objected to this treatment, and was told she would not be allowed out of bed unless she ate the breakfast first.

'But what of my boy? Who is looking after him?' she asked.

'Mr Wilson had been with him since yesterday, and a young girl called Florrie has been assisting him.'

'With they two he be in safe hands, so I will bide and take a little nourishment.'

After eating her breakfast, Fiona was persuaded to take time for the luxury of the hot bath that was prepared for her, and to put on the clothes that were neatly draped on a chair. She felt quite unlike she had ever felt before.

When she went in to see Phillip, Tug and Florrie greeted her as if she had been away for a year.

Phillip asked to be taken home, but the wounds on his back had not fully healed, and it was obvious he was still in pain.

Fiona gave him medicine that dulled the pain, but it made him drowsy. The journey home was thought to be too arduous for Phillip in this condition, but he begged his father to allow him to come home.

Not wanting to upset him in case it affected his recovery, they promised to see what could be done.

Tug constructed a harness that fastened across the interior of the chaise. The straps held Phillip in an almost-standing position, with all his weight forward on his chest. Feather pillows were wrapped around his body to stop the chafing, and to soften any jolts.

The journey home was long and tiring for Phillip.

His room, next to his parents' room, was at the front of the house and shared the same view. The chair Tug had made for him was placed near the window, from where he could see the water glinting through the trees, and sometimes the sails of ships.

He seemed to have lost all interest, causing great concern to his parents and those who loved him. He was often in pain, crying out at night. Fiona would come to give him a sleeping draught, and stay with him until he slept.

Thus it was for many weeks, until one morning, when Tug, who came to dress the boy, said that as it was a fine day, would he not like to sit on the balcony of his bedroom, and Phillip agreed.

Fiona and Aimee came to sit with him. He soon tired of Aimee's prattle, saying he wished he were able to paint, but in his reclining chair it would be difficult.

Fiona asked Aimee to run and fetch Florrie. Florrie came.

'Take the bairn wi' ye and go and bring Tug back tae us!' instructed Fiona.

When Tug came, Fiona told him of Phillip's wish, explaining that to paint from the position he was in would be difficult.

'Leave it tae I, Mistress Fiona, I'll think on it, and be back directly.'

Not ten minutes passed before a cavalcade came. Tug carried a dining chair, Aimee a cushion, Florrie carried Phillip's easel and paints, and his mother brought long, silken sashes.

Tug helped Phillip to sit on a soft cushion astride the chair, facing its back, then the sashes his mother brought were tied around his waist and the chair-back to support him while he painted.

The whole family was delighted. At last Phillip was taking an interest in something. At first he soon became tired, but Fiona watched over him like a mother-hen. Now that Bess Toomey and her mother, Martha, did most of the kitchen work, Fiona had freedom to spend most of her day with 'her boy', bringing her herbs and plants up to his room to sort them out, along with a tattered old notebook containing rough drawings.

Sharing a mid-morning drink and freshly-baked biscuits,

Phillip asked if he could see the notebook she had been drawing in.

One drawing was obviously of a person holding the lower back, and underneath this were some cyphers. Phillip asked what they meant.

'That be saying oil of Juniper berries be a cure for the back and kidney pains.'

On another page was a drawing of two circles with a dripping sausage in between. Phillip had an idea what this meant but, feeling a little mischievous, asked anyway.

Fiona thought for a second, then said, 'That be parsley tea, it be gaed for the waterworks and other things.'

He laughed at her embarrassment, showering her with crumbs from the biscuit he was eating.

Fiona felt warm that her boy was truly on the mend.

So it was that Phillip started cataloguing Fiona's cures. She brought the plants, and he compared them with a book on Botany that was brought at his request, then drew them with coloured crayons. He copied Fiona's sketches, but also neatly wrote the Latin names as well as the names Fiona called them.

Often, when unable to sleep, he would sit at a table working on this, until with sheer exhaustion he sank into a deep slumber.

15

Tug and Alex Toomey procured a small pony and governess-cart. Again thanks to Tug's ingenuity, the seating was arranged so that Phillip, although sitting, had no pressure on his back. For he knelt on a frame, looking like a young gladiator driving a chariot.

Tug, Alex, or Simon his son, led the pony at first. Phillip said he would like to go alone after having practised driving his chariot close to the house.

Mr Peel often visited, bringing good wishes from Phillip's student friends, and other news of current affairs, for these were difficult days on the whole for Britain, at the beginning of the year 1798.

Napoleon was sent to Brest, there to work out the feasibility of an invasion of Ireland, but Napoleon dreamt of an Eastern conquest, of capturing Egypt, and marching on to India.

If Napoleon had invaded Ireland at this time, it would have been disastrous for Britain. The British seamen were, not without just cause, as records show, rebelling. They were given very little money as a result of its embezzlement by the paymasters, issued with insufficient food, which was mostly unfit for consumption, and had to suffer sadistic punishment for the slightest misdemeanour.

A man named Parker became their leader, and he hoisted the red flag of anarchy, urging them to select their own officers. But he was captured and hanged.

Lord Howe, nicknamed Black Dick, was highly thought of by the mariners. He promised then redress. Lord Howe's audacity had gained everyone's admiration, for the magnificent victory he had gained over the Dutch, with Admiral Duncan.

The crafty Admiral Duncan made a show of signalling to the mutinous ships as if they were still in his command, but in fact he commanded the only two ships that were not involved in the mutiny. Thus he made the Dutch believe the whole fleet was blockading them, so they stayed where they were.

Duncan manoeuvred between them and the shore, attacking them from that side together with Lord Howe, winning a magnificent victory.

By October, conditions had improved on board ships and with further improvements promised, the mutiny came to an end.

Britain was still desperate, having failed to crush France in the year 1797. France held the whole of the Netherlands, and controlled all of the Spanish fleet. Britain had no allies on the continent and, with Ireland on the brink of rebellion, and Scotland highly dissatisfied, England was indeed in a bad way.

Phillip was hungry for every piece of information. Determined to get himself fit, he longed to do battle, especially after hearing of Lord Howe and Admiral Duncan's exploits.

The British Navy, as in other times, started to improve matters.

Admiral Jervis beat the Spanish off the Cape of St Vincent, and was then honoured by the name Lord St Vincent.

It was at Cape St Vincent that Nelson distinguished himself, too, for the Spanish fleet was in two divisions, with Jervis trying to keep them apart. At a critical point, without orders, Nelson took his own initiative. Swinging his vessel out of line, he attacked the leading ships just as they were on the point of joining up with the others.

Phillip's parents were against him going out on his own in the cart. So, helped sometimes by Tug, and other times by Simon, carrying his easel, paints and seat, they would set out on foot.

Phillip would pick a suitable spot, then whoever was with

him would leave him and return to the house.

There was always a haversack containing sandwiches, and instructions from Fiona that he should never overtire himself, and always take with him a phial of the pain-relieving potion.

It had rained heavily for two days, and Phillip was impatient to go out.

The rain had stopped, and the weak sun was trying to break through. Phillip asked his mother's permission to go out, and she said he could go on condition that he did not stay late, for his friend and tutor, Mr Peel, was coming that evening. She did not tell him the reason for Mr Peel's visit, as it was to be a surprise for him.

William had engaged workmen to help Alex Toomey erect the domed glass from the old orangery in one of the attics. Now that the school had a fine new telescope, Mr Peel was giving the old one to Phillip for his personal use.

Anxious to go out, Phillip rushed through to the kitchen to find either Tug or Simon. He was about to go outside when Fiona called him back.

'Ye have not had any breakfast this morning, Master Phillip.'

He told her he was not hungry.

She told him he must take his medicine with him, and she would get Mrs Toomey to make him some sandwiches.

He promised he would come back for them as soon as he had found Tug or Simon.

Phillip returned with Simon, who picked up Phillip's chair, easel and paints.

Again calling to Phillip, Fiona told him not to forget his medicine or the sandwiches on the dresser before leaving, and to put the catalogue of cures he was compiling, safe out of the way of busy little fingers.

The catalogue was on the dresser, where Martha had put it after rescuing it from Aimee and Kate, as they were going to scribble in it.

Impatient to be away, Phillip grabbed the catalogue and his medicine, pushing them into the bag around his neck, but he omitted to pick up the sandwiches.

The river was swollen after the recent rains, and seagulls swooped to investigate the flotsam. Some perched on a fallen tree, pecking at the carcass of the dead animal caught up in it.

This upset Phillip, making him feel queasy so he went further downstream towards the ironworks.

At the quayside stood a large ship. Phillip had heard that Royal Navy ships now came to Scotland to have their hulls sheathed in copper, and the work was perhaps done at this factory.

Two soldiers stood guard at the foot of the gangplank, looking very smart in their cocked hats and red-and-white Marine uniforms.

Phillip brought out his crayons and started sketching one of them.

A call came from the deck and one soldier answered, 'Right, we will come as soon as we move a young fellow away.'

One moved towards Phillip and pointed his musket at him. 'What be ye a-doin', an' what have ye there?'

Phillip showed his drawing.

''Ere, Billy, come an' have a look at this, 'tis a dead spit o' ye!'

Billy came and laughingly agreed.

Billy said, 'Ye are not a Frenchie spy, are ye lad?'

Phillip shook his head to deny this. 'I just love ships, sir, and if you would like the drawing, you are welcome to it.' Tearing out the page, he handed it to the delighted Billy.

'He is not a-doin' any harm, matey, so what say we leave him be, eh?'

Billy's compatriot agreed, leaving Phillip, to go on board, wishing that the lad had done a likeness of him also, so he could show it to his wife when, and if, they went home.

Phillip stayed and was fascinated, watching the ship being loaded. Lads not much older than himself coiled up ropes and did other things mariners do. He wished he were up there with them.

It was well past noon when he looked in his bag for the

sandwiches, and realized he had left them behind. He did some more sketching, and the pain started. He drew out the potion and took a good swig.

Leaning forward against an upturned boat, he felt drowsy. He knew it was far too early for Simon to come and collect him. The bustle on board ship had died down; there was no one on guard, or to be seen on deck, just a chain across the gangplank.

Hiding his easel and paints behind some loading platforms, he slung his bag around his neck and crept on board.

Suddenly there was a pounding in his ears. He realized it was his own heartbeat. Voices floated up from below, then seemed to come nearer. He dodged behind a coil of rope, but this did not hide him completely. Sliding across the deck, he entered a locker containing tins of paint and sundry other items.

The pain started again. Taking out the phial, he swallowed another large dose.

Semi-conscious, he thought he heard orders being shouted, the creaking of pulleys and winches. Then he sank into a whirl of near-oblivion.

When he awoke his head swam and his limbs felt like lead. He had forgotten where he was. He struggled to his knees, feeling nauseated, with a very bitter taste in his mouth.

He remembered, and pushed at the door which opened onto velvety darkness, with pools of light only where lanterns hung. On his knees, keeping in the shadows, he crept out, and the deck rushed up to meet him.

There was not a soul to be seen. Rising, Phillip again fell to the deck and lay on his belly for quite some time, fearing someone must surely have heard him fall.

On all fours he crept towards a light above a large cask lashed securely to the mizen-mast. To his dismay he found the lid of the cask firmly fastened with a heavy bar and sturdy lock, to stop anyone taking more than their ration. At the base of this cask, on the peg of wood hammered half-way in the bung-hole, hung a small can to catch the tiny droplets that leaked.

Phillip saw the glint of liquid in the bottom if this can, and eagerly lifted it to his parched lips. It hardly wet his tongue.

A raucous sound like sawing came to him. Creeping along sideways like a crab, he worked his way towards the noise, and arrived at the galley.

The ship's cook lay in his hammock, sleeping blissfully. In the dim light, all Phillip could see, at first, were a sack of potatoes and a half-empty bottle.

The ship lurched again, as waves hit the vessel's sides.

Phillip froze, but the cook slept on.

Phillip picked up the discarded bottle, the contents of which smelt richly fruity. To quench his thirst he took a mouthful, gasping at the strength of Navy rum, which only seemed to increase his thirst.

Feeling pangs of hunger, carefully he lifted the lid of a large stewpan at the side of the stove. He dipped a ladle into the mixture and tasted, then ate, the gritty oats which were steeping overnight prior to cooking later.

The cook grunted loudly. Making a hurried escape, Phillip reached into the sack and grabbed a potato.

He arrived back at the locker unchallenged. Using a bundle of sailcloth as a pillow under his arms, he lay forward across it, and nibbled away at the peel of the potato. The earthy-tasting vegetable eased his thirst and to some extent, the rumbling in his stomach.

The pain in his back started up, so he felt in his bag for the bottle of medicine, and took a dose. The swish of waves against timbers, with the motion of the ship, at last lulled him to sleep.

He dreamed a terrible dream, that he was being stirred around with a huge paddle in the syrup vat at his father's sweet factory. He choked in the vortex. Articles were being thrown in on him and striking him, he was upside down, then the right way up, a rushing crashing sound almost deafening him.

Screaming, he awoke. He was upside down, then he was hurled sideways as far as the limited space allowed. Tins of grease and paint became missiles as they took flight around him.

Then he felt his feet against the door. Kicking at it, he tried to escape from his torture chamber.

William arrived home early in the afternoon, bringing Mr Peel with him. Alice greeted them, saying she had delayed sending someone for Phillip, so that they would have a little time to take the telescope to the observatory to complete the surprise.

At first, Alice was not over-enamoured of the prospect of entertaining a common schoolmaster but, finding the young man to be well mannered, pleasant and an excellent conversationalist, she now looked forward to his visits.

Mr Peel was impressed with the attic conversion, complimenting Tug and both Toomeys, saying it was even better than the one at the school. A shelf of technical books was above a desk, and a large blackboard with chalk at the ready to work out calculations.

Tug explained it had been a simple job really, as Master John, the master's brother, had sent drawings of an observatory in London, along with the astronomical maps for the walls.

Bess came with a tray of refreshments asking, was it time to send her son, Simon, for the young master?

As they waited in the sitting room, chatting about world affairs, an hour passed, and then another.

They were beginning to be concerned when Alex Toomey arrived. He stood wringing his cap, finding it difficult to speak.

'What is the matter, Alex, is there something wrong?' William asked.

'Aye, sir,' he stammered. 'Our Simon has searched high an' low, but can find no trace of the young master. Tug and I have been lookin' for more than an hour, an' we canna find him either.'

Phillip's easel and the things he had hidden were found, but there was no sign of the bag containing his medication and notebooks. Boats with grappling-irons searched revealing nothing.

Tug went to challenge one man who was airing his opinion that the boy might have taken his own life, for hadn't he a loony grandfather.

Fiona was insistent that 'her boy' was alright and alive, but her grey face did nothing to lift William's anguish, he thinking that some dreadful accident had befallen their son.

Alice collapsed, and a doctor visited her daily to keep her under sedation.

Alex and Tug refused to give up the search, Tug asking all seamen and dockworkers to make inquiries for him, passing the message up and down the coast, promising that genuine information would be rewarded.

A terrible day arrived when a message came from a ferryman near Clackmannan.

A body had been found by some fishermen at Rosyth.

Unashamed, William wept in front of Tug and Fiona.

Tug told him it was good to weep, but that he was jumping the gun for it might not be Phillip.

Fiona reassured him that she knew in her bones that their lad was alive.

William blessed them both for their support, and was greatly relieved when Tug said he was going to accompany him.

The ferryman was most respectful, but he did not have much information. He told them the body now lay in a kirk less than half-a-mile away. Showing them which direction to take, he wished them well, and gracefully refused the coins offered him by Tug.

When they arrived at the little kirk, the cleric there took them to a small vestry, saying he hoped they could identify the departed as he had lain there some days, and the decomposing body was keeping away his already small congregation.

Tug asked if he could go in first, so as to save William more pain. Trembling, William said it was his duty as a father, and entered the ill-lit room.

The cleric drew back the sailcloth draped over the form.

William held a kerchief to his mouth and nose to allay the stench that came to him, forcing himself to look at the bloated face with empty eye sockets. The light was not good, and he asked for a lantern to be lit.

The light fell on the calloused upturned palm of the hand, and William saw at once these were not the artistic hands of his son. Tug said this poor soul had the hands of a mariner or a fisherman.

The minister was most disappointed, saying he had hoped the body would be claimed, for it sorely needed burying.

William suggested he record all the details he could about the corpse, any marks; Tug reckoned the age would be 18 to 20, to keep then, and bury him, placing a marker on the grave.

William left money so that this could be carried out properly.

On the journey home, both men were deep in their own thoughts, having no knowledge that the one they sought was a long distance away, working as he had never worked before in his young life; forming new friendships, starting a new future that would take him onward to a memorable battle.

16

Phillip vomited. He longed to escape from his prison, and wished he could die as his head spun and the storm raged. He thought the ship had sprung a leak, and panicked, when he felt dampness in his breeches, then felt great shame, among other things, on finding the dampness was his own body fluid.

A sudden blow to his head rendered him unconscious.

The storm had ended and the sea was calm when a 'veteran' seaman of more than five years, 16-year-old Robert Murray, was sent to the locker for a tin of grease to lubricate pulleys.

It may have been his soft, Scottish voice asking, 'What the devil?', or the fresh night air that brought Phillip, moaning, to his senses.

On board there was much activity, everyone working by lamp, inspecting and repairing storm damage.

Phillip was unable to focus properly as Robert pushed him back into the locker, whispering he was to stay there until he returned.

At last Robert came with a pail of water. Taking the pail, Phillip raised it to his lips.

Robert, snatching it away, said, 'This be sea water. Dowse thysel' wi' it for tha is in a sorry state.' Then he asked, 'Are ye a stowaway?'

Phillip denied this, saying he had come only to look, and the locker had got jammed, so he could not get away.

Robert told him that before the storm had started, all lockers and hatches were battened down, but thought he would still be treated as a stowaway anyway, and that was not pleasant.

Thinking everyone was too busy to see, he told Phillip to keep to the shadows, keep his head down and follow him below. But alas, someone did see them; a man called Ratty Leary.

Ratty Leary claimed he came from the port of London. There was much speculation about how he became named Ratty. Some said it was because of his ability to scale up the ratlines between the shrouds, where he hung like a bat most of his time, this being the best vantage-point from which to see what went on aboard ship.

Ratty Leary seldom took shore leave, choosing to stay aboard, scuttling around like the rodent after which he was named. He only left a ship, so it was said, if it were sinking.

One person knew the reason Ratty never went ashore; his partner-in-crime, Ben Sewel. For he knew Ratty Leary had more enemies on dry land than afloat.

On board, these two were adept at finding things out, so they could blackmail their ship-mates into parting with their baccy, rum or other possessions. These were minor crimes for this pair of villains.

On the lower deck, Robert told Phillip to hide in a corner behind a hammock he said was his. Phillip shivered as he stooped, his face twisting in pain. 'Please, sir,' he asked through chattering teeth, 'I have a bag in the locker, with medication inside that I have need of, if you can bring it to me.'

Robert threw him a blanket, 'Take off those wet things and wrap up in this. Mind ye speak tae no one.'

He returned with the bag, and another pail of water, soap and a clean flour sack. 'Wash and dry thyself properly, before ye put these on.' He threw him a rough sweater and a pair of calico trews.

Phillip was unable to get a lather in the sea water. After rubbing himself vigorously with the flour sack, he put on the clothes and crouched between the hammock and the ship's side.

In semi-darkness, men came and flopped onto an assortment of beds and pieces of sail tied and stretched in criss-cross fashion. Phillip was grateful for the water Robert had brought him, and the blanket he threw down, telling him, 'Lie there til I call ye, and do what ye are bid and ask no questions!'

Ignoring the snores, and his hunger pains, Phillip turned his face to the bulkhead and was soon asleep, but he seemed to have slept only a few minutes when he was being shaken by Robert, who stopped him from pulling on his boots, hissing, 'Leave them, they be a right give away, ye have tae work barefoot on board like the rest, excepting officers.'

Phillip's limbs were stiff as he followed his rescuer and recognized the cook, dressed in badly stained calico and a hat that appeared to be made of paper. Sitting at a long table, half-awake young mariners waited. Phillip did not see Robert taking a bowl and a tin mug from a bath of water, as he was pushed onto the bench.

The cook ladled grey, glutinous porridge into each bowl, and a rating poured grog containing a mixture of water, rum and lime juice to combat scurvey, a fairly new concession since the mutinies.

There was a moment of concern when the cook arrived at the end of the table, where a bewildered lad argued to no avail, as the cook cuffed him, saying, 'Ye lazy young varmint, again ye have not fetched a bowl and mug. No pots, no vittles or grog.'

Ashamed, Phillip looked at Robert and saw him busily eating his porridge and shaking his head slowly, as a sign to say nothing, and just get on with eating.

Phillip was now able to see Robert properly. He had a pleasant freckled face beneath a thatch of reddish hair, and he was not much taller than himself, for Phillip was tall for his age. Robert's shoulders were broader, and he was of a sturdier build.

Having eaten, Robert nudged Phillip, whispering, 'Do what I do!'

Phillip threw the tin mug and wooden bowl into the bath of

water that he should have taken them from. Following Robert out on deck, Phillip understood from the signals coming from him that he was to join three youths and do exactly what they did.

He was handed a pail and scrubbing brush. A thick-set man threw a pail with a rope tied to it overboard. Withdrawing it, he slopped sea-water into each pail held by the boys. Arriving at the fourth boy, the man shouted he was stupid, for he was on the wrong deck.

Feeling guilt for the second time that day, copying the others, Phillip fell to scrubbing the deck as if his life depended on it, while the man stood over them, swinging a knotted rope down onto the palm of his hand.

Unaccustomed to labouring, Phillip's body became soaked with sweat, his arms and shoulders ached, and his back felt as if it were bleeding.

At last they met up with three other ratings doing the same job, coming to the end of the port deck.

The water in the pails was now thrown overboard. Phillip followed suit, but forgot to remove the brush first.

He failed to hear the threat that the cost of the brush would come out of his wages, as the knotted rope slashed across his back, and he slumped to the floor in a dead faint.

Robert tried to find things to do near Phillip to keep an eye on him. Seeing him collapse he ran to him, but Bo'sun Arthur Gammon got there before him. Robert and the bo'sun had been on many voyages together, and were very friendly.

'What are ye goin' tae do wi' him, Mr Gammon, sir?'

Once attention had been diverted away from them, the other boys disappeared.

Mr Gammon and Robert lifted Phillip to a sitting position, and the bo'sun spoke in his soft, West Country accent, for he had been born and bred in Somerset, the same county the captain hailed from.

'I don't recall this fellow-me-lad's jib an' oi did see all new hands an' volunteers come aboard. It be a bit o' a mystery.'

Robert then broke the rule of all soldiers and sailors: never volunteer information. 'I found him locked up in a locker, sir. He were there all through the storm, an' in a terrible state.'

Nearby, Ratty Leary listened and, knowing all personnel were on deck about their business, he crept below. Searching, he found Phillip's bag. Meanwhile, Phillip had come around, and was being helped to his feet by the bo'sun and his friend.

'We had best go an' see Mr Webley, lad,' said Bo'sun Gammon.

Robert's tan faded for he knew harbourers of wrong-doers suffered the same punishment, and stowaways were most severely punished.

Mr Gammon, seeing Robert's concern, said, 'The First Officer be a fair sort o' fellow, one o' the new lenient kind o' chaps, so no frettin' until needs be, eh!'

Ratty, annoyed at finding nothing he thought valuable, being illiterate and not knowing a cypher or a mathematical symbol, and thinking to ingratiate himself with the officers, screamed, 'We have caught ourselves a Frenchie spy!'

The First Officer, Mr Webley, said stowing away was too serious an offence for him to deal with, and the Captain had to deal with it.

The two boys were told to stand to attention in front of officers, but there was no need in Robert's case for he was already standing rigidly to attention.

The Captain had just finished breakfast and was puffing on a long-stemmed pipe his turbanned blackamoor boy had filled and handed him.

Phillip's bag was put on the table when the used dishes from the meal had been cleared away.

'Mr Webley, sir,' said the Captain, pointing with the stem of his pipe, 'please examine the contents of this bag.'

The First Officer examined Phillip's notebooks with interest. 'Methinks we have captured an artist and a scholar, sir, and if he be a spy the French be engaging talented young ones of late.'

Phillip denied emphatically that he was a spy, and was told

sharply by Arthur Gammon not to speak unless spoken to.

The Captain flicked through the pages of a sketch-book with interest, stopping at one page. 'I know this fellow's jib, there cannot be two of his like.' Turning the book around so Phillip could see who he was talking about, he asked Phillip if he knew who the person was.

Proudly, Phillip said, 'That is a likeness of my very good friend and mentor, sir. He is a loyal servant to my father, and his name is Tug Wilson, ex-Royal Navy.

'Aye, I knew Tug Wilson very well, one of the finest, bravest seamen I have had the privilege to serve with. An' if ye be friend to Master Wilson, I am certain ye will be no spy.'

Turning his attention next to Robert, the Captain asked, 'And what about ye, Mr Murray? Being a seasoned mariner ye should know, all unusual happenings aboard ship should be reported.'

Robert, standing with eyes downcast, remained silent.

The Captain knew of Robert. He was liked by all, and more than once had been commended for bravery. The Captain himself had mentioned the lad for his actions at the Battle of Brest in 1794.

When just a youngster he had shown great bravery and compassion, helping the wounded during and after the battle. Eventually he had collapsed with a wound to himself that was not reported or noticed, as his clothes were already drenched with the blood of others.

The Captain had a problem. Although punishment had been relaxed a little since the riots, discipline had to be maintained.

Bo'sun Gammon asked if he could have a word with the prisoners. The Captain gave his permission.

Arthur Gammon whispered to Phillip, 'If ye say ye came aboard as a volunteer, ye canna be a stowaway.'

Thus it was recorded, but then Midshipman Murray was charged with the following offence: 'not reporting unauthorized persons, who might have been enemies of King and country at time of war'. The punishment for such a crime was severe, and once had been hanging.

Phillip, on hearing this sentence, for the second time that day, slipped to the boards.

The ship's surgeon, on examining him, diagnosed that the collapse was due to a combination of shock, hunger and the terrible beating the boy had been subjected to, and that he was undoubtedly in great pain.

Captain Hood was a man who had come up through the ranks, always ready to recommend promotion when it was deserved, and it grieved him to demote Robert and order his flogging. He disliked Ratty Leary and his type, but knew that if he appeared to do nothing, there would be dissention among some of the crew.

The orders had come through for the ship to join Nelson, but the storms had delayed them. All the crew were present when the charge was read, and the flogging commenced.

Phillip winced at every stroke and sobbed silently. When it was over he asked permission to go with Robert, who was being carried to the surgeon. Blood had appeared on the angry weals criss-crossing Robert's back where the lash had fallen more than once.

Bo'sun Arthur Gammon remonstrated with the man who had wielded the whip, who had insisted on being one of the men to carry Robert, telling him he had been told to go easy and not use force.

'I tried, honest Arthur, but had to make some kind o' show. The lad has skin like a lass, so it were bound to break.'

Phillip felt overwhelming guilt, and his own back started to throb when he saw Robert arch his back and bite into his lip as they applied white crystals.

'Please, sir, may I ask what it is that you are applying?'

He was told, salt.

'But that stings dreadfully. Have you some potato that can be sliced? I have been told it will take all the inflamation away and help with the healing.'

'Well, I'll be blowed!' exclaimed the surgeon. 'We have someone here who is trying to teach his granny to suck eggs, but I am willing to learn. Fetch some potatoes, for I believe I have read somewhere of a man called Culpeffer, who treats maladies with stuff from the garden.'

The seaman holding Robert's head was Sid Rosser from Wales. He begged the surgeon's pardon. 'The boy might be right, sir. I remember when my brother got scalded real bad, and my granny was cleaning taters at the time, she did cut some up and put them all over the scald. Next day, not a blister did he have.'

Slices of potato were carefully placed on the marks that were already discolouring.

Phillip requested his bag and, when it was returned to him, he asked the surgeon if some pain-killing medicine could be given to Robert.

The surgeon examined it first, by sniffing the bottle with only a small amount left in it, then put a little on his finger-tip and tasted it.

'There be opium in this, where did ye get if from lad?' Phillip told him of Fiona.

Robert was given the last remaining drop of medicine and was soon asleep.

The surgeon wanted to know more of Fiona, so Phillip showed him the catalogue he was preparing. The surgeon was fascinated, and came to the page on the medical use for the potato, where *salanum tuberosum* was written above the drawings of a knobbly brown oval, flames, the sun and a blistered hand. He became excited, declaring even the most ignorant person could understand this, and begged to borrow the book.

When he looked through it with the Captain and other officers later, they discussed the owner, who was newly christened Tommy Cole. For when he had given his name as Phillip T J McCall, the Captain had said there were too many men on board with similar names, and asked what they stood for, to be told 'Thomas.' Phillip McCall became known in the Navy as Thomas Cole, but his friends still called him Phillip.

The day after the flogging Phillip was allowed to stay at Robert's side. He was dozing when suddenly Robert, catching hold of his wrist with one hand, felt under his pillow with the other. Withdrawing a pouch he gave it to Phillip, saying it was his.

'This were in the trews that I washed for ye, and there be nay need tae keep sayin' sorry, for I did wrong and had tae be punished.'

Phillip was proud to know someone so brave, and hoped one day to be able to repay his new friend for the pain he had caused him.

Ratty Leary was in the shadows and saw Robert give the pouch to Phillip. He waited until the ship's bell announcing food was rung, and Robert told Phillip to go and eat, and ask the cook for a drink to bring back to him.

Ratty pounced, catching Phillip by the throat, hissing, 'I think ye have sommat for Ratty. Hand it o'er or I'll break yer scrawny neck.'

Taking out the pouch containing a few coins, Phillip felt the hold on him loosen, as Ratty was lifted off his feet and held in the air above the head of the mighty Glyn Rhys, cousin to Sid Rosser, and the undefeated wrestling champion of the Welsh valleys.

Banging Ratty's body against the overhead timbers, Glyn said it was a good thing he had come to tell them food was ready, and asked if this creature had taken anything from them or harmed them.

Both said they were all right. Glyn dropped the villain roughly to the deck and, stooping, grabbed the rag that Ratty wore around his neck. Again he lifted him in a throttling hold. Ratty struggled like a puppet that had had its strings cut.

'Listen hard, boyo!' snarled Glyn. 'If picking on small boys you are, and I find out, I will crush you like I would a bilge rat, so be warned.' When released, Ratty slunk away, his face a shade of green.

All the officers thought Phillip would make a fine officer. His caricatures amused them greatly, and the Captain often asked about Tug Wilson, telling Phillip that Tug had saved his life once. But Phillip desired to spend most of his little free time with his new friend, Robert.

The bo'sun kept Phillip busy, thinking the boy came from

the upper classes who had oppressed him and his family before he ran away to sea. But he was so impressed by the way he did all menial work without complaint, and by his knowledge of seamanship which Phillip told him, speaking with such respect for his old shipmate, Tug Wilson had taught him, Mr Gammon was soon treating him as he would a son.

The surgeon and the Captain expressed interest and wanted to study Phillip's notes on Astronomy. They asked him how he came to be aboard, so Phillip told them it had been his wish for as long as he could remember to become a seaman, and he could not resist coming aboard to see a large ship.

When the surgeon asked him who had whipped him, Phillip told of the schoolmaster who had gone mad, and the surgeon treated his back, giving him the treacle-and-brimstone treatment from Fiona's book to help clear up the carbuncles that kept erupting.

Thus Phillip T J McCall, aged 12 years, now named Thomas Cole, started his naval career; fulfilling a dream of going to sea, on a voyage he might never return from. For he was on his way to join Rear Admiral Nelson and his fleet, to do battle on the River Nile.

17

The McCall family grieved at the loss of their son. William the father was relieved no more bodies were reported, although the search was carried out for many weeks with no success. A reward was posted. Tug and Alex sorted through the informants, most of whom had invented information in an attempt to get the reward offered.

Alice lay in her bedroom with drapes closely drawn to keep out the late August sun. Nothing and no one seemed to interest her.

At William's request Fiona sat with her, and it was she who spooned the little sustenance that kept Alice alive.

Young William was fretful, having a bad cough, and he was brought to his mother's room at Fiona's request, so she could attend to him. Then Fiona told his mother it was not healthy for the child to be in such a hot room with no fresh air, and asked permission to draw back the drapes and open the big window.

Alice drew the sheet over her face, shielding her eyes from the light. Her son thought she was playing peek-a-boo with him and, chuckling, he snatched at the sheet, saying, 'Boo!' The effort brought on a fit of coughing, but before Fiona could reach the child, his mother was rubbing his back.

Fiona encouraged the little boy to climb on to his mother's bed. If Alice found excuses to be occupied with other things when it was time for the child to eat, the spoon was given to her for her to feed her youngest son.

As often happens with children, the child made the one who fed him take mouthful for mouthful. For a few days this went well, until a bowl of soup spilt, soaking the bed and its occupant.

From the landing Fiona called for help. When Florrie and Bess came, she asked them to delay the changing of the bedclothes; she would like to keep the mistress out of her bed for as long as possible.

They washed and changed the child, and took their time washing the mistress, putting a clean nightshift on her, then a robe that hung loosely on her wasted frame.

'Where would ye like tae sit, my lady? Perhaps ye would like tae sit on the balcony for a wee while, for 'tis a glorious day,' said Fiona.

Alice allowed herself to be brought out to the balcony, and sat in the sunlight there with young William, who waved to Aimee his sister, and young Katie, playing on the lawn making daisy chains.

Waving back, Katie was heard to ask, 'Who be that wi' Willie, be that yer mammy?'

Aimee tossed her curls, saying, 'That is no mammy, my mammy is much more bonny tha' that!'

Whether it was this statement, or Aimee copying Katie's rural way of speech, or her reflection in her mirror when she returned to the bedroom, Alice, for the first time in weeks brushed her own hair and placed some cream on her face.

Everyone was delighted, no one more than her husband, to have her take notice, even asking him to find a governess for Aimee, and Katie, to at least teach them the correct way to speak.

William, remembering the last governess, was not keen to engage another, but to please her, he made inquiries. He discovered a very genteel, well-bred lady, living with her invalid father, who was an ex-British officer, and she was looking for a part-time teaching position to supplement their meagre income. He engaged Mary Gilchrist to teach the children a few mornings each week.

In the fine days that followed, Alice rested in the shade of an old tree while the children had their morning lessons with Mary Gilchrist. Mary asked if she could stay some afternoons and take the three children for walks around the grounds.

Mary was lucky, having been given the best education her parents could afford, for they were not of the general opinion that males of the species should have all the opportunities, and the females trained only in the arts of caring, and entertaining their menfolk.

The Gilchrist family had lived for many years in North America, where Mary spent her childhood. Her nanny came from further north, generally speaking in the French language, so Mary became bilingual at an early age.

Alice still thought that to speak French was very fashionable, although France was the enemy. She asked could the girls, at least, have tuition in this language. Strangely, it was young William who picked it up soonest.

Alice still had fits of depression, and sometimes wept bitterly. Fiona remonstrated with her, saying she had to pull herself together.

Alice cried, 'You should know that when he was a baby, I withheld affection from my son Phillip, and never once did I say I loved him. Now, it may be too late.'

'Nay, lass, ye munna fret, the lad loved thee, and he knew how ye had grown tae be proud o' him, and the pain ye shared wi' him when he was hurt.'

Aimee, seeing her mother's tears, ran to her, closely followed by William, who garbled something Alice could not understand.

'I wish I knew what you are saying, moppet,' she sobbed.

'He wants tae know why ye are cryin', and wants tae kiss ye better,' said Fiona.

Amazed, Alice asked how she understood him.

'Weel, he be speakin' French, an' ifen ye remember, I told ye I travelled a few years wi' my Portuguee friends, in that place.'

'I remember you telling me before. You have led such a varied life, Fiona, perhaps you will carry on telling me about it, and take my mind off the tragedy of losing my child.'

Fiona became a little cross, snapping, 'Ye are buryin' off our lad afor ye know he be deed, an' ye are no' the only one tha' has lost bairns. Some folk would rather ha' their childer in a grave, than see how they become. 'Tis true what is said. When they be babes, they do make yer arms ache. When they grow up, all-too-often they make yer heartache.' She sighed heavily.

Alice apologized, 'I am so sorry, dear friend, I know how you loved our son, but he knew you loved him, and I don't believe he knew how much I had begun to love him.'

'There ye go agin, talkin' as if he be gone for ever. Aye, I loved, and still love him, better than my ain flesh an' blood, and I know in my bones my lad is coming back tae us one day, just like Tammy Floyd came back tae my friend, Annie.'

Alice again apologized, and quietly asked, 'Tell me again of Annie. I remember she was a very good friend of yours, and she left to go back to her husband's birthplace.'

Sighing heavily, Fiona said that was correct.

Alice was contrite.

'Please, dear friend, forgive me. When you are ready, maybe you will talk of Annie. Her tale will take my mind off my worries for, as you say, Annie lost *all* her children, but her husband returned.'

18

In the night, Fiona had nightmares, screaming out. The whole family rushed to her room, where Florrie was trying to comfort her. William wanted to know what had upset Fiona, but no one seemed to know.

Next day, Fiona was made to sit out in the sun, with her feet up, and Alice sat with her.

The lad Simon was sent to ask Mary Gilchrist to come in an extra morning, that she might see the children. She immediately came, asking could she take them to visit her father, and go for a picnic.

Bess and her mother hurriedly packed a basket with all sorts of goodies. Old Martha wagged her finger, saying she wanted every scrap to be eaten. Excited the children were going out, Bess told Katie to mind her manners, when young William solemnly promised he was going to be a good boy for his *madamoiselle*.

Alice was attempting to do some embroidery. Seeming to find difficulty settling, Fiona twitched and fidgeted.

Alice asked what was bothering her.

''Tis just old memories, lassie, and I had no' the right tae snarl at ye t'other day, when I, above all people, should know what ye are sufferin'.'

'Well, if you can speak of it, why don't you tell me? It might help to ease the anguish you are suffering.'

'It be difficult tae know where tae begin. Ye know of my early tragedy. The rest don't bear tellin'.'

'Well, tell me of your friend, Annie. Did you ever see her again?'

'Not alive, but I learnt about the paer soul when I came back frae abroad, where I had been mony a year.'

'Tell me of your travels, and of your return! The telling would help me, maybe, out of my depression.'

Fiona reminded Alice of how the Portuguese performers had taken her away, affording her escape from the place of horror that had robbed her of her memory and all her loved ones.

She was unaware her gentle, feeble-minded mother had been dragged away by the crazed man who had murdered her husband and would have battered her screaming child to death, had not her gentle mother shielded the babe with her own body. She had clung to the child as the drunken lout dragged her by the hair, her only thought to protect her little granddaughter.

Manuel headed the group. His family consisted of his wife, Pillar, her mother Teresa, and her husband Jesus who suffered ill-health, the two children, the boy Juan, just a little younger than Fiona herself, and lastly, his sister Maria.

The family wandered as nomads, earning a living by making things out of wood, hand-weaving and entertaining, travelling all over Europe, calling no country their own.

Strangely, France was the friendliest country. During winter months, the warm beaches of southern France provided them with many things; driftwood for carving, shells the women fashioned into trinkets. The mild weather was less cruel to folk sleeping under canvas or the stars.

Rich aristocrats spent months there to avoid the rigours of wintering in their draughty old chateaux further north. These people were generous with money and rewards to entertainers. It was a hard life with good days to compensate for bad days. Fiona travelled with them, with no memory of home or past events.

The old woman, Teresa, kept Fiona busy; her young body healed. She soon picked up the French language, and a little Portuguese.

For 12 years they moved around Europe. Fiona, in her twenties, often wondered why she had sad longings seeing young children. Many men made advances to her, but she shunned them.

Manuel's son, Juan, was never far from her, jealously protecting her against other suitors. He wanted to marry her himself, but his mother, Pillar, was strongly averse to her son marrying a *Gringo* woman, and was jealous of the attention and care her husband Manuel also gave Fiona.

They had passed through Bordeaux to a place where peasants were burning the stubble left after harvesting, when a sudden change of wind blew sparks on to the thatch of a cottage which was soon alight.

Jesus, Teresa's husband, Manuel and Juan helped to fight the blaze. From inside the building, the terrified screaming of a child was heard. Teresa's husband, before anyone could stop him, dashed into the flames.

Staggering, he soon emerged holding a child, his hair and clothes aflame.

Fiona sank screaming to the ground. The pain, loss and memory returned with consciousness.

The child was treated for minor burns while Teresa, sitting with her back to the wheel of the wagon, held Jesus all through that night. The gallant man died just as dawn was breaking. Teresa lost the will to live after Jesus died.

Fiona wanted to return home to Scotland, but as it was autumn, it was not the right time to make sea journeys. She was persuaded to go and winter with them in the south.

On a wet May day, Fiona waved a tearful goodbye to friends she was never to see again.

The captain of the vessel taking Fiona to Weymouth was a fellow Scot, and as she had been away for so long, she inquired if he had news of Scotland.

'Nay, lassie, frae it were eight year to this very day I were in Firth o' Tay at the May Day fair, where a man were killed by a mob as he tried tae auction a paer simple-minded creature he said was his wife. Havin' nae takers he dropped the price tae one shillin'. Mind ye, that included a wee bairn.

'The crowd cried shame on him, strikin' the wee child for weepin'. The woman was shieldin' the little one for maer blows, when he raised his heavy staff tae strike her, a blow that might well hae brained her. He was dragged frae where he stood, and beaten tae death.'

'How horrible!' cried Fiona, covering her face with her hands.

'I set sail that night, never to return tae Scotland, but I shall ne'er forget that day, for I still dream, and hear the man screamin' that he was Angus McCready, who killed many British at the battle o' Culloden. They kept on beatin' him until he was silent.'

'What became of the woman and child?' sobbed Fiona.

'I dinna ken, lassie, I did not stay. The crazed crowd started fightin' among theyselves, so it were wise tae leave, I bein' a stranger tae the place.'

Fiona was confused. Could her father have been alive eight years ago, and not died in battle? Could the woman have been her mother, and what of the child? If the child was her baby, what were the bones that were buried?

All these questions made her head spin. She was still in a whirl as she was being helped into a small boat, to be taken ashore to England.

Sick and frightened, Fiona hurried away from the quay through narrow streets. At last she came to the open road, with deep ditches on each side full of muddy water from the recent rain.

A fast-travelling coach came up behind her so close she had to step sideways, and lost her balance, falling headlong into the ditch. She pulled herself out, squatting on the verge, sobbing out of anger and self-pity in French.

An old biddy leading a mule came along, also cursing the coach-driver for spattering her already grubby clothes. She consoled Fiona, being a fellow sufferer, and helped her to her feet.

'Ye come along to the Sisters Of Mercy, they happen will be able tae fathom yer lingo,' she said.

Fiona allowed herself to be led off the road, and down a rough track until they arrived at a stone building surrounded by a high palisade.

The old woman pulled the rope hanging at the side of the stout door. A bell clanged within, and a face peered through the grill.

"'Tis I, Sister, wi' a poor creature fallen by wayside. She is a foreigner an' not o' these parts.'

Bolts were noisily drawn back, and they were beckoned to enter an overgrown courtyard, where tethered goats, chickens, geese and pigs squabbled for food thrown out amongst the scrub.

The pale-faced young woman brought a bowl of water and mimed washing her hands. They did this, and followed her to what appeared to be the kitchen, where women wearing coarse-spun robes sat.

Silently the nun motioned them to sit. Prayers were said, then they were served with dark bread and some hot liquid ladled into bowls.

Fiona awoke next morning feeling stiff, for she had slept on a pallet in a narrow cell. Memory came flooding back to her, and she heard shuffling and rhythmic breathing in the corridor outside the door. Peering out, she saw the backs of the last two shadowy creatures disappearing around a corner.

Back in the bare chamber, a grey light was coming through a narrow window-slit. Shivering, she searched for her top-clothes without success. All she found were rough grey robes like those worn by her hosts. On discovering the belt with a hidden purse was still round her waist, she breathed a sigh of relief. Manuel had given her a third of all their money, and the purse also contained the five gold coins Annie had left for her daughter.

Her heart leapt at the thought that her daughter might not have perished in the fire, but, what were the charred remains? She must not let her hopes rise. The Captain might have been mistaken, and eight years was a long time. He might have the wrong name, there were so many men named Angus, and surnames beginning 'Mac' *(the son of)* were common enough.

Pulling on the robe she went down the corridor in the same

direction as the shadowy figures.

The chapel had rough benches, and the floor was strewn with straw. Everyone knelt on the bare floor, except for the Abbess, who was prostrate in front of a large cross. Chequered shafts of light from the big window behind it surrounded her with mystical, dust-laden beams.

Fiona waited. She watched them file out of the chapel, the Abbess first, then two by two the others following. As the last pair were passing her, she touched the nearer one on the shoulder and asked in English where her clothes were.

The novice turned, her finger on her lips. Fiona followed them back to the kitchen where the old crone who had brought her, sat with a milk stain all around her mouth, The Abbess shook her head at her in rebuke.

Fiona realized she was hungry as she was motioned to sit down. All bent their heads. The Abbess said prayers of thanks for the food, then one shrouded figure placed grey porridge in each bowl, another pouring creamy milk from a pitcher into clay beakers.

All ate and drank silently, except for the old woman slurping noisily. She held up the empty bowl. 'Be there more, kind sisters? It's bin days since I ate afore these vittles.'

The Abbess nodded, and the sister who dished up, scraped the remains from the pot into her dish.

While she was licking the bowl for the last morsel, Fiona asked her how she could find out where her own clothes were.

Smacking her lips, the woman said, 'Been taken for washing, I suppose.'

The Abbess looked surprised, 'You are not foreign, but Scottish, I believe.'

Everyone looked up as Fiona answered, 'Yes, Mother, but I have been abroad many years.'

The young novice sitting next to the old woman put down the beaker of milk she had taken just a sip of, to look at Fiona. She also hailed from Scotland.

As quick as a wink, the old woman slyly replaced her empty beaker with the novice's almost full one, gulping down the contents in seconds.

Forgetting the woman had been kind to her, Fiona scolded her. 'Ye greedy besom, ye had maer than anyone, and tae take frae someone wi' less than thysel', ye aught tae be ashamed.'

She offered what was left in her beaker to the young woman, who shyly shook her head, withdrawing into her habit.

Fiona helped clear the bowls and beakers, washing them in a pail of cold water. All were then allocated their daily tasks, and the old woman was given a parcel of food and sent on her way.

Fiona stayed, for she had not had her own clothes returned. She was summoned to the room of the Abbess. The large room had a bed set against one wall. Another wall had a cabinet full of bottles, which stood between rows of shelves holding many books.

Facing all who entered, the Abbess sat at a large, polished table, which held a stand containing an inkpot and fresh-cut quills.

'Come in, do not fear. I should like to talk with you, for we seldom have visitors such as yourself.'

Fiona nervously asked, 'Could I be havin' my clothes? Then I will be on my way. There be nae need tae wash them?'

'They are already washed and hung to dry, but will take time. Stay with us a few days! I know you are troubled, for you cried out in the night while you slept.'

'Nay, Mother, it is best tae be on my way, for there be far tae travel, and 'tis anxious I be tae gae.'

Again the Abbess pleaded with her to stay, for she longed to talk with Fiona, and find out where, and how, she came to speak a foreign language.

Asking Fiona where she was going, and where she had come from, Mother Georgias said it was not curiosity, but eagerness to gain fresh knowledge of the outside world.

'Here in this cloistered place we have contact with few folk, and have taken a vow of silence, for speech interferes with thought and prayer, but when you have sick people to attend to, for we also attempt to heal the sick, we have to converse.'

She spoke with a slight accent. 'The old woman thought you were foreign.'

'Aye, I was talkin' French tae mysel' when she came upon me. That is the tongue I have used these last years, but Scotland is my hame, and I have need tae return.'

'I, too, have been away from my birthplace for many years. My grandparents, with their family, fled from their home because of religious persecution, and my mother found refuge at the Abbey Lyon, there giving birth to me, but sadly she died shortly after.' The Abbess sighed, 'Did you ever visit Lyon?'

'I'm not sure, we went to many places.

'Do ye think my clothes will be dry soon? I must be away,' said Fiona impatiently.

'Please forgive me, but won't you stay with us a little while, then maybe we will find someone to accompany you on your journey. A woman travelling alone is so vulnerable.'

A knock at the door interrupted Mother Georgias. A very flustered nun came in, bowing, and whispered to the Abbess, who became concerned and excused herself. She told Fiona she had to go to attend to a young girl who had been savagely attacked, the fourth victim they had treated in as many weeks.

Fiona asked if she could help as she knew a little of Medicine, and accompanied them to a room with white lime-washed walls.

The girl lay on one of four narrow beds. The clothes torn from her body revealed many abrasions, bites and scratches.

Fiona thought of her daughter, and asked would they permit her to look after the girl.

Bathing the bruised body, she applied salve made from oils and herb extracts as Teresa had taught her. The bite-marks on the girl's young breasts brought to mind Annie when they had first bathed together, and she wondered how her dear friend fared.

When the girl awoke in the night, screaming, Fiona cradled her in her arms, rocking her like an infant. For two days and nights she left the girl for only a few minutes, eating her food when she had force-fed her charge, for the child wanted to starve herself to death.

On the third day the girl rallied, and willingly took a little nourishment.

The nuns brought Fiona her own clothes. She asked for a bowl of water to bathe, and after bathing, ate a little bread and honey. She was starting to dress in her own clothes when fatigue overcame her and she collapsed. Two nuns picked her up, and lay her on one of the beds, covering her with a blanket. There she slept until past noon the next day.

When she awoke, the girl she had been attending was sitting at her bedside staring at her. Smiling weakly, the girl asked, 'Be ye alright, mistress? I thought ye were one o' they sisters, but they say ye bain't one o' they.'

'Nay, I be travellin' tae Scotland. What be thy name, child?'

'I be called Rachel from Osmington, an' I were goin' home from Weymouth market. They took the master's money.' She shuddered. 'Then the three o' them took me. Will I have a babby, mistress?'

The girl looked so fragile and young in the calico shift, Fiona was unable to answer her. Silently she cursed the beasts who had violated, and possibly ruined, this child's life.

She wondered if she had made a wise decision coming back to this cruel land, leaving her friends and the protection of Manuel and Juan behind. But once her memory had returned, there had seemed a force pulling her back.

Throwing off the blanket, she got out of bed. She felt giddy, but soon collected her wits.

'Go ye back tae bed, lassie, ye will catch a death o' cold.'

Rachel returned to her bed, thinking of facing her master with no money for the produce she had sold, and the possibility of an unwanted child. She wished she were dead.

Fiona dressed in her own clothes, and went to find the Abbess.

The Abbess was conversing with a man dressed like a

farmer. She beckoned Fiona. 'This is Master Simmons, who employs Rachel. He is most upset at losing his money, and her labour, but is a kindly man, and at a loss to know what to do.'

He greeted Fiona with relief. He was nervous speaking with a holy person. 'Ye see, mistress, we live from day to day, wi' wars an' tithes, an' wi' little enough tae survive. The lass is a foundling wi' no kin, septten we. My lad fancies she, but the lass be tocherless, wi'out a marriage portion.'

Fiona asked if they would wait just a while for her. She would return shortly.

Going back to the cell they had taken her belongings to, she closed the door, and withdrew from her hidden pouch one of the gold coins.

During all the years of travelling, Fiona had not known why she had these coins, why she had saved them, or what they meant to her. She now knew that they were her daughter's inheritance, and felt that if her child were alive, she would not mind a part being given to help secure a poor, unfortunate creature's future.

'Wi' this be enough dowry for the girl?' she asked Mr Simmons.

He nodded his head furiously. 'Do ye mean if Rachel marries, this dowry be handed o'er?'

Fiona said this was correct.

Mr Simmons left in haste, returning the next day with his son.

The 18-year-old youth, unlike his father, was slim and tall, his bright face tanned from working out-of-doors.

A solemn priest performed the ceremony. Rachel wore a plain gown which, Fiona suspected, the nuns had put together. A wreath of flowers crowned her shining hair. The youth looked down at Rachel with loving eyes.

Merrily the wedding party moved away, watched by the shadowy figures whose features were hidden by their habits.

Fiona was asked to stay another night. The Abbess was preparing a route of hospices for her, where she might have shelter. She had asked Dick Simmons, Rachel's new husband, if he knew of someone to accompany Fiona on part of her journey.

Next morning, Fiona said goodbye, thanking them for their hospitality. The Abbess thanked her for her help and generosity to the girl Rachel.

Outside the gate, Dick and Rachel sat waiting on a cart loaned by Mr Simmons, so they could journey for two whole days and nights, with Fiona.

During the two days travelling together, only once did the trio have an awkward moment, when a dubious character jumped out at them. Seeing the stout staff Dick wielded, and hearing and seeing two screaming dervishes ready to do battle, he soon scurried back to the undergrowth.

Hospices on Mother Georgias's list refused Dick entry, so Rachel insisted on sleeping with him under the cart. At dawn, Fiona brought out the bread and milk given her to break her fast.

Gently she woke the pair, asleep in each other's arms, and shared the food with them. They had to start the return journey that day, having only four days altogether.

Dick showed such affection towards Rachel, that Fiona had little fear for her future.

They were very concerned about her travelling alone. She told them not to worry, asking if they would wait a little longer for her to return to the hospice. They waited as she took her bundle, and requested re-admittance to the hospice.

Minutes went by, then the door opened and a filthy, old, hump-backed crone stepped out. The couple waiting, wondered what had become of Fiona.

The old crone, smelling like a pigsty, came and spoke. 'We had best be on our way,' Fiona cackled as recognition dawned. They were still laughing as they waved goodbye at the turnpike.

Mother Georgias had put the town of Wells on her list, so Fiona headed for Wells on the way back to her past.

The young couple, on their way to a new life, were never again to meet up with the person who had made it possible.

19

Alice was still suffering from depression. William looked ill, for there was still no news of their son. Meanwhile, Fiona made Alice smile, describing how she had looked when she 'borrowed' the disguise Annie had used, how no one had bothered her on the journey north, and even dogs snapping at the fly-infested biddy's heels, went whimpering back to their own territory.

Four months had passed since Phillip went missing. Mr Peel had become a frequent visitor, doing a great deal to help William get through Sunday, his worst day. They walked and discussed current affairs.

It was October, and everyone became excited, hearing of Nelson's victorious battle of the Nile. William's brother, John, had arranged that as soon as the latest news was available it should be sent to Bruce Peel, for John was greatly obliged to him for helping his brother.

Christmas was not the merriest of times. William's hopes of ever finding Phillip were waning, and he was getting as depressed as Alice. Fiona was still confident that her boy was alive, but she was confined to her bed with a very bad chest cold.

Florrie was diligent in her care of Fiona, and Bess and Martha prepared special dishes to encourage her appetite.

William visited her room every evening, sitting with her, and bringing the children to see her.

Fiona had lost a good deal of her sparkle. Alice was worried, and asked if there was anything she could do to help. 'Is it going over old memories that has upset you, dear friend?'

'Not altogether, lass. Aye thinkin' about Annie, and her troubles, bless the dear angel, along wi' other things, but it's mainly seeing the maester so down lately, and I canna be much gaed at cheerin' ye all.'

'Oh, Fiona, if not for you I'm sure I should have died, for it was you and your tale that pulled me out of the trough of despair I was in. Now hurry and get well, for you have not finished your tale yet, and I should like to hear more, if you will tell it.'

It was early one afternoon in the middle of February, when William came home from his factory, his face flushed with excitement.

He rushed into Fiona's room, where Alice sat near the fire, doing needlework, and Fiona sat across from her, mending some hose. Waving a letter, he almost shouted, 'At last some news, I had to rush home to tell you!'

Hurriedly, he told them that Major Folland, who had bought their old house, had sent one of his servants around with the letter he held in his hand.

'Oh, Willie! Don't keep up in suspense! Tell us what the letter contains. Is it about our Phillip?'

'Well, it comes from a shipping clerk, name of Davey Wells from Portsmouth, and he is inquiring after information of a Thomas Cole, a young lad who has somehow acquired one of Phillip's note-books. That is how the letter came to the old house, for the name and address in the book were Phillip T J McCall at the address of our old home. The letter was brought to Major Folland, who sent it post-haste to me.'

William decided he must go to Portsmouth, to see for himself what this brief letter was all about. Feverishly he made plans and arrangements, getting quite excited after the months of anxiety and waiting.

He left Tug in charge of the factory, with a young man named Alun Breamer, son of one of his oldest employees. Alun had already started training to take over for him when he was away, but William felt he was not quite ready to do it on his own.

The weather was not the best for travelling, for the winter

snows were starting to thaw, but William was keen to get away as soon as possible.

He reassured Alice and Fiona that, in such bad weather, there would be few scoundrels to molest him, as he hoped to do most of the travelling early in the day, and had heard or read somewhere, that most footpads and highwaymen liked to lie in bed on cold mornings. At any rate, he would keep a brace of pistols and a musket near him at all times.

He set out at dawn, riding his horse Blue Boy, with a trusty mare he had recently bought in tow.

On the second evening, he stopped overnight at the apartments of his brother, John, in London. John was so pleased to see William a little more animated than when he had last seen him, and begged him to stay a few days. But William explained that he wanted to get to Portsmouth as quickly as possible.

John wished he could have accompanied him but was very busy with an outbreak of chills and colds. Bidding him 'God speed', he made William promise to call on the return journey with any news, and perhaps then he could stay a little longer.

It was late evening when William arrived at the noisy taverns around Portsmouth harbour.

William had been away just a day, when someone from Fiona's past appeared.

A crippled man approached Alex, who was clearing the driveway of some branches that had broken under the weight of snow. He asked if there was any work he could do, wanting no payment, just a little food.

Alex explained he could not say if there was any work, but if the man went up to the kitchen door, and asked for Bess, his wife, she might find him a morsel to eat.

Before Bess would give the man anything, she told him she would ask the mistress if she could, and perhaps the mistress might have some work for him to do. She thought to herself there might be something the poor, lame fellow could do in place of Tug, him being away at the factory. Before closing the door on the man she asked his name.

'Matthew Wilkie, but most folk call me Matt. And I am willin' tae do anything.'

Telling her mother on no account to let him inside, Bess went to see Alice who was, as usual, with Fiona.

'Beg pardon, ma'am, there be a man at the door who be askin' for work. He doesna look like a beggar, an' says his name be Matt Wilkie. If there be nay work can I give the paer chap a bite tae eat? He looks fair starved.'

Before Alice could answer, Fiona, practically shouting, asked, 'Did ye say Matt Wilkie? I used tae know a man o' that name mony years ago. Be he old or young?'

'Old, I would say, older na my Alex, but younger na mother.'

'Take me tae him, it canna be the same mon, for he went north, when I went south!'

Opening the back door they discovered Matt, slumped on the doorstep.

They dragged the limp body inside, along the floor up to a chair near the fire, and rested his back against the chair legs. Martha dribbled water into his mouth. Spluttering, he came to, with three pairs of eyes staring down at him.

Awkwardly, he tried to rise. Fiona pushed him back, peering into his face. 'Are ye the same Matt Wilkie that came tae Perth wi' my friend, Annie Floyd?'

Looking up, he did not speak for a few minutes, then he gaped, 'Mistress Fiona! Oh, Mistress Fiona! It is ye, I know it is! Aye, it were me that came tae Perth with Mistress Floyd, and it were me that gave ye a rabbit frae the Lady Ruth, God rest her soul. So many years have passed. I never dreamt I should see ye again.'

'Help me lift him up, Bess, and gie him the food that were for me this day. I'll be back, for I'm awa tae see the mistress. Mind ye be gaed tae this mon, he not only saved my life but my sanity as weel!'

Fiona introduced Matt to Alice, in turn, telling her how she and Matt had met, and how Matt had helped her to discover some of her past that had been a mystery to her.

Alice was intrigued, wanting to know more.

Fiona promised she would tell her how the threads of Fate had brought Matt, Annie and herself together. But first, what could they do about Matt? For he looked in a very poor way.

With Fiona to vouch for Matt, Alex took him in, and on her advice, prepared a hot mustard bath for him. As he soaked, he was fed hot chicken soup.

Dressed in some clothes Martha brought, he was introduced to Tug, who said he would be honoured to share his accommodation with any friend of Fiona's.

As William had left Tug in charge of the factory, he also felt responsible for the running of the house while the master was away.

Tug normally looked after the horses, saw to the maintenance of the carriages and acted as coachman. Besides feeding the stock of goats, the milk cow and the poultry, he supplied most of the vegetables for the kitchen from the stock he had stored during the summer months.

Alex and his son, Simon, were a great help to him, but sometimes they were able to get a few jobs at the quayside, and there were still a lot of building repairs to be done around the grounds.

Katie, the little daughter, was doing so well with the schooling she was receiving from Mary Gilchrist, that Alex asked William's permission for his son, Simon, to sit in on a few lessons to learn the rudiments of reading and writing. He said he and his wife would be prepared to take less of the wages William paid to the family, to put towards the lady teacher's salary.

William readily agreed, saying there was no need for them to pay anything, as long as Miss Gilchrist did not mind an extra pupil.

The lady was happy, saying there was no extra work involved as the lad was extremely bright and an apt pupil.

She was, in fact, willing to take a reduction if she were allowed to bring her crippled father with her to share the schoolroom fire. As he was only able to walk with the aid of crutches, he had great difficulty attending to their own fire.

She had returned home late one day to find he had fallen, and was almost frozen to death with the cold.

Matt Wilkie took over most of Tug's household chores, and started going in the shay to pick up Miss Gilchrist and her father.

Alice was not at all keen to have Major Gilchrist under her roof. After all, he was the enemy. But William, before engaging his daughter, because of the Noani Burns woman, had made intensive inquiries into her background, and when Alice remonstrated at him for giving permission for the man to be there, he told her that while investigating Miss Gilchrist, he had found out a great deal about her parent.

Major Gilchrist was an Englishman, one of the few who hated the terrible treatment and punishment served to the Scots. His mother came from the hills of Wales.

Once he had been court-martialled, accused of allowing Scottish prisoners to escape. Nothing had been proved against him, but loudly he had made public his views. Shortly after, during the night, he had been shot in the back.

He refused to return to England, choosing instead to send for his daughter to come and live with him in Scotland.

Oddly, their humble dwelling was close to one of a new friend who, to help them stretch their meagre pension, brought kindling and fresh fish. He was one of the men who had escaped prison, and execution, miraculously evading his British captors.

Tug, Alex and Matt were getting on well together. They sat around the table in the kitchen at the gatehouse during the last hours of the evening, yarning, drinking just one jug of home-brewed ale between them, and blessing the day they had come to the McCall household.

Bess, while placing out a bite to eat for them, said, 'I feel for the Major. I'll be bound he would enjoy to be wi' ye and ha' a chin wag. An' he's bin so gaed tae our Simon, he gae him books tae read, and ha' helped him no end.'

Often business acquaintances and local squires had words with William about the spoiling of his minions, but William turned on them, stating he himself would starve before he treated his workers the way they did, for they would not treat their horses and dogs as they served their tenants and workers.

When a man died, his family were thrown out of their dwelling the very day he was buried, to make room for the next stockman, or farm labourer. The grieving family were then taken off to rot in the workhouse, often dying from ill-treatment and starvation, unless work could be found to pay the warder of the establishment for the little food given to them.

William had given instructions that the Gilchrists were to partake of lunch each day with the family. On hearing that Major Gilchrist had declined to eat, William asked if he would like to earn a little money and therefore pay for his lunch, by doing something William intensely disliked doing, keeping accounts.

The Major was delighted to do this, and made such a good job of the household accounts that William asked if he were up to doing the factory accounts as well.

The Major asked William to check the supplies of sugar, molasses, coconut and cocoa, all expensive items, for the entries of deliveries being meticulously kept by William's deputy, Alun Breamer, were far fewer than the bills that had been paid.

The merchant, when accused of charging for the same goods more than once, pleaded he could not repay the money, but promised to repay everything obtained by fraud, by making each alternative delivery free, if William did not notify the authorities of his crime. Major John Gilchrist was happy. Having believed he was a useless invalid, he now had a new interest in life, besides saving his benefactor quite a deal of money.

One of his great joys was a fine collection of soldiers he had made himself from moulds, with beautifully painted uniforms. He brought them to young William. Having set them out, they fought battles Royal with the enemy, Aimee and Katie, whose bloodthirsty cries brought the mistress to the ground-floor study converted to a schoolroom, to save the

Major climbing stairs. Alice escaped in mock horror on being shot at with dried peas fired from a cannon.

Matt had been there barely five days and proved an asset, especially on the day the Toomey family asked him to bring Miss Gilchrist and her father to the gatehouse for supper, and spend a few social hours. They accepted with alacrity.

William had now been away a week.

Bess prepared oat-cakes, scones, jam and cream to spread, sliced meats and cheese and pickles, before returning to the main house to prepare the evening meal for the family there.

After playing, and winning, two games of cards, using buttons for gaming chips, the Major asked if Simon would read aloud for them to hear how he was progressing. Simon asked if he could read from a chronicle he had found about the war and all said they would be delighted. He brought the paper over to the Major for help with long words.

In the warmth of the lighted room no one noticed how dark it had become, until old Martha went to the window to see what had delayed Tug, and saw the snow falling.

Mary asked could her father stay there, while she went to see all was well at the house. Matt and Alex said they would escort her.

Struggling through the snow, the three arrived at the back door. Pushing it open they found all the occupants huddled around the fire, Florrie cuddling Aimee, Alice nursing William in a thick blanket, and Fiona holding Katie on her knee.

Both Alex and Fiona asked simultaneously, 'Is Tug wi' you?'

When it was discovered he had not come home from the factory, Alex said he was going out to search for him.

Matt said it would be best if Alex stayed to look after his family, for *he* was more experienced in this kind of weather, having worked as a shepherd in the far north, where it often snowed for nine months of the year.

To lighten the atmosphere, he declared he knew of a place where you could get a snowball in June, but that was a story he would tell them another day.

He wanted to go on foot, but Alex made him take a sure-footed little cob with him. Aimee jumping down from Florrie's lap, went over to Shaggy the St Bernard, who hauled the carriage that Tug had made for her.

'Take Shaggy, too, for he comes from a place far away, where there are mountains of snow. Mistress Gilchrist told me, dogs like our Shaggy go out and find folk who are lost.'

Mary Gilchrist confirmed this, but Matt said he did not think that Tug was lost. He was going to check that the old fellow was safe at the factory, and tell him all was right at home, so he should stay there until the storm was over and clear.

Wrapped up well with borrowed clothing and fortified with a flask of the master's best brandy and a packet of food from Bess, Matt set off, leading the horse, as Shaggy lolloped in the snow that was deepening by the minute.

Two miles from the house, in blinding snow, Shaggy stopped. He started to bay in such a mournful fashion that Matt thought he had never heard such a sad sound.

At the side of the road he saw something sticking out of a snowdrift. Halfway along the drift, Shaggy was digging furiously. The tops of the fences were just disappearing when Matt helped the dog scoop away the snow to find the shay on its side, and Tug's body.

Matt cursed himself that he had not set out sooner. Shaggy licked Tug's still-twisted face, which showed a bluish tint in the light of the lantern. Matt imagined he saw a flicker of the snow-flecked eyelashes then, like a tiny serpent, the tongue through the white lips. Frantically brushing away the snow, Matt rubbed the body. Tug moaned.

Forcing the brandy through Tug's lips, Matt said, 'We shall soon hae ye hame auld comrade, ifen this brave hound will keep us on the road.' Wrapping Tug in a thick rug the women had made him bring, Matt lifted Tug into the saddle, giving him another sip of brandy.

Quickly digging where he thought the horse would be, and

finding the poor animal with its neck broken, he unbuckled the reins, looping them through Shaggy's collar. Fastening the other end to his horse's bridle, he called to the dog, 'Lead us hame, laddie!'

The two-mile journey was a nightmare, but Shaggy seemed to sense where the road was floundering less than three yards in front of Matt, who had abandoned the lantern, he needing two hands to coax the wild-eyed horse through a sea of white, until at long last they arrived at the gatehouse.

Alex came out to help Matt lift Tug down, but Tug gasped, 'Take I tae Fiona!'

Alex shouted to Simon, 'Stay with your grandmother and the Major! Keep up a good fire and make sure they are warm!'

It stopped snowing. Shaggy went on ahead, and his scratching at the door brought out Mary, with a lantern.

Bess had plenty of hot water at the ready. Tug was carried into the kitchen and placed on the table.

Matt, before taking off his wet clothes, asked, 'Could someone rub that hound dry, and please tae gie him a reward o' some kind, for wi'out him, we would niver ha' found the way back.'

The children vigorously rubbed the dog with a blanket, feeding him the biscuits Bess had brought for them to nibble on, to keep them quiet, for they were far from sleepy.

Fiona asked Alex for a pail of snow to be brought, and told Matt to remove his boots and hose, and massage his hands and feet with snow to bring back the circulation and stop frostbite.

Bess, following Fiona's example, rubbed snow into Tug's right hand and foot, while Fiona did the same on the left side, avoiding pressure on the shattered leg.

Even Alice helped fill a bath with hot water. Fiona instructed that an amount of mustard, menthol and drops of eucalyptus be added to it, telling Matt he was to sit near the fire, his feet in the bowl and a blanket over his head and shoulders, breathing in the fumes.

Tug's trews were cut away. Fiona asked Alice, could she use

sheets as bandages? Alice told Florrie to bring anything Fiona needed, and quickly left as Tug groaned loudly when Alex pulled the shattered leg straight, for Fiona to bind the wooden beating paddle, and the stick used for lifting clothes from the boiler, to it, to act as splints.

William went back the way he came, not fancying the waterside inns, and remembering passing a hostelry a little way up the hill that had looked clean and quiet.

Going into the cobbled yard at the side of the Jolly Mariner, William tied his horses up outside the stables which, in the evening light, appeared dry. He called for a groom and, as no one came, went to the front door and entered.

The only occupant was a shadowy figure sitting on the settle-bench by the inglenook.

William called for service, and the figure at the fireside called to him.

'Ye'll hae to call louder na that, matey, to get the lazy landlubber o' a landlord tae hear.'

William could not see much of him as he hollered, 'There be a gen'leman here needs service, Seth Grundy!'

Minutes passed before a burly fellow, whose apparel looked as if it had been slept in, appeared. 'There be nay chance fer a fellow to take a rest i' this accursed place!'

A loud, wicked chuckle answered him, ''Twere no resting ye were, ye lecherous toad, an' tha best put thy breeches on the right way round afor our Maggie seed them!'

The fellow fumbled with his trousers, only to find they were the right way round. He crossed the room, and kicked away the table in front of his tormentor. Picking up a thick piece of wood from the firewood box, and screaming loudly that he was but a jealous, crippled half-man that no woman could stand the sight of, he rained blows on the head and shoulders of his seated adversary.

William was glad he had rushed forward to snatch away the weapon, and seeing that the man in the shadow had but his left arm to protect himself with. When William threw the wood in the fire, the sparks lit up the seated man. He had a sabre-scar across his face, very similar to the one Tug had, and this poor fellow had only one eye.

Horrified, William then saw the two roughly carved wooden stumps strapped to the man's knees. He apologized for staring, and snapped at the landlord to send someone out sharpish, to see to his horses and bring a jug of ale.

The fat man sidled away, and was heard to call for someone called Sam.

William asked permission to sit on the settle opposite the crippled man, who nodded his head. William picked up the table the landlord had kicked over, and was about to sit down when a buxom wench brought a jug of ale.

She leant over him, pushing her barely covered bosom in his face. The stale, sickly odour of her unwashed body offended William, who choked, and demanded another tankard for the gentleman, if he would oblige him by sharing the beverage.

The man thanked him, civilly, introducing himself as Gabriel Foley, ex-master gunner, Royal Navy.

William asked where he could get something to eat.

'Ye can do nay better na here. My sister Maggie be a fair cook, an looks after me fine. The thing that be wrong wi' our Maggie be the scoundrel she married.'

Gabriel rang a bell and called, 'Maggie, love, can ye come?'

A wisp of a woman came. Gabriel asked could William have food. She nodded.

William asked if there were a room he could rent. Again she nodded.

Silently she left them, to return to wipe the table before placing on it plates, spoons, bread and a tureen of delicious-smelling mutton stew.

Maggie silently ladled the stew into a dish, breaking bread to float in it. William noticed the meat and vegetable were also cut into small pieces. Without a word, she tucked a napkin into her brother's collar and placed a spoon near his left hand. Still silent, she left.

William admired the dexterity with which Gabriel ate the stew, spilling not a single drop.

The stew finished, Maggie took away the dishes and came back with large meat pasties. Once again, she cut one into pieces small enough for her brother to cope with.

The front door was opened with a flourish, and a large, jovial one-legged man came in. A strong gust of wind blew behind him.

Maggie, turning her face, twisted it into a lop-sided smile, and William could see that one side of her face was stiff, as if she had suffered a stroke.

The arrival pushed the door shut with his crutch, and cheerfully greeted them. Maggie beckoned him, offering the plate containing the pasties.

'Thank ye, Maggie, my fair love. Although I have not long eaten, I cannot resist one o' your pasties.'

Asking William's permission, he sat down next to Gabriel.

Maggie hurried away, her sallow cheeks betraying a faint blush, whilst Gabriel introduced the newcomer as Daniel Turtle, an old shipmate and valued friend, who was once betrothed to his sister.

'The weather has started to blow rough, old matey, for even wi' three legs, I had a struggle to come along.' Dan seeing William's puzzled expression, pointed to his crutch, his peg leg and his good leg. He said he would not be stopping long as there was a storm blowing up, but he stayed long enough to find out why a Scotsman had journeyed so far, and offer him his assistance.

A few other seafaring types arrived. All sat near to Gabriel and Dan, passing the time of day with them, and they, in turn, were introduced to William. William asked to be excused for a few minutes as he wanted to check his horses had been bedded down for the night.

With a walking-stick, Gabriel hooked down a lantern off the wall and Dan lit it with a taper, before handing it to William.

He went out into the strong wind, which pelted sea-spray into his face.

The horses had both been rubbed down, and had sacking

thrown over their rumps. Blue Boy was still munching on bran and oats when his master softly wished them goodnight.

William, hearing a sound behind him, turned and saw, in the light of the lantern, a small urchin blinking his eyes.

'These be yorn master? They be fine beasts. I gave them a good rub down, and they will come to no harm, for I sleep here wi' them.'

William felt a lump in his throat, and wondered if his son had a safe harbour. He patted the lad's head, giving him a few coins.

As he was leaving Maggie came, clutching her shawl which the wind was trying to whip away, as she struggled to hold a pastie she had brought for the boy, who scoffed it in seconds.

Going out, Maggie stumbled, so William clutched her arm, and together they battled their way against the torrent, back to the tavern.

She uttered not a word of thanks, only looked into William's face with her doe-like eyes, lowering her lashes.

Gabriel asked the man who now sat in the seat William had vacated, to move, saying it was William's place.

Seth Grundy shouted that *he* was the landlord, and broken-down sea-dog cripples had no right to say who was to sit anywhere.

The fellow sitting in William's seat arose, apologizing.

William, thanked him but said that he was very tired and asked the landlord if he could be shown to his room, instead.

Seth Grundy told him the room was not ready, for they had only just that minute gone up to light a fire in it. He would be called when all was prepared.

Seth was in no hurry for a fellow to leave, who had bought a round of drinks for all there. The trade in the Jolly Mariner was poor, the few regulars being Gabriel's friends and shipmates.

Wiliam drew up a stool and called for more ale. Bringing it, the blowzy barmaid leaned over him again, one grubby palm held out for payment, her arm around his shoulders.

Dan Turtle lifted his crutch and pushed her away with its end, telling her to take herself off, and not to bother decent folk.

Disgruntled, she went back to the bar. She and Seth Grundy held a whispered argument, then he slapped her painted face.

Gabriel, grinning, said, 'That be a lovers' tiff, no doubt.'

Bringing out the letter, William showed it to Dan, telling him of Phillips's disappearance, and that the letter was the first scrap of information they had received.

They all knew Davey Wells, a decent enough young fellow. He was bookkeeper-clerk to a man called Thadious Tully, a slimy, rogue shipping agent known to be in league with press-gangs.

Davey, a foundling, had been brought up and educated by monks near the city of Wells, from where he had got his name. Delivering papers for the monks, he had been caught by the press-gang, starved and beaten almost to death until, unfit for work, he had been pushed overboard near the shore and was washed-up on the beach, more dead than alive.

Maggie came and tapped on William's shoulder, indicating that he should follow her. He wished them all a good night, and went up the rickety stairs.

Holding a candle aloft, Maggie showed him into a room where the floorboards were bare, and squeaked as he trod on them. The room was full of smoke blowing down the chimney, so William opened the window but had to struggle to close it because of the gale blowing in.

Maggie propped open the door and flapped her apron. William believed she was trying to tell him the smoke would soon disperse. He knew that, although she could not speak, she could hear, for she had heard her brother call to her to bring food.

'Would it be possible for me to have a lamp or lantern for light, for the draught will blow out a candle, and I need to write a letter?'

Maggie nodded. Within minutes she brought him an oil-lamp.

The fire brightened and the smoke thinned. William sat at a small table and wrote a letter home, saying he had not made any fresh discoveries, but he *had* met with people who knew the writer of the letter.

Fatigued, he drew back the blankets on the extra-large bed, which smelt of damp and age.

After closing the door and pulling the larger of the two chairs up to the fire, he removed his boots and sprawled out. His loaded pistols down at his side, he was soon asleep.

Suddenly he was awake, pistols at the ready. Creaking boards had awakened him. He made out the figure creeping towards the bed behind a flickering light.

Jumping to his feet, he caught the prowler around the throat with his forearm, and pressed a pistol-barrel at his temple.

There was no news of William, and the whole household was worried. Fiona tried consoling Alice, telling her the weather was so bad, only a fool would venture out in it.

It had been 12 days since William had left during a freak thaw due to mild south winds, but then the north winds had returned, bringing blizzards, sickness and death.

Tug was in a great deal of pain, and fretting that he had let the master down, not being able to see what was happening at the factory.

Young Alun Breamer was too young, Tug kept saying. 'The Maester would niver abandon his workers.'

Tug had been carried, on Alice's orders, to one of the guest-rooms in the house, making it easier for him to be nursed. His condition did not improve, however.

Fiona thought it was worry, for in previous winters, William had arranged that his workers be given credit for essentials for life, and he had paid the traders.

Alex, Simon and Matt made sure there was a stock of food in the house, and fires were stoked up day and night.

Florrie was kept busy with hot drinks and warming-pans, and helping Mary Gilchrist to keep the children amused.

Mary and her father were invited by Alice to stay in the house. It was a problem moving the Major up from the gatehouse, but a solution was found when he was seated on the children's sleigh, one of Tug's construction, with Shaggy pulling, the children pushing. The gentleman declared he had not had so much sport for many years.

Matt suggested that to ease Tug's mind, he should try to get through to the factory. Tug told him what to do, Alice gave him money, and Aimee insisted he took Shaggy. Matt constantly praised the brave dog, vowing he had saved the lives of himself and Tug.

Matt had only been once to the factory, but he had no trouble finding it, for Shaggy stopped at certain points, sniffed and headed straight for it.

Matt was surprised to see it was a hive of activity. He asked to be taken to Alun Breamer, telling the sharp, bright-faced 20-year-old that he had come on behalf of Master Tug Wilson, Matt was given a tumultuous welcome.

Alun had been worried that Tug had not survived the terrible storm, and was concerned when told about his injuries, and that his condition was not improving because it was thought he was worried about the factory and its workers, believing he had let the master down.

Tug had left a little early on the day of his accident, wanting to get back home before the storm broke. But the blizzard came just after he had left.

Some of the workers were too frightened to venture outside, so Alun had held a meeting, suggesting they all stay there until the storm blew over.

Many had elderly folk and babies at home. So Alun had organized the strongest men to take carts and collect all the people at their homes, asking them to bring food, warm clothing and blankets with them back to the factory.

Two volunteers had gone out again, to buy as much food as they could with the money that was available. To keep warm they worked all day. At night, boilers were kept alight and filled with water.

Next day the storm raged on. A man had asked could he go to see to his stock, for he had two goats and some hens. Another had asked could he go to see his cow and hens.

The strongest had again been sent out to bring back the animals with any available feed.

The stores became a sleeping area where grannies cooked hot meals for everyone, besides looking after the babies.

Matt was most impressed. The children seemed happy enough; at least here there was less danger of them freezing or starving to death, which was a common occurrence in harsh winters.

He asked if there was a doctor nearby who could visit Tug, for Fiona said she wanted someone professional to examine him. Alice had asked if it were possible for him to call and see their financial adviser, Andrew Savage, and arrange funds for the factory, and also tell him William had travelled to Portsmouth. Alun had met Andrew Savage – William had brought him to tell him that if he needed financial help or legal advice that's who he should contact. Matt was a stranger to the area, so Alun asked a young male worker to go with him to show him the way, and then bring him back to the factory.

It was afternoon when Andrew Savage, Matt and the youth came. They looked very weary for they had battled against the elements, and deep icy snow. An old woman brought them hot soup and oatcakes, which they were grateful to accept.

Andrew said he was sure that William would be pleased and proud at what had been achieved by his young deputy. True, they were running low with stocks, but he would go as soon as possible to the supplier. It might be best if they eased a little on production, and thoroughly cleaned the premises instead, do minor repairs to the property and paint it.

Matt spent a very pleasant evening listening to tales from the old folk. He was even invited to dance to pipe and fiddle by a very pretty girl, but had to decline because of his gammy leg, and set out for home at early light.

Matt arrived back at the house very cold, very weary, but safe. Before he would accept any assistance, he pleaded that Shaggy should be seen to first.

Alex helped remove his boots, and Mary and Florrie each rubbed one of his hands. Bess had put a poker in the bright embers while she went for a tankard of homebrew, adding a pinch of cinnamon and ginger spice to it. Pulling out the hot fire-iron, she plunged it into the mixture, which sizzled loudly. She handed it to Matt, telling him to drink it down whilst she got him some food.

All were anxious to know how he had got on, and were very pleased with what he told them, except that the doctor had refused to come that distance until the weather was better.

Matt had been given presents to bring back with him; treacle toffee and gumdrops for the children, brittle nut candy and peppermint fudge for the adults. Alice was overcome with a beautiful lace piece an old lady had made for her.

There were so many good wishes for Fiona, and Matt had to admit he was getting quite confused by how many lasses had been given her name, as it was she who had delivered at their birth.

For Tug there was a special present; long, thick, knitted socks. It was difficult to tell what he thought, with his odd, twisted face.

He declared he was pleased young Alun had proved more than his worth, and was delighted the workers were safe and well, and that he had been so kindly remembered. But he did not believe he could find a use for the gift, and would be pleased, rather than they should be wasted on him, if Matt would have them, to wear them in good faith, and health.

20

A blanket of despondency as well as snow rested on the house, for Tug lay taking little notice of anything or anyone.

Alice and Fiona watched and tended him together or in turns, for the mistress and Fiona had become great friends. Whereas Fiona had been reluctant to speak of her past, now that Alice, in Fiona's opinion, had become more natural and softened, she did not mind her inquiring how she had come to know Matt.

'Weel, ye remember I telled ye how I came back frae France, and went tae the convent, where the young couple did travel wi' I?'

Alice said she remembered.

'Weel, I wanted tae find out what had really happened when my hame were burned, and I lost all my family, so I went to the place where it happened.'

Fiona told how she had left the couple to travel north, dressed in rags, uncomfortable in her filthy state, but never washing since she was convinced it was being that way which kept her safe.

Three long months it took her to arrive at the moss-covered ruins of her old home.

She wept at the overgrown, neglected graves, tearing at her rags, loathing the odours that came from them. She removed the pack from off her back, her mind a turmoil. Going down to the river, she jumped in. Stupidly, she watched lumps of filth float from her like frog's-spawn in the waist-high water.

She climbed out and went back to her pack, taking out the

soap she had many times looked at longingly. In her undergarments, she jumped back into the cool water and soaped herself.

Removing her wet clothes, she threw them on the bank, and soaped her body and hair, feeling suddenly exhilarated. She dried herself and put on a clean shift. She spread out her wet clothes, then lay on stones that were warm in the early September sun, closing her eyes.

Memories came flooding back. How happy they had been! Then there, in front of her, was the house in flames. She screamed again, seeing her young husband lying against a tree.

It was dusk when she hurriedly pulled on her kirtle and shawl, and gathered up her damp clothes, running to escape from the nauseating stench of burning flesh which filled her nostrils.

Unheeding, she ran, falling over a crouched figure, who jumped up and grasped her tightly, else she would have fallen into his fire.

She struggled like a wild creature as he pulled her away from the flames.

'Hold hard, mistress, for I mean ye nay harm.' The voice was gentle as he released her.

She was still shaking when he asked if she would like a drink. She did not reply, just stared into the fire with her arms held tightly across her chest.

'What frightened ye, that ye ran so madly?' he asked.

Her gaze fell on the branding-irons and, as if coming out of a dream, she sensed rather then saw, hazy shapes of cattle moving in the gloaming, and began wondering whose cattle they were, so close to the cottage.

In the fire's glow she took a sideways look at the man. He was quite young, younger than herself, she thought. A waft of the rabbit he was spit-roasting came to her, making her realize she was hungry. She stammered, 'I be Fiona Brown. I once lived in the cottage yonder. And who might ye be?'

'My name be Matt Wilkie and I have heard Mistress Annie Floyd speak of ye often.'

'Ye know my dear friend Annie? Is she back in Perth?'

The man's voice saddened, 'Nay, Mistress Floyd died three year since.'

'Annie dead! I canna believe it! The last time I saw her she were travelling back tae her husband Tam's birthplace.'

'Aye, but they ne'er got there. It were after Mistress Annie's husband died I met her, and travelled with her to this place.'

Fiona thought she heard a sob in his voice as tears sprang to her eyes. They were silent. He then asked if she would like some rabbit meat. It was a shame to waste it in these days of want.

After eating, Fiona asked who the cattle belonged to. Matt said they now belonged to the authorities, taken for non-payment of taxes and such-like. The land they were on once belonged to a Lady Ruth McGregor.

'I know Lady Ruth. She showed me great kindness,' said Fiona. 'Be she still alive?'

'Aye, she lives in the rambling house wi' an auld woman servant, the only one left to serve her; infirm and old, so not wanting any wages.'

'But why? Lady Ruth was surely rich.'

' In the past, maybe, but she having no heirs, the land and property were not entailed. She selling some property and land she were not allowed to sell, the government demanded full repayment of the money the lady had left, which was little, her having spent most of it redressing wrongs her lord had committed.

'Annie and Willie Haig tried to fight her cause, but to no avail. Before they both died, they ensured she had food, and fuel for her fire.'

'Willie Haig be dead, too!'

'Aye, he died within hours of Mistress Annie dying.'

Sobbing until there were no more tears left, Fiona fell asleep, and Matt covered her with a jacket.

The mist lay on the ground like a thick blanket when Fiona awoke. Matt had finished skinning a snared rabbit, and was rubbing his hands on a clump of grass before scooping up some water from the animal-drinking-trough. He then offered Fiona a hot drink.

She sensed an urgency in the way he rushed packing up, and poured water on the fire.

'Ye have tae go soon so I'll no hinder ye,' she said.

'Ye take time, but I must be away tae toon for the agent tae ship off these cattle. If ye need tae find me, I am lodgin' wi' the tanner who was friend tae Willie Haig.'

Fiona remembered the tanner, for it was he who had supplied the skins and leathers that her husband Edward had used in his shoemaking.

'Will ye be goin' tae toon? Ye can come wi' me. It be a slow, dusty job drivin' this lot,' he said.

'Nay, as I am so near, I will call on the Lady Ruth tae pay my respects.'

'If ye do, will ye do me a service, and take this rabbit tae her? But don't say I gave it tae thee, say ye found it by the roadside, perhaps dropped by a poacher!'

Taking the rabbit, Fiona was puzzled by this. She accompanied him part of the way, then said goodbye as she turned off towards the big house.

The driveway had almost closed up with the overgrown hedges and fallen tree branches. As she arrived at the house, it looked eerie, neglected and forlorn. The once fine steps up to the front door were broken, and weeds grew through the cracks.

Fiona banged on the door with her fist. Receiving no reply, she picked up a piece of broken masonry and hammered with that.

She waited, then sadly turned to leave.

There was a rustling sound like dead leaves being raked together, then, with much creaking and scraping, the door was opened the merest chink.

A head of hair, looking like storm-blown thatch, covered by a tattered shawl, peered out. The cracked voice asked what was wanted at that early hour of the morning. It was no good begging there, for they had nothing left to give.

Fiona, thinking this was Marie, the old servant, told her she had come to see the mistress of the house. If told the caller was Fiona Brown, the wife of the shoemaker who had once lived in the burnt-out cottage, she would see her.

The old dame struggled to pull the door open further, and in the light, Fiona realized it was not Marie dressed in rags she was addressing, but Lady Ruth herself.

'Fiona, my dear, is it really you, after all these years? I'm sorry you have found me in this state. Come in, but have a mind where you step.'

Inside, Fiona helped her to push the stiff door, which closed with a thud, and lumps of plaster fell down, sending spirals of dust up, and rats scuttling along the wainscotting.

Fiona yelped, almost treading on one rodent who sneezed and rubbed his whiskers right in her path.

The smell of decay and mildew prevailed as they crossed the baronial hall, where once Malcolm McGregor's boots had resounded.

The cobweb-festooned stairwell was littered with chunks of masonry, rusty armour and weaponry, hung drunkenly or lying where it had fallen.

Fiona understood why she was warned to watch her step as they slowly descended the dark, slippery steps to the kitchen, for they, too, had all manner of obstacles to avoid.

In the cold, lower kitchen, although there was a small wood-fire burning, it was not sufficient to give out much heat.

Sitting in one of the two large armchairs drawn up to the fire, an old wizened creature squinted at them with her pale, half-open eyes.

'Marie, do you remember young Mistress Fiona Brown?' Lady Ruth faltered and thought for a second, wondering how she could jog the old woman's memory without bringing too much pain to Fiona. 'You remember, her husband used to make those lovely slippers for me.'

But tact is not the way of the very old. 'Oh, ye mean him that were murdered by a madman who set fire tae that cottage ye had tae pay back a' that money tae the government for sellin' tae them?'

Fiona felt dreadful. This gracious lady had been penalized for her good deed and generosity.

She placed the rabbit on the table, saying she had found it, as she had been instructed by Matt.

'Did you skin it?' asked Lady Ruth. 'What did you do with the skin?'

Fiona remembered Matt scooping a hole at the very edge of his fire, putting the pelt in the hole, and drawing hot embers over it. 'It be buried.'

'Good, for poaching is an offence, even for wild creatures.'

Fiona then understood Matt's odd actions.

Standing in corners were two beds, each looking as though they had recently been vacated. Fiona asked could she prepare the rabbit for cooking. Quickly Marie said, 'Aye, for I canna see much and my lady be no much tae the art o' cookin'.'

Fiona, searching the cupboards for a pot, and finding plenty of utensils but little in the way of food, just a few dried carrots and potatoes, realized why the two ladies were so thin.

Placing the rabbit in water and salt, Fiona looked for wood to put on the fire. There was none. She asked if there was an axe or chopper so that she could go out and get some wood.

Lady Ruth showed her a small cleaver. 'I have to use this, the axe is too heavy. It is not right that a guest should work. *I* will go to get the wood. Marie used to do this, but now she has severe stiffness of the limbs and cannot walk.

Fiona said she was a friend, not a guest, and if shown the way out, she could at least help to gather some firewood.

Through a door at the back, Fiona followed Lady Ruth up steps leading to the kitchen garden. Someone had been digging at a small patch, but there was no evidence of anything growing there.

'I have tried to plant some carrot tops and bits of potato sprouts, but nothing came.'

What Fiona first thought were mittens she saw, as Ruth gestured hopelessly with her hands, were bandages of rag.

In the overgrown garden, there were many thick branches. Fiona told her friend to sit on a low wall, whilst she hacked away with a will.

Lady Ruth, with great effort, dragged the pieces nearer the steps.

Fiona suddenly stopped, listening. Raising her hand to her forehead, she looked up and saw starlings lifting and quarrelling in the air a short distance from them.

Working towards them, slashing at the undergrowth she made a path, and laughed loudly on coming to an apple tree where birds pecked at the ripe fruit. Shooing them, she called to Lady Ruth to come and hold up her skirt as she picked, until there was no more room in it, holding her own skirt with one hand, and picking with the other, she worked until her own skirt was also full. Fiona was pleased with her find.

In the daylight she could see how transparently thin this gentle lady was, and how she staggered weakly back to the house with her burden of fruit.

Putting the fruit in a large laundry basket, Fiona told Lady Ruth to rest, while she threw the wood they had gathered down the steps.

Lady Ruth did not take a rest but dragged the wood into the kitchen, and only sat at the table, panting for breath, when it was all inside.

While they had been in the garden, Marie had brought a pot from the oven and ladled watery oatmeal into three dishes. Pushing the salt-cellar towards Fiona, she said, 'If ye put some salt i' it, it nay be so bad.'

Fiona swallowed the oatmeal that was no more than thickened water, and asked could she see if there was anything else to be found in the garden.

Taking the machete-type cleaver, she again chopped at the overgrown foliage, finding a fruitless cherry tree and a pear tree bearing quite a few pears.

She was about to go back to fetch a container to hold them, when a familiar smell came to her nostrils. She cleared a path to where this odour wafted from, and in a corner where two walls met, she came upon a mound where garden refuse had once been thrown.

Excitedly she dug at it with a broken pot, pulling up a dozen small potatoes, and the four onions which emitted the smell she had picked up.

These safe in her tucked-up skirt, venturing further she came to the old herb garden, with mint, thyme, parsley and rosemary. Much had gone to seed, but was still usable, dried, for tea and flavouring.

In the neglected salad-garden, she was elated to find animal droppings.

Returning to the house for the second time with her skirt full, Fiona had an idea, and hoped the ladies would agree to it.

Marie was scraping the dried potatoes and carrots, while Lady Ruth was building up the fire.

Fiona showed her treasures to them. They were speechless for a second, then Lady Ruth started apologizing for being so useless, and Marie scolded her, saying she was never born to work, for she was a lady.

Fiona washed the herbs and vegetables, and said she would have to leave soon, to go to town, for she wanted to see Matt Wilkie.

Lady Ruth said she knew Matt, as he had been with Annie while she lived, and had brought her many things from that wonderful woman.

'Aye, them pies! My mouth do still water just thinkin' o'them,' said Marie.

Lady Ruth explained that Annie had had a bakery, and asked why Fiona had to go into town that day. Couldn't she stay with them for a little while? She was more than welcome to share what they had. She could even have the lady's own bed and she would sleep in a chair, as she often did, it being warmer near the fire.

'Besides, there be this food ye have provided. It only be right an' proper for ye tae hae a share,' croaked Marie. 'My stomach is fair gripin' at the thought o' it. Stay, lass, and gai tae toon on the morrow.'

The mention of food made Fiona feel hungry, too, as there had not been much nourishment in the thin oatmeal. Placing her pack on the table, she emptied the contents. Wrapped in a cloth was half a loaf of very dry bread, a small pouch containing a few grains of tea, and another of dried herbs.

After requesting a knife and saucepan, Fiona sliced one of the onions finely, also chopping up the green leaves she had left on. She put them on to boil until soft. Having cut the bread into pieces, she added it to the onion and water, with a good pinch of herbs and salt. When the bread was well-soaked, she placed it in the washed bowls the oatmeal had been in, and offered it to her hosts, saying, 'There be not a great deal o' nourishment, but it will help tae ease the hunger.'

Both Marie and Lady Ruth scraped their bowls.

Fiona then peeled and cleaned some bruised apples, cutting them into slices on a plate. Lady Ruth declared them delicious. Marie grumbled just a little at them being hard for her toothless mouth, so Fiona said she would bake or stew the next ones for her.

Fiona thanked them for the kind invitation to stay, which she would accept on condition that Lady Ruth would not give up her bed, for Fiona was used to sleeping on the floor. And for as long as she stayed with them, Fiona would try to provide their food.

With a few mild objections, this was agreed.

Fiona hacked at the bigger pieces of wood, she and Lady Ruth stacking it in the large, empty larder.

Amid the noise of the chopping, they failed to hear the hammering at the front door, and were startled when a man's voice called down from the garden.

Clutching the small hatchet she had chopped the wood with, Fiona cautiously opened the door.

At the top of the steps stood Matt Wilkie. 'I had to bring some heifers this way for grazing and branding, so I thought I might call to see if ye were still here, and safe.'

'Fiona called over her shoulder not to be frightened, it was only Matt, Lady Ruth told her to invite him in. She knew of Fiona's meeting with Matt, and was not as surprised as Fiona when Matt brought in a bag, saying to Fiona, 'I hope these goods are what ye wanted, mistress?' taking out flour, salt, potatoes, carrots, parsnips and a bladder of lard, amongst other things.

Lady Ruth asked him, whilst he was there, would he do a service for her, and go down to the cellar, which had been locked up for many years, and see if there was any wine there, so she could offer him a drink.

He was given a bunch of keys, and shown the cellar door.

Fiona held a lantern while Matt tried keys to find the right one to open it. Inside the door, facing them, was a shelf holding another lamp, which Matt lit. He asked Fiona to follow close behind him with the extra light. He being lame, was cautious of going down uneven steps.

Slowly descending, Matt stumbled as he brushed aside cobwebs. The lower they went, the colder it became.

At the bottom, the lanterns illuminated the Gothic arches, and wine racks, some empty, others containing shattered bottles. In the end racks were some intact, full bottles.

Matt picked up an old basket and placed a bottle in it. The rotten wicker crumbled, the bottle crashing to the stone-slab floor. A rich, fruity aroma floated up. After dipping his finger in the drop left in the thick base of the bottle, Matt tasted it. 'Mistress Fiona, I canna be sure, but I think I have destroyed a bottle o' fine brandy.'

Fiona told him to stay there, she would go above to find something to carry a few bottles back upstairs.

Putting three bottles in each pail, carefully they carried them up the stairs. They left one lantern hanging on a hook, for they wanted to investigate further.

Marie, peering hard at the dusty bottles, practically yelled, 'I knowed these, for my man brought me many o' these bottles tae clean off the dust, in the old days, afore bringin' they tae the maester.'

Marie's husband had been butler to Lady Ruth's father.

When the lady had married McGregor, he had taken over the estate. Malcolm McGregor had been too lazy to go down to the cellar himself, and Lady Ruth would never venture there, having been taken down once as a child, and shown a dark pit where, she was told, in years gone by prisoners had had their food thrown to them as they rotted in the dungeons below.

She remembered this, now and warned Matt and Fiona to take extra care, for she had forgotten exactly where the pit lay. Often at night she heard noises from below the floor, and that was the true reason she wanted Matt to inspect the cellars.

They lit large candles with the lanterns, to take down the second time to give more light. As they turned into a chamber on their right, where four large casks stood on a stout stone platform, they heard the tinkling of water.

Matt lifted his candles and saw, to the left of the casks, a spring coming out of the mouth of a carved stone head in the wall, and disappearing into the ground two yards from where he stood.

At the edge of the thick planks of timber set in the stone floor, Matt took a step forward and the candle he held went out. Fiona had been clutching the back of his jacket. When he lurched forward she jerked him back, just as the timber crumbled and went crashing into the pit below.

Retracing their steps back to where they had left the first lantern, they stopped to get their breath back. Relighting his candles, Matt said, 'Now that we know where the pit be, shall we see if there be aught in the barrels?'

Fiona, trying not to show her fright, nodded her head. Holding the lantern in one hand, she kept a tight hold on his jacket with the other. They returned to the casks.

Running a little wax to hold the candles firm, Matt tapped each with a piece of timber. Two sounded hollow, the third had a different sound, but the fourth was a dull thud.

'I believe the first two are empty, the third has some liquid inside, and the fourth is full,' said Matt. 'But we need a mallet and taps tae try them. But wait, I see pegs at the top. Hold up your light, mistress!'

Taking string from his pocket, he loosened the plug at the top of the last barrel, then threaded the string in the hole. After a few minutes he withdrew it, running it through his fingers and licking them.

'That be a drap o' gaed auld ale,' he declared, smacking his lips.

Placing a few more bottles in a bucket, he blew out the candles. They picked up the lantern and returned upstairs.

There was an air of excitement around the two women in the kitchen. On the table stood six bottles, with the dust of years cleaned away, three fine sparkling glasses that had been washed and polished, and a slightly rusty corkscrew with ash clinging to it, where someone had tried to clean it.

Fiona asked what the three glasses were for. Lady Ruth told her to try the brandy.

'But there be four on us!'

'I have no taste for strong drink,' Ruth replied. Matt said he would prefer water to drink. The bottle remained unopened.

Matt said he would have to go to see to the stock, grazing not too far away. He had to brand them with the government mark, then take them to town for shipment.

This was the last batch, as there were not that many beasts in the area at this time. Those left were not worth paying him to do the job for, and an agent would just collect what he could through the winter, then send them down south.

'What will ye do then, lad, wi'out your work?'

'I could go back up north where I came from. It were not much o' a job anyway. I had little stomach for it, being nowt but legal stealin'. The way the poor beasties were marked, was no tae my likin'.' He did not have to enlarge on the method of branding. Having to work on his own, he was ordered to drive each animal into a narrow box-like pen, restricting its movement. Forcing the creature to go where he wanted it to go, he went behind it, holding two long, metal rods with heated ends, which scorched its sides to make sure it went in the right direction. Matt used this method when all other means failed, or he was desperate to make up essential time.

When the beasts were corralled in this way, it was simple for one man to do the branding.

Matt asked Fiona what were her plans.

'I thought o' goin' tae toon afor ye came, but then thought o' somethin' else that I must work out, with my lady askin' I tae stay this night. If the offer still holds I will stay.'

Lady Ruth asked Matt could he come back next day. He said he would try. She was asking if he knew of anyone who would discreetly buy some of the bottles, when Marie spoke.

'Gae tae the Caledonian Tavern and ask for Dougal. He be my kin. Ask him tae buy the bottle. Tell him I sent thee, but be careful.'

At midday Matt returned, bringing with him Marie's great nephew Dougal, who was the landlord of the Caledonion Tavern. Fiona had cleaned the kitchen, washing was festooned on bushes, and a batch of griddle-cakes cooled on the side bench.

Marie was pleased to see her relative, asking why he had not come before. He told her he had to work hard to pay taxes, but had he known the dire circumstances Matt told him they were in, he would have tried to come sooner.

Marie mumbled youngsters would never be like their elders.

Dougal said he would love to buy the brandy but would not be able to sell it in his tavern. He knew a gentleman who would buy as much as they wanted to sell, however. It would be dangerous, and the buyer would have to believe the brandy was obtained from smugglers.

Fiona asked Lady Ruth, could she speak for her in this matter.

'Certainly, my dear.'

'We dinna know how many bottles be in the cellar. There may no' be a lot, for there be mony bottles broken, but there be some barrels that need checking, and we hae not the tools ta do this job.'

'Oh, aye, we have!' said Marie. 'There be all the tools i' the butler's pantry, weer yon corkscrew came frae.'

Marie led the way to the butler's pantry. 'This were al'ays

locked tight, an' no one were allowed i' here. But my Saul allowed I tae clean the silver i' the auld days, when Mistress were a babby, an' for all were sold by the McGregors.' She spat on the ground as she spoke the name.

Inside were all the accessories for tapping barrels and decanting wines.

Dougal promised to come again early on the sabbath. Lady Ruth wrapped up a bottle in some rags, asking could he bring some food in payment.

Matt asked had they any oil to make torches to light the cellar on the Sunday. Lady Ruth did not know. He then asked could he do anything before leaving for Perth.

Fiona said there were many things a man could do there, but if he must go, at least stay and have something to eat and drink with them, for she had made a salad of onion, young dandelion leaves and nasturtium. There was also soup made from the remains of the rabbit, and the juice it had been cooked in.

Besides, she would like him to be there while she put a proposal to her hostess.

Matt agreed to stay for a short time, but it was essential for him to return to collect his money from the agent, and settle up with the tanner before he started travelling.

When they had eaten, Fiona put forward her idea.

'There may be a chance my child did not perish in the fire, and I must search for her,' she began. Then she related the story told to her by the sea captain.

She did not see Matt's face lose its colour, or his unease as he gasped, 'It were a long time ago. Ye might be hopin' falsely, and bringin' a deal of sorrow for thyself.'

Fiona said she could not rest until she found out the truth. She asked if she could stay with Lady Ruth for a time, for the people there were all the friends she now had in Scotland.

Lady Ruth told her she could stay for ever, for had not she, and Matt, improved things for them.

Fiona said she would pay for her board by selling in town, health and beauty preparations Teresa had taught her to manufacture.

Lady Ruth asked Matt if he could also stay, and make a home with them. 'Wi'out work, how can I pay for my keep?'

'Dinna ye worrit on that, lad, a way will be found,' Fiona told him.

21

Fiona told Alice how Matt had come back in the early evening, bringing her the swede and raw brown sugar she had asked him to get. He gave her back the money she had given him to purchase them. She argued with him, to no avail.

'Be there some job ye need doin' outside, afor it gets dark?' he asked, hoping to get away from the subject.

Fiona had been so busy all day that she had had no time to replenish the firewood. Still arguing, they moved outside, and soon collected a pile of wood.

Fiona then showed him the animal droppings, which he said were rabbit, and possibly deer. He set a few rabbit traps, for they were on private ground where no one could accuse them of poaching.

As it was getting dark, he put up a rough shelter in one corner of the garden, spreading out his sleeping-blankets.

While Marie dozed, Fiona peeled the swede. Lady Ruth, on Fiona's instructions, then cut the washed swede into small slices, putting them in a very large mixing bowl. Fiona then covered them with the raw sugar. Finally, the large bowl was covered by a cloth, and Fiona told Lady Ruth it would have to be left for two days.

Early next morning Matt had arisen and skinned two plump rabbits he had found in his snares, by the time Fiona called him for breakfast. She asked him if he would accompany her down the cellars.

With the torches burning brightly in the wall-brackets, the cellars did not seem half as menacing. Matt, being unsure of Dougal, for he was partial to drink, suggested hiding most of the full bottles, just in case.

He was puzzled by Fiona wanting so many empty bottles. Later he was to find out why.

'What *did* you want empty bottles for, Fiona?' asked Alice.

'It were tae put my cough medicine in, almost the same as the one we keep for the bairns when they have a chesty cold, and we gave young Aimee when she had that dreadful, choking whoop. But the syrup I were making then, had sommat secret and special added tae it, that made folk clamber for it.'

'Oh, do tell me what, Fiona!'

'Bide yer time, I be telling the story!'

Fiona told how there had, indeed, been a barrel and a half of ale, and how Matt's intuition had been right about Dougal. For Fiona had seen him secrete one of the few bottles of brandy left in the rack, under his clothes, although Lady Ruth had already given him two for his services tapping the barrels.

The swede and sugar had now turned to a very sweet liquid. It should have contained raspberry vinegar, but Matt had failed to get some for her, as raspberries were out of season.

Lady Ruth suggested, as they did not drink it, and it was rather difficult to dispose of, why not add a little of the brandy to the syrup?

Selling fruit cup made from the fruit found in the garden, the medicine and home-made balm cakes, using the ale as leavening, they built up quite a trade for a time.

The kitchen being such a hive of industry, Lady Ruth began to look, and feel better, working well with them. Marie did a little, but her eyesight had gone.

Matt cleared the ground-floor of the house, removing all the armour and cleaning three rooms. He brought two beds into one room, for Lady Ruth and Marie who did not want to be on her own. Then there was a room for Fiona, and the third became somewhere for them to relax when not working.

'It were durin' weather like this I learnt about Annie, the

friend I telled ye about. It were Matt told me as much as he knew, and the rest what Annie told him.'

Alice was eager for Fiona to carry on with her story as she sat watching the snow fall. It was late afternoon, and there had been no word from William.

'I were kept busy wi' cookin' and preparin' my medicines and such, that I had nay time to gae to toon, so Matt took o'er the sellin'. Not that there were much o' that, for the same folk seemed to buy and order more. Often there were squabbling, and we were runnin' out o' bottles. The brandy, too, was gettin' low.

'Matt made one delivery each week, for the weather was bad, although he said he did not mind. He became quite angry when I said I would go in his place one day, when he had a pain in his leg. I didn't know he were tryin' to save me bein' hurt.'

'Why should he want to save you from being hurt?' asked Alice.

Fiona was silent for a second, 'Well, bein' there, in the place where I used tae be, wi' friends that were now all dead.'

Alice felt Fiona was keeping something back, but did not pursue the matter. 'Well, what of Annie? She left to go north wi' her husband, and that was the last time you saw her.'

'Aye, I hated to see them go, but she looked so happy with her Tam. But Tam was still pale, havin' not gotten o'er bein' a prisoner in a foreign land. What happened next, is what Matt told to me.'

They travelled some miles. Annie asked could they stop as the movement of the cart made her feel sick. She did not remember feeling so terribly ill when she had been pregnant with her other children. Maybe it was because she was older.

After two nights sleeping out in the open, and eating the food from the hamper, their rest was frequently disturbed by Tam's fits of coughing.

They decided to stop at an inn, but were bitten badly by bed lice and unable to sleep. Arising, they went to the stables.

In the morning, refusing the breakfast of cold, fat, saddle of mutton, Tam asked the landlord for bread, cheese and a flask of ale, instead.

They decided they would not waste money staying in hostelries, to be eaten by bed bugs and given food they could not eat, but would buy food for two or three days and sleep under the cart or, if they were lucky a barn, or some such building.

Their progress was slow, for Tam sometimes had difficulty breathing, and Annie suffered sickness.

Around noon on the fifth day, Tam slumped, letting go of the reins. Annie, taking control, drew up in the bracken and helped Tam down. His knees buckled, almost bringing them both to the ground.

She sat him down among the fronds, then tethered the mare. Not more than 30 yards further on, she thought she could see a glint of water coming down the hillside. Leaving Tam, and walking on, she found a stream.

Returning, Annie gently coaxed Tam to sit on the back of the cart as she led the little mare to the stream at the foothills of Ben Wyvis.

On a grassy slope she spread out blankets, and helped Tam down. In the sunshine in a small hollow she lit a fire, bathed him, and then herself.

They ate boiled eggs they had bought that morning, and drank the sweet water. Tam started to cough again. Leaning against the slope, having wrapped a blanket around them both, she held him until his coughing stopped, and they both fell asleep.

Annie awoke. There was something wet touching her hand. In the early morning light, she could just make out the dog licking her. She sat up and saw they were surrounded by sheep.

Someone in the distance whistled, then shouted the order, 'Bring them back lass!' and the dog immediately started to round up the flock.

A shepherd came into view, dressed in tartan so old it was impossible to tell the clan. Ian Tansy could not tell you his antecedents either, for he was found when a baby by a small terrier called Tansy, whom he was then named after.

Tansy was always finding strange little creatures for her master, old Jock the shepherd, to look after. She was a marvel at finding lost sheep. Jock and Tansy had raised Ian like an orphaned lamb, and he had known no other parents.

Tam's head nestled on Annie's lap, causing her skirts to rise to her knees. Hastily she adjusted her skirts, shuddering at the sight of dried blood on Tam's pale lips.

Ian Tansy was not accustomed to many folk, and stared at the pair.

'Can ye help us?' begged Annie.

Silently, Ian helped her to place Tam on the back of the cart. He then led the gentle mare, who did not appear upset at being in the midst of a herd of sheep.

Over hills they journeyed, ever upward, coming to a building that looked as if it were built into the hill itself. Grass had grown, sweeping down the hillside across the roof to the front of the house. A nanny goat dragging a rope, grazed happily on the grass of this rooftop.

The dog had raced on before them, and now lay before a pile of logs, with six puppies suckling, and clambering over her.

In a daze, Annie helped the stranger carry Tam's unconscious form inside.

A young deer pushed its way past them through the open door, and two squirrels chattered noisily as they scampered through a broken window. They carried Tam inside.

Gently they lay him on the rough bed covered in sheepskins, causing other creatures to scuttle from under it.

It was obvious to Annie no woman's hand had been nigh the place for many years, if ever, but it was far more wholesome than the inn where they had spent the first night, even with wildlife around.

A morning mist was sweeping down the hill, mingling with the smoke from the fire Ian had lit. Although he had not spoken, Annie knew that he was able to speak, as she had heard him calling to the dog to bring back the sheep.

Still without a word he went outside, and she heard scratching, scraping sounds coming down from the roof, as if something were being dragged. Then, for the second time she heard the shepherd speak. The voice was soft as it chided the goat for being a stupid animal eating through her rope, and getting up on the roof where she could fall from.

Time passed. Annie sat on the edge of the bed removing the boots Edward, Fiona's husband, had made for Tam, then rubbed his feet and hands in turn as he lay motionless and pale.

Tears sprang to her eyes as she was thinking again she might be losing her man, when Ian entered with a large pan of thick, dark, creamy goats' milk. He poured some into two wooden bowls which he had first blown into, then wiped on a ragged cloth before handing them to Annie.

Annie brought out two spoons from the pack she had with her, and attempted to feed Tam through his pale lips.

Tam came to, choking, and started to cough, bringing spots of blood onto his chin.

'N-n-nay, mistress,' Ian stammered. 'Leave him be, tae rest!'

Ian's voice was high-pitched and strange. Annie later discovered he was so nervous talking to humans, he hardly ever spoke with them except when he went to sell stock or buy supplies. He preferred to be in the company of animals.

'Wilst take a mite of bread? 'Tis barely a week old.'

Annie thanked him, copying his action of dipping the coarse, stale bread into the warm milk, and was surprised to find she had eaten a lot worse things in the past. She wondered why the dogs were making such a fuss at every mouthful their master took, she not knowing it was their dish he was eating from.

Again he went out, returning with a frame that held the fodder off the ground to prevent it being trodden on.

He lifted Tam to the front of the bed, and placed the wooden frame sloping against the wall at the head of the bed.

Covering it with soft, white lamb's skin, without effort he

lifted Tam up against it, so that he was almost sitting in an upright position. As Annie struggled to take Tam's top garments off, Ian stammering shyly, asked if he could help.

Between them they undressed Tam, and Ian sponged away the blood around his mouth with such gentleness, Annie again felt tears come to her eyes. Through the blur she could see Ian Tansy was not a young man, but seemed to know how to care for the sick.

She asked him where he had gained this experience. Slowly, he told her that, for more than two years before his death, he had nursed the only parent he had loved and known.

For two days Tam fought for breath. Each attack Annie thought would be his last.

Ian Tansy, their host, said the cottage was not the right place for Tam to be, but he knew of a place where the air was so fresh, and the water so clear, way above the morning mists of the glen.

Annie cleaned the cottage, made cheeses and prepared oatcakes and griddle scones which Ian swore melted in his mouth.

Annie was puzzled where he went to buy supplies, for he seldom moved far from the slopes. She had been told the town was some distance away when she had asked.

Tam rallied and wanted to be helped outside. Fastened into a large armchair, he was carried by Ian and Annie out into the hazy sunshine which, he complained, hurt his eyes. Annie wrapped his legs in a thick, woven rug, and removed her apron to place on his face.

'Ye just wait, my bonny lad, I have just the thing,' she said.

Indoors, she sighed heavily, for the bright daylight showed the hollowing of his cheeks, and how his skin had the look of old, yellow parchment.

Returning with a broad-brimmed bonnet, she tied it on his head, telling him to take care lest marauding fellows should take a fancy to him, for with half-a-look he could be mistaken for a lassie.

Annie had made mutton stew and scones, for there was no shortage of any of the supplies that Ian brought her. Tam was now sleeping peacefully. She could see the flock on the slopes a short distance away.

She put stew in a basin, and scones in a cloth, and quietly went towards the flock. Lass, the collie, slid on her belly, welcoming her, licking her hand as she had the first day. But there was no sign anywhere of her master.

Annie never questioned where Ian was, she was so grateful Tam seemed to be improving.

She kept herself busy. Ian had brought her great bundles of lambs' wool, saying she could fill bags to make pillows. She asked if she could use it for another purpose, and he told her she could do what she liked with it. She combed and spun the undyed wool on the spinning wheel she had brought with her, then knitted it up.

As Ian came home at sunset, he saw Annie sitting at her husband's side, her tawny hair gleaming in the golden light. For the first time in his 60 years, he felt a great emptiness, knowing that this might end all-too-soon.

Tam thanked him for his hospitality and kindness, saying he felt much better.

'It be nothin',' mumbled Ian. Stooping down, he lifted Tam out of the chair as if he were a child, and followed Annie indoors where the evening meal of stewed rabbit with vegetables awaited them.

They ate in silence, Tam eating well. When Ian rose to go outside, Annie asked him not to leave yet, as she had made some cakes with cream and jam.

'I must gae and see to the goats, they need milking and feeding.'

'Sit down, it be all done, and milk be in cooling place.'

'What be this cooling place, mistress?'

'Wait 'til morn, ye shall see. Come, eat!'

With bread, a little meat and juice from the stock-pot in one dish, and water in another, Annie took them out to the dogs, where the bitch almost turned herself inside out in her welcome.

215

Annie, laughing, scolded the pups for climbing up her feet and legs, making her spill the food. She threw bones from her tucked-up apron to older dogs.

She was unaware of the turmoil Ian felt, as he pondered on how much was missing in his lonely life.

Just before dawn, Ian crept into the house from the byre where he slept. He was busy tending the fire when Annie came from behind the blankets he had hung to screen the bed for privacy. Ian stirred the fire embers, put on fresh wood, and pushed the kettle on to a swinging bracket nearer the flames.

The goats started bleating. Ian went outside, Annie followed, waiting until he led the goats to stakes by the stream bank. A pink glow could be seen in the east, but the waters of the stream were steel-grey in the half-light.

Annie, pointing upstream, said, 'There be the cooler!'

Ian peered where she indicated, shaking his head. She caught his sleeve, and drew him to where the bank had been dug away.

The cooler was a very large pot with a wooden lid kept firmly in place by a rock. The waters rushed in between rocks spaced around the pot, allowing water to flow between them and against the pot's side, thus keeping the contents at a cool temperature.

Ian wondered at this woman. How she must have had to struggle to bring this here, wrestling with those rocks, standing in water he knew could chill you to the bone even in summer-time.

He did not find out she was pregnant until later, then wondered what was in her mind to do such a dangerous thing.

Going back, he stopped at the byre, or old cow-house, which looked as if it were built right up against a sheer rock wall.

Beckoning her to follow him, he went into a narrow space behind a boulder, and entered a dug-out cave that was completely hidden.

Removing the lids from casks, he showed her oats and other

cereals. Cages were suspended from the roof to deter animals. He told her to use all the supplies as if they were her own.

Tam's coughing lessened. Each evening, Ian brought pine cones and pine bark back to burn on the fire. Once or twice when Tam had a bad attack, Ian put pitch-tar on a large spade which was heated until the tar boiled, and bubbled. Then, he supported Tam, shielding his body from the heat of the fire with his own, making him inhale the fumes.

Annie had heard of this treatment before, as a cure for bronchial horses, and as gentry thought as much, if not more of their horses than folk, it must be good.

She knew Ian would never harm anyone, having seen even the most timid of creatures like deer, and squirrels, eat from his hand.

The days were golden. Tam gained strength and a little weight.

A few times Annie went to look for Ian among the sheep, only ever finding the dogs. There was no sign of their master.

One evening, he came home excited, 'Mistress, it be ready!'

'What be ready?' she demanded.

'The place I spoke of, better for the man.' He still could not use their name. 'On the morrow we will go, if he be fit.'

Annie was puzzled, and thought that he might want to get rid of them to return to his solitude.

Next morning, Tam was safely secured on the cart, and Ian led them up a road that was winding and steep. The higher they climbed, the rougher it became. After climbing for some time, the road widened for just a short way, then tapered to a path of a few feet. Ian told them the cart could go no further.

Lifting Tam down, Ian placed him on the back of the sure-footed little mare. Leaving the cart, he filled a basket with goods and slung it on his back. He led the horse, Annie following behind.

22

The telling of Annie's tale had to be put aside, for there was great excitement as a letter had come from William.

William wrote that he was well, and not to worry; the weather being so bad, he would be delayed. He was not wasting his time, but had many inquiries to make.

He sent love to all the family, regards to everyone else, and would they tell Tug he had made friends with two old shipmates of his, named Gabriel Foley and Daniel Turtle. These two, amongst others, were proving to be of great assistance to him.

William said he was not quite sure the letter would arrive safely, as it would be delivered to Scotland in such a strange way.

As the whole country was in the grip of such atrocious weather, it was feared the mail could not get through, but a mariner on a ship sailing up to the port of Glasgow had called in to the tavern where William was staying, and was asked could he take it with him, and send it on to the factory.

The letter had been brought to them from the factory by a young man on a sleigh. It contained a few more pleasantries, but little else, for this was the letter William wrote on his first night, the night he was disturbed in his bedchamber by an intruder.

William suddenly realized the person he held around the throat, his pistol at their temple, was a female. He knew it was the barmaid, by the nauseating body odour he had smelt before.

Spinning her around he demanded to know what she

wanted. She did not seem at all upset at the rough treatment she had received, but just gigled, 'Oiy be here to bring ye a little extra comfort.'

Indignantly, William told her he had everything he wanted and she should return to her own bed.

'Ye mean Seth's bed, don' ye? He be snorin' like the fat pig he be, after he had his way wi' I, never botherin' fer my feelin's, but ye have the looks o' a proper man who could please a girl besides himself.'

His stomach churning, William gasped, 'Please, madam, leave and go back to whence you came!'

'Oh, don' be mean to I now, it will only cost a penny, an' if ye are good, I might give the penny back.'

Bundling the barmaid out of the door, William discovered there was no way of fastening it. The woman cussed and swore during the struggle. He pushed her onto the landing and wedged the door shut with the armchair. Quickly he pulled on his boots, and collected his belongings.

He was pushing past her at the top of the stairs, when voices began to question what was going on. Maggie came out onto the landing, then Seth emerged from a different room and waddled over to the wench, glaring at William as he rushed down the stairs. Seth shouted after him that this was not a whore-house.

Gabriel lay on a straw pallet near the fireplace.

'Thet Polly bin up tae her old tricks again, eh? Set ye down by me, an' ye will no be bothered agin this night.'

Gabriel and William talked for a while, discovering they had a mutual acquaintance, for Tug Wilson had once served alongside Daniel Turtle and Gabriel.

Gabriel had told William that Maggie Grundy, the landlady, was his sister. William said he did not understand why she should put up with her sad lot.

'Ah her sufferin' be not as bad now as it were before. Then, poor lass, she went through hell!' Gabriel talked briefly of when Maggie was young and pretty, and betrothed to Daniel Turtle.

When he and Daniel came home from sea, they put all their

savings together and bought the Jolly Mariner, planning that Daniel would retire from the sea after their next voyage, to make a home there for his wife and her brother.

Maggie waved goodbye, and God speed, not aware she was with child.

Being pregnant, and trying to run a tavern alone, she was glad of the assistance of Seth Grundy. Then the news came that her brother and future husband had perished at sea. Grundy took advantage of her sorrow, he offering marriage and to give the child she was expecting his name.

Soon after the wedding he brought other women into his bed, and started ill-treating his wife, beating her so badly she lost the child.

Gabriel, with both legs and his arm gone, near to death, and Daniel who had lost a leg, were picked up and taken ashore at San Domingo in the West Indies, but were unable to get a passage home for two years.

Seth started beating Gabriel as well, Maggie tried to protect her brother. One day Seth, striking her, smashed her jaw, severing her tongue, so robbing her of her speech.

Daniel arranged for some able-bodied shipmates to beat up Seth, warning him to toe the line. In fear of his life, Seth also knew of the small pistol Maggie always carried on her person.

William was awakened by water tinkling, and was amazed to see Gabriel urinating in a tin can. Apologizing, Gabriel told him the thing he missed most, was to stand up to pass water.

William asked if Gabriel wanted assistance back to his bed. Thanking him, Gabriel said he could manage, and with a sort of roll landed on the mattress.

'It won't be long afor the lads will be here and maybe then we can find out sommat o' that letter ye have.'

A light came from the kitchen, then Maggie brought a jug of warm milk and some toast spread with butter. She made signs to Gabriel, who told William to drink and eat up, and should he want more, to just call out.

William thanked her, saying he was sure there would be

enough. Maggie curtseyed, her mouth twisting into what William thought was a smile.

She came back later for the used dishes, followed by two youths who made a chair of their crossed arms and carried Gabriel away to do his ablutions, he said, and prepare him for the day. William thought he had seen these lads the night before.

When Gabriel was carried back by the two boys, and placed on the settle where William had first seen him, he was wearing his wooden stumps.

'The lads says it be not too bad underfoot for someone who is pretty sure-footed, that I ain't, and your letter has come from the office of Thadious Tully, a rogue of a shipping agent who would sell his own mother to the press-gang, so it be best ye don' go alone.'

Gabriel spoke with the youths so quietly William only caught the last sentence, which was to tell them to get something to eat from Maggie before they went.

Within an hour they were back, accompanied by the jovial Daniel Turtle who, laughing, said he had had great fun getting there, for the boys had brought him on their sledge.

Daniel and Gabriel talked at length, explaining to William how all the local folk hated Thadious Tully, knowing he was a bounty man who worked with the press-gangs.

Gabriel wished the weather were better, so that he could go with William to the office.

'It be best if we could get Davey Wells to come up to us, for him to make inquiries,' said Daniel.

'Who *is* Davey Wells?' asked William.

'Davey be clerk to Thadious Tully, a very clever young fellow who does most of the work in the office.'

'Aye,' said Gabriel, going on to tell how Davey Wells, a foundling, had been brought up and educated by the learned monks in the city of Wells, and named David because he had been found on the first of March, the Welsh saint's day, and Wells after the city.

Davey had been on an errand from the monks to a local clergyman when he was shanghaied. For many months he then worked as a galley slave.

The unusually strenuous work, coupled with his less than robust constitution, meant that when a fever broke out on board, he soon contracted it. He was thrown overboard, but then picked up by a fisherman.

On finding his way back, he was afraid to return to the monastery, for he knew that what he had been carrying for the monks was valuable. He had also acquired some learning while on board the ship of Thadious Tully so, with the hope of discovering something about the monks' missing papers, he begged him for a position.

With his literary skills and fine writing, he was soon running the legal side of the office, and was in a good position to warn certain people to go and rescue the poor souls sent by his employer to cheap lodgings where they were drugged and then collected by the press-gangs. Thus he saved many from the fate that he had suffered.

Daniel was told of William's experience with Polly, the barmaid. He, not wanting to go through a similar night, thought it best to look for other accommodation, and asked their advice.

'Well sir, if ye don't mind, and it be not too humble, ye could stay along o' me. There be two bedrooms, and there be nowt stoppin' ye comin' to meals down along o' Gabriel here.'

So it was that William moved into the neat, little home of Daniel Turtle, overlooking the harbour. They spent most of the days making inquiries and the evenings with Gabriel, partaking of Maggie's good fare. William agreed his horses should stay stabled there, for they were well cared for.

The two lads who dressed and attended Gabriel, were told to take William to the offices of Thadious Tully and to tell that gentleman that Mr McCall was an acquaintance of Master Gabriel Foley and Master Daniel Turtle.

Daniel wanted to go with William, but the bitter wind blowing in from the sea, and the slippery pathways, were bad enough for man with two good limbs.

Maggie brought strips of rough sacking for William to wrap

around his boots to give extra grip. She also pinned small shawls around the head and shoulders of the two lads, as Daniel followed her every movement with a look of adoration on his tanned face.

The wind and sleet tore at their clothes as they battled up a narrow, cobbled street. They climbed up the steps outside of stables, and entered the dismal, dank, workplace of Thadious Tully.

The oldest lad introduced William to the oily individual behind a high counter, as he crouched over a belly-pipe stove which only gave out heat to that very small area.

Sniffing, Thadious Tully glanced at the letter and denied any knowledge of it. Turning his back on them he shrugged his shoulders and pulled at the thick scarf he wore around his neck, hunching back over the stove.

Coughing came from a dark, raised recess. Turning to his right, William saw a figure he had not noticed before, with stacks of paper bundles around him, leaving just enough space for the little desk and a high stool, where sat a thin figure in clothes a size too small for him.

The thin man spoke quickly. 'Will ye give my kind regards to Master Gabriel and Master Daniel, sir? And will ye tell them that Davey Wells will try to come to see them one of these nights?'

William was not quite sure, but he thought he saw the thin man wink. It might have been a flicker of the candle that fluttered in the draught from the broken window at his back.

Disappointed, William left as Thadious Tully snarled at his clerk that he was a lazy good-for-nothing, and to get on with his work, for he was not paying him to socialize.

Back at the tavern, Gabriel and Daniel told William not to lose heart, for there might be something in Davey's message. The only time Davey went to any tavern or inn, was for a purpose other than drinking.

By early afternoon, the wind had dropped and there was calm. Daniel said it was the calm before the storm.

There were a few folk in the bar, and the talk was of the

wonderful victory over the French in Egypt, and how lucky they were to have such a hero as Nelson.

One old salt said how proud he was to have a nephew who had fought in this battle. They had heard the boy was safe, but had stayed in Alexandria to keep the French at bay.

The storm broke. Some of the men left to help secure the boats, and be at the ready if there were a ship in distress.

William begged to be allowed to go with them. They tried hard to dissuade him, but Gabriel had seen how frustrated he had been all that day, and shouted to Maggie to bring oilskins.

Down near the quay, they made boats secure. William suddenly realized that they had been joined by the shipping agent's clerk, Davey Wells, who was talking very earnestly to a burly fellow, one of the men had brought him there.

The burly man told William there was nothing more to be done and, thanking him, said it would be best if he returned to the Jolly Mariner. He told Davey he had better go home as well. Davey said that he would accompany William up to the Jolly Mariner, however.

The wind made it impossible to talk as they hurried up to the warmth and comfort of the tavern.

Maggie appeared with blankets to place around them as William was helped off with his wet things. But Davey held a whispered conversation with Gabriel before disrobing, and Gabriel called loudly for the two boys to come quickly. William wondered, as they were always there, if they lived on the premises.

Maggie swathed them in large oilskins. Gabriel told them names, and William thought he heard the word 'headland' being mentioned.

The boys left, and Maggie brought scalding hot broth and pasties to eat, before disappearing once more into the kitchen.

Seth Grundy shouted, 'Be there anybody buyin' drink this day? It is a tavern ye know!'

On being ignored, he soon disappeared also.

Davey Wells said it was he who had written the letter. A

ship's surgeon from Nelson's fleet had asked him to make inquiries about someone called Phillip T J McCall. The doctor had returned to England with the wounded from the Nile battle.

Every time the surgeon was in the vicinity of Portsmouth, he would visit Davey to make inquiries about a young nephew who had gone missing. The boy's widowed mother was demented, like many others who had lost their menfolk.

A group of men Nelson called his 'Band of Brothers' decided they would try to uncover information about young people coming aboard their ships, especially under unusual circumstances, which was often difficult as someone who had run away did not want to be discovered.

William became excited, bringing out the letter. 'There is mention of a notebook with my son's name in it.'

'That is so, sir,' said Davey. 'But I do not know any more details, for we did not have the opportunity to converse at length, as my employer returned.'

'Aye, the less that serpent knows the better,' said Daniel, Gabriel nodding in agreement.

'Has the surgeon returned to sea? Are there means of getting in touch with him?' asked William.

Davey told him he did not think he had sailed as yet, for he had arrived on a badly damaged vessel, and would be ashore to wait for a fresh berth. The surgeon had told Davey he would be back in case the letter had any news.

'Do you know this man's name?'

'Aye, his name be Trowbridge.'

The weather was not fit for travelling, and the inquiries made bore no results frustrating William until Davey turned up saying he had discovered where the surgeon lived.

There was great jubilation when William came home. The only thing that blighted the homecoming for him was Tug's accident, and the old fellow was very slow getting better. But Tug did brighten up a little to see his employer and friend.

William was pleased to meet Matt, and thanked him, as Alice had told him what a great help and comfort Matt had been to them.

After the evening meal, William told them of the new friends he had made and how glad he was that the surgeon lived in a small town, for all Davey Wells had found out was the name 'Singleton', which was not too far distance away from Portsmouth.

Arriving at the small hamlet, William had inquired at the first cottage he came to, and was directed straight away to the home of the doctor's sister. Again he was disappointed, for the one he sought was not at home.

The gentle lady of the house had asked what William wanted with her brother, and given him a letter to take to the naval hospital at Portsmouth, just six miles from where he had been staying.

As a result of this letter William had been granted an immediate interview with the surgeon, who told him that on a ship anchored at that time off the Bay of Aboukir, a few miles north-east of Alexandria, was a youth who was now called Tommy Cole.

This lad was very bright, of Scottish origin, and had come to the notice of the surgeon aboard for, although he was young, no more than 14 years old, he had quite a knowledge of herbal cures, and was extremely good at drawing. The lad appeared to be fit and well, although there was evidence he had been severely whipped.

Alice cried. Fiona asserted she had known all along her boy was alive and safe. William said they had no definite proof, but the description was too much of a coincidence.

William was very worried about Tug. He looked so ill. Fiona had told William that Matt was an old friend of hers, and seeing his caring way with Tug, William liked him immediately. Tug now asked what else could be done to find out if this lad was, indeed, Master Phillip?

William said he had done as much as he could do, and had left letters to be sent on to the lad, Tommy Cole, begging him to write to him, and if he were to come back to Portsmouth, to go to the Jolly Mariner tavern and contact a Master Gabriel Foley. There would be funds available there for his use.

William choked with emotion, telling how he had written

that, if indeed, he were Phillip McCall, he was very much missed and loved.

If he were not Phillip McCall, he sent him his regards, and if he should be in need of help, he should contact the above-mentioned gentleman at the Jolly Mariner.

William sent for a doctor who was an orthopaedic specialist to examine Tug, and he said that he would have to operate to relieve the pressure on Tug's spine.

After the operation, William was told there was not much hope of Tug ever walking again. There were many pieces of gun-metal in his body, which the accident had dislodged, and all that could be done for the old chap, was to try to make him comfortable.

For many months, life settled down as well as could be expected. Spring passed, and summer was starting. Fiona resumed the story of her friend, Annie, for Alice.

23

The narrow path around the escarpment came to an end and the beauty of the small hollow took away the little breath Annie had left.

Coloured lichens clung to the granite rocks, where a crystal stream cascaded into a rock pool before journeying down to the loch, gleaming miles below.

The house was no more than a large hut, its roof extending over the front door and window to cover the verandah, where a chair stood, complete with a footstool attached, its sheepskin-upholstered arms held out to welcome an occupant.

The green sward spread before them like an emerald carpet, dotted with bright, yellow-eyed daisies and golden buttercups.

Arriving at the house Ian, helped by Annie, lifted Tam off the horse, lowering him into the chair. Annie followed Ian inside.

The interior belied the exterior, for it was much larger than one would have thought. A large bed stood against the farthest wall on the left. In the centre stood a table and four chairs. Shelves on one side and above the narrow door at the back of the building, were filled with supplies, as were the shelves above a stone slab holding a bowl to do the washing up on the other side of the door. A large earthenware container filled with water stood with a pail by its side, to carry and refill it. On a hook there hung a handled drinking skillet.

A fire had already been laid in the magnificent stone fireplace with its oven, dominating one corner. The place smelt fresh and clean.

Annie thought she knew why Ian had been missing when she took out food for him. He must have been preparing this place, and she marvelled at his kindness, and his labour.

Ian put a light to the fire, and placed on a log from a neat pile in the deep recess at the side of the grate.

'Mistress, if ye be wantin' maer wood, if ye will come along o' me, I will show you where tae get it.'

Going through the door at the back of the house, she was delighted to find a neat little garden, where sweet thyme, rosemary and mint perfumed the air.

On stakes laced with string against the rock face, runner beans grew in profusion. At their roots in the dark soil, cabbages, late lettuce and carrots grew. There were enough split logs piled against the building for two or three winters.

Annie said, 'There be wood enough tae last a few years.'

'It becomes cold come eventide. Ye will need gaed fires.'

She heard Tam call to her, his voice sounding strange. Suddenly she turned to rush to him, losing her balance for a second. Ian grasped her arm to steady her, withdrawing it sharply as if he had been burnt.

Tam demanded to know where they had been, and what they had been doing. Annie told him they had been lighting the fire, and Ian had been showing her where to get more tinder. She felt hurt by his attitude, after the kindness shown to them by their host.

After Ian had given the little mare some hay and water he quietly said, 'I had best be away doon to get more supplies, so I can return afor dark, mistress.'

Thanking him, Annie watched him leave.

Tam grumbled that the journey had wearied him. Annie asked if he wanted a drink. He did not answer her, so she went into the house and took a drink of water from the jar, refilling the skillet and bringing it to Tam. He swept it from her hand, sending it crashing to the verandah floor.

Stunned by his unwarranted anger, she watched the water disappear through the wooden boards. Stooping slowly, she picked up the skillet, whispering, 'I be goin' tae make up the bed, and start somethin' tae eat. If ye be wantin' anythin', just call.'

Once inside, she was unable to control her sobbing, placing on the bed sheets and blankets, then plumping up the pillows.

A strange feeling welled up inside her. She dragged off the bedding and pillows, roughly throwing them to the floor. The mattress followed them, then she knelt with clenched fists, punching and pummelling them. Picking herself up she started to dance wildly on top of them until, exhausted, she fell to her knees, chuckling to herself.

'Ye best pull thyself taegether, Annie Floyd, for sake of the bairn ye carry. After all ye've been through, it be not time tae get demented.' With her skirt up to her knees, legs apart, she flopped onto a chair.

From behind the wall at the back of the bed, there came a scratching, kicking sound. She went to investigate. As she passed him, Tam appeared to be sleeping.

Going in the direction where the sounds seemed to come from, she entered a byre and there found a nanny-goat who had twisted and struggled so much, her tether was entangled, and she was strangling herself.

Annie thought if she undid the terrified creature's head first, she would surely bolt, so she untied the rope from the ring in the wall first, crooning softly to distract the animal. At last, she had almost unwound the full length of rope, when the goat rushed straight for her, butting her backwards into a pile of hay.

Annie was not badly hurt. Still maintaining a firm hold on the rope, keeping a wary eye, she arose and worked her way around the stout upright supporting the roof. Winding the end she held around the timber of the stall, she regained control.

Pulling on the rope, she eased it until there was enough to tie back onto the ring again, and the goat was securely fastened, but with not much length for freedom of movement.

Looking around, Annie saw more rope coiled on a hook. She tied one end of this firmly to another ring, while the nanny started chewing on some hay, allowing Annie to tie the new rope to her leather collar. Once this was done, Annie loosened the first rope.

Uncontrollably she laughed, thinking it was not yet noon, and today was turning out to be one of the most emotional she had experienced for a long time. For Annie always steeled herself against showing her emotions. She who had been through a furnace of tribulations and trials, to break down over just a few harsh words and a sharp action! She told herself, 'It must be the pregnancy.'

As she went past Tam into the house for a pail to milk the goat, Tam again demanded to know where she had been.

'Tae see tae the goat!' she snapped.

Returning with the pail, silently she showed him the milk, and went indoors. Later, she brought out a bowl of bread and cream cheese, soaked in milk, liberally seasoned with salt and pepper.

He accepted it grudgingly, mumbling it was food fit only for toothless old folk, but it did not stop him from scraping the bowl clean.

Meanwhile, Annie ate at the table and, although it was warm inside, and sunny outside, suddenly she shivered.

She must have dozed off, for she awoke hearing Ian's voice.

Ian led the horse carrying sacks on her back, and two crates slung like panniers. The black and white collie at his heels, he came up to the house.

'I've brought Laddie up for ye, he be a gaed hound. I couldna bring Lassie on account o' the pups. Should ye need I, just say, 'Go for the man!', for he knows this command and he will come for I,' he told them shyly.

Lass was never far from Ian's house, as her pups were there, but Laddie, on the other hand, came only at feeding time.

Ian was unfastening the ropes of the crates, and a crate started to slip. Annie darted over to steady it, or it would have fallen. Accidentally, her hand brushed against Ian's for the second time that day, and his hand moved sharply away from hers. Annie thought the men were acting very strangely.

The atmosphere was very like that when Tam had first come home, and he had forced her to tell of the rape. She winced remembering that time, and the bad names he had called her.

Had his illness turned him against her? Surely he would not be so cruel as to malign her to their host? So much so that even he could not bear to touch her? No, this could not be. Ian had shown no sign of this, only kindness and respect. It must be something else.

Each of the crates held two hens. The sack held grain, flour, fats and fresh meat.

Ian said he would come again on the morrow with more supplies, and if there were something more they needed, to tell him then.

Annie invited him to take a bite to eat. Politely he refused the offer, and bade them goodbye until the next day.

Annie hoped Ian would stay for something to eat and drink, and perhaps stop for a while to talk with Tam to cheer him up, and take him out of his morose mood; not that Ian was much of a conversationalist. But he said he needed to go back down before it grew dark, to see to his flock.

She wondered why she felt reluctant, at this moment, to be alone with the man she loved above all others. Tam had been sullenly silent while Ian was there, with only a brief nod, hello and goodbye to him.

Annie was busy seeing to the hens and checking and putting away the supplies, thinking Ian had thought of practically everything. He had even brought up most of their personal belongings.

The sunset was magnificent. Tam was so moved by the beauty that the mood he had been in vanished.

'Come sit with me, and see this wonder, lass.'

Slowly Annie emerged, drying her hands on her apron. She leant against the door frame, gazing at the sky's splendour.

Tam slid his feet off the stool. 'Sit here with me, for I need the touch of you, and have been in bad humour this long day.'

Annie sat on the stool, her back resting against his knees. Contented, they watched the sunset together. Clinging to each other, they went inside and ate the food she had prepared.

At the edge of the bed she undressed Tam and made him comfortable.

She washed the dishes and put them away, made the fire safe for the night, and stripped off her clothes to wash herself.

Annie felt Tam's eyes follow her every movement. She pulled on her night shift, threw the water out at the back door, and wearily climbed into the bed beside him. Annie lay with her back to Tam, as he slid his arm around and gently caressed her breasts. Within minutes she was in deep velvet sleep.

She awoke, feeling smothering restriction from something tight around her abdomen and neck, terrifying her, and realized it was her shift that was pulled up at its hem, and her own weight trapping it on one side. Squirming, she managed to free the garment.

Annie was surprised at Tam's strength as he pulled her over onto her back, and rolled on top of her.

Struggling, she tried to release her arms from the sleeves, easing the restriction to her breathing.

'Please, Tam,' she groaned, 'bide a wee while.'

'I doubt ye asked the others tae bide a while,' he snarled.

'What others?' she asked breathlessly.

'The laird who so kindly bequeathed ye land and a cottage.'

He penetrated her roughly, painfully. Freeing one arm, she pulled the shift behind her head. Her body throbbed, and there was a pounding in her ears.

'Ye did'na think I'd notice the carry on 'twixt ye and that auld shepherd, either? Ye are nay better than a whore, selling thysel' for gain.'

At his final thrust she heard a bubbling sound as the bright, frothing blood he coughed up, splattered them.

Dry-eyed, she sponged him and cleaned the bed as best she could, then washed herself again, thinking she must be accursed to lose her children, and have men, even her own husband, treat her in this way.

Her head on the table, she was overtaken by merciful sleep until she awoke with a start, her face stiff from shedding tears. Tam lay so still, she took a candle to look at his ashen face with its dark eye sockets. Sobbing, she thought the night's efforts had taken their final toll.

Suddenly the eyelids fluttered. Annie brought a cup of water and held it to his colourless lips. He tried to speak, but she shushed him, holding him. She rearranged the pillows, and fell asleep.

Annie dressed. Although it was not dawn she went about the morning's chores. Between each task she crept back to look at him, not knowing what to expect.

With only firewood to replenish, the morning's work was done. She entered the house with her arms full of logs. Weakly, he called to her. Dropping the logs she rushed to his side.

'Annie, my ain sweet love, can ye forgive me? I am sure that I have not been this day in slumber, but 'tis the sleep of death I have just awakened from, to come back to ye, plead for your forgiveness.'

His tears flowed, as he asked her to hold his hand. He needed her courage and strength, for he was sorely afraid. As he spoke his eyes burned, and a light shone from his wasted face.

'I walked in a shining valley, where blossoms I have never seen on this earth bloomed. A river of golden water flowed between banks of beautiful trees, that dipped their branches into the waters.'

He started coughing. Annie held him in her arms as he looked up and pleaded, 'Not now, Lord, I havena finished.' Annie stifled her sobs. The coughing stopped.

'Three beautiful lads, so tall and fair, came out of the haze towards me. Two seemed familiar, and the taller one carried a bairn he told I was my ain wee babby, and they were our ain sons, Tammy and Jamie. But the third I did'na ken. He said his name was Edward, and he was waiting for Fiona.'

Again he begged her forgiveness. She told him there was nothing to forgive.

'Nothing to forgive, calling ye names, when ye are the purest of women! Our bairns told me ye must give me absolution, or else I will not join them in that beautiful land, and we shall not be together when it be time for you to come to us, as they told me you would.'

'Hush, dear husband, let me hear no more. I forgive you. Having loved you, and no other, you were my life. When you were gone, our bairns kept me sane. They went, taking with them my reason, for I tried hard to join them.'

'Aye, lassie, and nae one would have held ye to blame, for the horrors that were done tae ye, they made me see and look at, in the reflection of the shining waters. For ye tae survive a' that, an' then tae be reviled by such as I!'

'No more! No more! I beg of ye, let it be, and pray the good Lord may let us bide in peace for some time, if only for the sake of the little one I carry.' Looking up at him she saw the eyes that had held such scorn, were now filled with adoration.

Picking up the logs she had thrown down, she stacked them neatly, and went out for more.

The dog followed her outside. When they returned, Tam seemed to be dozing. She looked across at him as she poked the fire to heat the pot of porridge. Was it the flames that gave his face that glow? For all around his head there was a bright halo, and on his countenance a look of contentment such as she had never before seen on any face.

When Tam awoke, Annie fed him a little porridge. When she rose to wash the bowl, he begged her to sit with him. As he was propped up on the pillows, she sat facing the bed. Feeling a little weary, she rested her head on her arms as gently he stroked her hair.

A scratching and faint whining awakened her, and although stiff, she felt refreshed.

Opening the front door she found Laddie on the doorstep with a large rabbit between his front paws. His head was down as he did not know if he would be praised or scolded.

Annie threw her arms around his neck, kissing his head. She told Tam later she was sure the dog was embarrassed at this show of affection.

'Nay, lass, I have seen the love the hounds have for thee, like their master.'

'Nay, Tam, Ian has kindness for all creatures, and be old enough tae be faether to us.'

'Today, I can speak with nae malice, knowin' ye now, as I never knew ye before, and bein' sore jealous of the man, he bein' well an' hearty, an' seein' the love he has for ye.'

'Oh, Tam!' she interrupted.

'Let me finish, for there must be nothing left unsaid. I know the man is true and honourable, doing more for me, and he be a stranger, than anyone's kin would do. But my reason was poisoned, grossly misjudging your nature, and his. This be another thing I must beg forgiveness for.'

'No more talk of that. I forgive you every ill deed or thought. All I desire is tae look after ye, and tae get ye well.'

'I pray we will have a wee time to spend afor I go tae wait wi' our bairns for ye, in a far better place.'

As she skinned and cleaned the rabbit, Annie realized that Tam had seen what she had not, Ian's affection for her, and she was a little sad.

Ian brought more supplies. Annie was unaware of his approach as she was busy making bread, flour up to her elbows, a smudge on her nose, tendrils of hair escaping from the cloth she had tied on to restrain it.

Tam hailed Ian, calling to him, 'Come awa inside, mon!'

Hastily, Annie dragged off her head-gear and wiped her face with it. She looked embarrassed, being caught that way.

Ian apologized for startling her, and told her to carry on with what she was doing. She noticed how he sniffed at the air. 'I'll be wi' ye in one second, but I must first take a batch o' bread oot o' the oven.'

'It will be no hardship, mistress. There be nay need for ye to come, I can manage fine.'

The next batch of loaves were in the oven, the potatoes were almost cooked, and the rabbit meat was falling from the bone when Ian came to ask Annie could she spare a few minutes for him to show her where he had put the meat he had brought for her.

He led her to a cleft in the rock behind the garden, and removed the wooden gate at the entrance to another cave, similar to the one down in the valley. This cave, he told her, had been hacked out by his father before he was born.

Cold air met them, and once accustomed to the gloom, Annie could see cages with sides of mesh hanging from the roof.

'The meat be always fresh here, for 'tis cold, summer or winter. The cages are oot o' the way o' creatures and such.' Ian went on to ask her what she had been cooking besides bread.

'Oh, Laddie brought a fine rabbit that is ready for the eating, if ye will join us,' Annie replied.

It was Tam who finally persuaded Ian to stay and eat with them, telling him that, rightfully, it was his food, and they were his guests.

Even Tam ate well of the rabbit and cooked vegetables.

Ian shyly asked if he could have another piece of bread. Annie said not only could he have more, but she had already wrapped up two loaves for him to take down with him.

The two men watched her breaking bread into the juice from the cooking, adding the remains of the meal, then feeding it to the dog.

When Ian declared he had tarried long enough, Tam asked if he were coming on the morrow.

'I thought not to come for a few days, that is, unless ye have need of me, and the mistress, she knows what tae do then.'

'Oh, please come, for 'tis good to have thy company,' pleaded Tam.

'Aye, please come!' Annie coaxed. 'But bring no more food wi' ye, for there be more than enough to last for many weeks.'

Ian agreed to come the day after the next. Annie asked if he could make it as late in the day as possible, then she would cook a joint of lamb that he had brought, for it was much too large for just two of them.

As he was leaving, Tam called him over and whispered to him.

Ian nodded his head, and cautioned, 'Be ye sure it wi' nay harm ye.'

Ian's protestations brought on a fit of coughing. As Annie rushed to Tam's side, she was relieved to find he had not coughed up any blood, and it occurred to her how little he had coughed that day, or since that peculiar dream he said he had experienced.

Looking back at Annie, framed in the doorway, Ian wished he were younger, thinking again of the things he had missed in his life.

When Ian next came to visit, Tam asked him if he would do the greatest service of lifting him out of bed, so he could sit at the table. He had already persuaded Annie to help him get dressed.

The meal of lamb, flavoured with thyme, honey and rich mint sauce, followed by a thick egg custard tart dessert, was declared by the men to be a meal fit for royalty.

Annie flushed with pleasure and was starting to clear away, when Tam asked, 'Would it be warm enough to sit outdoors, do ye think?'

'Oh, Tam, ye will catch yer death,' said Annie.

'Lassie, 'tis not possible tae catch what has already been caught. Nothing will alter the inevitable,' he told her.

Ian carried Tam out on to the verandah.

With the dog at their feet, they sat outside in the sunshine.

Annie threw some dried fruit and a beaten egg into some dough. The iron griddle-plate, an essential part of every Celtic kitchen, was already heated.

As Annie cooked, an unusual odour wafted in from outside. When the cakes were ready, she took out a few on a plate, and was shocked to see the two men puffing contentedly on pipes.

'Oh, Tammie lad! Ye are smokin', ye with the lungs that are shredded.' She scolded Ian, saying she thought he was their friend, yet he would give Tam such things as tobacco and a pipe!

'Dinna blame the man, Annie lass, 'twere mysel' that told him how I longed for a puff on a pipe, and pleaded wi' him. He were loath tae give they tae me, an' see, I be none the worse.'

Returning to the heat of the room, Annie offered up a silent prayer for the miracle she thought had happened, and sang to herself, hoping this happiness would last.

The shadows of the afternoon lengthened and Ian thanked them heartily for their hospitality, saying how pleased he was Maester Tam was better.

'Ye who are friend, must nay call me maester, nor any man maester, for ye are an honourable free man, who I be proud to have met,' said Tam with emotion.

'We all have maesters of one sort or other. For me, they be my animals, which I must be away tae tend, for they hae no one else.'

Before leaving, he lifted Tam back onto the bed, Annie having freshened it with clean linen scented with lavender.

As they waved goodbye, Tam shouted, 'Make your return soon, friend, for it was pleasant tae hae your company.'

The dog, Laddie, followed Ian part of the way down. The shepherd first noticed him when the path was wide enough for him to walk at his side. He chided the dog for leaving his new mistress, and made him go back with his tail between his legs.

Ian had been day-dreaming, which was one reason he had not noticed the dog following him. But he knew they could only be dreams for him, he that had been brought up by the old shepherd afraid to go among folk in case someone should claim the child who had brightened up his lonely existence. Ian had been raised with only the dog that had found him and sheep as playmates.

They had survived on what they themselves produced, doing without what they had not grown or reared. Jock went into town rarely.

Ian had had no experience of the softness of women, the warm scent of the female body. Nor had he seen the light of love in their eyes as they looked at a cherished one, until now. Bitter loneliness overshadowed the warmth he had lately been bathed in.

Tam lay on the bed, a look of serene contentment on his face as he watched Annie wash her hair in front of the fire. Next she dried and combed the strands, the flames shining through and turning her lustrous locks into burnished copper.

She dampened the fire with kitchen waste and peat then, sitting up on the bed, ran her fingers through the still damp strands.

Tam kissed her tenderly, and told her, 'Ye are maer beautiful than when we first met.'

'Even wi' grey hair and a swelling belly? Oh, Tam!'

He placed his head on her heart and, with a start, declared he was sure he heard another heartbeat, and felt a tiny hand, or foot push him away. 'Dinna push thy faether awa, little one. I would love to see ye grown up, but it is not for I tae say.'

With a lump in her throat, Annie turned to blow out the lamp.

'Not yet, leave the light, so I can have more of the sight of ye. And can ye move the blanket off, too, so that I see all of ye.'

Later when he slept, she blew out the light. In minutes she, too, was asleep but had slept for barely an hour when she was awakened by Tam's writhing.

Rising, she lit the lamp with a taper from the fire. His face was flushed, hot with fever, yet he shivered. Gently shaking his shoulder, she begged him to wake up.

Once he was awake she wrapped him in a blanket and held him.

'I walked with our bairns, and Fiona's husband, Edward, who I did not recognize. He walked so straight. He nae be Scottish by his speech. He says Fiona be sorely troubled.

'What did ye say? Edward be with our bairns? They have

long since gone, but Edward be surely still alive?'

But she received no answer, for Tam had fallen asleep in her arms, leaving her pondering and worried.

Shivering, Annie awoke. Laddie was howling in a most unusual and mournful way. She went to the door where the dog lay, his sad brown eyes gazing up at her, and she told him to be quiet and not to disturb Tam. The dog crawled on his belly and his rough tongue licked her bare feet. Stooping, she patted him before going inside to stir the fire into life.

On a chair near the bed were her clothes. She had started to dress when she looked at Tam's still form. There was not enough light to see him properly, so she lit the lamp, and saw the waxen pallor of his serene features. Her hand touched his cheek, feeling the marble coldness of his skin.

She knew her Tam was with their children, in the shining place he had spoken of.

When she had finished dressing, she took Laddie to the path. Pointing down, she instructed the animal, 'Go for the man!'

Tenderly she washed Tam, put a clean shirt on the stiffening limbs, and pulled on his trews and the boots that Edward had made for him. She combed his hair and kissed the cold lips, telling him to wait for her.

Feeling numb, she automatically went about her daily duties, then sat at the bedside looking at her man.

Ian arrived. His shabby Tam o' Shanter in his hand, he stood in the open doorway until Annie asked him to come and sit a while.

'Nay, mistress, we best be seein' tae get him doon.'

Carefully they lifted Tam, wrapped in a blanket, across the little mare's back. The fire was doused. Slowly they descended to where Ian had left the cart, and gently placed the body on it. Ahead of them, Laddie yapped, as he shepherded the goat to the meadows far below.

Ian said they needed to be away for a few hours. The dogs lay at her feet, their soulful eyes watching for her, but she did not seem to be aware of what Ian had said, nor did she heed him drive away the horse and cart.

She did not look up when he returned with the minister's wife, and men carrying a wooden box, or when they placed Tam in the coffin, resting on two chairs.

They were about to fasten the lid when, suddenly, Annie sprang to life, 'Dinna ye cover him till bidden by me!' she screamed. Her eyes were red-rimmed burning coals, that had want of the comfort of her unshed tears.

Outside the men spoke softly, but she heard mention of the sin eater and flew out to them.

'My man doesna need a sin eater. Look for thyself, that face is sin-free. Ye save the service for they that need it!'

The sin eater was someone paid to eat bread and drink ale placed on the bier or coffin, symbolically eating the sins of the deceased.

Throughout the service conducted by the doleful minister, Annie was dry-eyed and silent.

The minster's wife, at Ian's request, stayed a few days with her, so she would not be alone, whilst he returned up the mountain for the livestock and supplies left there.

The minister's wife, Mrs McKenzies, was happy to oblige, for she hoped to discover something of the mysterious Ian Tansy, and the widow, to report back to the narrow-minded gossips in her circle.

Ian was surprised to find the woman dressed and ready to leave when he returned, demanding angrily to be taken to her home: this was no place for a decent person to be. She had discovered nothing from Annie, and when her inquisition had become too much, Annie had cursed her loudly.

'If ye must go now, mistress, ye will hae tae go by foot,' Ian told the cross little woman. 'The mare canna take a step more afor droppin' in her tracks, an' I, too, am bone weary.'

Reluctantly, she agreed to stay, but only until morning.

Mrs McKenzies sat glaring at Annie, smarting at being told she was a nosey old biddy who should attend her own business.

The woman ate the cheese, bread and mutton brought by Ian, who tried to get Annie to eat, but failed.

'Please, mistress, eat, if only for the sake of the bairn.'

Mrs McKenzies pricked up her ears. She had known there was something. So, the widow was with child. She wondered who the father could be. She scrutinized Ian. No, he was too old to be the father but, there again, the husband had had the wasted look of a long illness.

Trying to find out more, the minister's wife agreed with Ian, saying, 'If ye are wi' child ye had best eat, my lass. How far gone are ye?'

'There be a few weeks yet tae go, if ye must know. When we came tae this quiet place a few moons ago, there were nay nosey folk about.'

Not deterred, Mrs McKenzies kept on, 'Oh, ye are not frae these parts, then?'

'Nay, and soon I will be back tae the place whence I came, where folks dinna ask questions, and mind their ain business.'

Mrs McKenzies fumed, speaking no more that night, but not so the next day on the way back to town with Ian, who wondered how the woman took breath with her non-stop talking of the evils of all southerners, who were not true Scots at all, but more like Sassenachs.

Ian was extremely relieved to get to the kirk, and be rid of her at last.

Annie had milked the goats, collected the eggs and prepared dough ready for kneading. The house had been cleaned and the bed-linen washed. Ian returned and told her she should have been taking a rest.

'Mistress, there be nae need tae work as ye work,'

'I would hae left yesternight, but ye spoke of the little mare droppin', and I could not bear losin' any other livin' thing,' she almost sobbed, but still the tears did not come.

'I wish ye would stay and bide here, mistress. 'Tis not much, I know. Ye will be left alone. I will sleep in the shelter on the hill, come down only if ye call, or need me.

He longed to say he wanted her to stay forever, giving his life for her, if she wanted it, but felt he was too old, unsure and worldly.

'Nay, I must go, for there is a friend who maybe has need of me.' She was thinking of Tam saying Fiona was troubled.

Ian wanted to shout out that he had need of her, too. Silent and feeling awkward, he went outside, cursing the pain he felt, then went up the hill to his flock.

It was well into evening when the two dogs bounded into the house. Unlike humans, they had no inhibitions about showing their affection.

Asking them softly, 'Where be thy maester, then?' she fondled each in turn.

When packing her belongings, she had held Tam's clothing, breathing in the body smells that still clung to it, and at last the healing tears came. On the bed she had put a neat pile containing a sheepskin jerkin, a shirt, a scarf, a hat and two thick-knitted sweaters. One for each of them, she had made, but her Tam would never wear his now.

Drying her eyes, she went to the door and called Ian to his supper.

'Come away in, mon, the food is gettin' cold,' Annie told him, as he seemed reluctant to enter. An appetizing aroma rose from the mutton soup she was dishing up. Silently they ate, he pleased she was eating, she thinking he looked old and drawn.

Then he broke the silence, asking for more bread, ''Tis so fresh and soft, manna frae heaven must taste like this, 'tis so sweet.

'The old bread was nae wasted, it be fed tae hens and animals.'

'They will miss ye when ye leave, mistress. Cann ye bide? We'll bring a maid in tae help and keep ye company, least 'til little babby comes.'

'Nay, there be nae time, just seven weeks afor I be confined, and it must be in Perth, where I have kin.'

'If gae ye must, it nae be safe for ye tae travel alone.'

'I would not hear of ye comin' with me. Ye would shrivel and die away from this place.'

Ian, pulling on his old tammy, and fastening his tattered scarf around his shoulders, told the bitch Lassie to stay, and called the dog Laddie to heel.

'I will be awa tae the toon. Favour me by waiting until I return. Ye will come tae nae harm with Lassie here with ye.'

'Wait,' she called, 'I beg ye not tae take offence, but it will please me if ye will wear this jerkin, scarf and tammy.'

He removed his hat. She took off the tattered scarf, draping the new one around his neck.

At her touch, he started to shake violently. She asked if he were ill.

Choking, he said, 'Nay,' and stumbled as he hurried out.

Late in the morning, accompanied by a youth who walked with an odd gait, Ian came back. He called out to Annie, 'This be Matt. The minister says that although lame, he is strong and trustworthy. He has promised to travel with ye and protect ye.'

The lad seemed pleasant to Annie, answering respectfully when she told him he would have to return north alone.

'There be nae need tae return, I'll seek my fortune south.'

Ian told Annie to take as much food as they could carry, such as cheese, eggs and things that would keep on the journey.

He placed out a large sack of fresh vegetables and a carcass of lamb, cut up and wrapped in cloth, making certain there were cooking pots, so that they could cook on the way.

Annie protested he was giving the food out of his own mouth, as he placed a large bundle of animal pelts, the skins of fox, sheep, stoat and other animals, under the driving seat, telling them, in the town of Inverness, if they were going that way, there was a tanner who would give them at least a guinea for the skins.

'How shall we get the money back to ye, Maester Tansy, if the lad be not comin' this way again? For 'tis doubtful I shall be back,' said Annie.

'Use it for your journey, if there be aught left, and buy things for the bairn.'

They were ready for off. Ian hurried away up the hill,

muttering that he had delayed tending his animals too long, and had no time for goodbyes.

Hidden from them, he watched until they were out of sight, a hand on the head of each dog, not realizing the pressure he was using to fondle their ears, until Laddie yelped loudly.

They travelled, and talked little. When Annie found out the lad called Matthew Wilkie limped after receiving a bayonet wound, she warmed to him and spoke of her two sons' death.

For two nights she dreamt she and Tam were young again, and back at the cottage with their three children. Edward, Fiona's young husband, came to them. She asked him where Fiona was and Edward replied, 'Gone away, far away.' She awoke, not knowing of the tragedy that had befallen the young family.

Matt was a great help to her, and Annie admired his sharpness when dealing with the tanner at Inverness. He haggled, getting two-and-a-half guineas for the skins. One thing upset her as they were leaving the tanner's establishment. Matt brought out a pair of boots from his bag, offering them for sale.

The boots were the ones she herself had placed on her husband's cold feet. Hysterically, she screamed, snatching them from him, accusing him of robbing the dead.

She staggered from the place, shrugging off Matt's helping hand. Outside she was physically sick. Matt asked her what was wrong. Slowly she recovered, and told him the boots belonged to her dead husband.

'I be so sorry, mistress, I were given them by the minister for payment for digging graves, an' such. They be too small for him or me, so I thought to get some money for journeying.'

Annie handed the boots back to him, telling him to get what he could for them.

That evening, Matt told how he had been left to die after a battle, just surviving to get back to his home, to find all his kin had died of starvation. He had to work for little food, and hand-outs at the church.

Traders had left piles of rubbish in the market square. Annie had pains in her breast. She walked over to her cousin Willie Haig's butcher shop. He was sweeping out the soiled sawdust when, looking up, he saw her.

'Annie, my wee dove, wheer hast been, and why so wan?' He looked behind her for Tam, and asked for him.

Annie requested a drink. The smell of meat and stale blood nauseated her, so she stayed outside.

'Tam died five weeks ago.' She swayed. Willie told her to hold on to the door frame as he went inside to bring out a stool, then made her sit down whilst he brought her a cup of water.

Annie, sipping it, thought it tasted nothing like the Highland water near Ian's mountain cottage. She had doubts if there were water anywhere as wondeful as that.

Matt led the mare and cart across, and Annie introduced him.

'This be Matt. The journey has been long and tedious, and I have been a great trial to him.'

Matt shook his head, denying this.

'Can Matt bide wi' ye? I'll awa tae see Morag.'

'Morag be not at the old place, but wi' her kin, Poxy Meg, and tha doesna want tae gae theer,' Willie told her.

'I must gae there, for 'tis nae place for Morag, poor gentle soul. Why did not young Fiona let her bide wi' her?'

'Fiona be gone, her man, all gone, this many weeks.'

His voice ringing in her ears, Annie swayed. Matt caught her before she hit the cobbles.

Two days later she awoke, in desperate pain, aware of a faint mewing sound as if there were a hungry kitten somewhere. Then darkness again overtook her.

24

Fiona had been relating as much as she knew of Annie's tale to Alice. Alice stopped Fiona when she became upset, and often both would shed a few tears.

Alice had softened, becoming very concerned about Tug, even making a point of taking him special treats she herself had requested Martha to make for him. Everyone gave him particular care, especially Fiona and Matt.

All of Tug's duties had been taken over by Matt. Fiona thought Tug was very slow recuperating and, knowing how he loved the children, encouraged Aimee and Katie to visit.

At first, he complained of being tired, taking little notice of them. They stayed away for a few days, and Tug asked Fiona what was wrong. She told him. Little ones did not like being ignored by miserable old codgers.

He begged her to ask them to come back, and made an effort to be cheerful.

The snow disappeared and the garden borders became filled with pastel colours. William and Alex went to the house of the governess, Mary Gilchrist, to fetch some of her personal things. On returning, William told Alice it was in a dreadful state; part of the roof had collapsed, and there was water everywhere.

Without hesitation, Alice said they must make their home there with them, for Mistress Gilchrist was a treasure. When last Mr Peel had come to visit, inquiring if there were news of Phillip, she had asked him to examine the children's schoolbooks, and give them a verbal test. In his opinion, the three children were well in advance of pupils twice their age.

Then, William received another letter from Davey Wells. Enclosed in Davey's letter was another from a Dr Rhys, the surgeon who had spoken to William at the naval hospital. He wrote about how Davey, Gabriel and friends had been most diligent and fervent in their inquiries, contacting him often in their efforts to find his son Phillip. They had at last been able to discover an officer by the name of Lieutenant Thomas Duval, who could be reached through the Admiralty in London, and who might be able to give him some information regarding a Thomas Cole who had documents in his possession which contained the name Phillip T J McCall.

Davey sent regards from himself, Gabriel and Daniel Turtle, and said that if they could be of service again, not to hesitate to ask them.

William immediately wrote back to Portsmouth, thanking them all for their trouble on his behalf. He thought of the pitifully shabby little clerk, vowing that he would do everything in his power to help release him from his dreary existence.

William decided writing letters to London would take too long, so started making arrangements to go there personally. Alice did not want him to travel again, alone on horseback; she would rather he went by coach, accompanied. A new coach had recently been bought to replace the carriage so badly damaged during Tug's accident.

Tug was upset that he could not be William's driver. When Alex asked if *he* could be the driver, Matt promised to do his best to keep everything under control in the house and garden. Alun Breamer the under manager at the factory had already proved himself very capable at the factory. William set off in style. Simon, the armed attendant, sat up tall and straight, next to his father, Alex. William booked two rooms in a hostelry near to his brother John's establishment. While Alex and Simon unpacked and saw to the horses, William went to see John.

A pleasant young man William had met once before, and who shared apartments with John, answered the door. He invited William in, telling him John was out seeing a private patient, but would not be long.

'He has private patients, then?' asked William, in surprise.

'Oh, yes, he had become very much in demand, with a growing clientele,' answered the young man.

'Has he finished working in the hospital, then?'

'No, he still works there, but the pay is minimal, and hours are long. As soon as we are ready, and that will not be long, we shall be going into private practice, he and I.'

Rupert Doyle went on to say how both he and John had been studying hard to specialize, for John had gained a reputation as an excellent pharmacologist, using ordinary herbs.

Here is Fiona's influence again, thought William, for she and John had spent a deal of time in each other's company when he visited. He had often accompanied her when she went doctoring, he making notes and many scribblings.

John greeted his brother warmly, but did not like the idea of him staying in a tavern. William explained he was not alone, but had two staff with him, and explained the purpose of his visit.

'My uncle has a fine house near the Admiralty,' said Rupert. 'He is leaving for the country tomorrow. I will take a cab and go and see him straight away. I am sure he will let you and your servants stay there.' He pulled on his boots as he spoke.

Next morning, William was installed at the house with its gardens leading on to St James's Park, and its facade almost directly opposite the Admiralty. It was the large town residence of Sir Francis Bayard, the uncle of Rupert Doyle, whose portrait hung in the study, and if the painting were a true likeness, the subject was a jolly fellow who was as generous as his form.

At 9 a.m. sharp, William presented himself at the Admiralty and was bewildered by the hustle and bustle. He inquired at a desk in the foyer and was told he had to wait his turn until called.

Having waited until 11.30, William became impatient. He

marched up to the desk, tapped on the top with his cane, and told the pompous individual sitting there reading a news-sheet, that he was Mr William James McCall, who had travelled down from Scotland for the particular purpose of contacting a Lieutenant Thomas Duval. As he spoke he slapped down his business card.

The pompous individual sat up, taking notice when William declared he could be reached at the residence of Sir Francis Bayard, across the way, where he was a guest.

All that afternoon William waited, anxiously, but no one came. In the evening John and Bertie, as Rupert was fondly called, insisted on taking him to dinner at their club.

After an excellent meal, William politely refused to join a game of cards that was in progress in the salon, saying he would prefer to wait in the club's library, and read one of the many newspapers there.

Within 30 minutes Bertie came and introduced him to a marine officer who claimed to know Lieutenant Duval.

Around noon the next day a naval officer presented himself to William as Lieutenant Thomas Duval. Sir Francis's manservant asked if they required refreshments, but both declined and they were left alone.

William learnt the Lieutenant had come to London more than five months previously, having been sent from Egypt. He had had many adventures on the journey overland from Bombay, carrying duplicate dispatches for Nelson's commander-in-chief, Lord St Vincent, and for the East India Company.

He had served on a ship that was, as far as he knew, still standing guard with five or six ships of the fleet in the Bay of Aboukir.

Thomas Duval had been told why William was so keen to speak with him, and without delay told him that there was a lad called Thomas Cole aboard, and the Captain and officers had taken a particular interest in him, especially the ship's surgeon, because of the boy's knowledge of herbal cures. The boy was not the normal stowaway, having a good knowledge of Mathematics, Art and, among all things, Astronomy.

William became very excited, and brought out a sketch that Bruce Peel had done of Phillip. 'Would the boy, by any chance, resemble this drawing?'

Taking the drawing, the Lieutenant said if it were not a likeness of Thomas Cole it was his twin.

William was jubilant and fired all manner of questions at the young man. Was his son well and fit? Did he fit in with the rest of the crew?

'Aye, sir, as far as I know, the surgeon has really taken to the lad, and I believe the boy will, in time, become an excellent mariner. But sir,' asked Thomas Duval, 'why did this lad run away from home, and who, or what, gave the boy those terrible scars on his back and rear?'

'If you say this lad bears the scars of a whipping, you have given me positive proof that this be my son, Phillip. I do not know why he should have run away. The scars he bears were given to him by a schoolmaster, who was out of his senses'.

'How can I contact my boy? Could we have him brought home? It matters not what it costs.'

'Let us take one step at a time, for the boy, to save dire punishment, has been listed as a volunteer, and I am not sure for how long a period.'

There was a tap at the door. William bade the manservant enter, who said Dr John McCall was waiting to see him.

'He is my brother. Would you mind if he joins us?' William asked Thomas Duval.

'I should be delighted to meet him,' said the Lieutenant.

The butler showed John into the room, and asked would the gentleman like to partake of lunch, for Mr Rupert Doyle had sent a message saying he would be around for lunch and would be pleased for them to join him. They said they would be delighted.

William was almost certain now, that the lad Thomas Cole was his son, Phillip.

Bertie wondered why Phillip had changed his name. Lieutenant Duval said this was often the case with seamen, but it was not the lad's choice. His fellow officer, who was there at the time of the interview, told him it was the Captain who had named him Thomas Cole, as his own name was very similar to a few others on board their ship.

After a pleasant lunch, John and Bertie said they had to leave soon, as they both had appointments. William was in a state of euphoria, so John took it upon himself to query the next step.

'Your brother could write a letter to the boy, and I could have it sent on to him,' the Lieutenant suggested.

Excited, William asked, 'Was my son there in the battle on the Nile?'

'Yes, indeed, if this boy *is* your son, and he did very well for a young one, as did they all. They were in the fore, in the thick of the battle. We lost but one life and only seven were reported wounded, but Tommy Cole worked alongside the surgeon, tirelessly tending the many wounded saved from the sea.'

'Oh I wish I could have been part of it all,' declared William.

'I will try to get you a copy of the battle plan, and the reports,' said Thomas Duval. 'But it might take some time.'

William said he would stay a few more days if Sir Francis did not object, for he wanted to shop for some gifts for his family.

Bertie assured him his uncle was agreeable for William to stay as long as he wished.

William said he would write letters straight away, one to his son Phillip, another to Sir Bayard thanking him for his hospitality, and inviting him to come to Scotland any time he chose. The invitation was extended to the Lieutenant and Bertie.

Ten days later, William was back with his family. The children were excited on opening the presents, but all the adults were thrilled on reading and hearing the reports brought back by William.

25

The 74-gun vessel hugged the coastline, sailing west. The officers and crew were glad to be free of the storms that had kept them anchored. They sailed due south, past the Spanish coast.

Phillip marvelled at the blue of the Mediterranean after the grey-green of home waters.

Porpoise performed close to the ship. Two men, held with ropes by others, were hanging over the side trying to club the gentle creatures, when Arthur Gammon and Sid Rosser hauled them in, punching and shouting that porpoise were the friend of man, and they themselves had seen a group swim alongside a man who had fallen overboard in shark-infested waters. Their squeaking and the fuss they made did drive the sharks away, then two fish, one on either side, appeared to support the man and bring him alongside the boat sent to pick him up.

Phillip had heard such a story before, from old salts back home. He wondered what his family were doing. They would be deeply worried about him. When he had the chance he would try to write to them to let them know he was alright. He was kept so busy from morning 'til night.

One of Phillip's duties aboard was to tend the live-stock. Robert sensed he was not very keen on this work, and told him that the Captain and officers needed fresh meat for their table, and happy officers made a happy ship.

Robert could remember the old days of harsh treatment and insufficient rotten food. At least the men on this ship sometimes had stew from morsels of meat, and bones, and their Captain visited the sick and wounded, sharing with them fruit and food from his own table, and insisting all had lime-juice added to their drinking water to keep scurvy at bay.

Nelson suspected that Napoleon was heading for Egypt, and was anxiously waiting for his frigates, for they supplied him with advance information, and had been held up due to the storms.

Heading for Sardinia with his fleet, Nelson set a course for Alexandria. Napoleon left Malta for Crete, also bound for Egypt.

Nelson's ships were faster than the French. Strangely, the two fleets travelled parallel courses, approximately 60 miles apart. The British ships arrived at Alexandria before the French.

Disappointed, Nelson thought he had made a mistake thinking that Napoleon wanted to conquer Egypt, when he received reports back from his ships, the *Alexander* and *Swiftsure,* that they saw no French ships before Alexandria.

Nelson doubled back to Sicily, not knowing the French Vice-Admiral Brueys, had anchored his ships of the line in Aboukir Bay, about 13 miles eastward.

The opening to Aboukir Bay was not an uninterrupted one, a semi-circular indentation northward between the Rosetta mouth of the Nile and from Aboukir Point, which had a chain of shoals and rocks.

Nelson was not to be down-hearted for long, for the Vanguard signalled it had sighted the French fleet, 17 ships of war, 14 of them formed in line of battle, at the mouth of the Nile.

Nelson and his Band of Brothers, as he was known to call them, immediately hauled up, heading east, under top gallant sails and a brisk breeze, and were sighted by the French ship *Heureux* at 2 p.m. on the first of August 1798, which reported the presence of 12 fleet of sail of the line upon them, but the *Alexander* and *Swiftsure,* out of sight, made it 14.

There were no trustworthy charts of the Bay, and the area was strange to every captain there. Nelson hailed, inquiring the depth of the waters.

Captain Hood of the vessel *Zealous,* answered 11 fathoms, and asked permission to go on ahead, sounding the depths as he went, and acting as guide to the rest of the fleet.

The *Zealous* cautiously rounded the head of the shoal, with the *Goliath* on her port or outer bow, but the *Vanguard,* for some reason, hove to, allowing several vessels to pass her.

Captain Miller of the *Theseus* approached, and Sir Edward Berry hailed him, telling him he was next in line.

It was 6 p.m. when they were signalled. The order of ships was *Goliath, Zealous, Orion, Audacious, Theseus, Vanguard* (Nelson's ship), *Minotaur, Defence, Bellerophone, Majestic* and *Leander.*

Considerably to the north lay the stricken *Culloden,* and to the west, under press of sail, the vessels the *Alexander* and *Swiftsure.*

At 6.20 p.m. the French ships, *Conquerant* and *Guerrier,* opened fire on the *Goliath* and the *Zealous.* The shore batteries began throwing shells, but to little effect.

Ten minutes later the *Goliath,* which had great difficulty keeping ahead of the *Zealous,* passed under the forefoot of the *Guerrier,* fired a raking broadside into her, then endeavoured to anchor on her port bow.

As the *Goliath's* anchor was let go rather late, she was brought up abreast of the port quarter of the *Conquerant* and, with the ships *Serieuse* and *Hercule,* firing on her.

The *Zealous,* guns blazing, retaliated, bringing down the *Guerrier's* foremast. All the advancing British ships gave a loud three cheers.

The French had made fatal mistakes, first not anchoring close to the shore, enabling the British to go around and between them, blocking them from the land.

Secondly, as they were not expecting an attack from the land, all their guns were trained out to sea.

Thirdly, their vessels were not chained one to the other, to prevent the enemy getting between them.

It was later reported the canvas bulkheads forming separate sleeping quarters on French decks had not been cleared, restricting the gunners' activities considerably.

The British ships took depth soundings before, and as, they

proceeded in the shallow waters, getting between the shore and behind the French.

One British ship, the *Culloden,* had the misfortune, as she turned, to get firmly stuck on a sandbank and, sadly, was unable to take part in the battle.

The *Orion* rounded the starboard quarter of the *Zealous* and, running along outside her and the *Goliath,* poured her starboard broadside into the *Serieuse,* dismasting her and cutting her cable. She started to sink.

The *Orion's* Captain Saumarez dropped anchor, veering away so as to bring up head to the wind, and executed a wonderful manoeuvre as he had to deviate his course not to foul the anchor of the *Theseus.* He came a little abaft the port beam of the *Peuple Souverain.*

In the meantime the *Audacious* cut between the *Guerrier* and *Conquerant* and dropped her bower anchor, so as to bring herself upclose, thwarting the *Conquerant's* hawser.

The *Theseus* took a short course around the head and between the French, coming about 300 yards from the *Spartiate.*

Nelson, in the *Vanguard,* followed, cutting between the lines, anchoring 80 yards to the starboard beam of the *Spartiate.*

The *Minotaur* was anchored on the *Vanguard's* disengaged side.

The *Aquilon* and *Defence* were anchored abreast of each other.

Captain Troubridge and his crew of the *Culloden* were mortified by the accident keeping them from taking part in the battle, but they signalled their sad position to the *Leander* to prevent her suffering their plight. Captain Thompson avoided the sandbank and proceeded on course to engage the enemy.

The stricken *Culloden* kept signalling to all the other ships, warning them of the danger in their path.

Darkness fell. In dense smoke, the wind changed causing the *Alexander* to tack, surrendering her lead to *Swiftsure,* and almost colliding with a dismasted unlit vessel, with no colours. By pure chance, the *Swiftsure* hailed before firing on the vessel, discovering it was the *Bellerophon,* disabled and going out of action.

The French ship *Peuple Souverain,* parted her cable, dropping out of line and, observing a gap left by *Leander,* with great judgement anchored in the space.

Leander raked the *Franklin* with a broadside from her port side. With her starboard side she also raked the *Aquilon,* sustaining little damage to herself.

At 8.20, something so awful happened, that for a time it paralyzed both sides. The *Bellerophone,* having lost her main mast overboard, lost her mizen-mast when many fires broke out on the crippled ship.

Cutting her stern cable, the *Bellerophone* set her sprit sail, and attempted to set her fore topsail, bringing down her shattered foremast. Thus disabled she somehow got clear, and pulled out of line, to retire totally from the battle. But the French ship, *Tonnant,* fired broadsides into her repeatedly, interfering with the attempts to extinguish the flames on board.

This ungentlemanly conduct greatly annoyed *Swiftsure* and the *Alexander* so, with zest they attacked the *French Orient,* battering her with broadsides until she was aflame.

Vice-Admiral Brueys, on his flagship the *Orient,* already had two bad wounds, but still kept command. He descended from poop to quarter deck, and was almost cut in half by a round shot.

Without the Admiral, and with her flag-captain, Comte De Casa Bianca dangerously wounded, the *Orient* was in a shambles. There was worse in store, however. Flames increased on board, spread along the decks, and leapt to the riggings.

Ships in her vicinity quickly shifted their berths, closing ports and hatchways and removing ammunition from the upper decks. Large bodies of men were kept at the ready, armed with fire-fighting equipment.

At 10 p.m. the *Orient* was blown into the air by an explosion in her magazine, the concussion sufficiently violent to damage ships some distance from her. Burning debris showered everywhere, some landing on the *Alexander* and *Swiftsure,* but the fires were quickly extinguished. The numbing shock, however, remained. Seventy of the *Orient's* people were saved by the British. All the others perished, including her captain.

The French ship *Franklin,* although damaged, was first to recover from the shock that stunned all, and renewed the battle, but not for long. For the *Defence* and *Swiftsure* brought down her main and her mizen-masts. She made no reply, but hauled down her flag.

By midnight, all ships of the French line, ahead of the *Tonnant,* had been struck or destroyed.

The *Tonnant* continued her gallant resistance. She had been engaged mainly with the *Majestic,* whose main and mizen-masts she had shot away. She had also been involved with *Swiftsure* and the *Alexander,* some little distance from her.

At length, with all her own masts cut off close to the deck, the wreckage encumbering her batteries, she was unable to fire and so continue. Instead of surrendering, she let out cable, dropped out of station, and moved away out of annoyance.

All greatly admired the *Tonnant* for the magnificent defence she had put up, and her most heroic captain.

Captain Dupitit Thouars, who had lost both his right and left arms, and had one leg shot away by a round of shot, refused to retire below, but insisted he be placed in a tub of bran at a vantage point, from where he continued to issue orders. One was to nail the French flag to the mast.

He implored his people to sink the ship rather than have the dishonour of surrender. He eventually became insensible through loss of blood, but his spirit fired all on board. Of his descendants his son Abel became a vice-admiral, protectorate of Tahiti, and his grandson a rear-admiral.

Everything possible was done to get the *Culloden* off the shoals where she was grounded. The *Mutine* had been standing by to lend assistance, but not until 2 a.m. on the second of August could she haul herself free. By that time she had bumped off her rudder and was making seven feet of water an hour.

At 6 a.m. the *Zealous, Goliath* and *Theseus* were signalled to weigh, then the *Zealous* was directed to chase the frigate *Justice,* which was making for the disabled *Bellerophone*, with a view to summoning her to surrender.

The other British 74s followed the *Heureux* and *Mercure* fired a few shots at them and forced them to strike.

The *Zealous* easily induced the Justice to abandon her absurd design against the *Bellerophone.*

Nelson ordered that Captain Hood should stand by Captain Darby's ship, to deter any other enemy ship from troubling her.

While the *Zealous* was thus employed, the *Goliath, Alexander* and *Theseus* chased *Heureux* and *Mercure.*

Five French ships, *Guilliaune Tell, Genereux Timoleon, Tonnant, Diane* and *Justice,* finding no British ships near them, seized their opportunity to make a bid for freedom.

The *Zealous,* observing this, chased after them, and was soon engaging five undamaged ships, and had cut off the rear-most frigate, when Nelson recalled her.

The *Tonnant* was now unable to move, and the *Genereux Timoleon* had entrapped herself among the shoals to leeward, and was running herself to shore. Therefore four French ships, only, survived, all others falling to the victorious British.

Phillip had learnt many things, one that Frenchmen were not as he had imagined them to be; effeminate, perfumed and wearing enormous wigs like the ones he had seen in his mother's boudoir. He found them to be exactly like the British; mainly brave, they bled the same and called for their mother and God when dying.

There was so much to do, excitement set adrenalin pumping in his veins, making him forget fear.

Robert kept a sharp eye out for him, telling him to keep out of the way, especially on the gun decks, for there many lost limbs and life with the recoil of the cannons, from mooring chains breaking and whipping through flesh and bone, and flawed or misloading gun barrels, besides exploding ammunition.

Seven only had been recorded injured, and one killed on their ship, but the surgeon was kept busy for more than 36 hours as maimed bodies were pulled from the sea, with no one asking which country they came from.

Working with the doctor, Phillip administered rum as an anaesthetic, held up heads, and passed dressings. His hands and arms ached from pressing to stop bleeding.

At last they were alongside the *Culloden*. Phillip's clothes were saturated and stiff with gore. The doctor said the stench coming from his own body sickened him, so suggested at least they should take time for a drink, and change of clothes.

Phillip had difficulty removing his breeches, for a large wooden splinter had penetrated the cloth, pinning it to the flesh of his right leg. A cannon-ball had smashed, unnoticed, into the bulkhead beside him while he was working, and without feeling it at the time, he had received his first war wound.

William read and re-read the reports containing the information that after the battle, 218 British were reported killed, and 678 reported wounded. He marvelled at the bravery of Rear-Admiral Nelson who, struck above his blind eye, insisted the wound be sewn up, so he could return to his duties.

Estimates of French losses, whether burnt, drowned or killed, were 3,500, showing Nelson not only defeated a superior force, he had in addition, struck a serious blow to the colossal schemes of Napoleon, thus saving a great part of the Ottoman Empire.

This also, at least temporarily, stopped India from becoming a prey of France.

Nelson sent Captain Berry with dispatches to London, and also Lieutenant Thomas Duval, of the ship *Zealous,* overland to Bombay, with duplicate dispatches and with messages of reassurance to the East India Company.

On the fourteenth of August, the main part of the fleet, and such prizes as could be removed, were stood out of the road, to proceed westward the next day. It was on this day, also, that Napoleon learnt what happened at Aboukir Bay.

Nelson, on his ship *Vanguard*, with the *Culloden* and the *Alexander*, sailed for Naples, leaving Captain Samual Hood of the *Zealous*, as senior officer with the ships *Goliath* and *Swiftsure*, and the vessels *Seahorse, Emerald, Alcmene* and *Bonne Citoyenne*, which joined them on the thirteenth of August, to stand in Aboukir Bay.

Thus Phillip, known as Tommy, deepened his friendship with Robert Murray and the ship's surgeon, gained knowledge and colour under the burning sun of North Africa, started his almanac, and wrote to his parents whom he missed greatly.

The news of the victory, travelling via Naples, did not reach the Admiralty until the second of October. Now praises were heaped on Nelson, whose popularity had been under a cloud. On the sixth of October, Nelson was created Baron Nelson of the Nile.

William received a letter from Phillip via the Lieutenant.

Alice came to the landing, to see that all the fuss was about.

William, bounding up ther stairs and waving the letter, shouted that their son was alive and safe. Alice sank to the floor in a faint.

William's heart swelled with pride to think that his son was a hero serving in His Majesty's Navy.

In the letter, Phillip explained how he had come to be aboard ship.

It had been difficult for him to contact them sooner, under the circumstances, but he was fit and well, and had made many friends, but two in particular; one, Robert Murray who had been a great help to him, another, the ship's surgeon.

He sent love to them all, and please could Captain Hood's regards and high esteem be passed to Tug.

Tug showed such admiration that Matt said if he were not careful he would do himself an injury.

'But ye dinna know, Captain Hood be one o' the finest next

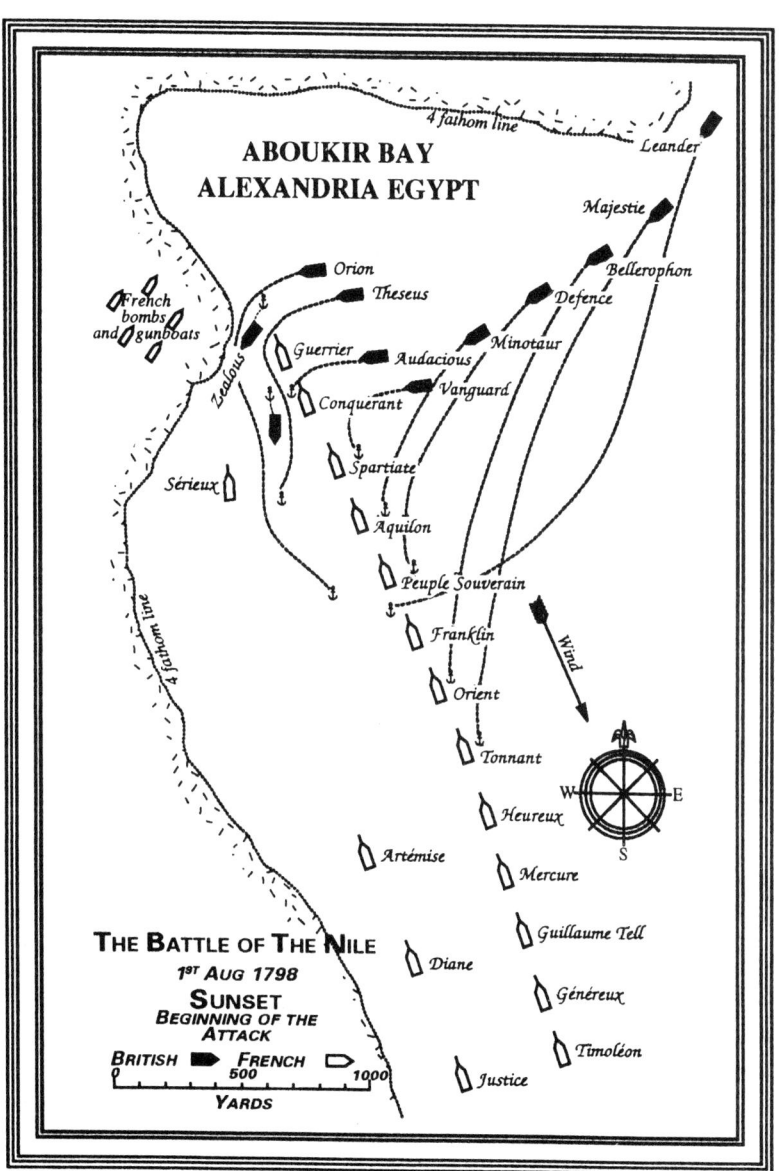

tae Nelson, an' I be less concerned tae know our ain lad be servin' under him.'

Alice wiped away tears which started the moment she became conscious, and understood that, at last, this was definite proof that Phillip was at least alive.

'Is he well? And does he say when he will be coming home?'

'No, dearest, he does not say that, but he does say he will write again, soon.'

Phillip settled down to becoming a first-class seaman under the watchful eye of his friend, Robert, and Bo'sun Arthur Gammon. He got on very well with all the crew.

The ship had seemed a better place of late, for Ratty Leary broke the habit of years by deciding to go ashore, but as he did not return after 48 hours, an order was issued to search for him.

The searchers had not been over-enthusiastic to find him, and had returned without him. After 28 days had elapsed, Ratty Leary was listed as missing, believed to be dead.

Eight women tried to claim a pension as his widow, with 32 children between them, saying they were his issue. His 'butty' and partner-in-crime, Ben Sewell, was the only person to miss him but, as he did not possess the scheming brain of Ratty Leary, was kept in order, and became servile to the rest of the crew.

Ratty Leary was never seen, or heard of, again.

Bruce Peel, the Art master, was noticed by Fiona and Alice to spend a great deal of time with Mary Gilchrist.

True, they were together checking the children's lessons, but when it was fine enough to go out-of-doors, they would take the children into the gardens to teach them a little Botany, or give them tuition in drawing and painting.

Once they were observed holding hands, and Bess swore Bruce looked at Mary 'Like a moonstruck calf'.

As usual, it was Fiona who, in her forthright way, asked him outright what were his feelings for the governess, whom she had grown very fond of, and, more to the point, what were his intentions?

Bruce Peel was flustered by Fiona's directness. Blushing, he said, 'I have fond feelings for Mistress Gilchrist, Mistress Brown, and I believe she has a little fondness for me, but a schoolmaster's low stipend is hardly enough to support one, let alone three, for Major John's pension is also small.'

'Oh, ye have thought about settin' up together, then? Have ye spoken of it, also?' Fiona quizzed the downcast young man.

'There is no point in speaking of it, for it is not to be.'

Fiona was later telling Alice about the conversation, and Alice sympathized with the young couple, but commented she would hate to lose the services of Mary Gilchrist. She was such a wonderful teacher and influence on the children.

Fiona was pleased to hear her mistress also say she would dislike the Major to leave, for he was such an entertaining and interesting person to have around.

How the years altered folk, Fiona thought, remembering how Alice used to be. Allowing her memory to stray, she wondered how her daughter, Nellie, was. It was no good wishing things could have been different, or thinking how often she had longed for her girl not to have been forced to be as she was, and for her to be there with her mother, who could never deny or forget her. Fiona was glad that Matt had come to be near her, for he had been a tower of strength. Not once did she hear him deride or scorn Nellie, although he knew what she was, but he also knew how she came to be that way.

Matt had told her that, in his journeying before he came there, he had found where Nellie lived and had seen her.

That night Fiona had a nightmare, and was screaming out in her sleep. Both Florrie and Alice arrived in her room at the same time, just as a tormented cry came from the bed.

'Thet painted creature canna be my bairn. My little Helen be a sweet, wee thing, not a painted harlot.'

Fiona tossed and writhed as if she were in a kind of fit.

Florrie tried to restrain and quieten her, saying it was only a bad dream. Alice came, wringing out a cloth she had soaked in the porcelain basin, and sponged Fiona's forehead.

It was minutes before she awoke, highly embarrassed, and

apologized, for causing a disturbance.

'Don't worry, old friend,' Alice reassured her. 'If you have anything, or anyone bothering you, please do not hesitate to let William or myself, know.'

Alice asked Florrie to check that the children were alright in the nursery, and to go back to her bed, for she had work to do the next day.

For the rest of the night, Alice sat with Fiona. William tapped at the door and looked in, and was told by Alice that everything was alright, and he should go back to bed. She was going to stay and sit with Fiona, until she settled down.

William asked if they would like a hot drink. Both shook their heads and thanked him.

At 5 a.m. Florrie passed the bedroom door. Hearing the low murmur of conversation, she tapped gently and was asked to enter.

Fiona sat up in bed, whilst Alice lounged on a small sofa. When Florrie asked if they required anything, this time Alice suggested some delicious hot chocolate, when it was convenient.

26

Fiona felt that at last she could unburden herself. She had been loath to tell Alice of the daughter she was so ashamed of. William, Tug and Matt knew of Nellie, though Fiona still thought of her as Helen, the name she had given her.

Fighting off sleep, Fiona continued the story of how she and Matt did extremely well selling the elixir for colds, coughs and winter rheums, made from swede steeped in brown sugar, with just a small spoonful of brandy added to it. This was far more popular than the fruit cup made from fruit and the water from the underground spring which they had found was was fresh, cool and sweet.

Fiona was desperate to go and search for her daughter, but was kept very busy preparing things for sale. Winter was almost upon them. She pleaded with Matt to search for her, and had the strong feeling he was holding something back.

The supply of brandy had almost run out. Matt was away in town. Fiona decided to go down to fill jars with spring water, ready for Matt to carry up to the kitchen, and she was searching the now almost empty wine-racks for full bottles.

Lady Ruth was coming down the steps, calling to her to come quickly, for Mary was having a queer turn.

Whether Lady Ruth slipped or felt faint, for she was not of a robust nature, Fiona could not be sure, but fall she did and lay moaning at the bottom of the steps.

Fiona rushed to her side and felt along her arms and legs, discovering her right leg to be lying in an unnatural way, and her right arm to be useless, as both were badly fractured.

Bringing the lighted torch nearer, she kindled the others

which Matt had placed in the many brackets, to bring as much light as possible to the prostrate woman. Fiona knew that it would be almost impossible to carry Lady Ruth up the steps without causing her extreme pain, and possibly injuring herself and Lady Ruth further.

'Stay there, do not move, my lady, I will return as quickly as possible.'

'I'll be alright, you go and see to Mary.'

Fiona groped her way up the steps as fast as she could without falling, for they were steep and sometimes slippery, then went straight through the kitchen to the sitting room that Matt had cleared for them, without glancing up. She had thought to find Mary there, but, it was empty, so she returned to the kitchen and found the old woman stretched out with her mouth open and spidery legs wide apart.

As Fiona went over to her, her foot kicked against an empty brandy bottle rolling on the flagstones, a bottle which, before she had gone down to the cellar, had been nigh full. Picking it up, she cursed under her breath, for this was the last but one, left.

From the linen closet she took sheets, from the bed, a pillow and blankets. On the way through the kitchen she took the last bottle of brandy from the cupboard, and blessed Matt for opening the bottles ready for use. For she had had difficulty removing the corks and wax.

Heavily loaded, she carefully picked her way down. Gently lifting her patient's head, she placed the pillow underneath, and covered her body with the blankets.

Into the bloodless lips she tilted the brandy, holding it away only when Lady Ruth choked and gasped.

'I know ye dunna take strong spirits, my lady, but ye must take as much o' this as I can pour into ye. 'Twill deaden the pain. There are things that must be done tae keep ye frae further harm.'

The bottle was half-consumed when the giggling started.

Fiona tore one large sheet into strips. Removing the blankets, she straightened Lady Ruth's limbs; brought the arm straight in line with the body, and the leg straight down against the other leg.

Easing the cut strips underneath, she bound and tied them around both limbs and torso. Alongside the now unconscious body, she spread out another sheet, placing a wide, wooden shelf on top of it. Lifting first the shoulders, then the feet, she shifted Lady Ruth onto the plank. Fiona folded the two sheet ends as tightly as she was able, again fed strips underneath all, then tied the whole like a long parcel.

She replaced the pillow under the head, and covered her friend with blankets, before going back upstairs to see how the old woman was, and bring down more blankets, one to wrap around herself, the others to place on Lady Ruth.

Twice she returned to the kitchen, thinking Matt had returned, only to find it was Mary mumbling to herself, and shuffling her feet on the floor.

Matt returned and, after a few minutes' thought, brought ropes which he fastened securely around the bound sheets, placing a loop, like reins, over his shoulders.

Laboriously they slid the plank with its burden up the steps, Matt pulling, whilst Fiona held the feet to prevent the Lady Ruth from slipping off.

Gently they lifted her onto the kitchen table. Matt said he would go for a doctor.

He had no sooner left, however, than Mary came to and vomited. Fiona was about to scold her severely, when Mary said, 'I dinna think a great deal o' tha' medicine o' yorn, ifen it make ye feel as sick as this.'

Fiona then realized Mary had drunk the brandy in mistake for the medicine, which was stored in an assortment of different bottles, including old brandy bottles. Even so, the dose was a spoonful, three times a day, and not half a bottle.

The doctor approved of the way Lady Ruth had been bandaged, but was afraid that nothing more could be done for her, except to keep her comfortable and occasionally examine the injury. He doubted the lady would make a quick recovery, for she was very frail, and her bones were brittle. This doctor had treated her for mysterious accidents before, when she had suffered broken bones in her youth, while her husband was alive.

He left the juice of the poppy to administer to her if she were in great pain, and asked Fiona to smell the broken limbs often, to see if there was putridness, for he strongly suspected there would be.

A week later Matt again went for the doctor, who came poste-haste. Matt held Lady Ruth down, and Fiona who found it most difficult, helping through her tears, dripped opium through cloth stretched over the top of a small wine funnel, with the spout held in Lady Ruth's mouth.

Her leg was amputated, but the poor, gentle soul did not survive the operation. Mary was bereft, wandering around like a ghost, refusing to eat or talk to anyone.

The doctor's fee and Lady Ruth's burial took most of the money Matt and Fiona had earned.

A man wearing McGregor tartan was at the funeral. He and another man followed them as they helped the almost collapsing Mary back to the house, where they asked to come inside.

Matt apologized, saying the front door could not be opened, and if they wanted entrance, they would have to do the same as themselves, and go to the back entrance and through the kitchen.

Once there, the man in the tartan said, 'There was talk that ye have done repairs here, man. Why did ye not fix the main entrance?'

It was Fiona who answered him.

'First, there were nay time, second, there were nay money, for my lady were nigh starved and penniless. And by the by, who are ye tae be asking such questions?'

The man who had asked to come in said quietly, 'Madam, this be the new laird, and owner of the hoose, the only blood kin tae the late Malcolm McGregor.'

'Aye, and I would like tae take possession o' my inheritance straight awa.'

'Gaed, firstly ye have tae settle the account o' the doctor, an' the burial,' said Fiona. 'An' we will be oot o' the way, for ye tae take o'er yer inheritance.'

'The money should come oot o' the estate,' said the heir.

'What estate?' asked Matt. 'There be a cabbage patch, an' a few vegetables, an' that's all.'

The quiet man spoke, 'That be right, Mungo, all land and stock were taken a few years ago.

It was then he introduced himself as Brian Mercer, solicitor.

'Where be Mary? She were here a minute ago,' interrupted Fiona.

They searched, but Mary seemed to have disappeared.

It grew so dark it was impossible to search further. Matt was convinced Mary could not have gone far in her condition. Fiona was worried for it was bitterly cold outside.

The solicitor, Mr Mercer, voiced the opinion that, hearing they were being evicted had upset the old woman.

In all fairness, as a local man who had worked for Malcolm McGregor in the past, but did not like him, he knew how Matt and Fiona had cared for Lady Ruth. He, with everyone around, had revered and respected that lady, whereas her late lord had been hated.

The feelings of local people would be against the new laird from the start, particularly since on his father's side he was related to the hated Campbells. So he had boasted when he had come to see Mr Mercer shortly after his uncle's death, to see if he had inherited something then.

After a whispered conversation, Mungo Laith, the new owner, said he would allow them a month to find other accommodation.

Fiona said that as soon as things could be arranged they would move out, but first they had to find Mary, and if he were going to town, would the solicitor notify Mary's kin, Dougal, at the Caledonian Tavern, that Mary had gone missing.

At dawn, Dougal said he had an idea in which direction Mary might be heading, for she had always said that she would like to return to Pitcairngreen, the place of her ancestors.

Matt joined the many men and dogs, asking Fiona to stay at

the house to keep a good fire going.

Two hours later they returned, bearing the stiff, small corpse.

Fiona told them to lay Mary on the sofa in the small sitting room. 'Paer wee thing, she be stiff wi' cold, and why be her clothes so wet?'

Matt told her the dogs had found Mary in the water near the river-bank, and it was a miracle that one so frail could have gone so far. Dougal had pointed out the trees on the other bank, saying that was where she had been heading.

'I hope she has found peace, and I am so glad that I had not the time or opportunity to rile at her for getting drunk, and bein' the cause of my lady coming for I. But I know she blamed herself, poor, pathetic creature, and would not believe it to be an accident.'

Dougal wanted to know who was going to pay for the burial.

'Dinna ye fret, we will find the money from somewhere, an' I think she should be taken where she wanted tae be, and be buried at Pitcairngreen,' said Fiona, with feeling.

Next day, Matt took the cow, goats and chickens to be sold, using the money to give Mary a Christian burial. This left them with just a few pennies to start afresh. Fiona still had most of the money that Manuel had given her, and the four gold coins she had kept for her daughter. At last, she had time to start searching for her child in earnest.

She and Matt called at the office of Mr Mercer, to tell him they had vacated the house. He said he was sorry the new owner had not been forthcoming with Lady Ruth's expenses, and as they knew, there was no money left in the estate to repay them. But what he could do was take them to a house where the owner had died, and they could stay there at least through the winter.

The house stood on the banks of the lower reaches of the River Tuminel. Mr Mercer explained that the river was rich with salmon and the spot frequented by poachers the keeper had to deter, and shoot if caught.

The previous keeper had died suddenly, and the solicitor

had been instructed to replace him as soon as possible, well before spring and early summer when the salmon did their run upstream to spawn.

Matt could not believe their luck, for there was a very small stipend with the job, an abundance of fuel, chickens and nanny goats for milk. He was also permitted to take the occasional fish as long as it was for their own table.

One of his main tasks was to look out for pike, and to catch these predators at all costs, not to eat them, but present them to the office where he would be given a bonus, for the pike was an avaricious hunter which preyed on young fish.

Fiona was a little upset as she had wished to be nearer the town, but common-sense prevailed, and she knew she should count her blessings for their good fortune. At least she was not a continent away, and she would be able to go into town often.

Alas, this was not to be. They had been settled in a few days only, when the dead man's dog returned to the door, thin and pining. Matt fed him, and immediately the dog licked his hand, accepting him as a new master.

Next morning, Fiona fed the hound, declaring he was a nice animal. As she watched Matt going on patrol of the banks, the dog at his heels, she thought his limp seemed pronounced that day. Preparing vegetables, she heard the dog barking, and thought she heard a faint cry for help.

Hurriedly pulling her shawl around her head and shoulders, she ran out. A hundred yards upstream, where a bridge crossed the river, she could see Matt on the other bank, almost under the bridge. He appeared to have both hands in the water.

She ran as fast as she could to him, and coaxed the dog away. Matt indeed had both hands in the water, trying to free his foot, and leg, which was wedged in between two stones.

It was then that Fiona saw the fish thrashing about in the tangle of net which trapped them.

The bank was very slippery. Fiona could not help Matt from behind and was moving around between him and the bridge when she slipped. Luckily, the water was only waist deep. Stooping, she worked fast as her fingers were getting stiff with cold, and with a tremendous effort she heaved, and fell backwards.

Matt pulled out his foot and the fish swam away, free. But Fiona was practically midstream, floating down like a discarded doll, her clothes ballooning about her.

She had almost reached the small, man-made waterfall when the dog bounded before Matt and leapt into the water. He fastened his teeth onto Fiona's clothes and dragged her towards the bank, and the edge of the wall of the waterfall.

Matt arrived and was soaked as the dog shook the water from his fur and, like a hunting dog pointing to the quarry, stood aside as Matt pulled on another poacher's net, which Fiona had become entangled in.

Matt carried her cold, wet body up to the house, wrapped her up in the thick tablecloth which draped the table, and sobbed, hoping he was not going to lose yet another friend.

Fiona opened her eyes and shivered, and through chattering teeth said, 'We had best get out of these wet clothes. How long have ye been standing there, lad? Hurry up and get changed.'

While Matt was upstairs changing, Fiona pulled the kettle to the flames and placed another faggot on the fire. She put the onions she had been peeling into a pan with water, then onto the hob to cook.

She felt strange, and again had the sensation of the icy water closing over her in a cascade of bubbles, then blackness as something struck her head.

Matt had to shout at her, for her to go and change her clothes that were steaming in the heat of the fire, while she shivered.

After helping her up the stairs, he was taking off her sodden boots when suddenly she snapped, 'I can manage the rest masel', thank ye.'

It was ten minutes later when she staggered down, dressed in her night attire, and fell at his feet.

Gently he lay her on the hearth then, making a few journeys, brought down her bed and put it up near the window.

This house had once been a hunting and fishing lodge for the gentry. There were two large rooms plus the kitchen on the ground floor, and three bedrooms. At the side and back of the house were stables and servants' quarters.

Matt had wanted to use these quarters himself and leave the house for Fiona, but she had said it was a waste of fuel to keep two fires going, and she did not mind him sharing the house if he didn't object.

Putting onion with pepper, salt, juice and a little oil in a dish, he mashed it with a spoon, as he had once seen Fiona herself do when old Mary had had a chill. Then he forced it through her lips.

For three days Fiona was in a fever. Matt fed her liquids and when she slept, he and the dog patrolled the banks, where the snow had fallen. He was pleased the only footprints he found were his own and those of the dog, who seemed to have been trained to go automatically where traps and nets could be set.

The fourth day was crisp and fine, with the wintry sun making icicles on the fronds of bracken and branches glisten like frosted silver.

Mr Mercer came to see how they were getting on, and became concerned about Fiona's illness, worrying that Matt could not do his job properly.

Matt assured him that, with the dog's help, it was not difficult but he was not over-keen to leave Fiona for too long.

Mr Mercer wondered aloud if there were someone who could help him look after Fiona until she was well again. Matt said he might know of someone, if she still lived in Perth; a woman named Kate Waters, who used to live near the Three Tuns Tavern. He had seen her, he was sure, when he was peddling the medicine Fiona made.

Mr Mercer said he would try to find her, and ask if she, or someone she knew, would come and help out.

'Thank ye, sir, for all yer kindness. If ye do find Kate, tell her I be Matt Wilkie, that were wi' Mistress Floyd in the bakery.'

'I will do that, for I well remember the bakery. Was not Mistress Floyd kin tae Willie Haig, the butcher? A fine man, he was kin tae my ain mother by marriage, I believe.'

Late in the afternoon, Mr Mercer returned with Kate, the same Kate who had been wet-nurse to Annie's baby.

Morag and Willie had brought Kate to wet-nurse Annie's child, Morag seeing the pain which Annie tried to hide, when she put the babe to her nipples to feed, and how the little one cried with hunger, as she was unable to digest the animal milk being fed to her.

Kate had just lost her baby, and had an abundance of milk. Annie's child thrived.

Kate Waters had had the misfortune to have a partner who beat her regularly, the last beating resulting in the loss of her full-term baby.

She was glad to be away from the brute and have Willie Haig in the vicinity, in case her spouse should come looking for her.

Fiona had never met Kate, but because she had worked for, and known Annie, did not put up too much argument about her staying. Kate was supposed to be a little slow of wit, but she was a good worker and enjoyed listening to stories, not that she was averse to chatter, for chatter she often did.

This was how Fiona learnt of Annie's later life, and the things she had questioned Matt about, but failed to get any answers.

Annie had been slow to recover after the birth, but insisted on getting up, although everyone said it was far too soon.

The lodgings Willie had brought them to, were cramped now that Kate had moved in with Annie and Morag whom Willie, having to use threats and much force, had rescued from the brothel of Poxy Meg. For Meg had not wanted Morag to leave, as she was of great use to them. She knew most of the locals, who had little or no money to spend, and had been told to entice strangers to the brothel.

Poxy Meg had been angry, shouting obscenities after them, and cursing Willie and all his kin, quite forgetting that she, herself, was a relative of his.

Willie sent around offal and cuts of meat which he told Matt to say were unsaleable. Annie asked where the vegetables, milk and bread came from.

'I bought them, mistress, for I could not impose more on Master Haig. He found me work, cutting up carcasses and hauling goods to and from the market frae traders,' said Matt. 'Master Haig did ask if he could come around on a visit tae see thee and the little wain.'

'Tell him, we would be pleased to see him tomorrow, in the evening, as I have a question for him,' said Annie.

Next evening, Willie came, his face beaming like a full moon.

'Will ye partake o' a little supper wi' us, seein' as it is ye that provided the main dish?' asked Annie. The three women had pushed the table to the only bed in the one-room lodging. The drawer that had been resting on two chairs, acting as a crib for the baby, was now placed on the bed close to the wall. Morag and Kate's beds were sacks of straw on either side of the fireplace.

The women dished up the scrag-end mutton stew, to start, as they sat side-by-side on the edge of the bed. The two males had the honour of sitting on the two chairs. After the stew, Morag brought a large dish of kidneys and liver cooked golden brown, with thickened onion gravy.

All were silent. Annie watched Willie, Matt, Kate and Morag mop up every vestige of gravy with bread.

When they had eaten, Annie asked Willie for permission to call her baby, Elizabeth.

Willie's eyes filled, 'Lass, ye have paid me such a compliment, I canna say Elizabeth, aye, indeed, aye.'

Willie had married his wife, Elizabeth six months to the day that Tam Floyd had taken Annie as a bride. He had hoped and prayed that Annie would grow to love him just a little, but was devastated when Annie became so enamoured of Tam.

Willie knew that every one of his kin had been upset that he should even think of taking a close blood-relation to wife, as many such marriages (for at one time it was customary to keep wealth and lands in the same family) produced malformed and retarded children. Not that he cared, it had also been pointed out to him that Annie was without dowry, and in hiding from the English authorities.

He was not unhappy with Elizabeth, for she was an orphan of good family, and of a very gentle nature. Although she did not possess Annie's vibrant good looks, her pale angelic face had a little-girl-lost look, which folk said had first attracted Willie to her. For he was always a fool for wee, helpless creatures, forever ready to protect and champion them.

Elizabeth adored her big, awkward husband, and both were thrilled when she became pregnant. But fate was unkind, and Elizabeth gave birth, after a long, painful labour, to a stillborn son, a few hours later breathing her last breath, declaring her love for her grieving husband.

Annie grew a little stronger, and baby Elizabeth, although tiny, appeared to be well. Her uncle Willie and Matt were besotted with her, but were afraid to hold her, even when assured she would not break.

Willie came to say that he had found new premises for them to see, as it was not good that they were in such cramped quarters.

The lodgings were much larger than the old one. The ground-floor consisted of a large window and door, facing the main street, onto the market square, just a few houses from Willie's butchery business. The shop did not look very large, as there were dislodged shelves and rubbish piled up everywhere.

Willie cleared a path for Annie to pick her way to the back and down a few steps, into a very large room where one wall was taken up by huge ovens.

'This be the old bake-house of Michael Scoony, but it canna be a place for us tae live,'

'Wait, lass,' Willie told her. 'Ye havena seen all, yet.'

He managed to open the large door at the rear of the bakery, and held out his hand to help her up the steps into a yard.

The stable doors hung drunkenly on broken hinges. Matt, who had followed them, said these were no problem to repair, nor was the clearing-out of the premises.

The water pump across the yard pleased Morag tremendously, for where they now lodged, water had to be brought from the street pump, and carried up 13 steep stairs.

Annie was greatly surprised to see the surplus water from the pump run down a deep gully to help wash out the pit of the earth privy, which had a door with two small heart-shapes cut in it. She had never known such modernity.

Willie led the way up the stone steps in the wall at the side and above the rear door, to an enormous chamber.

The upper room had two windows overlooking the square, both with shutters. The wall facing the fireplace was partitioned, like stalls in a stable. The door they had come in by was one of three, for double doors opened out to a platform overlooking the yard. The crossbar of a winch stuck out from the eaves.

Two weeks later, Annie moved in.

Thick curtains were placed across the stall-like sections, forming sleeping quarters. Matt wanted to sleep in the stables, but Annie would not hear of it, telling him he could sleep in the corner of the bake-house.

Using some of the money from the sale of the pelts Ian had given them, Annie bought two beds, one for herself, while Morag and Kate happily shared the other.

Willie brought the cradle meant for his son, and gave it to baby Elizabeth.

The three women and Matt set to with a will to clean up the ground-floor and stables. Under the rubbish they found baking tins and many other implements appertaining to the baking trade.

A sweep was brought to sweep the chimneys clean, and a trial baking session undertaken to test the ovens. All agreed the meat pasties and bread Annie made and baked, were as good as they had ever tasted, and far better then most. So it was decided the bakery should be re-opened as soon as possible.

The day before the opening, Poxy Meg and her husband, Foxy, brought some louts with them, who had been given drink enough to goad them into fighting mood, with the intention of causing damage to the premises and taking Morag back by force.

Shouting and howling they came, wielding clubs, They attempted to enter the yard by climbing over the gates, which Matt had repaired and fastened. Screaming, they rattled them violently, frightening the little mare who started shaking. Matt took her into the stable and double-tethered her, speaking softly to calm her.

He picked up a stout beam just as Willie came through the bake-house to join him, having been let in through the front by Annie.

Morag was on the platform above hauling up, with the repaired winch, pails of water Matt had filled for her.

Telling Annie to go upstairs and fasten the doors, Willie asked Matt if he were set. Removing the restraining bar from the gate, they stood back, weapons at the ready.

Poxy Meg and her spouse hung back, while three burly hunks staggered forward as Matt and Willie retreated slightly, until the attackers were under the winching platform from where old Morag emptied the night's slop bucket over them, followed by the pails Matt had filled for her.

Annie changed places with her, and emptied out a bag of rancid flour she had found that morning in an old cupboard. Spluttering and cursing, the bullies were soon routed.

Willie wanted to give chase, but Annie shouted down to him to stay. She laughing so much, warmed his heart, for he had thought that the heart had gone from Annie, she had been looking so ill.

First she stood inside the shop doorway behind a trestle-table, where she set out the pasties, pies and scones which were soon snapped up, people asking for more. Annie, Matt, Morag and even Kate, in between seeing to the baby, helped with the baking. Annie's bakery was a great success.

Elizabeth grew and played in the bake-house in a special playpen made for her by Matt. Willie adored and spoiled her, never calling without bringing her a toy or sweetmeat.

Annie, on the other hand, developed a stoop, her once bright complexion assuming a distinct yellow tint.

Willie and Matt were greatly concerned for her, so they hatched a plot that each Sunday they would go for the day to the country.

Annie herself had made requests to go to visit the cottage, to see her baby girls' grave as well as Edward and his child's grave, for she had forced Willie to tell most of the tale, and what he had left out Morag and Kate filled in, for the murder and fire had been talked about for a long time.

Many times before sleeping, Annie prayed for Fiona, and wondered where she was.

The day was bright. Elizabeth loved the green grass and picked the flowers, watched by Morag and Matt, whilst Annie and Willie pulled away the weeds from the graves.

Wandering in the ruins, Annie told little Elizabeth that long ago this was the house where Mama and her Papa had lived. Elizabeth wanted to know where her Papa was now.

'He is far away in a beautiful land with your brothers and sister,' Annie told her. Elizabeth could not understand, and soon forgot about it, wandering away and finding a small, blackened, wooden toy horse.

Annie asked Willie if they could call on Lady Ruth.

Annie was horrified at the decline the house and its owner had fallen into, crying out, 'Shame!', forgetting the misery dealt to her by its lord and master.

Each Sunday afterwards a pilgrimage was made, with a basket of supposedly unsold bread, pies and small cuts of meat, the pies and cakes having been 'slightly damaged' with the greatest of care and the best of intentions. Willie would sprinkle a little sawdust on the meat, saying it fell to the floor, but it could easily be washed out before cooking. Matt would cut wood for the fire, for the two old ladies.

Elizabeth was eighteen months old when Kate, her wet-nurse, who, besides looking after the needs of the child, worked in the bakery, and suddenly confronted by the husband who had disappeared after beating her, and causing her to lose her own baby. He turned up out of the blue, demanding that she return to live with him. The not-too-bright Kate was so terrified of him she allowed herself to be dragged off.

Annie was often so fatigued she begged to be excused from the Sunday outings. Willie asked Matt to make the delivery to Lady Ruth on his own, as he would prefer to stay with Annie and help to keep little Elizabeth entertained.

When the weather became colder, they would sit in the bake-house, breathing in the smell of the dough which was rising in large pans, and savouring the odour of the best cuts of succulent meat Willie had provided, cooking slowly, ready for the pies and pasties.

After they, themselves, had eaten, Elizabeth played with her toys and Morag dozed, whilst they sat quietly listening to the chirp of the crickets in the crevices around the ovens.

Willie Haig wished Sundays could go on forever, and felt great contentment in these halcyon days.

A few years passed. When Kate's husband needed money he would make poor, bruised Kate go and beg for work from Annie, who was glad of her assistance, as the business was excellent but very demanding.

Sometimes Kate would arrive so badly beaten she was unable to do a great deal, and she had to plead many times with Willie and Matt to stop them from going to give her man some of his own treatment.

Elizabeth had reached her seventh birthday when Willie saw the woman in rags, with a child, who was begging unsuccessfully. They were so thin and dirty it was difficult to gauge their ages.

A man came out of the tavern. The woman, approaching him, held out her hand, and he pushed her away roughly, causing her to fall into the gutter. The child struggled in vain to lift the woman.

Willie approached and lifted the woman, bringing her to rest outside his shop. He brought her water to drink.

Her eyes bright and burning, she pleaded, 'Di ye ken where be my Fiona, sir? I have searched long.'

His shock was tremendous. This was surely Fiona the elder. When he asked the child her name, she pertly answered. 'I be Helen McCready. This be me dafty granny, Fiona, who be always a-searchin' fer anaither Fiona.'

Hurriedly putting up his shutters, he took them to Annie.

Annie, crying and laughing at the same time, clutched the dirty child to her, smothering her with kisses, the child pulling away towards the shelf where pies were cooling. Elizabeth pouted, jealous of the attention this newcomer was receiving.

Fiona aimlessly gazed around as if searching for something or someone.

Annie, explaining to Matt who the strangers were, called Morag, and asked her to place a pie on a dish with a spoon. The scrawny little child fed her grandmother as if she were an infant, one spoonful for her, then one for herself.

Annie asked if Matt would prepare a bath upstairs, then come back to keep an eye on the customers, for Kate had not turned up that day.

The child struggled, fought and screamed at being bathed. The old woman was so docile, it was as if she were made of wax.

The child was clothed in a clean shift much too large for her thin frame, although it belonged to Elizabeth who was almost two years her junior.

Annie, smiling through her tears, watched as Helen scoffed half the plate of scones, while stuffing her grandmother with the rest. If she kept eating in this way she would soon fill out, Annie thought.

Helen did fill out and grow taller in the months that followed, even surpassing Elizabeth, but Annie lost weight. Willie put it down to worrying about the old woman, Fiona, constantly getting out and going wandering to search for her daughter. And the two girls were contantly squabbling over toys and possessions.

Matt, going in search of old Fiona, thought it strange that she was always to be found in the area of the burnt-out cottage, and wondered how she had the strength to go that distance.

Annie was getting very short-tempered, often cross and shouting at customers. Trade fell off. Folk seeing the gaunt hollow-eyed person she had become, were convinced she had some horrible disease, and refused to buy from her. It was obvious to those close to her that she was very ill so, ignoring her protestations, Willie brought in a doctor.

Kate, Elizabeth's old nurse, was soon being instructed by Fiona on what treatment she herself was to receive to get her fit and well, to enable her to go and search for the child she had believed perished in the fire.

Fiona wept bitter tears when Kate told her about her mother continually searching for her. She cursed the bad luck of losing her memory, and being abroad with Manuel's family. How she would have liked to be there to care for her gentle mother, and to see her daughter grow up.

Kate could or maybe *would* not say where her little Helen was at that time. Nor could Fiona get that information from Matt. She grieved again for her young husband, and dreamt of him stretched out under the tree that terrible day.

She reasoned that the tiny bones that were buried, thought to be her baby's, must have been one of the piglets, but how did the remains of the child's petticoat, with the coins stitched in it, come to be in the fire?

She did not know that her baby had been wallowing in a mud puddle, and her father had had to bathe and give her a complete change of clothes.

Fiona suffered a great deal of pain in her limbs, which she put down to bruising and aches from the ducking she had received.

It was not until she attempted to get out of bed and stand on her own feet that, with a scream of agony, she discovered she had fractured her leg. Through gritted teeth, she told Matt to pull the limb straight whilst Kate held her down, and bind two flat strips of wood tightly to it, to keep it straight.

Fiona was frustrated at not being able to start her search.

Kate continued with her tale of Annie, Willie and her mother, both weeping at their tragic end.

Examining Annie, the doctor gasped at the swelling and discolouration of her breasts. He shook his head as he turned away, later telling Willie, Matt and Morag that there was little hope, and she must have suffered horribly.

The only thing he, the doctor, could do for her, was to give her opium to try to ease her agony until the end which, in his opinion, was not too far distant.

Willie and Matt were bereft, wondering what to do without this woman; one had grown to love her and the other had loved her since she was a girl.

Old, crippled Morag was incapable of looking after two lively children and the bakery.

The feeble-minded Fiona had discovered how to undo the strong bolts of the doors, and went wandering out into the night.

Annie refused to stay in bed, struggling to carry on in a daze of pain, until she collapsed with loss of feeling in her left side.

She had been confined to bed for only two days when Matt returned, carrying Fiona's body. Her wandering was over.

Annie was too ill to attend the funeral, where Willie wept bitter tears, not for old Fiona, for whom he felt great pity, but for his beloved Annie, whose grave, he was thinking, might well be the next he stood beside.

He took old Morag and the girls home, and tried to keep a brave face when he went up to see Annie. She had shrunk. The head on the pillow was a mere skull, with dark hollows where her bright eyes used to be.

On returning to his own shop, Willie busied himself cutting up carcasses for next day. Blinded by tears, he missed with the cleaver, crunching through his left arm.

Willie Haig stubbornly refused to get professional help for his injury, saying he had no time, until a customer found him, collapsed, in his shop.

The doctor said he could not save the arm, and was afraid the poison had travelled through Willie's body, which diminished in size like a deflated balloon.

Willie tried to put his affairs in order. The money he had, he paid out for Annie's interment, and his own. Because of his injury his trade fell to almost nothing. He left a will, leaving all his estate to his aunt, Morag, and the two little girls, Elizabeth Floyd and Helen Brown.

He was glad Annie could not fully appreciate the state he was in, for she seemed unaware of anything in the haze induced by the opium he had refused to use himself.

Sitting at her bedside he held her hand, having asked Morag to put the children to bed to allow him to sit quietly with Annie.

Next morning Elizabeth came screaming to Matt that she could not wake her Mama, or her Uncle Willie.

Both were buried on the same day. Morag and Matt carried on as best they could until the property owner came, less than a week after the funeral. They were evicted for non-payment of rent. Bailiffs took everything of value, even the mare and cart.

Willie Haig had been covering the rent of the bake-house when Annie fell ill, but as his was a cash business, he paid from day to day for his meat, and monthly for his own rent, which had also fallen into arrears. The bailiffs took everything of value at his premises also.

Fiona could hear Matt and Kate arguing, but could not understand what was being said. She was surprised at the anger in Matt's voice, for he had such a temperate nature.

She heard Kate stomp up the stairs, then heard drawers and cupboards being opened and shut. Minutes passed. Kate popped her head around the door and said, 'I be away off then, for I'll no stay fer ony man tae shout at me agin. Hope ye are soon fit an' weel.'

She was gone as Fiona caught her breath, and called, 'Wait, Kate, don't go!' Tell I what be up!'

As she tried to get out of bed, the tangled bedclothes hampered her. Finally, freeing herself of them, she got out, and had to sit back on the edge of the bed, as the room spun around her.

The dizziness subsided. She picked up the crutch Matt had made her, and banged on the floorboards with it, calling, 'Matt, Matt, where be ye?' Matt came, bringing a dish of tea and a scone.

Silently entering, he put the tray on a chair near the bed which Fiona had climbed back into, as she was afraid she would have another giddy turn, and felt numb with cold after sitting up, listening. Matt was turning to leave the room without a word.

Fiona blurted out, 'What be wrong wi' ye, Matt? Hae I done somethin' tae upset ye, and what were that shindig wi' Kate?'

'She were gettin' tae forward, forever prattlin' of what did nay concern her, regards o' the feelin's o' other folk.'

'Oh, I didna notice. I thought she were a friend o' yorn, that is how ye sent for her ie the first place.'

Matt mumbled as he left, 'We worked alongside taegether, tha' be all, but leavin' were her ain choice, an' we can manage wi-oot her.'

Poor Matt tried hard to evade questions when Fiona badgered him about the time of Annie's death. He did not want to hurt her by telling he what had happened to her daughter; how circumstances had turned her into what she had become.

That was what he and Kate had rowed about. He had begged Kate not to divulge to Fiona, anything about where the girls lived, and especially how they lived, but Kate had argued that Fiona should know.

Poxy Meg and Foxy, immersed in their own business and often inebriated, only learnt about the death of Willie and Annie days after the funeral. Their informant also told them that Willie had left all of his estate to Morag and the two girls.

The tanner, Willie's friend, out of pity gave Morag, the two girls and Matt lodgings. He also asked the owner of Willie's shop and premises, to surrender the key to Matt and Morag, to see if the bailiffs had left anything they could sell, as they were penniless.

Morag and Matt were on the point of entering when Poxy Meg and Foxy, with two really tough characters in tow to enforce their argument, came down the street.

Claiming kinship to Morag, they told Matt he had no right to be there, and that they were going to look after their kinswoman themselves, and see to all her affairs. Matt was rough-handled and thrown into the gutter.

Protesting, Morag was forced to go with them to collect the girls Poxy Meg thought would have the bulk of Willie's wealth, she not knowing he had died penniless.

Taking Morag and the girls to the brothel, they left poor Matt lying comatose from the cuffs and kicks he had received.

Leaving Morag and the girls to be, as they said, 'looked after', but meant 'guarded' in case of an attempt at escape, Meg and Foxy returned to Willie's shop to find nothing of value. A man who knew them told them they were wasting their time as the bailiffs had taken everything of worth. They slammed the door on him, and started to wreck the shop.

Foxy went berserk, hacking tables and blocks and swinging on hooks. Meg smashed a chair, crying in anger, making so much noise neither of them heard the hammering on the door. Eventually the man kicked the door to attract the attention of the people he knew were inside.

Due to the piled-up rubble, Meg and Foxy had difficulty opening the door to a red-faced man with a pot belly, puffing with exasperation.

'Did ye no hear me knockin'? 'Tis neigh on 15 minutes that I hammered on this door.'

'And what is it ye be wantin', fatty?' sneered Foxy.

'Keep a civil tongue on yer heed, ye varmint, I came on business wantin' to buy tools of the butchery trade, that I hope tae set up in. There be nothin' here worth a farthin'!' He stormed out.

Meg, still holding the leg of the chair she had smashed, beat Foxy with it, raining blows on him, as he staggered out to the street.

The crowd that collected jeered at them, making Meg

angrier than before, at the realization they had gained three more mouths to feed, with no financial gain.

The two little girls were put to begging and fetching ale for the clients, getting beaten if they spilt any, until they grew wiser, and made up the spillage at the water pump in the street outside.

Matt was picked up from the street and taken to the lodgings before Poxy Meg and Foxy arrived at the shop. The kindly tanner and his wife tended his wounds, but could do nothing to ease his anguish at having been unable to save the girls and Morag. He had no thought of how he could feed and support them all, but in his mind they replaced the family he had lost.

This was another reason why he did not want Fiona to find out about her daughter from him. He believed it was his failure to care for them better, that was the reason they had such a degrading future.

He did not think of the many beatings he had received, or the time and energy he had spent trying to get them away from the brothel. Especially after the tanner got him a job herding and branding cattle for the authorities.

Matt racked his brains to find a way to answer Fiona's questions without lying. After a number of attempts he came up with something which, having gone over and over it, he thought might satisfy her.

'Before, when ye asked about what happened after Mistress Annie and Master Willie died, I was ashamed to tell ye. I was incapable when Morag's kin came and took the three away to stay wi' them.'

'Ye were incapable, ye say? Matt Wilkie, ye are nay mon tae take strong liquor, so how be it ye were incapable?'

''Twere a fight, mistress, and I was knocked insensible. When I came around they were all gone.'

This far from satisfied Fiona, but at least it gave him respite from her questions for the time being.

27

It was late March before Fiona went to the square where she used to trade. Everything had changed except the tavern.

An old woman scurried out carrying a jug of ale. There was something very familiar about her. Fiona gasped. The old woman was wearing the shawl Annie had woven and worn before her journey north with her husband Tam. But Annie was dead.

Ah! thought Fiona, it must be old Morag.

Running after her, Fione called, 'Morag, Morag!' for she had not been told Morag had died a tragic death.

The woman hurried on, not looking back, as Fiona followed her down a narrow lane, and remembered Morag's laboured way of dragging her poor legs. But this woman was neigh running before she entered a dirty hovel.

A man's voice came from inside, cursing the woman for taking so long, asking where was the tater pie. Fiona failed to catch the woman saying she had no money for a pie, hearing just a crash of something being thrown. The poor woman almost fell through the door to prevent more missiles from landing, as the first one had found its target.

Fiona helped the woman and mopped away blood, snot and tears with the corner of her dirty shawl.

They staggered back to the square, stopping at the waterspout the market traders used. Fiona bathed the deep wound on the woman's forehead. A young lad came over to look. Fiona asked him if he would fetch a tot of gin from the tavern, and gave him a penny.

Returning with the gin, he offered Fiona her halfpenny

change, but she told him he could keep it for going.
'It be alright, thanks mistress, but this woman be my kin.'
Pouring a little of the gin onto a clean cloth, Fiona held it to the wound. The cloth was soon saturated. A few spectators gathered, but walked on, uninterested. Fiona found out later that this was a common occurrence, where this woman was concerned. An old fish-seller came to look, seeming more interested in Fiona as she stared into her face.
'Do I know thee?' Fiona asked.
She had a bad squint, her breath was foul and her clothes bore the stale smell of the wares she sold.
'I once lived near here, and had a stall on this market. My man used to mend shoes and saddlery. Do you remember Annie Floyd, and Willie Haig, the butcher? They were my friends.'
The injured woman spoke, shakily, 'I knew them well. Morag was a cousin tae me, and would shelter I when my mon, Hamish, had the horrors. This be Annie's shawl, given to I after Annie died.'
The old fishwife, sniffing, said, ''Tis high time ye left yon braggart afor he kilts thee.'
'He were never the same after bein' in the wars,' said the injured woman, falling against Fiona.
'Is there anywhere we could take her? I will pay,' said Fiona, not wanting to lose touch with a woman who had known Annie, and who also might have known her mother. Holding on to one of the woman's arms, the fishwife holding on to the other, she helped her through the squalid streets. They were familiar to Fiona, being the same ones Willie and she had trodden when they unsuccessfully went to rescue Morag from Poxy Meg, the first time.
The injured woman's knees buckled, and she fell to the ground, dragging them with her.
Telling them to stay there, the fishwife scuttled back the way they had come. Fiona was afraid, having spoken of payment when a squeaking, rumbling sound came to them.
Fiona was considering propping the woman up in a

doorway and running away, when she caught sight of the old fishwife trudging a rickety cart from which she sold her wares.

Awkwardly, they loaded their charge onto it, oblivious of the rough shaking as they pushed the unsteady conveyance.

They came to a gate with a huge padlock which Daisy Fish, as she was called, unlocked. The outside yard was stacked high with stained fish boxes.

The old wife told Fiona to push, while she pulled and guided the cart through the narrow channel between the boxes, and into a chamber, very like a stable.

Lighting a lantern, for it was gloomy inside, they saw a large table and two chairs that had seen better days. Across one corner, blackened and shining with the grease of many fish smoked and cooked there, was a fireplace with a deep chimney and hooked wires hanging. In another corner lay a pile of straw and old blankets.

Sitting their charge down on one chair, the old woman told Fiona to sit on the other and from behind boxes, brought a stone jar, then poured a measure into a cup with no handle.

Tilting the injured woman's head, she forced the cup between her lips. She spluttered a cough and opened her eyes.

Halving the bed straw, Daisy Fish asked Fiona to help her lay the woman down. Daisy then proffered the stone jar to Fiona, first rubbing its rim with her sleeve.

Fiona thanking her, declined. Daisy shrugged her shoulders and took a large swig. Then, surreptitiously, using her body as a shield, she replaced it in a secret hiding place.

Daisy had refilled the cup before putting the jar back. With her back towards Fiona and the wounded woman, she drained it.

Turning, she leant over Fiona, asking if she were hungry, and if she were, being she had mentioned payment before, she could pay a little something now.

Fiona turned away from the odour coming from the woman's mouth, shaking her head, saying, 'I am not hungry, but I will gie ye something, if ye will tell me all about Annie's death and, more important tae I, what ye recall of the two bairns, Helen and Elizabeth.'

The injured woman spoke, 'Annie is surely turning in her grave, for all the care she and Willie gave those wee lassies. And poor Morag grieved tae see what was happenin' tae them.'

'Whisht yersel' woman, if there be onything tay tell I will do the tellin'!'

Fiona was getting impatient, 'I don't care who does the telling as long as someone tells me.'

Daisy, squatting on an upturned box, started, 'Ye knowed that Annie and Willie Haig be deed?'

The injured woman intervened, 'Aye, and were buried on the same day.'

'I telled ye tae be quiet!' Daisy shouted. 'If ye don' stay still I'll chuck thee oot. I be gettin' paid 'tis hoped, for this.' She held out a dirty claw for Fiona to place a few coins in it. In a slurred voice, she continued. ''Twas said that Willie Haig was wi'out a penny and bailiffs came and took everything to pay his and Annie's debts.'

Fiona broke in. 'I have been told all this. What I want tae know is, what happened after.'

But she could get no more out of Daisy, for she had slumped to the earthen floor and was snoring loudly.

Fiona was so angry she went over to the sleeping woman and shook her violently. The only thing she achieved were louder snores from her. Taking her legs, she dragged her to a pile of straw.

The other woman had fallen sideways. Fiona straightened her, dragging some straw under her head to form a pillow. The rags around her wounded head were saturated.

Fiona, taking the lantern, looked for water thinking to bathe the wound, but found the pail empty.

With the pail and lantern she went to look outside for a well or water pump, but if there were one in the yard, so cluttered up with fish boxes and rubbish, she could not find it.

Cautiously, she crept out into the dark street, and heard the sound of running water and a pump being used. Not a dozen yards away there was a lad filling pails from a pump set against the wall.

Hurriedly, she filled the bucket then, cupping her hands to hold water, drank deeply. She shivered, for the night was cold and there was ice around the trough under the water spout. She snapped some ice off, putting it to float in the pail.

Returning indoors, searching, she found some kindling and a tinder box in her bag. She got a fire going, and soon there was a good blaze in the grate from the timber of some broken boxes she brought from the yard.

The fire gave extra light, enabling Fiona to see pots and also a kettle hanging on the wall. Filling the kettle she placed it to boil and turned her attention to the woman's wound. The woman woke as Fiona bathed it and put on a fresh dressing.

There was a strong odour of cooking fish coming from the chimney breast. Fiona peered up the chimney to find some herrings gently grilling on a wire shelf.

Suddenly she felt hungry, for she had not eaten since the small amount of oatmeal she ate before leaving the riverside lodge. She had left plenty of cooked meats and pies for Matt, and was sorry they had argued so heatedly.

Matt had been most unhappy she was going into town, and she was sure he knew far more than he had told her, when she snapped at him sharply that she might be away a few days. She still believed Morag was alive, and she would find her a place to stay.

Again, not to grieve her because of the sad circumstances, Matt had omitted to tell her of Morag's death, on learning how fond she was of the old woman. For months he had found an excuse, or made up ruses, to prevent Fiona coming to town.

Fiona cleaned tin plates she found, then shared out bread she herself had made and brought with her. She was unable to rouse Daisy, so she put her share aside.

She and Doris, the wounded woman, ate the succulent fish with their fingers. When finished, Fiona threw the bones into the fire, then sponged her face and hands with a damp cloth. She tipped fresh water onto the cloth, and offered it to Doris to wipe her face and hands.

The woman seemed much refreshed, and asked Fiona if she minded her coming nearer the fire as she felt a little cold.

Placing a wooden box opposite her, and spreading straw on the ground in front of it, Fiona helped Doris to her feet. She then sat her down, with her back resting against the box.

When the kettle boiled Fiona made an infusion of herb tea in a little pewter pot old Teresa had given her in France.

Looking around, for the first time since her return to Scotland, she thought of the brightness of the beaches, and the colourful and fuller, although not easy, lifestyle of the Portuguese family.

Doris accepted the cup that Fiona had rinsed out yet again, throwing the rinsing water on the floor in front of the hearth. She seriously contemplated the cockroach that came out to investigate the sudden dampness of his territory.

Doris spoke, 'Ye were askin' about Annie Floyd. I knew a deal about her when she came back after Culloden, especially when her man, Tam, came back, for Morag my cousin would come and sit wi' I, tae leave them on their own together.'

'Well, surely ye remember me, for I came back with Annie with my mother an' a wounded lad that I married,' cried Fiona.

'Aye, I do recall ye now.' The woman stopped, drawing her breath before going on, recalling the tragedy of the fire and the murder.

'Aw, ye paer wee thing, ye who have seen such tragedy. If I were ye, I should gae awa' from this place, for there be no happiness here for ye.'

'What do ye mean, nay happiness here for me?' demanded Fiona.

Doris was obviously flustered as if she had said too much. But Fiona was determined to find out, no matter the cost.

'Ye know what happened tae my bairn, Morag, and Annie's

child. In the name o' God, woman, tell me, for the doubts and fears I have are tearin' me apart.'

'I canna tell ye,'

Tell I what? That my child be dead?'

'Nay, worse tha' that, she were taken tae Poxy Meg's brothel.'

Fiona was stunned at first, then she rocked herself, sobbing dry sobs. She cried out, 'If that Meg or Foxy have harmed my child, I will kill them.'

'They be already dead, murdered with their throats cut,' said Doris.

'What happened to the girls and Morag?' asked Fiona.

Daisy, suddenly awake, sniffling and scratching herself, angrily snarled at Doris, scolding her for abusing her hospitality by talking to Fiona. 'Who lit thet dang fire?' she almost screamed.

Fiona said it was she, for it was bitterly cold, and handed her her share of bread and fish.

'I hope ye knows this fish be my livelihood, an' 'tis no gotten fer nowt.'

Fiona threw two pennies on the table, much to Doris's disgust. Daisy crawled over and snatched them up.

'Morag be deed.' Daisy spoke with her mouth full, almost choking on a fish bone.

Fiona, rising, slapped her back dislodging the bone, and Daisy spat out a half-chewed mouthful. Spluttering and scattering crumbs, she said, 'Ye dinna want tae gae tae that place, fer 'tis a place o' thieves, whores and beggars, even worse than it were afore.' After eating, and wiping her mouth and hands on her skirt, Daisy curled up and was soon snoring again.

Fiona had made up her mind. She was going to find her Helen and little Elizabeth, and make a home for them, whatever it cost.

She was beginning to realize why Matt had been so secretive about it all, and was a little ashamed.

Fiona was awakened by someone touching her, and found Daisy bending over her, trying to reach into her pocket.

She jumped up, sending the chair she sat on backwards.

Daisy fell back on her rump as Fiona stood astride her and threatened, if she ever touched her again, she would be sorry.

'Who are ye tae threaten I, when ye are the daughter o' madmen, and mother to a dirty little harlot? Get oot o' my hoose, and take that one wi' ye!' She pointed back at Doris.

Fiona collected her things and helped Doris drape her shawl about her. They departed into the dark, cold hour before dawn.

In the distance there was a glimmer of a fire. Stumbling, they were drawn to it, finding it was the blacksmith's forge.

Fiona asked the smithy if they could rest there in the warmth for a little while. On receiving permission, they sat together on sacks that felt as if they were full of horseshoes.

Fiona asked Doris what she was going to do, for it might not be wise to return to her husband. Did she have somewhere else to go?

'Aye, I have a sister living out towards Tibbermore. Maybe she would take me in.'

The smithy must have overheard the conversation, for he apologized for interfering, but he was shoeing a horse for a carter who was coming later to collect it, and he was almost sure he had said that he was heading for Crieff, and Tibbermore was in that direction. He thought the carter would take Doris, for he was a kindly man.

Taking no notice of her objections, Fiona gave Doris a few shillings, and the smithy a few pennies to give to the carter for his trouble, if he would convey Doris.

Fiona then left, going out into the steel-grey of the early morning.

For more then three hours Fiona stood in the cold, leaning against a wall on the opposite of the studded door leading into the late Poxy Meg's establishment.

Then the small door set in the large one opened, and a

cripple dressed in filthy rags emerged. For a brief second, Fiona froze.

As the cripple hobbled up the road on his crutch, she ran after him, calling to him to wait. She meant him no harm, only wanted to ask him something.

He turned and grinned at her, showing his broken, blackened teeth. Holding out his grimy hand, he whined through the spittle on his sore-covered mouth, 'Spare a coin fer a paer cripple creature!'

'I will gie ye something if ye tell I if there be twa wee lassies named Helen an' Elizabeth in that place ye ha' just left.'

Suddenly his hand grabbed her arm in a steel-like grip. She realized this was no crippled beggar, but an accomplished thief who wore a cunning disguise. Looking down she saw he had two good feet.

One hand held on and spun her around. The other, that had been secreted under the ragged jacket, with one sleeve hanging vacant, giving the impression he had only one arm, held a knife to her throat.

She gasped for air. Her breath was like smoke in front of her eyes. She was sure she was dying, as the vapour first turned blood-red, then gave way to blackness.

Slowly, she regained her senses as someone was leaning over her, rubbing her hands. Looking up she was relieved to see Matt's friendly face.

'How came ye to be here?' she asked.

'I was sure ye would come tae this accursed place sometime, so I came and waited for ye.'

'Will ye help me up, Matt? And I beg ye tae forgive me.'

As Matt put one arm, under her armpit, a well-dressed gentleman she had not noticed before, leant forward, placing his arm under the other armpit. 'Please allow me, madam.'

On her feet, Fiona dusted herself down and looked to see if there were anything amiss, mumbling her thanks to the stranger.

'Would you both like at accompany me to my warehouse, which is but a stone's throw away on the canal bank, where I can offer you some refreshments?'

'Thank ye, sir, but we could not presume to put ye, a stranger, to so much trouble.'

'I am not quite a stranger to Mr Wilkie. We have met a number of times, and he can vouch I mean you no harm. Nay, quite the reverse.'

With one either side supporting her elbows, Fiona was taken to a very large building with boards bearing the name Victor Peckway Importers.

Inside were rows of shelves in banks and bins, and many packing cases. Some were being emptied of an assortment of different items, from china vases to pieces of furniture, which were being carefully packed in paper and wood shavings, before being loaded onto carts where a pair of magnificent horses waited patiently between the shafts.

Fiona and Matt followed Mr Victor Peckway up a flight of stairs, into an airy, well-lit office where a male clerk slid off his high stool and touched his forelock, bidding his employer good day.

In the inner office, a cheerful fire burned. Shelves on the walls were heavily laden with thick ledgers and files overflowing with documents.

Mr Peckway asked his clerk if he would please arrange for refreshments to be brought. Some hot chocolate and biscuits would suffice.

Fiona found the hot chocolate and biscuits much to her liking, and could not help but compare the fine china cups with the cracked, stained cup of Daisy's.

She pondered how Matt had come to know this man. Suddenly she felt drowsy. Not having realized she had pushed herself so soon after her accident, now she began to feel the full effect of the trauma of being attacked. Her eyelids drooped and she started to sway.

Matt jumped up to steady her.

'Please, mistress, lay down a little while on this sofa. Or would you care to be taken home?' asked Mr Peckway.

Shaking herself, Fiona said, 'I will nay gae hame until I can do what I came tae do, thank ye, sir.'

Matt said he could not stay much longer as he had already been away too long from his work, and the dog had to be seen to. Matt had left him enough food, but the poor beast was locked up in a shed.

'Sir, if I may, I would like to rest a little on your sofa, and then I will go and rent a room at the tavern.'

Neither man would agree to this. It was far too risky for a lady to be alone in a tavern. Victor Peckway asked if she and Matt would wait for a few moments. He returned with a bright-faced girl.

'This is Mattie. She lives with her widowed mother, not far from here. She is sure you can have a room in their house, if you would care to come there with us. Mattie's blind mother greeted them cordially at her clean modest house, saying she would be delighted to have the company of a guest for as long as Fiona wanted to stay.

Matt said he was far from happy leaving Fiona, but he made her a promise that if she would not go near the brothel again that day, he would come on the morrow and accompany her.

Feeling weak, and seeing how clean the neat, little house was, made her feel dirty, so she agreed to his request.

Matt and Victor said goodbye to her. Victor told Matt if he would come back to the warehouse with him, he would arrange transport to take Matt back to his work.

Next day, true to his word, Matt turned up at Fiona's lodgings.

Fiona said she was much refreshed, having bathed and had a good night's sleep, but Matt was worried as she was pale and seemed to have a heavy cold. He asked if she were really fit enough to go, suggesting she should take a few days to get over her chill, for she had developed a hacking cough.

Telling him not to fuss, that she was alright, and had taken a good dose of medication before retiring, and again in the morning, she pulled her shawl tightly around her, bade good morning to her landlady and hurried out.

Matt had to ask her to slow down, for he had difficulty keeping up with her. They arrived at the gate to find Victor

Peckway there before them. She thought this man was most kind to worry about strangers like this, but hadn't Matt said he knew him before? But still, it was a little strange.'

Matt hammered on the small, inset door, but received no reply. He hammered again, and bolts were heard being drawn back.

The door was opened just a little by the bogus cripple who had tried to rob Fiona. He wore a bandage on his head where Matt had struck him the day before. Seeing who was there, he tried to shut the door, but Matt had anticipated his action, pushing with his shoulder and putting his leg inside. Falling back, the rogue ran off to hide.

Matt stood in the littered yard, and bellowed he wanted the girl Helen. Someone yelled back there was no one there of that name. Fiona spotted a girl peering down at them from the top of the steps as she was cautiously descending.

Victor Peckway suggested they should try calling for Nellie.

'I wonder who that be, up there?' Fiona asked.

The thin girl with dark circles around her eyes took a few more steps as Matt rushed to meet her, crying, 'Ye be Elizabeth!'

Nervously, she whispered, 'Aye, but I be called Betty, here.'

'Where be Helen?' he asked.

'She be called Nellie, now. Please go from here an' leave us be.'

'Don' ye remember me? I be Matt, the friend o' thy mother.'

Once Elizabeth had been ashamed for folk to know the way she lived, but now all she cared about was where her next meal came from.

Fiona showed her a coin, 'If ye fetch Nellie, ye shall hae this.'

They waited. Betty pulled at a figure who seemed most reluctant to come with her. A caricature of a creature, who wore only a thin, wine-and-food stained chemise, which was no protection from the elements, nor did it conceal the small body underneath. Her face bore the remains of white powder, and her heavily rouged lips and cheeks were streaked with the deep black that encircled her half-open eyes.

'Who be asking for I?' she asked, sulkily.

For the second time in as many days, blackness overtook Fiona.

Fiona soon recovered, and looked at this shivering person who was very like the grotesque puppets she had seen with street performers abroad. She could not believe this painted harlot was the sweet, little child who had held out her arms to her when she returned from her day at the market.

Shaking, she questioned her.

'What be thy name, child?' Fiona heard Matt take a deep breath, catching at her arm to support her.

'I be called Nellie, and who be asking?'

'Were ye ever called Helen?'

The frail Betty looked nervously around to see if anyone were watching, before asking for the promised coin. Fiona gave it to her and she clutched it close, scurrying away as if someone would stop her.

'Aye, if ye must know I were called Helen, and left wi' a mad-woman when I was young, who dragged I around, she always a-searchin' for someone named Fiona, same name as hersel'.'

The sneer on her face made it more distorted. Fiona felt such pity for this poor, pathetic child. Removing her shawl she placed it around her shoulders, but the girl shied away from her, telling her to keep her hands to herself.

'Dinna speak tae thy mother like that, lassie,' scolded Matt.

'Me mother, ye say? The selfish sow o' a mother I had, left I tae starve and be beaten. If this be her, take her away' afor I scratch oot her een.'

Matt let go of Fiona to hold the girl back as she lunged forward, shouting that her mother did not abandon her, but had thought her to be dead, and the shock had robbed her of her memory.

Fiona was racked with sobs as Nellie screamed abuse and

obscenities at her, saying, 'Aye, that Betty's mother, Annie, told I the same tale, but I dinna believe it. Clear off, afor I call for help!'

As Matt held the quivering Nellie, Fiona fell to her knees, and begged her to come away from this dreadful place. She wanted to care and look after her, and Elizabeth, too.

Nellie screamed and spat at her, shrieking she only wanted Betty and herself to go away and set up their own whorehouse.

Victor Peckway added his pleas to Nellie, that he also would look after her if she would leave that place.

Nellie spat in his face and said something that was a mystery to Fiona for many years, 'Ye want I tae leave so as tae ease thy ain conscience, but it be far tae late, maister.'

Creeping and crawling like insects from rotten wood they came, then rushed, screaming, kicking, waving all manner of weapons, to surround Fiona and Victor Peckway. Getting the better of them, they threw them roughly out into the street.

Fiona was in a state of collapse. She wanted to stay there, on the street, but was so weak after coughing violently, that Matt was able to half-carry her back to the blind woman's house.

As they arrived, Mattie, the woman's daughter was waiting for them, sent by her employer to assist them in every way.

Although Mattie had left after them she knew of the quick way home and, Matt being hindered by Fiona's struggles to return to the brothel, she arrived at the house before them.

At last Fiona was persuaded to go to her bed. She was obviously ill, burning with fever, and was racked with coughing.

Matt searched her bag for a remedy, bringing out different bottles and herbs, but Fiona was incapable of telling him which ones to administer.

Mattie was sent to bring a doctor, who prescribed a strong inhalant and forced Fiona to take medication. Matt waited until she was asleep.

He asked the girl to thank her employer for his abounding kindness, and said he would return the next day if his work would allow it.

Early next morning Matt returned, bringing all his, and the rest of Fiona's belongings with him.

When he asked Mattie's mother how Fiona was, she said she must still be sleeping. Her daughter had taken up food and a drink before she went to her work and, as Fiona appeared to be asleep then, she did not disturb her. Since then, she herself had not heard a peep out of the guest.

Matt asked could he go up to see Fiona himself. Given permission, he crept up the stairs to the darkened room. On the bed, he could just make out a still figure. Crossing, he gently touched where the shoulder should have been. Finding it hard and ungiving, he drew back the faded window curtain and saw that form in the bed was just pillows.

Leaving his belongings well out of the woman's way, in case she should fall over them, and telling her he would return, he hurried away in the direction of the river.

Matt fought his way through the group led by her own daughter, who were tormenting Fiona as she cowered against the wall of a derelict building, across from the brothel gate. She was covered in rotting fruit and bad eggs, and someone had even emptied the contents of a slop-bucket over her.

Matt fought tooth and nail until he managed to drag Fiona away. As their route back to town was barred, he backed his way down the river bank where a group of barge-men came to their assistance.

The bargees were really rough with the rabble who were soon driven off. One even wished they had stayed longer so that the fight would have lasted. Another took off the kerchief around his neck, and after dipping it in the cold water, warmed it between his hands before handing it to Matt, telling him to wipe away the filth from the bewildered Fiona.

It was a few of these barge-men who had discovered Morag's emaciated, bruised body, after she had been thrown out to starve to death, later to be buried in a pauper's grave.

Many of these men had known Morag as a poor soul who would never have harmed a fly, and did not easily forget the people and place connected with her ill-treatment and subsequent death.

Fiona lay unaware of anything for almost a month in the house of the blind widow. She did not know that, when Matt returned to the fish lodge, two men were waiting for him; the solicitor who had given him the position, and an official-looking man with an angry face.

They took him to the bank, and showed him the slaughtered body of the dog, who had escaped from the shed to be killed by poachers, who threw fish they thought too small, high up on the banks, and left them to die, instead of throwing them back into the water so they could live and grow.

Victor Peckway was overwhelming in his kindness. He gave Matt a job loading wagons, but Matt realized there was not sufficient work for him and the other two loaders, so he decided that, when Fiona was strong enough, he would ask her to journey north with him, and follow in Annie's footsteps.

Fiona was better, but far from well. A number of times she had been back to try to persuade Nellie to come away with her. Often Victor Peckway, or one of his hefty workmen, was in the near vicinity.

At last, Matt persuaded her that she was doing harm to herself, and she should try to forget that she had a daughter. Fiona swore this she would never do.

Spring was well on its way when they set off. Fiona still had a hacking cough.

They came at last to the house of Ian Tansy, and found it neglected and deserted. They made camp for the night. Fiona was very weary, saying she was too fatigued to eat the food Matt had prepared for her.

Matt lit a fire in the grate and found straw in the byre to make a bed for Fiona in one corner of the cottage. He wondered what had happened to Ian, for when they had left him he had looked so hale and hearty, but Matt was forgetting that almost ten years had passed.

Next morning, Fiona again had a fever. Matt carried her outside to the sunshine, and started to clear out the house, then repaired the bed that Tam had been placed on when they first arrived there.

He opened the windows and carried Fiona back inside. She was wet with perspiration, yet she shivered.

He bathed her face, and covered her with all the blankets they had, finding some tonic that she had made in Lady Ruth's home. He forced some through her quivering lips.

For four days and nights Matt kept his vigil by her side, only leaving her to fetch water, and wood for the fire.

Matt sat at Fiona's side, looking down at her thin, pale face.

'Eh, lass, ye have been through a great deal of sorrow, but do not go and leave me alone now, for I have no one but ye, and I have grown gae fond o' thee.'

He was not sure, but he thought he saw her tongue lick her lips. He sprang to his feet when she moaned.

Weakly, she asked how long she had been ill, and where were they?

Matt told her they were in the cottage of Ian Tansy, who had helped Tam and Annie, and it was where Tam had died.

Fiona tried to sit up, but fell back with weakness.

'Ye lay there, we will soon get your strength back.'

Matt had set some traps and caught two rabbits. One was in the stewpot, and the other was slowly cooking on a spit. He spooned some stewed rabbit to Fiona, who asked him what he had seasoned it with. He told her nothing but a little salt.

Again she tried to get up, but was unable, and her effort brought on a fit of coughing. When the coughing subsided, she asked him to pass her bag over to her.

Taking out little pouches, she smelt the contents, giving one to him and telling him to sprinkle a little in the stew. Then she gave him a tiny clove of garlic, telling him to peel the outer skin and rub it over the roasting rabbit first, then crush it and add it to the stew. She asked him would he make a tea for her from other herbs she gave him.

He asked what they were.

'This be horehound, and peppermint. They be good for heavy chest colds. 'Tis not pleasant tae take, but be a wee bit better sweetened by honey.'

Fiona, doctored by Matt under her instruction, improved, but the cough remained.

They had been there for nine days, and were running short of supplies such as flour and salt. Matt went into the cottage from the barn where he slept, to ask Fiona if she would be all right if he went to town to buy what they needed.

Fiona said she would be fine, and he was not to worry.

He was about to leave when a black and white border collie appeared on the doorstep, snarling at him and barring his exit.

A whistle was heard. The dog drew back, and Matt was able to take a few steps forward, seeing an ancient-looking fellow leaning on a shepherd's crook coming towards him.

When the man was face-to-face with him, even with his flowing beard, and even having seen him but a few times, Matt recognized the friendly features of Ian Tansy.

Standing aside for Ian to enter, Matt apologized for intruding, saying he had thought the place was deserted.

Fiona was bending in front of the fire.

Seeing her, Ian's face lit up. 'Mistress Annie, ye have returned, as I prayed ye would.'

Fiona, rising, turned to face him and was deeply touched by the disappointment he displayed.

'I be Fiona, Annie was my best friend, and ye know Matt, that ye asked tae travel wi' Annie.'

'Be Mistress Annie well? And the bairn, was it a lad or a lassie?'

Matt helped Ian to a chair that he had repaired. 'Master Tansy, are ye well?'

'As well as three score years and twelve years can be. Ye did no answer my inquiry.'

'Mistress Annie had a little lass, but –' Matt halted, and choked.

'The fair Mistress Annie is no more, ye dinna ha tae tell I.'

Fiona and Matt were glad he asked no more of the child, for he was distressed enough.

Ian told how he had sold most of his flock after Annie and Matt had left, going up the mountain to live like a hermit with his family of dogs. He rarely came down, only when it was really necessary to get supplies, as that day, for he hated to go into the town.

He told them he was pleased they were using the cottage, and they could stay as long as they wanted.

Matt said that if Ian did not desire to go into town, he would get what he was wanting for him. He was so pleased Mistress Fiona had company, for she had been ill and he was concerned about leaving her on her own.

'Can ye ride a horse?' Ian asked. 'If ye come along o' I, we will see if it still be there.'

'Do you mean that fine horse in the fields belongs to you?'

'Not exactly. He be fine noo, but when I found him on my way back frae toon last autumn, he were near tae death. Someone had shot the paer beast, thinkin' he had broken his leg. 'Twas not broken, but just bad-sprained, and the ball had only grazed him.

'I had bought a bottle o' whisky, ready for the chills o' winter. I poured some in tae the frightened beast, swabbin' and bindin' the bleedin' from his neck, I staying all night alongside him.'

Ian went on to say that, after asking in the town, the only information regarding a horse, was that an Englishman, the worse for drink, had tried to acquire a cheap mount for the saddle he carried.

The horse whimpered a welcome for Ian, and brushed up to him as he put on the bridle, and a rug on his back.

'Ye'll hae tae ride bare-backed, I'm afraid,' said Ian, as he cupped his hands to help Matt up.

It was difficult to say who enjoyed the ride more, the horse or the rider.

Ian invited Fiona and Matt up to the mountain retreat. Fiona rode the horse as her breathing was so laboured she found it difficult to climb.

Like Annie before them, they were enchanted by the beauty of the place. They were surprised to see so many animals there, especially sheep, for Ian had told them he had sold his flock. He explained that he had overlooked a few strays which had multiplied, however. There were also chickens, five or six goats and three dogs.

The oldest dog was a bitch and she sniffed at Fiona, then immediately rolled on her back with her belly up.

'Well, I be! She does want ye tae scratch her tummy, mistress. The only one she has ever done that for afore, until the noo, was Mistress Annie. By, how Lassie here, and old Laddie loved that lady. These twa be Lass's pups that are grown, but Laddie died three year since.'

They left him in his retreat, driving down two goats in front of them, and a crate containing four hens. He tried to persuade the young dog he called Trooper, to go down with them, but he hung back, cowering, as if he had done wrong. Ian said he had given him that name because the animal had a slightly stiff hind leg, causing a gait very much like a march when walking, but it had never hindered the dog from running, or any other activity.

Now, with eggs and milk, life became much better. Fiona made bread, cheese and cooked meats, which Matt took up to Ian.

Ian asked Matt to drive the sheep down to the meadows below, as the grazing was not sufficient for them on the mountain top.

Matt became a shepherd.

The next few months went by very quickly. The dog Trooper was at last persuaded to stay with Matt, and became very attached to Fiona, who fed him.

Between them, they cleaned and repaired the cottage and outbuildings. Matt made himself a bunk in the shed at the side of the house. Fiona worked hard, and appeared fit, but he often heard her coughing at night.

Matt repaired an old cart, eventually coaxing the horse he now named Star, for he had a star-shaped blaze on his face, into the shafts.

On his last visit up to Ian, the old shepherd asked Matt to accompany him into town the next time he went in. So it was arranged.

Ian came down in the morning, and was pleased to see the horse and cart ready for them to go.

In the town, when Matt helped Ian down, he noticed his movements were slow and laboured. Ian asked Matt to assist him to the notary's office, then told him to go about his business.

Ian did not speak on the homeward journey, and appeared to be asleep. Matt had to lift him from the cart, calling Fiona to help him.

They laid him on Fiona's bed, but Fiona was unable to give him a drink as one side of his face had dropped.

Through her tears, Fiona said he had suffered a seizure, as she bathed his face with lavender water. Matt said he would go for a doctor, but Ian held him back, struggling to say something.

Fiona thought he was worried about the animals on the mountain.

Saying he would go and see what he could bring down, and feed and secure the rest, Matt leading Star still in the cart shafts, went up the path to where it narrowed. Then on foot he brought a few hens in a crate, two goats, some clothes and bedding. But he failed to get the dogs to follow him.

Making three journeys up the mountain the next day, Matt taking Trooper with him, loaded all he could into the little cart. Trooper drove the flock, the geese and the two goats down in front of him.

On the second journey, Trooper's brother, Cal, slowly followed them, but Lass remained stretched out on the verandah, as if waiting for her master to come home.

When Matt went up on the third day, the food he had left for Lass had not been touched, and she looked very weak. Gently he lifted her, carrying her down to the cart.

Lass lay, barely moving, looking at her old master, who seemed to rally a little at seeing his hounds about.

That evening he became quite animated, pointing first to Fiona and then to Matt, tapping his two forefingers together.

'I think he be askin' if we are wed,' said Fiona, but Ian shook his head, again pointing to them and clasping his hands together.

'Nay,' said Matt, 'he knows we are no wed, for I did tell him. What I thinks he is trying to say is, we should get wed. What do ye think o' that? Would ye consider marryin' a penniless cripple like myself?'

Fiona was quite taken aback, and did not answer.

'I suppose, as ye are no answering me, the answer be "no",' said Matt, sadly.

'I canna say aye or nay, for ye have fair taken me by surprise,' said Fiona. 'Ye will hae tae gi' time for I tae think on it.'

Matt went to his bed happy, for she had not turned him down completely, and that meant there was some hope.

During the night Fiona came to him, to ask if he would go to town to bring the doctor, for Ian's condition had deteriorated.

For two days and long nights, Fiona waited for Matt to return.

Ian passed peacefully away in the early hours of the second morning. Fiona prepared him for burial, fed the stock and the dogs, and was fetching water when two men rode up, and asked to speak to the master.

'I be sorry, sirs, he died this morning. If ye will come awa inside tae pay respects, ye are welcome.'

Doffing their caps, they entered. One crossed himself, while the other looked around, asking. 'Be this man father to ye?'

'Nay, sir, a good friend tae I, and Master Matt Wilkie, who went to fetch a doctor two days since.'

The elder man of the two was kneeling at the bedside, praying, and had not spoken until then. 'I remember now, I did think the name of Wilkie was familiar to me, but it was a few year since I myself introduced him tae Ian Tansy, tae travel south wi' a widow-woman, but my memory be not that gaed these days.' His bones creaked as he rose slowly to his feet.

He introduced himself to Fiona as the Reverend McKenzie. 'I remember well, tha noo, the lad used tae be my grave digger, and not for a moment did I think he would become a horse thief.'

Fiona almost shouted, 'What are ye on about, mon?' She started to cough again. 'Matt be no horse thief!'

The other man, whose sharp eyes were everywhere, said haughtily, 'Madam, he was caught red-handed riding a horse that belonged to an English officer. Not only that, he almost ran the rightful owner and his friend down.'

'Where be Matt now?' she asked.

The haughty one said, 'In the lock-up, awaiting sentence at the next assizes.'

28

The sharp-eyed man told Fiona he was a representative of the government, and asked all manner of questions. What was her relationship to Master Tansy?

When told she was not a relative or a servant of the dead man, she was instructed to stay there to look after the animals and property until such time as they were sold.

'Ye can find someone else tae do that for I am awa' tae toon tae be near Matt, who be no thief, I can vouch for that.

The minister had helped Fiona to a chair. Old Lass came and put her head on her lap, and looked up at her with soulful eyes.

'How long will it be before Matt comes up for trial?'

'Maybe three weeks, maybe two months, who is to say? It depends on the Judge's calendar.'

'Right, I will stay here for a while, if ye will arrange for I tae seek legal advice for Matt.'

'Have ye money for this child?' asked Reverend McKenzie.

'If, sir, ye will find a lawyer, I will find the money.'

'I will see about it. And what about the funeral of Master Tansy? Can I see about that also, and can ye say, who is going tae pay for that?'

The government official replied, 'That cost will no doubt come out of the estate.'

Ian's burial was a sombre affair, conducted quickly in the rain. There were but seven, Reverend McKenzie, Fiona, four bearers and a dog, present. The dog was driven away until it was over, and two bearers and Reverend McKenzie hurried away, leaving Fiona to watch the other two shovel wet soil onto the plain box in the water-logged hole.

She tried to coax and pull Lass away from the wet mound where she lay, above her old master.

The courtroom was full when Matt was brought forward. He looked haggard and dirty, and Fiona's heart went out to him.

She had managed to get a barrister by the name of Pollard, to act on Matt's behalf. And he told her Matt had ridden into town that early morning, and collided with three drunken men who had been forced to leave the tavern for causing a disturbance.

They had dismounted Matt, as one man was sure the horse belonged to his officer, a Captain Wallace Willerby, who owned many horses, all were branded with the character 'W'.

They called the watch to have Matt apprehended. In the morning light, amongst other old scars from the whip and spurs, the letters 'WW' could just be made out.

Matt had groomed the horse many times, but its rump and sides had so many deep criss-cross weals, he had not noticed the brand.

It was not known how two Sisters of Mercy came to be in court that day but, as the Judge was saying that horse-stealing was a hanging offence Fiona, screaming, fainted and was helped from the court by the two nuns, who looked after her for three days.

The legal adviser came to see Fiona. In terror, she asked if the sentence had been carried out on Matt.

'No, my dear, he has been kept in prison for the Judge to decide whether he will show leniency, as the Reverend McKenzie came forward, saying he had known Matt as a young man, and he was always of good character.

The Judge had declared that Matt should be deported to the colonies instead of hanged.

'But he is innocent!' cried Fiona.

Fiona tried to visit Matt, but was not allowed to, as she was not a relative.

The nuns were well disposed to her, and begged her to accompany them, for they wanted to learn of the herbal cures she knew about.

Even Ian's dogs were sold along with all the rest of his chattels and equipment, the land being taken over by the government. Old Lassie stayed, and died on her master's grave.

Mr Pollard, the barrister, was contacted by the notary to help him bring to the notice of the court, how the horse had been in Matt's possession, for Ian had asked his advice on the matter, and told him how he had acquired the animal in the first place.

When Ian had come to his office for him to draw up the documents, he had made Matt and some girl, child of a woman called Annie Floyd, his heirs.

The notary was not allowed to present his evidence in court. The word of Scotsmen was not acceptable against British authorities, who declared the documents did not matter a jot as they bore no signature, and alive or dead, the horse was still the property of Captain Wallace Willerby.

Among strangers, with nothing to bind her to the place, Fiona journeyed with the nuns, thinking it would be best for her, with her weak chest, to leave the rigours of winter for the slightly warmer climate of the south. The nuns had been on a pilgrimage to many places, including the church at Balnakiel in the far north, but were now on their way back to a convent outside of the town of Glasgow.

Fiona did not stay over-long in the convent, but made a living, and a name for herself, out of her cures and knowledge of herbs.

Fiona's skill at doctoring was what had brought her to young Mr William McCall's notice. He had recently taken over the running of the family business. Fiona called at the factory, bringing with her a young girl, and insisted on seeing him personally.

When he had granted her an audience, she told him that all the night before she had been attending to the girl's mother, who was employed by him, and had given birth to a stillborn child.

'I see, you would like me to pay you for your services, eh?'

'Whisht, hold yer horses, 'tis not for payment I came, but tae ask ye tae let this lassie take her maether's place until she is fit tae return tae work.'

'That is very good of you, I will see if it can be done. I would like you to take something for your trouble.' He placed a few coins on the table in front of him.

'Thank ye, no, all I ask is that ye do yer best for the lass, for there be five more mouths tae feed in the hoose.'

'I wish you would take something for your trouble, ma'am.'

'What be these?' asked Fiona, pointing to a dish of sweets.

'Oh, those! They are a new cough lozenge we are trying out.'

'Can I try one, as I have a terrible cough maself?'

William offered her the dish. She, taking one, popped it into her mouth, only to spit it out straight away on her hand.

'My, that is diabolical. What are ye tryin' tae do, mon, poison folk? Aye, if ye kill them, that is a sure way tae stop they coughing!'

William, could not help laughing, and agreed that if she could bring in some of her cough linctus, he would try to turn it into confectionery.

That was the start of a very long and wonderful friendship for both of them.

The McCall family had a surprise visitor; Sir Francis Bayard uncle of Rupert Doyle, in whose apartment William had stayed when in London.

He was travelling home, he said, in the company of someone he had been staying with, it having been necessary for him to curtail the visit as he was in such agony with an attack of gout.

He had remembered William's invitation, and hoped he did not mind himself, and his companion, making a short stop, for the coach's movement had aggravated the pain.

William was delighted, telling him they could stop for as

long as was necessary and, furthermore, he would ask Fiona to attend to Sir Francis immediately.

Fiona sat on a footstool, unwinding the enormous bandage around Sir Francis's foot, when the patient called out, 'I'm in here, my dear fellow.'

Fiona gasped with surprise on recognizing who was being invited in.

Framed in the doorway was Mr Victor Peckway.

He was also surprised at seeing her, greeting her as he would an old friend. Florrie had been asked to bring in a large bowl and a pitcher of hot water, to which Fiona added some oil of pine and rosemary.

She asked if they had eaten, and was told Sir Francis had been in such pain he had eaten only a little rare steak the day before.

'That be the worse thing ye could have eaten. If ye want tae get better ye should keep off red meat and eat only vegetables,' said Fiona.

Sir Francis almost exploded, 'Demmit, I am not a rabbit, and cannot survive on such things.'

Fiona, laughing, told him, 'Them rabbits don' do at all bad on it. Ye don't see they hop about wi' a great bandage on their feet!'

Fiona was kept so busy doctoring Sir Francis, and arranging his diet, she had little chance of conversation with Master Peckway, who tried many times to get her on her own.

He and Matt had often talked of when he was placed in irons, Matt thanking Mr Peckway for all his efforts to save him from being deported to America.

The ship he had sailed on was boarded by pirates, and those in irons had had the choice of joining them, or being thrown overboard. While in Jamaica, Matt had feigned illness and was left behind.

While he was working on a sugar plantation, the owner, seeing he was European, took him on as a deckhand on his ship, but off the coast of Africa, in a terrible storm, ship and crew, with the exception of Matt, were lost. But he had had the good fortune to be picked up and cared for by some natives.

After many adventures, Matt had found a berth on a vessel bound for England.

Fiona went again to Perth when travelling with the nuns, to attempt to get her daughter to come away with her, only to find the brothel full of barrels. The cooper working there did not even look up, cursing and telling her not to bother him, and to 'clear off'.

She was seen and recognized outside the warehouse of Victor Peckway, and taken inside. Victor took her to a house where Nellie, with others, carried on their trade. It was Victor who took Fiona away from the abuse yet again, persuading her to rejoin the nuns.

When Fiona ran away from the McCalls, she thinking that she was being accused of stealing, she went to Victor to ask him to find Nellie for her.

Although abusing her, Fiona's daughter allowed her to stay until all the money she had, even the gold coins she had saved, was gone, and she was too ill to earn more.

Fiona often wondered why Victor Peckway had been so helpful to her, and taken such an interest in her daughter, whose every move he knew about. When she was treating Sir Francis, she remarked that Master Peckway was a very nice, quiet gentleman.

'Aye, he is all of that,' said the lord.

'Be he a friend, or a relative tae ye, sir?'

Sir Francis, pleased to be almost free of pain, as Fiona gently massaged his foot and ankle with a mixture of oils of lavender and winter-green, became very talkative as he sipped tea made from dandelion sweetened with honey.

'Victor be relative to me by marriage, he being wed to my cousin, Hortense, who everyone nicknamed Horsy. By Gad, the name suited her, for I have seen better looking camels and mules than she.'

He went on to say that Victor was a descendant of a noble house that was loyal to Mary, Queen of Scots, the family being devout Catholics.

Fiona recalled the Abbess Georgias, and the kindness of the nuns she had met. Once she herself had thought of embracing their religion, but felt shame for the way her daughter lived. Fiona firmly believed she was to blame for not being there for Nellie as a child, which was the cause of what she had become.

Sir Francis broke into her thoughts. 'Poor Victor were trapped into marriage wi' Horsy when she managed to get him into her chamber, on the pretence she was unable to open a valise. Then, locking the door, she tore her clothes off, screaming, "Rape!"

Victor stood no chance when told he was responsible for the child she carried, for with her looks and form no other man would bed her. Therefore Victor had to be the father, no matter how he protested.

Victor Peckway was an excellent catch for any woman, having inherited a fortune and a business from his father. His men friends at the time thought him a dull, queer fellow, who never went carousing of wenching, and were totally surprised at the union with this gross female. They were convinced he was either around the twist, or in need of assistance from Horsy's very powerful political family.'

Sir Francis stopped what he was saying to watch Fiona deftly bind up his foot with soft linen.

'My dear lady, ye are a marvel. Three days ago I would have gladly shot my foot off, so bad was the pain. Now I can hardly feel it.'

Fiona placed a large, knitted boot on top of the bandage. 'This be tae keep thy foot warm, not, mind ye, tae walk on.'

'Did ye construct this footwear, my dear?'

'Nay, that were Florrie's doing. The one thing that I do not do well is needlework.'

Tug was having quite a lot of pain with his injuries. To make time to see to him, Fiona taught Florrie to attend to Sir Francis. She still supervised his diet, and often went to check everything was as it should be.

Matt and Tug shared the coach-house, which had been repaired and refurbished. It was very comfortable, for the tackle-room had been converted to make a room for Tug, who was unable to climb the stairs to the rooms above.

Fiona began to look tired, so Tug suggested that he go and stay with his widowed daughter, Ally.

William would not hear of it, and immediately sent his coach to see if Aileen would come there to look after her father.

Ally and Matt were attracted to each other straight away.

Sir Francis and Master Peckway had been there almost a week. The improvement in Sir Francis was amazing. Not only had his health improved, but he swore he felt years younger, for his waterworks were functioning better than they had for ages.

Fiona explained it was a combination of many things causing the improvement. The gallons of barley-water he grumbled at taking, tincture of juniper, herbal teas and refraining from red meat, eating instead, only vegetables like leeks, onions, carrots and greens' all combined to ease symptoms that were connected.

Victor Peckway asked Alice and William for permission to have an undisturbed conversation with Fiona. They both said that as long as Fiona did not mind, they certainly did not, for Fiona was not a servant but a revered member of their family.

A sitting room with a cheerful fire was put at their disposal. Victor Peckway started by asking did she know anything about his private life.

'I knowed ye were married tae a cousin o' Sir Francis, for he told me, and that thy wife had a child.'

'No, Fiona. I hope ye do not mind me calling you by that name?'

'Nay, I dinna mind, for ye have been naught but kindness tae I.'

'Have you never wondered why I was so?'

'Nay, I thought it were the kind nature that ye had.'

'Not a bit of it. It was a guilty conscience, for what I did to your daughter. I am partly to blame for her downfall.'

'Ye talk in riddles, sirrah. It were Poxy Meg that took my lass awa' tae that place o' sin, and I, for my shame, was no there tae protect and look after her. If blame there be, it be mine, not yorn.'

'Please do not upset yourself dear lady, or I will not be able to tell you something that has weighed so heavily on me, a guilt that, once or twice, if I had had the courage, would have compelled me to commit more mortal sin, and done away with myself.

'I have no children, for my wife of five months had a fall from her horse. The doctor who came to examine her afterwards said the extra padding she wore had cushioned the fall. When I asked if the child were harmed by the accident, he told me there was no child as far as he could tell, but would examine my wife again, to make sure.'

Bitterly he went on, 'I had been tricked into an unwanted marriage, that had no escape. Religion forbade divorce, and her powerful family threatened to ruin me.'

'But what has this to do with my girl and me?' asked Fiona.

Victor asked how much did she know of her daughter's life after she had been taken to the brothel. She told him that all she knew was that her child was a prostitute, for Matt and others had kept it a secret from her, thinking not to hurt her.

Victor Peckway started to tell her the sad story.

At eleven years of age Helen, now called Nellie, was given to men. At first she cried bitterly and Annie's daughter, Elizabeth, who had had her name shortened to Betty, would try to comfort her companion in misery. They grew, for a while, closer together.

Old Morag had complained bitterly about their using one so young. For her trouble she was beaten, kicked and thrown out into the street, finding shelter under a bridge, where the bargees found her poor, cold, broken body. She was buried in an old sack for a shroud in an unmarked pauper's grave.

Nellie was only twelve years old when she gave birth to a boy.

Poxy Meg sent messages to the few clients who had used the services of young Nellie, claiming each one was the father, and threatening to notify their families of their use of young children for their perversions and carnal pleasure.

At first only two men paid handsomely, but one of them stopped and did not return. The other, a merchant, came with his donations, also bearing gifts of sweets and fruit. He asked if he could see the child, and was told the infant was asleep, as was the young mother, after a very difficult birth.

They persuaded him not to come too frequently, because the girl was so young. Neither he nor they wanted to be involved in a scandal. But if he sent a regular stipend, they would make sure his child, and the mother, had the best of attention. When the man insisted he wanted to see them, he was told the mother was far from well and should not be disturbed.

Poxy Meg said she would send him a message as soon as it was convenient. A few days later the merchant was brought into a darkened room where Nellie lay on a bed, nursing a baby.

For six weeks he brought money and gifts, and did not see the girl, or the baby he thought was his. He began to get agitated and was told the child was being fostered with a respectable, childless couple, for a brothel was hardly the place to bring up a baby.

The man argued the best place for a child was with its mother. He would set her up in a house with a maidservant, and recompense them for her loss and their trouble.

The irate man was forced to leave by two roughnecks.

A well-dressed man watched the merchant being thrown out of Poxy Meg's, and went to his assistance. The man asked what the fuss was about, but the merchant would not divulge anything.

'Have ye been cheated by they blackhearted villains, sir? For if ye have, I would like tae know.'

As they walked together, the man said he had been paid to watch, and he had seen the merchant coming and going often in the past weeks.

The merchant was suddenly frightened, on learning that he had been watched. For he was married to a woman of high birth, and foul temper, and did not want it known he frequented such places, although it was his wife's male relations who had introduced him there at first.

Angrily, he said, 'Ye look like a decent fellow, but you are no better than those rogues in that place.'

'Forgive me, sir, I was not spying on ye, and do not want your money. I am only in the business of finding information, so it can, accordingly be acted upon, for there are a few interested parties involved.'

He continued that he was indentured to a well-known family who had only one son. This son had been betrothed to be married, but like many young men of his class he had 'sown wild oats'.

A prostitute had been with child, and the son approached to pay maintenance, but the young man's father had refused to advance him any money, except a settlement on his wedding day.

As the bride-to-be was deeply enamoured of her fiance, he thought to confess to her. The young lady had been horrified, saying she wanted nothing more to do with the youth.

In deep despair the youth had thrown himself off a cliff. His bride-to-be was so distraught she had slashed her wrists and ended her own life.

The merchant was aghast at this tragic tale, and apologized, asking if there were anything he could do.

'Well, ye could say what trouble ye had wi' those creatures, sir.'

'I am sorry, it is far too personal to speak of.'

'Well, sir, it has been more than a year now since this happened. As ye might well know, both families were fraught wi' grief losing their children like that, and have spent time and money to find the reasons.'

When refreshed by a drink at the merchant's premises, the man resumed his tale. Five other men had been duped into supporting the same child, until one discovered the babe was definitely of Asian origin, so could not be theirs.

'That is not like my case. The child I was shown was white and I knew the mother, in the biblical sense.'

'The same thing has happened to ye, then, sir?'

The merchant was annoyed with himself for being so stupid as to give himself away like this.

'Well, sir, we would be obliged, if ye find out anything, if ye can contact me at this place.' Leaving his address, he left.

Going through another part of the town, the merchant saw a girl in rags, begging. She looked so old and haggard for her tender years he hardly recognized her as Nellie. Attracting her attention he leant from his carriage to give her a coin, whispering, 'Meet me at the old church ruins outside town!'

Looking behind her stealthily, she approached. Pulling her into the shadows, he felt her tremble.

'Ye are a frail lassie. Are ye well? Do ye ken how our bairn be?'

'I hae nay bairn, 'twere born dead. Because o' that I ha' tae beg, frae the bleedin' hasna stopped an' nae mon wants blood on him when he be pleasuring.'

His fingers gripped her bony shoulders.

'Let go, maister, ye are hurting.'

He apologized for hurting her, feeling hatred for the people who had done this to her, and disgust at himself for having abused one so young.

His was a dreadful marriage. He had very little contact with his wife, or the hunting, horse-riding people she filled their home with. He had become the butt of their lewd humour, with his wife jeering that he was but half a man, and boasting about how she had trapped him into marrying her. There were remarks passed by some that most men would have killed her for less than she had done and said.

When two of her male relatives decided they had had enough, it was they who persuaded the husband to go to the town with them. After much drinking, they ended up in the brothel, where they had had more drink. Next day the merchant woke up on a bed, being attended by Nellie.

He was sick, not only from the alcohol, but from his great remorse at having slept with a child, and being told by his companions, that at least in one direction, he was certainly a man.

He visited the house of ill-repute many times afterwards, but only to take gifts and pay for Nellie's services. He never once had sex with her after that night, but talked with her while she ate the fruit and sweetmeats he brought.

Now he told Nellie to return, but not to say that they had met. He gave her money in case they had been seen.

The merchant contacted this man who had been spying, and he arranged a meeting with four other angry men. A fifth was a naval man who asked to be informed of the proceedings, as he was unable to attend that night himself.

At the meeting, they decided to take affairs into their own hands, for they had complained to the authorities, and suspected they were collecting bribes from Poxy Meg, when told by them not to interfere for many officials were frequent customers of the establishment.

A week after the meeting, two seafaring men came to the brothel. One asked for Nellie, insisting he wanted no other. The other boasted how they had managed to get by Customs with the contraband he had in his large bag, bringing out a bottle of good Dutch gin.

Meg and Foxy were well-known as purchasers of stolen goods, so invited the men into their private quarters.

Nellie had her rags exchanged for other clothes, and was brought to wait outside the closed door, while Meg and Foxy had a drink and discussed business.

The men came out, shouting their thanks, saying they would see them later, and closed the door behind them.

As this was quite a frequent occurrence all there went about their normal business, knowing Meg and Foxy did not want any interruptions when hiding, and gloating over their ill-gotten gains.

When Nellie was asked if she were truly Nellie, she nodded her head, and was bundled out to a waiting coach and told to put on the warm cloak on the seat.

They drove speedily out of town for many miles before coming to a stop at a large house. In the open doorway stood a woman dressed in a crisp white apron over her gown, with a cap covering her hair. She led Nellie to an upstairs room.

Unprotesting and very weary, Nellie allowed the woman to remove her clothes and place them on the fire burning in the grate.

Nellie was placed in a hot bath and scrubbed from head to toe by two giggling housemaids. When she had been dried, she was dressed in a clean, white shift and helped into a narrow bed.

A man came in and smiled at her. She was really frightened on seeing a small table on wheels bearing shiny implements. Girls at Poxy Meg's suffered all sorts of indignities, as long as they were paid for.

She thought she may have been seen talking to the merchant, and overheard saying her child was stillborn and that he had been duped.

The man drew back the sheets, telling her not to be frightened. He was trying to see what was causing the haemorrhaging, which he explained was the bleeding, and he would try to stop it.

'Ye can close you eyes if you wish, I'll try not to hurt you. Bend your knees and bring up your legs.'

She winced at the coldness of a type of pincers that held the lips of her vagina apart.

'Ah, I see the trouble. We will have you right in no time, and you so young, should heal soon.'

Nellie enjoyed her stay in bed, being fed rich food and receiving a lot of attention. On the third day the tin bath was brought in and she was bathed yet again, although she protested she was clean.

As soon as she was back in bed, the woman who had met her on the first night stood beside the doctor as he examined her.

'Good,' he said, turning to the woman, 'let this young person sit up today, and give her something light, like mending, to do. Maybe in two days she will be fit enough to leave us.'

Nellie felt sheer panic. She did not want to leave this heaven.

One of the maids brought her a pile of socks to darn. Nellie made an awful mess of the mending, never having been shown how.

The woman the maids called Matron was very cross, demanding to know if Nellie could do anything useful at all. Nellie said she thought she could clean taters, and was pleased to be taken down to the cheerful kitchen, and given vegetables to clean. At first, she cut off too much peel, but the kitchen maid was pleased to have someone doing a task she herself disliked, and taught Nellie to cut the peel sparingly.

Nellie offered to wash the dishes next, and clean the cutlery, anything, as long as they would let her stay. The matron had left strict instructions she was to do only light work.

Next day Nellie begged to be allowed to work in the kitchen where she cleaned vegetables, folded sheets and clothes, and was eager to please. After lunch she was taken back to the bedroom and told to rest.

Nellie's dreams were interrupted by a gentle shaking of her shoulder. The doctor was again there to examine her, saying he was very pleased with her progress. She would be able to leave next day.

With tears in her eyes she begged to be allowed to stay.

Sadly shaking his head, he told her he was sorry, it was not possible for her to stay. A place had been found in service for her. It was afternoon. Hugging a basket containing new clothes and wearing a new cloak and bonnet, Nellie was helped into a carriage. After a very long drive, the carriage stopped and the driver held up a lantern, telling her to follow him down the steps at the rear of the house and into the kitchen.

A thin girl, a little older than herself, was cleaning the fire range. She stopped and stared until the fat cook struck her on the side of the head for stopping her work.

The cook snapped at Nellie that she should not stand there idling, but get her cloak off and clean the pile of dirty pots and pans. The journey had tired the girl, and she soon flagged.

The cook crossed over to her and shook her vigorously. Tears of defiance sprang to her eyes, and the cook gave her a resounding slap across her face, saying, 'That'll gie ye somatt tae cry for, and dinna gie I evil looks, fer tha' ye'll hae nay supper.'

When all was done to the satisfaction of the cook, who had guzzled on mutton and ale, lounging at the table, with slurred speech she told Nellie to take her things and follow the thin girl May, who led her up narrow stairs behind wainscotting.

Her basket and outdoor clothes grew heavy, so she clutched at May's ragged skirt for her to slow her pace. From behind the panelling came the sound of two men arguing. One voice sounded very familiar to Nellie.

At last they were beneath the eaves. May shared out a pile of straw, bringing old newspapers, their edges chewed by rodents.

May told her, 'These will keep ye warm in place o' blankets, for it gets so cold up here.' From under her skirt, she brought out a chunk of bread. Breaking off a piece, she offered it to Nellie, who declined it. Nellie pulled her cloak over her.

Thinking she had hardly slept at all, May shook Nellie awake, saying they must hurry, for cook had a bad temper, especially when she had a thick head.

By candlelight, for it was not yet dawn, the kitchen fire was seen to, floors swept, water drawn, kettles filled and trays set for breakfast. May collected a bucket of kindling, and a brush and pan, beckoning to Nellie to follow her.

Cold and half-starved, Nellie did the most menial, dirty jobs. May and she became friends, while she and the cook shared a mutual hatred. She saw the family only from a distance.

Nellie made up her mind that as soon as it was warmer, for it was now late February, she would escape and get back to town.

The kitchen was in a turmoil when Nellie had been there but one week. The cook called the footman to deal with a tradesman who had refused to leave a cartload of supplies, unless he was paid in cash, and there was something paid off the account, for the order was strictly cash-on-delivery.

The footman, James, said haughtily that all bills would be

paid forthwith, as these paltry items were wanted to entertain the young master's fiancée, and she was very rich, bringing an enormous dowry.

Nellie had just come back from emptying slop buckets and washing them out at the pump, when cook grabbed her.

'Ye will ha tae do. Yon May has look o' poverty. Get scrubbed clean, keep yer trap shut, and do as ye are bid.'

A bowl of water, with a block of soap, was put in a corner, amidst a hive of industry in the kitchen, for Nellie to wash. As she started soaping her face, the cook pulled her back by her hair.

'Strip, there be no one will take notice of ye, take a look at him!' She pointed to a boy of ten or eleven who wore nothing but a greasy apron, as he turned the spit, roasting a great pig on the huge, open fire.

'While ye are at it, wash that carroty thatch o' thine, ye dinna want tae take yorn lice in tae yer betters,' the cook sneered.

Nellie asked for clean water to wash the soap from her eyes and hair. The cook laughed loudly as she threw a bucket of cold water over the almost naked girl.

Someone shouted that the boy turning the spit had collapsed in the heat. The cook screamed to May to relieve him as she yanked him to his feet then grabbing a jug of ale from the table, poured the liquid down his throat. Almost at once he revived, and urinated on the floor in front of the cook, who cursed him for being a dirty varmint, saying he should do that at the back of the grate.

Dressed in clothes given her, Nellie ran her fingers through her wet curls. The cook was too busy to see Nellie dip her fingers in a bowl of cream, to rub on her face. It was a trick learnt from Flora Dougal, top girl of Poxy Meg's establishment.

Nellie was taken by the footman, James, up the back stairs to the first floor, then into a chamber containing a huge bed.

The hangings were old and threadbare, alongside dusty, faded portraits concealing some of the damp and crumbling plaster. A fire barely warmed the musty room.

Nellie was shown a trunk at the foot of the bed, and told to take out the gowns therein, then hang them up in the large cupboard. James warned her, on peril of her life, that damage would come out of her hide.

His last words before he left were, 'Keep out of sight, this be the room o' the master's betrothed.'

The hooks in the cupboard were too high for her to reach from the floor, so Nellie had to climb inside to hang up each gown. Inside the cupboard when someone entered, she stayed hidden. Unseen through the door crack, she saw the outline of a man and a woman.

The open lid of the trunk prevented her getting a full view of the couple.

The man spoke, 'Why wait, me pretty? I hunger for ye and we will soon be wed.'

Nellie drew in her breath, although he spoke softly. She knew from this man's voice that he was one of Poxy Meg's regulars, and one of the first men who had used and abused her.

The couple were now on the bed, the girl giggling. Craning for a better view, Nellie overbalanced, falling out onto the floor.

The girl screamed, and the man struggled to release his hands from the tangled ties of her drawers.

Nellie stayed on all fours as the girl hastily rearranged her clothing, and the man fastened the buckles of the kilt he wore, in spite of the garment being banned by the government of the day.

Nellie started to crawl along the floor in a bid to escape. On reaching the door she found it to be locked. The man brought across the key and hoarsely whispered, 'Ye tell, and ye are dead!' Nellie knew then that he had recognized her as well.

Later she was summoned to the drawing room, where an old man sat on a high-backed chair. He was wearing a very old robe and a tasselled cap that looked as if it had been chewed by the enormous hound at his feet. The young master stood with his back to the fire, one hand resting on the mantelshelf.

The footman, James, took her there, and he held on to her

shoulder, his fingers biting into her flesh.

'So, ye were caught rifling our guest's possessions, eh?' spoke the old man. Nellie made to protest, but James's fingers bit deeper as he hissed, 'Stay silent!'

'Search her and lock her away,' sneered the young man.

Stripped naked in front of all in the kitchen, Nellie winced and shivered as James's hands touched her body.

Throwing the old clothes she had worn before her bathing, at her, and not waiting until she were fully dressed, he pushed her down the steps into the cold dampness of the cellar.

A little light came from a grille high up on the outside wall, filtering through the thick cobwebs. Someone was calling her from the grille.

Nellie arose from the stairs where she sat and, stumbling over rubbish, cringing as she swept away the cobwebs, for she had a dread of spiders, she arrived beneath the grille.

'Catch these papers! Put them under thy clothes next tae your skin, 'twill help tae keep ye warm, for I almost froze tae my deeth when they locked ma away, and 'twere June, then.' Among the papers, the kindly waif, May, had wrapped up a crust of bread and a piece of hard cheese.

As preparations were under way for the guests, all the morning food for staff had been cleared away as Nellie was being scrubbed to act as lady's maid.

Hungrily, she was chewing at the bread and gnawing the cheese, when she heard rats squeal, tumble and plop towards her. She hated rats even more than spiders.

In the dim light, she saw large barrels up on a platform. The front of one was knocked in.

Kicking at the rubbish, yelling out, she scrambled inside the cask and wedged as many pieces of wood as she could find in the opening.

The dank smell of decay and mildew vaporized in the haze, as she stuffed the newspapers under her clothes. She longed for a drink, wishing she were back at the doctor's house. Even Poxy Meg's was much better than this.

29

Nellie thought of Elizabeth, and how the brothel had changed for the better. It had all come about indirectly through poor, old Morag, and the way she had been ill-treated.

Many townsfolk objected to having such obscenities as Meg and Foxy in their midst. Many had been cheated by them or theirs, or some relative had contracted vile diseases from the services provided by the sisterhood at Poxy Meg's.

But who could say what really started the riot?

It was a few hours after Morag's burial they came, carrying torches, shouting, trying to gain access through locked doors. Failing to gain entry, they hurled their torches over the walls into the courtyard, which was piled high with rubbish.

A fire broke out. The crowd, concerned that deaths might occur, soon dispersed, not wanting to be caught and hanged, or deported.

In fairness, a small change occurred in Meg's even before the fire, brought about by Meg's envy of Flora Dougal, her top girl.

Flora, a beauty with skin always cleansed with cream off the top of milk, took frequent baths, and cared for her raven-black hair.

Flora was the favourite of English officers, and one in particular who, having seen brothels in other parts, abhorred the squalor at Poxy Meg's. He had a passion for Flora, always telling her she was wasted in such a place and saying he could provide her with her own house, and every luxury.

Flora, seeing the house, immediately left Poxy Meg, who sent around her bully-boys to persuade her to return. But they soon showed their heels rather than tangle with the British army officers who frequented Flora's new ménage.

Nights of merry games and drinking made Flora popular. She was seen around town in her fine carriage and expensive clothes by two of her old friends from Meg's, whom she invited to see her new house. Flora asked them if they would like to join her.

The clients increased. Flora's officer became suspicious and angry when Flora did not ask him for any money, saying he wanted 'La Belle Flora' for himself alone, and it had not been his intention to start a brothel. Flora laughed, telling him he was selfish.

He left in anger, shouting he would withdraw his support of her.

A whole month elapsed before, begging forgiveness, he returned.

Poxy Meg was furious about losing her best girls and customers. She and Foxy watched near Flora's house, and collared a previous client of theirs on his way to a night of relaxation. They forced him to tell them why he and others had deserted them, asking was it cheaper at Flora's?

'Nay, 'tis not the cost. Lads dinna like rollin' in filth, wi' dirty wee molls nay mear tha' babbies. They like a bit o' comfort an' experience. When we live and work in muck, 'tis good tae ha' a bit o' style.'

Meg and Foxy made an effort to clean up, buying a tin bath and replacing soiled mattresses with proper beds and fine linen sheets which were now being woven in Scotland. For more privacy, drapes were hung between the beds.

Where the girls slept, or in the entertaining rooms, there were no cupboards to hide things. The only cupboards in the place were in Meg's private chamber.

The fire, put all this expense to waste, blackening drapes and scorching sheets and beds. Even worse was the smell of soot, combined with the virulent anger that hung in the air.

As soon as the fire started, Meg rushed to her hiding place, stuffing valuables into the deep, front pockets of her skirt, and loading Foxy with bags that were also crammed full.

Everyone was rushing around, throwing water they had obtained from a trough in the street onto the flames.

Through the big, open door, a watching youth shouted and jeered that it would be better to let the fire burn the place to the ground, and the owners with it.

This was too much for Meg, who picked up a stake and rushed towards him, screaming she would smash his head in. The weight of her filled pockets pulled her forward until she overbalanced, landing face down in a pool of sooty sludge.

Everyone tried to hide their mirth at the sight. Meg was grotesque, with scraps of charred paper clinging to her collapsed nose and her scraggy hair. The weeping sores on her face were more sickening, dripping mud.

Refusing Foxy's help she struggled to get up, but alas, fell onto her rump. Sitting with her legs apart, trying to conceal them unsuccessfully, she emptied the contents of her pockets.

'Get I a builder and joiner!' she snarled at Foxy. 'And ye sniggering monkeys, get sharp a-clearing up this mess!'

The girls put evil-smelling rubbish into a truckle-cart, trundling it to the canal where they tipped it.

Nellie was on the point of giving birth, so was unable to be of much help. The roof and floors were repaired, the bedding was replaced, and there were a few more bowls for the girls to wash.

There, in the cellar, Nellie wept, remembering the birth of her baby, who had been washed in a new bowl before he was taken away, wrapped up in newspaper.

Victor Peckway was unable to continue telling Fiona this part of Nellie's story until the next day, when they sat in the garden.

Fiona wept. 'How did ye know all these things, fer my girl told I nothing o' this, jest blamed I for abandonin' her. I would ha' been maer tolerant if she would ha' told I all this, instead o' cursin' and wishin' I deed.'

She sobbed, and he let her cry for a while.

'Do ye know if she be alright the noo? I mean, be she as well as she can be with the life she do lead?'

Victor took his time answering, 'I suppose she is alright, but will never be a fit person, for she has abused herself, besides being abused by others.' He was going to add something but had not the opportunity, for the children Aimee, Katie and William came bounding towards them.

All three children were upset to see Fiona' tear-stained face, and young William was about to raise his small fists to fight the man responsible, when Fiona told him Master Peckway had said or done nothing to upset her.

'Why have you got tears, then?' he asked, the two girls demanding to know why, as well.

Thinking for a second, Fiona said, ' A fly flew into my eyes and made them water.' For the first time ever, she wished the children would leave her presence.

Within minutes their interest was drawn in another direction, when Matt arrived pushing Sir Francis in a kind of wheelchair.

Then Mary Gilchrist came in search of her charges. She had been told by her father to keep well away from the two guests.

Sir Francis greeted her, begging to be introduced to her, as he said she seemed very familiar to him.

May's voice was calling her. Nellie thought she was dreaming, but she had failed to catch her sleep with the scratching and gnawing of the rats, and the sounds from the floor above that now seemed to have subsided.

Moving a little of the timber she saw a glimmer of light at the grille, and heard the urgency in May's voice.

'Nellie, listen hard, there be not much time. Get tae the steps up tae the hoose, I must go now, else I be missed.' Wielding a piece of timber as a club, in darkness she bumped into obstacles until at last she felt the bottom step. Her legs were stiff with cold, so she rubbed them, touching the boots given her at the doctor's, pleased they had not been taken from her. Close by, she heard squeaking. Kicking backwards, she hurried up the stairs.

For what seemed an eternity, she crouched on the top stair,

the damp like a clammy blanket around her. She heard scratching, then the door opened.

May stood in the flickering candlelight and helped her out, re-locking the cellar door. She was glad of the warmth of the cape May had brought, and put on her shoulders.

Whispering to follow her and be quiet, May crept past the cook with her head on the table, still clutching an empty bottle. The footman, James, was sprawled in an armchair, snoring noisily.

At last they were outside. The night air in their faces, they could not travel fast, as Nellie complained of stiffness, then, as if panic gave her strength, she found she was racing, and May could not keep up with her, having to stop for breath, when Nellie saw the bundle May carried.

'What ha' ye there, we will be followed and hanged for thieves.'

'These be all brought by thysel', but the basket were too bulky tae carry.'

They left the road just as dawn was breaking, and came to a stream where Nellie gratefully slaked her thirst.

Keeping low, they were creeping along a low wall skirting a hill, when May saw the rough shelter of branches and turf. Warily, they approached it. Although neglected, the bracken inside was dry. As it was in a dip and blended with the terrain, it was pure chance they had seen it at all.

Deciding it was an ideal place to rest, they pulled loose branches over the entrance. They sat back-to-back, Nellie asking if May knew where they were heading. May told her first on to Perth, and then Dundee.

Pangs of hunger woke Nellie. She felt warm as May held her around the waist, her head resting against her neck. Her stomach rumbled as the branches they had placed across the opening were pulled away. They were discovered.

A dog's cold nose sniffed at her hand. Looking up, she almost screamed, seeing a man's weather-beaten face peering in at them.

Removing May's arm, she nudged her awake. The man spoke.

'What be ye twa sparrows a-doin' here? 'Tis na a place for young maids to bide.' He stood back whilst they scrambled out.

May quickly gasped, 'We be on our way tae Stirling, tae our kin,'

'Thy sister there, has the look of sickness.'

Nellie's face had turned a shade of green.

'She be just hungry, for we have had nay food for twa days.'

'Come along o' me!'

Following the man, both thought of escape but the chance that there might be something to eat was irresistible.

The dog yapped and snapped at a ewe with her lamb, as they journeyed over a couple of hills to a hollow.

The two girls must have slept, for it appeared to be well past noon. Long fingers of shadow and mist were spreading down the hill.

The man held open the door of the dwelling, which was sparsely furnished. It was not dirty, but far from clean. He spoke.

''Tis luck Blackie found ye, 'twill be a heavy frost this night. She's gaed finding lost lambs.' He patted the dog.

The stewpot bubbling near the fire, mingling with the aroma of sheep, set Nellie's stomach rumbling again.

'I don't suppose either o' ye lasses can make dumplings? I've had nay dumplings for years.'

'I can't,' said May. 'Ye need things like flour, suet and leavening.'

'There be plenty o' flour an' mutton fat, but none o' t'other things,' said the crestfallen man.

'Ha ye stuff for cooking?'

'Aye, there be vegetables a-plenty, mutton, maize and corn. There be seasonings, tae. Come look for thyself.'

In the back storeroom, she asked what the jars contained. Embarrassed, he toid her, 'That be ale. There be whisky too. I nae touch masel, but 'twere given in trading.'

'Cook used ale as leavening, I recall. I will try,' said May.

'Thanks, lassie, ye'll please an auld man if ye does.'

Blushing, May thought he was not that old, and he was the first man in her life to treat her like a human being.

Nellie swayed, and would have fallen had not the man caught her.

''Tis the sickness of hunger,' said May.

The man warmed some milk from a jar, and cut chunks from an odd-shaped loaf of coarse bread, telling them to eat and drink.

'I be called Shaune Ansty. I ha' a feeling ye lasses be running awa' and it be none o' my business. Ye can rest up here if ye want.'

May rolled the dough into balls for the dumplings, placing them in the boiling stew. Shaune Ansty had left them to attend to his flock, but could not have been far away, for he returned, sniffing the air, almost as soon as they had finished cooking.

He swore they were the best he had ever tasted. May blushed at his praise.

Nellie thought she had eaten too fast after being starving, and that was the cause of the severe pains in her lower abdomen. When bleeding started again she fainted.

May was happier than she had ever been in her life. Besides attending to Nellie, lying in the only rough bed, she having to constantly replace covers Nellie threw off in her raging fever and delirium, she bottle-fed three orphan lambs, cooked, cleaned and started to have roses in her sallow cheeks, and a sparkle in her eyes.

Each morning, Shaune brought in milk, enough wood for the fire and meat for the pot. First asking how Nellie was, he then told May shyly that he thought she was a marvel, as they ate their breakfast.

After five days and nights of sponging Nellie down and changing her nightclothes, which were old shirts of Shaune's, May had found, repaired and washed, he saying she could use them, and of trying to feed her, wetting her lips with whisky and water sweetened with honey, again brought by Shaune, Nellie's fever broke. But not before he had heard her shout

out more than once in delirium, 'I dinna want tae gae tae Dundee.'

May felt such guilt, lying about their destination, especially to someone who had been kind to them as no other living soul had been to her.

Nellie was sleeping peacefully, so May took the opportunity to wash, having placed a blanket over the window, and a chair at the door. Shaune always gave plenty of notice when he was approaching, banging the mud off his boots, always removing them to enter in his stocking feet, then knocking and waiting before asking to come in.

Never having been treated in this way before, May felt a stirring inside herself such as she had never experienced.

The smell of fresh bread greeted Shaune as he came in, May placing a steaming bowl of porridge at his place on the table.

Shaune was grateful for hot food, it having been a hard, cold night. 'Weel, lassie, I am glad your sister has gotten o'er the worst and the lambing is at last finished.'

May choked. 'Nellie be no sister tae I. We worked at the same place, but I was there all of my life. She came but a few weeks ago.'

Gaining confidence, she apologized for telling him a lie about their destination, and went on to tell him why.

Once before, May had tried to run away from the household that had treated her like a slave for as long as she could remember. She had been caught and beaten by the young master, then imprisoned in the same cellars she had helped Nellie to escape from. She was beaten daily, and neigh starved.

'But why did ye not leave? Had ye no parents?'

'Only my mother who worked in the place before I was born. She came frae Dundee, and once told me I had kin there, and if I were ever in trouble tae go tae them.'

'If it were such a terrible place, why did your mother not take ye herself tae Dundee?'

'She was too ashamed tae return herself, because o' I.'

'Why should you be the cause of shame tae thy mother?'

339

demanded Shaune, angrily.

May was silent for a few minutes, looking away, then she stammered. 'It were old master who faethered I, but refused us recognition. He provided us wi' food and a roof, and did tell us we had tae be grateful, and to count it a privilege tae work in bondage to such a fine family.' A little sob shook her voice. 'Then my mother died.'

Shaune knew of these things. Young girls no more than children were taken into the service of the upper classes, defiled and degraded, then they and their offspring were unpaid slaves until their children, and their children, ended their days.

May then asked him something he was not quite sure about. What was incest?

'I do believe it be a mortal sin,' he replied, asking why she wanted to know.

Before I ran away last time, the young master came tae my bed.' Again she hesitated, as if doubtful she was doing the right thing by telling him, or the memory were too painful. But she had to explain to this man why she had lied to him about where she was going, and the look of compassion on his face prompted her to carry on.

'He tore at my shift and he bit and hurt me. As I screamed for him to stop, the noise brought the auld maester carrying a whip that he thrashed his son with, and it was he who kept screaming that word.'

Shaune's face was dark with anger as she counted on her fingers. 'That were six winters ago, a few days after mother died, and I were eleven summers old.'

'Did the swine bother ye again?'

'Nay, not that way, but kept callin' I a bastard. Then one day he accused I of stealin', same as he did wi' Nellie. They did shame her somethin' awful, locking her up in the cellar, 'til I got her out, like old Sarah, who worked wi' mother got me out.'

'How did ye gae back tae such a place?'

'That is why I told ye a lie as to where we were going.'

She told how she had met a group of gypsies on her first

escape. They had taken pity on the poor child, feeding her. She, thinking she could trust them, had told them the way she was heading, and where she had come from. They told her, they being seasoned travellers, and as she was on foot, that they could show her a route that was much shorter.

The directions they had given were false, and by the time she had returned to the place from where she had started, they had sent a message to her masters, offering information as to her whereabouts, in return for payment.

The young master had caught her, binding and dragging her back, again to be locked up and beaten into submission for so many years that no one suspected May dreamt of escape, let alone that she would attempt it ever again.

Shaune was deeply angry, wishing he had his hands around the man's neck, to squeeze the life out of a person who could treat a sweet little being such as the maid, so.

He said he had to go to town, to take some rams in for sale, and get supplies. He left his dog, Blackie, on guard, and rode away on his mule, his dog Hunter driving the rams in front of him. May was nervous, with all sorts of thoughts in her head.

Shaune was approaching crossroads on the road to Buchanty as one ram turned on the barking dog, who snapped at the ram's heels, trying to make him move from the middle of the road.

Two horsemen rode up, the younger one taking his whip to the animals. Shaune leapt from the mule, trying to snatch the whip, but the rider then turned it on him.

The other man shouted, 'Hold hard, master, this fellow might have some information.'

The seedy-looking whip-wielding individual snarled. 'Have ye seen anythin' of two thieving runaway wenches, sirrah.'

Shaune drew himself up to his full height of six feet and six inches. He assumed this was the young master May had spoken of, and had to control the strong impulse to drag the fellow off his mount and beat him to a pulp.

Shaune had been lonely for many years, since the death of his Scottish mother, who said he had inherited his father's temper.

His father, a man of Irish descent, had distinguished himself fighting for the British, but he had almost killed an officer who was molesting his wife. Hastily he had retreated to the Scottish hills, until the British military traced him, forcing him to fight with them at Culloden.

Severely wounded, he had been brought home to his young son and his wife, who never forgave him for fighting against her countrymen.

Shaune's father had died a sad man, leaving his wife grieving for not having forgiven him for doing what he had been forced to do.

Shaune, calling Hunter to heel, said, 'I have not seen any thieving wenches, and even if I had, I would not tell the likes o' thee.'

The pair rode away, leaving Shaune inflamed. The man had not argued, thereby giving Shaune no excuse to smash his face in.

May was very concerned when Shaune left, thinking she might be betrayed again, and started to collect Nellie's belongings.

The only things she owned were rags. She took off the shirt belonging to Shaune, and the skirt he had found for her to wear. She tried to get Nellie up, but her friend was too weak.

Looking out, she saw the flurry of snow sweeping down the mountain, and sobbed. For flight was now impossible as she had no apparel for bad weather. True, Shaune had fashioned some moccasins for her, and she had started to knit herself a shawl of rough-spun wool. She wondered now who the skirt and needles she had been using belonged to.

Nellie was awake, asking for a drink. May confided her fears to her.

'If we ha' tae gae back tae that hell, I will find a way tae kill masel',' Nellie said with feeling.

May agreed she would do the same, and thought that at least the days she had spent here were the happiest of her life. She remembered how angry Shaune had looked when she spoke of her ordeal. 'No, Shaune Ansty was too fine a man to betray anyone.'

At that moment Shaune came into the house loaded with food and provisions. He was excited, telling them of the encounter with their old master. When he described the other man, the two girls together gasped, 'James!' May was deliriously happy, singing as she dished up the food.

For four days it snowed. Although it made work for Shaune, he said at the least, no one would come searching for them, and maybe it would be believed they had perished in the bitter cold.

30

Shaune fashioned warm jackets of sheepskin for both of them.

Nellie improved daily, but was a little impatient. The rural life did not suit her, and secretly she longed to return to Perth, having forgotten how ill-used she had been there.

She missed the company of the other girls, finding the quiet May dull.

Nellie was unaware that on the night she had been taken away from Poxy Meg's, the couple were brutally murdered. The murderers had escaped unpunished. It was believed the killers had abducted Nellie to prevent her from identifying them.

The general opinion was that Foxy and Meg, being the villainous pair they were, had had their just desserts, and why bother over a missing prostitute? At first, the girls at the establishment were like headless chickens, until Sally, a sharp fifteen-year-old, brought in Flora Dougal.

Flora, weary of the jealous rages of her officer, and finding it harder each day to hide the ravages of her profession with make-up, decided to consider the job of the new madam.

Flora had learnt that the punters would pay more for a little luxury and comfort in pleasant surroundings. Anton, a French-Italian nobleman she had befriended, and two hefty army deserters, Mick and Tolly, accompanied her as bodyguards, when she went to examine the premises.

Anton was most excited, prancing around, fussing and uttering phrases in a foreign tongue that only he understood.

Demanding paper and pens be brought, he immediately drew up plans for the 'most excellent and most beautiful bordel.'

The day Shaune was dreading came. The girls had been with him for five of his happiest weeks. Before dawn, heavy-hearted, he brought the mule and cart to the door. Nellie and May, dressed in their sheepskin jackets, climbed in the back, and Shaune covered them with hay.

Shaune led the mule, followed by Hunter, who was herding some sheep. The journey, on the roads that were merely rough tracks, was uneventful. Near to the town the road became busier, for this was a market day.

The moment arrived. Shaune, pretending to inspect a wheel, whispered to the girls to jump out, and if they needed him he was to be found in the market square where he would stay until sunset.

Quickly saying goodbye, Nellie led May through narrow back streets. May felt sick at the filth and odours as they dodged slops hurled from upstairs windows.

As they got near the river, a breeze sweetened the air. They came to the large, studded door of the brothel.

The hour early, Nellie hammered the door with her fist, then with a stone she picked up, before a large, mottled face came to the grille.

'Tell Meg 'tis Nellie, come back with a friend.'

'There's no Meg here, clear off!' The grille door slammed shut.

Nellie banged again, screaming that she wanted to be allowed in.

The main door opened, and the huge man threatened to beat them sorely for disturbing folk at this ungodly hour.

Tears of temper came to Nellie's eyes as she and May headed for town. Then they heard running footsteps behind them.

They broke into a run when a voice called, 'Nellie! Nellie! Wait, 'tis I, thy friend Betty.'

Annie's daughter was so pleased to see Nellie, as everyone thought she had been killed.

Betty hugged Nellie, who introduced May as a new friend.

'Flora sent I after ye, tae bring ye back,' explained Betty.

'Why be Flora back? When did this happen?' asked Nellie.

'Ye did no see Meg and Foxy killed on the night ye were took, like everyone said? Come, Flora be waiting for us.'

May was reluctant to return to the brothel, wanting instead to go to find Shaune. She was not over-keen on the man who drove them away, or the premises, but Nellie persuaded her she should at least come to meet her friends.

'We ha' better times now, since Flora came to us after Meg and Foxy were killed.' Betty chattered all the way back. Nellie could see for herself that she looked much cleaner and better fed.

Arriving inside the yard, Nellie gasped at the transformation. On one side, arbours had been constructed with seats half-hidden by climbing plants clinging to trellis-work. In the centre of the yard was a pool, where a marble Greek goddess poured water from the vase she held, into the lilies and the carp swimming lazily around her feet.

This was the work of Anton, trying to re-create a part of the garden of the home he could no longer return to.

Flora was delighted to see Nellie, for her benefactor, the rich merchant, had been a frequent caller, and had even offered a reward for information of Nellie's whereabouts. Flora was ever ready to have a little extra money.

The girls were invited into Flora's apartment, which used to be Meg and Foxy's quarters. Nellie and May were dumbfounded at the opulence.

There were large, ornate wardrobes built in one wall, their doors ajar with gowns hanging outside, as there was not enough room inside for any more.

On a richly brocaded four-poster bed, wearing a monogrammed shirt, lay Anton, who asked, in his heavily-accented voice, 'Who are these leetle peegeons?'

Flora introduced them.

'Sharmed, I'm sure.' The small man, still on the bed,

bowed from the waist.

Anton may have been small in stature, but his talents were immense. He could run rings around Tolly and Mick when they were refurbishing the place. It was he who had found Meg and Foxy's hoarded wealth, hidden in a cavity behind the hinged cupboard.

He was also an expert swordsman. When two rowdy fellows refused to pay or leave, making sport of his effeminate ways, he calmly brought them each a foil, and invited them to a little sport, two-to-one.

First he slashed their jackets and shirts into ribbons, then he cut the straps that held up their breeches, pricking at each on his bare bottom as he danced them to the exit.

Flora swore he was by far the best, and most experienced lover she had ever had, for he aimed always to please her before satisfying his own needs.

Young Betty was sent to bring chocolate and fresh biscuits, which she daintily brought on a tray with fine cups and saucers.

Flora and Anton insisted the girls at their academy be trained to wash often, mend and cook, all young ones to act as maids to those who worked, so they knew of other things besides their profession, if the need arose.

After breakfast Nellie and May were taken across the courtyard and up the steps to the first floor. They went along the balcony and entered a kind of dormitory where, on six narrow beds, young girls lay.

They were soon awake, and their excited chatter brought a few others to join them as they listened with awe to Nellie, relating her adventures for the second time, having already told Flora and Anton.

May had hardly spoken except for greetings. Sitting near the fire she was bewildered, not knowing what to make of this place. Since everyone was so friendly, why did she feel so uncomfortable?

The morning passed with the girls gossiping, dressing each other's hair and trying on clothes. Lunch of cold meat and potatoes was eaten at a large table in the centre of the room, the older girls and young women being waited on by youngsters of eight to ten years.

The eating done with, and the dishes cleared away, mirrors and items of make-up, ribbons and folderols were taken out of a large cupboard. The girls experimented, painting their own and each other's faces.

The smell of cheap perfume and a little body odour wafted towards May as she whispered to Nellie, asking what kind of place it was.

''Tis a place where men do come for pleasure wi' lasses.'

'I did hear James and cook talk of these places. They be bad, and sinful.'

''Tis gettin' paid for somethin' men take withoot askin',' said Sally, who was now Flora's lieutenant, coming into the room. 'Flora said ye are tae come along o' me to a room ye are tae share for the noo.'

Following her to a chamber with a bed with white sheets, Nellie lay down, feeling contented.

May knew there was nothing to be frightened about, but as the day wore on she started to experience a kind of panic. This place was a paradise compared with what she had been used to and the people here were so kind. What was wrong?

Suddenly she realized she was missing the cottage, and was unaccustomed to being idle. The cloying smell of cosmetics and cheap perfume was not as familiar as the smell of sheep.

Already she longed to be back in the hills, to share food that she had prepared with the shepherd, to sit at his fire, and to see the contentment on his face as he rested, with Blackie's head on his knee, and Hunter at his feet.

She awoke with a start. She must have fallen asleep, as it appeared to be dusk. Then she saw the curtain drawn to keep out the daylight.

She shook Nellie.

'Please, Nellie, will ye no take me to the square? I need to say farewell to Shaune, and thank him. We had nay time this morning.'

Sleepily, Nellie said she could go on her own, for she was

too tired, and did not want to leave such a comfortable bed.

Panicking, May pleaded with her. 'But I will not know the way there. Please come with me.'

Not answering, Nellie turned away from her.

Leaving the room, May bumped into the girl called Betty, and asked her did she know the way to the market square.

'I can take ye there, but I must ask Flora first.' Flora had strict rules about girls going out, and asked Mick, her bodyguard, to take May, and to wait and return with her when she was ready.

Hurrying through the streets, May stumbled. Mick, sensing her urgency, lifted her up and tucked her under his arm, like a rag doll.

Folk hurried out of Mick's way as he tore along.

The square was already in shadow when Shaune raised his bowed head and slowly rose to leave.

May uttered a strangled cry as Mick set her down. Hearing her cry, Shaune rushed over to do battle with her captor, followed by his dog, Hunter, who sank his teeth into Mick's breeches.

May screamed, 'Stop, call off the dog! Mick be a friend.'

Ashamed, Shaune apologized. Mick, being an amiable chap, said it was alright, the skin was not broken.

'Ye are Irish, with that accent?' said Shaune.

Mick asked how he knew. 'My father was Irish, he fought with the British.'

'And so did oiy, but left, having no stomach for things I were ordered to do.'

Shaune asked him, man-to-man, was the place where the girls were staying a safe place, where they would be cared for and looked after?

''Tis best ye come along and sae for yourself,' said Mick.

After collecting the mule and cart, the three made their way through streets only just wide enough for the small conveyance, Hunter padding behind.

Coloured lanterns, alight, hung on walls. A lute was being played, and already some arbours were occupied.

Flora, decked in all her finery, greeted them warmly, offering Shaune all the establishment entertainments free-of-charge.

He requested water only for his dog, but when a bowl was brought, it was accompanied by a large bone. Hunter would touch neither until his master gave him the command.

Nellie appeared, dressed only in a scant, beribboned shift, rouge on her cheeks and lips.

Shaune, aghast, asked May did she know the kind of place it was.

'I have no finery that is the like here, tae offer the two o' ye, but I can and will provide food, an' a roof over thy heads, if it is your wish tae return with me. That is, until ye find homes o' your own.'

Pursing her lips and shaking her head, Nellie said she was staying where she was.

May, blushing, asked shyly, could she come back home with him?

'It must be the two of ye, for it would be improper for one maid to come tae stay wi' a single mon.'

Flora and Anton, listening and watching, whispered to each other. They perceived the tender looks passing between Shaune and May. Flora came and whispered into May's ear. Her blush deepened.

Taking a deep breath, she heard herself say, 'There would be no shame in a maid staying with ye, if she were your wife.'

Shaune could not believe his ears; this lass was proposing to him. His heart was bursting, saying it couldn't be, she was far too young and inexperienced to know what she was saying.

Nellie giggled, upsetting May. She felt shame on seeing her friend's lack of dress-and-decorum.

Shaune suggested that May go to eat the food that Nellie said was waiting for her, while he had a word with Flora and Anton. All three talked, and Shaune said he thought that he, at thirty-five, was too old for May, who was not yet seventeen.

'Rubbish,' Flora replied. The age difference was nothing, and age made no difference if they cared for each other.

Shaune assured her that he had come to care greatly for May, and if she held even the slightest regard for him, it would be beyond his wildest dreams.

Shaune was asked to stay the night, as there was plenty of room in Mick and Tolly's quarters. He said he had to go home, however, as there were animals needing attention.

His mind was in a whirl, thinking that sweet, little May could consent to marry him three days hence.

Anton and Flora had promised him she would be protected and kept well away from their clients.

Shaune chided himself for thinking bad thoughts about them, having discovered they were caring, intelligent and generous folk.

May was to stay there until his return, with both Mick and Tolly, as fellow Irishmen, vowing she would not be molested or harmed in any way.

Shaune said he would return in three days, and if May changed her mind it would make no odds. He would understand.

Mick offered to accompany Shaune back to the market square. May begged them to take her with them to enable her to say farewell to Shaune alone. The two men led the mule, chatting like lifelong friends, as May sat like a queen up on the cart.

Shaune lifted May down gently, and she kissed him softly on the cheek, while Mick looked away.

As Shaune left, Mick called, 'Don't ye worry, me Bucko, 'tis wi' my life I will guard your maid for ye.'

Flora asked Shaune to return on the third day, so there would be time to arrange for the minister and other things.

Shaune had brought two sheep the day before, to cook for the feast, declining the invitation to enter. He was afraid to take the risk, it being unlucky to see the betrothed the day before the ceremony. In the fireplace where Morag used to sleep, a spit was prepared.

May said the silk Flora chose for her gown was far too good for a shepherd's wife, and asked for calico. Flora would not hear of it, however, and eventually accepted a very fine, yellow muslin, on condition that many yards of cream lace to trim it were taken as well.

Flora then insisted on buying a tiny straw bonnet. While May was trying on the bonnet, Flora secretly told the draper to wrap up a beautiful cashmere shawl as well.

The girls got busy with needles and thread under the watchful eye of the dressmaker, Anton supervising them all.

Two girls treated May's skin and hair with unguents and creams, rubbing oil and salt into her hands and feet to remove the ingrained stains of hard work.

The evening before the wedding, May's hair was being curled up with strips of rag. It was fine and dry, so they sat on the balcony outside the bedrooms, not to be in the way of those completing the making of wedding finery.

Flora gave strict instructions that no clients were to be allowed in for business, except those specifically invited.

Tolly was busy putting up bunting, and answering the door to any callers who did come, such as the client, a baker by trade, asking for the order for bread and cakes for the coming event.

A loud knocking and shouting brought Tolly tumbling down from the ladder, entangled with bunting. It hampered his blocking the entry of the young squire who was May's half brother, thus allowing him to push past.

Looking up he recognized May, and raced up the stairs before anyone could stop him. Grabbing May by the hair he pulled her to the ground, screaming, 'Thieving bitch, ye have now turned to whoring, have thee?'

Tolly was soon on his feet, racing after the man, shouting at him. The noise brought Anton out, foil in hand, to May's attacker, just as he was raising a foot to kick her.

Anton slit the cloth covering the raised leg, and the foil was at his throat. 'Tsh, mon ami, you are no shentleman, treating ladees thees way.'

Anton stood back while Tolly, who had been joined by Mick, picked up the young squire like a sack of coal, he struggling and yelling abuse, as they carried him towards the stairs.

It may have been his struggling that loosened Mick and Tolly's hold, but he fell head-over-heels downward, as the two bodyguards slipped after him picking him up and throwing him into the street, almost at the feet of Nellie's benefactor, who had been informed she had returned.

The evicted man screamed vengeance, almost insane with fury that Nellie's friend was allowed to stay.

Mick went to see if May was hurt, and was told she was only shaken. Outside the gate the commotion became intolerable, so Flora asked Mick and Tolly to go and see what could be done.

Picking up the man between them, each holding one arm and a leg, they carried him down to the fast-flowing river. There, holding his legs, they immersed his head in the deep water, then brought him out, gasping for air. This they did four times before he croaked he would leave quietly.

Each holding an elbow, they dragged him to the stables where they asked which was his horse, as there were two strange mounts, one belonging to Nellie's merchant. With a nod of his head, the squire indicated his own.

He was then thrown onto the saddle, facing backwards. The horse, headed out of town, was given a sharp smack on the rump, sending it careering madly away.

The little April rain did nothing to dampen the gay spirit. Nellie's merchant arrived early, with gifts of bolts of cloth, cotton hosiery and some fine pottery. He said they were for the bride, in gratitude for helping Nellie escape.

Nellie was so pleased with the gifts and the attention she had received from him the previous evening, she embellished her dangerous adventure.

All was ready by noon. A large cask of ale stood beside smaller kegs of wine and spirits, these beverages being the gifts of senior officers of a ship which was in port. They were such good clients of Flora's she had invited them to the festivities.

There was a knocking at the door. Mick asked who was without, throwing it open with a flourish to admit a very nervous Shaune. He had arrived at the very split second he had been requested to appear.

Waiting in the courtyard, his well-scrubbed face not showing the inward quaking, Shaune, flanked by Mick, stood in front of the sombre chaplain. From above and behind, the sound of pipe and drum caused the men to turn.

The drummer and piper led Sally and Nellie, half-turning to sprinkle petals in the path of the bride being escorted by Anton. As if to bless the event, a gentle sun came out to shine down on the lovely young bride. She was resplendent in her yellow gown and straw bonnet, festooned with lace and ribbon which formed a perfect frame for her small, bright face.

Flora dabbed at her eyes, and thought how often she had wished for such a marriage, a home, and her own children.

The minister disapproved of the surroundings and wanted to hurry through the ceremony. But before starting, he accepted a cup of what he was assured was fruit punch from Tolly and Mick, who were in charge of the liquid refreshments. They did not tell him that it was heavily spiked with rum, and soon he was quite happy to stay all day, and got quite inebriated.

Shaune and his wife ate little and drank only water. They were asked to lead the dancing, then sat quietly, holding hands, happy, watching the merriment of others. Shaune rubbed a callous on May's tiny palm, which the oil and salt had failed to remove.

He swore that if it were in his power, his wife would never skivvy for any man again, as long as he had breath in his body.

The pair were surprised when, with much jostling and jollity, they were taken upstairs to a bedchamber. Their embarrassment was pitiful to see, as May hid her face, and Shaune stammered, his weather-beaten cheeks burning.

Flora, generous to a fault, seeing their discomfort, called

Tolly and Mick to assist her. Taking all the bedding, sheets, silk cover, pillows, the mattress and the bed downstairs, she had them placed on the cart.

Loudly she called everyone to say goodnight to the bridal pair, who were going home, and told all others that, for them, the merriment was to continue.

The cart and mule, decked with flowers and ribbons, and heaped with the bed, bedding, gifts and hampers of food, was ready to leave.

May and Shaune were too emotional to speak as Flora, kissing May on her cheek, draped the cashmere shawl around her shoulders, before Mick and Tolly led them up the street.

In the twilight, the cottage seemed smaller to May. Shaune quickly alighting, asking her to stay a little while on the cart, as there was need for him to do something.

Unhooking the lantern, he went inside and came out carrying the cot she and Nellie had shared.

When he began to unload the bed and presents, she made to alight to give him assistance.

'Nay, me pretty, ye stay while I do work that is too heavy for a lassie.'

'But I feel a chill and it would warm me if I helped thee.'

'I be a thoughtless dog, not tay mind ye were not dressed for the travelling.' Then he was at her side, unsure where to put his hands to hold her.

Suddenly she was in his arms, as if it were an everyday occurrence. He set her down by the fire he had lit, saying, 'Ye stay there to watch kettle boil!'

She laughed. 'Ye know full well, a watched kettle never boils.' The room grew warm immediately.

Shaune went to see to his flock. May changed from her finery and set about making the bed given to them. She put away her wedding dress, and was removing the wedding gifts from the table, when she noticed a jar of flowers. Cupping the deep, blue violets and delicate yellow primroses between her hands, she thought: my husband is the most mindful of men.

355

She stopped, aghast. Her husband! She could not believe it.

Shaune also found it hard to believe the happenings of that day, as he went about his chores in a dream, thinking that he, of all people, should have the gall to marry a maid less than half his age.

He was trembling at the very thought of going indoors, when the front door opened, and he heard his new bride calling him to come.

31

The day that Fiona set foot on British soil, May gave birth to their second child, a son. She and Shaune had prospered, as Shaune was determined his family should want for nothing.

Flora and Anton were thrilled on hearing the first child was on its way, showering presents on the prospective parents.

Neither were to see the child born, sadly, for Anton's body was taken from the river, a bag over his head. He had been run through with a sword.

The authorities came. Tolly and Mick ran for unknown destinations, thinking they would be found out to be deserters, and hanged.

Flora grieved greatly for Anton, taking to drinking strong liquor. She neglected the business, then one morning one of the girls discovered her dead, her wrists slashed. Again the establishment was without its captain.

Nellie had been reprimanded many times by Flora, for breaking the rule about going abroad, moonlighting, with all and sundry. Her merchant friend stopped calling to see her, as she had become so grossly common.

Rogues, thieves and vagabonds took over Flora's empire, turning it into a den of iniquity.

Shaune doubled the size of his cottage to accommodate his family. Hearing of an auction at a large house less than a day's journey away, he asked May if she would like to come with him to see if there were any furniture there to suit her.

Decked out in her wedding bonnet and cashmere shawl, proudly riding with her husband and little daughter, Flora,

May's heart leapt. The auction was being held at the house where she was born, which Nellie and she had fled.

May was frightened she would be recognized and expressed fears to Shaune.

'My little dove, ye are not a scrap like that little sparrow Blackie found.'

May was in her sixth month with her second baby, glowing with the bloom of contentment. She remained out of doors, for her little daughter, Flora, wanted to see the penned animals.

A thin wisp of a woman came and knelt, cooing, in front of the baby. Protectively, May moved closer to her child as the woman spoke.

'Forgive me, madam, I envy you such a beautiful child, for I have none.'

She halted and frowned, her eyes burning in their sockets as she stared at May.

'Your features are familiar to me. Have we met before?' May grew tense, picked up her baby and looked around for Shaune.

'I am sure I've seen your likeness before. Ah, yes, I recall.'

May wanted to escape. She, too, had recognized the other person, a mere shadow of a girl who was to marry her half-brother, the owner of the things Nellie had been accused of stealing.

'Could you come with me? I will not take much of your time.'

May thought of excuses to escape, but the words did not come.

The woman held on tight to baby Flora's hand, mounting the front steps of the house just as Shaune appeared, asking where they were going.

May found her voice. 'This lady wants to show me something.' She introduced Shaune to the woman, who said she was now the owner of the place they were entering.

Halfway up the main staircase, the woman pointed to a portrait.

'There, sir, is there not a definite resemblance to your wife?'

Shaune agreed.

'That is an ancestor of my late husband.' Turning to May, she asked, 'Were you perhaps a relative?'

'My wife is of the same bloodline as your husband, madam, on his father's side, I believe.'

May was speechless. This husband of hers amazed her. He was talking like an equal to one she had been afraid to raise her eyes to.

'As soon as I saw the resemblance, I knew. Would you like this portrait? For if, indeed, you are kin, you must be the last of the line.'

May was again most fearful of being recognized, as one of the men lifting down the picture that the lady insisted she should have, was no other then James, the footman, who did not glance up at the comely mother.

She almost burst with pride to see haughty James touch his forelock, pouring forth profuse thanks for the coins Shaune gave him for lifting an old cradle onto the cart. His mistress insisted it was a gift she wanted them to take for the new baby, as it would never be used for future generations of that house. Shaune thanked her.

Riding home, Shaune told May what he had learnt at the auction.

It had taken less than six months to spend the huge dowry the lady had brought with her. The bulk was gambled and spent entertaining the husband, who had contracted more debts and a wasting sexual disease.

While gambling, in a drunken rage, he had almost killed a man who accused him of cheating. He had then run home and killed himself, causing his father to have a stroke and die.

The house, and grounds was so neglected no one bought it. When May's son was a year old, his father, being the son of a soldier who had served with the British, had his request to buy the property at a very low price, granted by the authorities.

Shaune then took his wife back to the house of her

childhood, for their children to inherit the lands of their grandfather.

Mary Gilchrist could not avoid being introduced to Sir Francis Bayard. Staring at her intently, he said, 'I am positive we have met before, my dear.'

Shyly she answered, 'I do not think so, sir.'

Fiona introduced them, giving only the governess's Christian name and occupation.

'May an old man be presumptuous and ask your surname?'

Blushing, she told him it was Gilchrist.

'Your mother's surname would not be the same as mine, would it, by any chance?'

Fiona and Victor Peckway gasped. As Mary ran away, they heard a tearful 'Yes.'

'Please come back! I have searched too long for you, dear niece.'

But instead she ran to her father, to tell him she had disobeyed him.

Sir Francis eventually persuaded Major Gilchrist to speak with him. He told the old gentleman that he had searched extensively for his sister, who had eloped with him on the day of her arranged marriage to the man her parents had chosen.

'Our mother, who your daughter so resembles, went to her grave crying for your wife, and longed to have her close. She made me promise to search for you and your family, to beg your forgiveness.

'I inherited my father's title when you eloped, for our strict father died of shock, that day.'

Within days, the two brothers-in-law became friends, and Sir Francis asked them to come and live with him, and he wanted to provide for them.

Bruce Peel, the Art master, came on a visit to see if there was news of his ex-pupil, Phillip. Everyone was excited that a family had been reunited.

Mary asked Mr Peel his advice on her move to London. Plucking up courage, he told her that if he had better prospects, he would beg her to stay and become his wife.

Major Gilchrist was not at all pleased about his daughter, Mary, wishing to marry an impoverished tutor. He seemed unaware that his circumstances were only better through the goodness of the family that engaged her and housed them. And now that his brother-in-law, Sir Francis, had promised to provide for himself and his daughter, their fortunes could be much improved again.

Mary was heart-broken, for she had often thought of her future as a lonely spinster, caring, if she were lucky, for other people's children, when she would have longed to have her own.

In the eight days he had stayed with the McCalls, Sir Francis felt as if he were experiencing a completely new life. The gout had all but gone, and he had found a niece who reminded him so much of the older sister he had loved so much, and searched for so long.

Mary's sadness hurt him, and he asked her permission to speak to Bruce Peel to get his own impression of the chap.

The following weekend, Bruce and Sir Francis talked for many hours, until William joined them. William said he and his wife were upset at seeing two people they admired and liked so much, so sad. They had no business or right to interfere, but if they could be of any assistance or support, they would be happy to help, as would Fiona and the rest of the staff.

A little more discussion went on between the three men, then Sir Francis went to see Major Gilchrist.

After the initial greeting, Sir Francis spoke rather bluntly.

'Do you remember what ye felt when ye were forbidden to marry my sister, Margarita, John?'

'Of course I do. I thought my very life would end and the feelings of inadequacy and frustration, of not being worthy of Margarita's love, all but destroyed me. I still blame myself today for the sacrifices she made, and I wanted much more for my Mary.'

'Oh, you are happy that she should spend the rest of her life a lonely spinster, serving and teaching others?'

'But the life you offered us with you would surely not be a lonely life for her?'

'My dear brother, now that we have found each other, do not let us argue. All I want to do is prevent anyone making the very mistake my parents regretted until their death, losing their only daughter by standing in the way of her happiness.

'I feel I cannot bear another family split. Just think for a moment of sweet Mary, when we are dead, as die we must.'

'If I could be sure her future were secure, I would gladly give my blessing.'

'Thank ye, that is all I wanted to know. We must all put our heads and hearts together and see what we can come up with.'

Father and uncle sat with the couple, who glowed with happiness just at knowing the affair was being discussed, and at being asked about their future.

Bruce said that as they were both teachers, the obvious thing to do was get a teaching post together, but it would be difficult because the sexes were segregated. He was not agreeable for Mary to take a position where her active mind would not be used to capacity, for that would, indeed, be a waste.

'Have ye thought of starting a school of your own, my lad?' asked Sir Francis.

'It would be my dream come true, to do that, sir, but I am afraid it would be impossible.'

'What are the drawbacks? I know it would take a great deal of money, and ye would need a suitable property. We will have no problems made, but I can help somewhat, financially, and try to get a few of my friends to invest, if it could be proven to be a feasible undertaking.'

William and Alice were thrilled to hear the Major had given his consent for the engagement of his daughter to their friend, Bruce Peel.

When William was told of the idea of starting a school, he was quite excited and promised to give his support, if they would allow him. He would like to ask the advice of Mr Savage, his legal adviser, who had been so immensely helpful to him.

Alice declared she did not know what she would do about the children's education if Mary left them.

Both Mary and Bruce said that if they were lucky enough to have a school of their own, they would be only too pleased to have the children as their first pupils.

Victor Peckway had to leave to see to his business. He had stayed over-long because of meeting, and talking with, Fiona, and Sir Francis having the treatment for his gout.

Victor had been invited to stay at the McCall home, but had elected to stay at an inn where he had already booked rooms.

Sir Francis was returning to London, sad that he was unable to persuade his brother-in-law or Fiona to go back with him.

Fiona, in particular, he had wanted to take, wishing to show his appreciation by treating her to shows and exhibitions, and he had especially wanted to introduce her to doctors who had extracted huge fees from him, without procuring the wondrous results she had.

Fiona confided in Matt that what she had learnt about her daughter had, as she put it, 'taken the heart oot o' her'.

When William and Tug found her by her husband's grave, she thought her life was over, never wanting to see her daughter again. But a longing came over her to be with Nellie once again, to try to get her to grant her mother forgiveness.

Victor Peckway called back on a short visit, en route to his home from London, where he had been concluding the business left unfinished the previous time, when travelling with Sir Francis.

This time, William insisted he should stay the night at their home. Matt, carrying Victor's case up to the guest room, asked if he could have a quiet word with him.

"'Tis mistress Fiona, sir. She be sorely troubled, and has a longing to see her daughter again, for her believes it be her fault that Nellie be as she is.'

'That is utter nonsense. There are others who are more to blame, and Nellie is her own worst enemy. She has spurned those who would help her.'

Victor told how he had found out Nellie was very ill. Believing she had a terrible disease, and pitying her, he had had her taken from the hovel where she dwelt, putting her in a small house outside of the town, with a woman called Sally, another unfortunate, to attend her.

The doctor Victor had brought in to treat Nellie, was appalled by her condition, and emphatically denied she was suffering from any disease, diagnosing the discharge she had as the result of pure neglect, and the ill-treatment of her wasted body.

Andrew Savage came to see William at his factory, with the news that he thought he might have found the right property for Bruce and Mary's school. It stood in its own undeveloped grounds, not three miles from Wychwood house, William's present home.

Andrew said he had had great trouble finding out who owned the property named Madison Manor. He had thought the name familiar, knowing that he had seen it mentioned somewhere.

Going through papers belonging to Alice's late father, Amos Ogilvy, he came across a deed of purchase for Madison Manor, bought by the rascally agent for himself, forging Amos's signature, and using his funds to buy it. It would take months of legal wrangling, but he was positive the property would be returned to its rightful owner, Mrs McCall.

The legalities did not take as long as expected, as Sir Francis acted on their behalf to get the matter settled in less than six months.

Bruce Peel gave notice to leave his employment, and within one year, the Madison Academy for boys and girls, opened its doors.

Fiona was not at Mary's wedding, for Victor Peckway came

to ask her to go with him to see a sick person who was asking for her.

On the journey north, Fiona shed many tears, thanking the merchant for all his trouble.

He, in turn, confessed he was the man supposed to have fathered Nellie's child, althought Nellie had told him many times that he was too drunk that night, to take advantage of her. The wife who had trapped him into marriage, fell from her horse and died. The guilt he carried about Nellie, and his unwitting involvement in a murder, would stay with him for the rest of his days.

Wychwood was very quiet during the day, for the children were at school, and Fiona had not been herself at all since her return home, having stood, with Victor Peckway supporting her, at her daughter's graveside.

For a whole month she had stayed in the same room as Helen, she refusing to call her by the name given at that evil place.

Helen had wanted to know what her father was like, and Fiona never tired of telling her about her baby days, and how she had been loved by all around her.

She had cried out in anguish, relating how her dear Edward had died, and how, for a while, she had existed in a dream world, believing all she held dear to have perished.

Mother and daughter had begged one another's forgiveness, each granting it to the other.

Helen had died peacefully, with two people who cared for her holding her hands.

Florrie was sitting with Fiona, when suddenly Fiona said, 'The only thing that be keepin' I alive, is tae see my boy come home safe and sound.'

Next morning, Florrie thought that Fiona's wish had been denied, and she had died. Old Martha came to Florrie's cry of distress, holding a polished tray up to Fiona's mouth, and crying, 'The Lord be praised, she be still breathing.'

The doctor brought by William said Fiona had suffered a stroke. She was nursed with the greatest care and love, the only hard words spoken being when Alice ordered Florrie to take a well-deserved rest from her vigil, and let her, or someone else, attend to their old friend.

Fiona became agitated when the children were driven from her room, but was obviously happy when they were allowed to stay for short periods.

32

Phillip and Robert's ship remained off the coast of Alexandria. The ship's surgeon, Charles White, took Phillip under his wing, and spent many hours with him, cataloguing Fiona's herbs and their uses.

When going ashore, Surgeon White always asked for Phillip and Robert to accompany him. Together they would purchase herbs they knew of, and some which they had no knowledge of, using an interpreter to ask the natives their names and uses. These were added to the catalogue, and the doctor's own record.

Phillip wished to learn as much as possible about seamanship, working hard at the duties allocated to him, and showed such enthusiasm he gained the respect of all his fellow shipmates.

At last they were told they were going home. He was now in his fifteenth year, his hair bleached by the sun, and his skin bronzed. A letter was dispatched straight away to his parents, telling them he was coming home.

William, on receiving it, immediately sent a reply to his son, saying that Fiona was very ill, and asking for him. Enclosed also were instructions to contact his friend, Gabriel Foley, at the Jolly Mariner tavern, Portsmouth, who would arrange finance forthwith, and provide him with all he needed for the journey.

As soon as Phillip's ship was in port, a much bruised Davey Wells came to watch, holding up a board with the name Phillip T J McCall written on it.

Davey became concerned when sailors passed him, shaking

their heads, saying there was no one of that name aboard their ship.

An officer and two young men came down the quay towards Davey. The youngest, a lanky, fair-haired lad, stopped in front of him, and asked what business he had with Mr McCall.

'Beg your pardon, sir, I have letters here from his father, and I am to take him to a certain place.'

The officer said he thought he knew Davey, inquiring if he were the clerk of the rascal, Thadious Tully.

'That be right, sir, but this has nought to do with him. I be sent by Master Gabriel Foley of the Jolly Mariner.'

The surgeon, Phillip's friend, was the officer and told him, 'It be alright, lad, if this man be sent by Master Foley, ye can trust him.'

All young seamen had been warned to be careful on shore, not to go off with strangers, and to avoid strange places where the press-gang might hang about.

When the doctor had first seen Phillip's injured back, he asked was it his father who had whipped him. Phillip had strongly defended his father, declaring him to be the kindest, most generous man in the world, who, with Tug Wilson, had first introduced him to sailing, encouraging his love of the sea.

When asked why, at first, he had seemed reluctant to go home, Phillip explained his fear that his father wanted him to follow in his footsteps, and work in the factory, he being the elder son.

Introducing himself to Davey, who asked the officer to verify that he was, indeed, Phillip McCall, Davey gave him the letters from his father.

Reading them there and then, Phillip said he must make haste to go home, for Fiona was very ill. The doctor and Robert Murray knew well who Fiona was, for Phillip had spoken many times of how she had cared for, and loved him since the day he was born.

No one spoke until they reached the Jolly Mariner, where Gabriel greeted them cordially, saying he was pleased to meet at last the son of, as he called William, 'a genleman o'the first water, he was glad to have made the acquaintance of'.

Will Turtle was introduced to Phillip and he, in his turn, introduced Robert as his very best friend, and shipmate.

Shipmate. Phillip could hardly believe he had said this, and in the hours that followed he began to understand why Nelson called the men the Band of Brothers, as he experienced the feeling of comradeship among naval men.

Bo'sun Arthur Gammon turned up suddenly, and greeted Gabriel like a brother.

Gabriel asked him, 'How be your son, Arthur.' With a sob in his voice, Bo'sun Gammon told him that his eldest son was killed while fighting with Admiral Jervis, at Brest.

'Ay, bad luck, but leastways he was wi' folk o' his own kind, not shackled in some scurvy hulk somewhere.'

Arthur Gammon junior, at the age of seventeen, had been saved by Davey Wells, Gabriel, Will Turtle and Co from being shanghaied after a visit to the offices of Thadious Tully.

The bo'sun would have liked to settle with the agent, but had been stopped by Gabriel and friends, and told he would get his come-uppance as soon as their ship had left, and it wouldn't be the navy to blame. A few days later, Thadious Tully was found beaten near to death.

The surgeon, on examining the bruises on Davey's face, was told they were the handiwork of his employer. Gabriel and Will Turtle said it was time the man Tully was taught another lesson.

Davey asked if he could travel with Phillip and Robert, as the beating he had received was the result of Thadious Tully discovering, at last, that it was Davey who had been leaking information about pending hijackings. No longer would he be in a position to prevent others from getting kidnapped.

The little Welsh cob mare, Sian, was happy as Davey held the reins for her to pull the cart Gabriel's sister, Maggie, had loaded up with goodies. She had even remembered bundles of hay for animal feed, while Robert now lounged on.

Phillip rode the other mare named Beauty, not for her looks, but for her placid temperament. She had been

Gabriel's horse, and at one time he had ridden her on a specially designed saddle. Stiffness in his limbs now prevented this, and she, having little or no exercise, had grown fat.

The boys had also been provided with weapons. A fine brace of pistols had been presented to them by the surgeon, with ammunition and instructions to keep them clean, and, whilst travelling, always loaded.

Gabriel had also given them a pistol and a sword of fine Toledo steel, and sent many warm greetings to Phillip's father.

Not to be outdone, Will Turtle brought a musket as a parting gift for them.

They had had a very early start, and were well on the way to Exeter. Travelling uphill, they stopped to rest the horses. The road was narrow with a clear stream running down one side, and sweet grass for the horses to feed on.

They too, decided to eat, and tucked into some broiled bacon and rolls Maggie had packed, finishing off with an apple each. They fed the cores to the horses, two for Sian, for she had worked the hardest, and one for Beauty.

When they arrived at a turnpike road, the keeper demanded a halfpenny for each man, and twopence for the horses and cart, but Davey pleaded they only had twopence between them, and the boys were not fully grown men. The man argued that it was not enough.

Davey leant back, whispering to Robert he had been this way before, and in a loud voice said, 'We will have to turn and go back.' With great fuss and awkwardness they tried to turn in the narrow road.

A coach with the driver and footman dressed in elegant livery drew up behind them. A large, bewigged head appeared out of the coach window, its owner shouting to them to get out of his way, for he was in a tremendous hurry. His purple face looked as if he were about to have a fit, as he screamed he would pay double if they could be moved out of his path. The coach had drawn up close to the boys, making it almost impossible to execute the turn.

The irate keeper, cursing, snatched the twopence and lifted the barrier, telling them to get out the road of their betters.

The road was wider this side, and the keeper's wife stood with filled buckets of water for horses, and mugs of homebrew ready to sell.

Davey pulled up to allow the coach to rush past. The sullen woman screamed at them to clear off, as the horses slurped in a pail of water.

A mile further on, the elegant coach, with its occupant lay on its side in a deep ditch filled with water. Its legs twisted and broken, one horse lay under the other wild-eyed beast as it struggled and kicked out at the coachman's bloodied body that had fallen between the shafts.

With difficulty, Robert at last pulled open the coach door, and heaved himself up. Inside, the occupant was upside down, his head in mud that had seeped through. His nose was in the mire, but luckily something was holding his mouth a fraction above the slurry.

Calling to Phillip and Davey to hold his feet, Robert leant further into the coach. With a slat from the seat he wedged a floating cushion under the head to raise it further upward to prevent drowning.

After pausing for breath, he managed to put another cushion under the first one then, with the shoulders in sight, put a hand under each armpit and pulled, telling Davey and Phillip to do the same.

The large man lay half-in and half-out of the doorway. They could see from the rise and fall of his barrel chest that he was breathing, as he was lifted out and put down on the grass verge opposite.

Davey placed his jacket over the head of the frightened horse. He and Robert freed it from the traces and helped it scramble out of the mud, apparently uninjured. They led it to be tethered to a bush on the other side of the road.

A pistol was placed to the head of the poor injured beast, whose legs hung loosely where its partner had fallen and kicked them. Robert looked away from its gleaming white eyes, as he pressed the trigger.

Nothing could be done for the coachman. Sian and Beauty were brought and fastened to the coach, and Robert and Davey coaxed them to drag it back onto the road. Mud-spattered and scratched, it seemed otherwise intact.

Phillip had been attending to the man, bathing him with water from their own drinking barrel.

The stout man regained consciousness, looking confused and asking who they were. Phillip explained that he had been in an accident, and was sorry to have to tell him his coachman was dead, as well as one of his horses. Phillip pointed to the bodies lying a few yards away.

The man complained his head hurt. Phillip gave him a drink. 'Sip this slowly, sir, it will do you good.'

'By Gad, sir, this reaches a spot. There be somethin' in this besides water.'

'Just a spot of navy rum, sir.'

Phillip swelled with pride when the man said, 'I thought ye were a service chap, by yer gib, ye and yon big chap. Gad, my head hurts.'

Phillip remembered, they had crossed over a river bridge just before coming on to the overturned coach. The road then veered sharply to the left, with a steep bank where trees grew with their thick roots spreading into the road and out of sight.

It had rained heavily in the last few days, the torrential water having washed away the road surface, leaving the roots standing proud.

The wheels of the speeding coach, careering over the bridge and turning sharply, caught against the roots. The coach had overbalanced, tipping into the ditch, pulling the horses with it.

Not wanting to use much more of their drinking water, Phillip went back to the river, where he carefully made his way down the slippery bank. He held the dock leaves he had picked on the way, in the brown water to cool. These he wrapped in his own cravat, then returned and bound up the cut on the man's head.

Thanking him, the man asked, 'Where be Henry, my footman?' No one had seen Henry since leaving the toll-gate, where he had been sighted clinging to the swaying coach.

Davey and Robert went in search of the footman. The cart and the coach had been drawn off the road onto a small piece of ground a little way from the scene of the accident.

The horses grazed on grass, fresh after the rain. The gelding, now calm, sniffed at the two mares, who were quite unconcerned.

Robert and Davey walked slowly back the way they had come, searching either side of the road and finding nothing.

Then, on the right-hand side they noticed a gate a little way past the site of the accident. Probing the mud with sticks, they searched the ditch.

Robert spied a fragment of material caught on top of the high hawthorn hedge. As he called to Davey, he heard a muffled cry for help coming from the other side of the hedge. On their side, the ditch was wide and deep, so they were unable to see over the hedge.

They raced back to the gate and climbed over it into a boggy field which had been churned up by hooves. From the far left-hand corner, they could see two dozen or more heifers slowly moving towards the hedge bordering the ditch.

The cries for help were getting more hysterical, and they made out a mud-spattered figure, down on all fours in the sludge, working his way towards them.

The cattle, having recovered from the shock of having a strange object hurtle into their domain, were now on their inquisitive way to investigate it.

Dragging their feet in the squelching mud, and waving their arms and shouting to scare off the animals, Robert and Davey reached the prostrate man.

Tired of the attention from the gelding, Sian had got loose and strayed. Phillip went to retrieve her. He found her drinking from a clear brook bubbling through a little rock-strewn clearing, less than 20 metres further up the road.

With abundant water, washing off the mud was no problem.

A fire was lit to dry them. The stout man had said he was Sir Ralph Lifton, and complained he felt strange. Davey told him it was shock and he must lie still.

Telling them he was in sore need of food, the man requested a large hamper of food from under the driving seat of his coach. Alas, along with the driver it had fallen into the deep mud of the ditch, and was trampled, the food mixed with the broken glass of the wine bottles, and fine crystal goblets.

They brought out Maggie's home-made cheese, strawberry jam and bread, serving the two survivors first. Sir Ralph found he could not use his right arm, and complained of great pain.

He cursed himself for his haste and felt deeply responsible for the death of his coachman, and a fine horse.

Phillip asked if he could look at his arm. Gently, he and Robert withdrew the left arm from the sleeve of Sir Ralph's tight jacket. Their attempts to withdraw the right arm were far too painful, so they asked permission to cut away the sleeve.

'If ye can ease the pain, as ye eased the pain in my head, cut away. Just leave enough to cover my modesty.' He laughed nervously to hide his discomfort.

With a sharp knife, Davey cut up the stitching of the cloth, trying not to damage the rich material of the jacket.

Sir Ralph's shirt was less trouble to remove, for it had voluminous sleeves. Henry, the footman, was asked to give his master drinks from a stone jar of rum.

Robert said he had seen this injury before, and had helped to put it right. 'It be called dislocation and has to be pulled back to place.'

Sir Ralph's elbow joint could be clearly seen sticking out at right angles. His hand hung limp, the broken wrist bone pushing its way through his skin.

They decided to attempt to pull the dislocation and the broken wrist back into place at the same time.

Phillip was amazed by Davey's fortitude. Having driven all the way from Portsmouth, he had then directed the righting of the coach. And now he was taking command of this operation.

Davey told Henry he was much stronger than himself. Would he mind if he took over the task of giving rum to Sir Ralph as they needed Henry's strength elsewhere.

Sir Ralph, now very drunk, was carried and put to sit with his back against a tree, a rope under his armpits binding him firmly to the trunk.

Near him, at the ready, lay flat pieces of wood obtained from the coach, his own cummerbund, a pile of muddy clay and dock leaves, and some mashed potato.

Henry sat behind the tree, his legs apart, arms stretched, ready to hold the bound man's shoulder still.

Robert sat at Sir Ralph's feet, facing him, his own feet planted firmly in the patient's armpits. With a deep breath, he heaved until both joints clicked into place.

Pulped potato on leaves was applied to the wrist, and the arm was plastered with mud and held straight by wood slats strapped to Sir Ralph's chest.

He was oblivious of all things as he had passed out.

Sir Ralph was unbound and his shirt and jacket replaced, the right sleeves stretched across, and fastened to his left shoulder.

They made a hot drink as Sir Ralph was coming around. Henry was forcing him to take a sip, when he vomited.

Davey jumped up to assist, but Henry pompously brushed him aside, for he thought he was of a better class than these rough fellows. Was he not Henry Smith, footman in the service of a county magistrate, owner of a large residence in the town of Wells, who was also squire of a big country estate at Lifton?

He felt embarrassment at being rescued by them, they seeing his lack of decorum and courage, wallowing in the field of cattle.

The afternoon was almost over. Davey and the boys had decided it was best to make camp there, where there was fresh water and grazing for the horses.

They emptied the coach of seat cushions, now fairly dry and brushed free of mud, putting them under and behind their owner for his comfort.

Henry, refusing to prepare his master for sleep, said it would be better if they were at an inn, and there *was* such an inn, but a few miles further on.

He refused to listen to arguments that it was getting late, the coach was too heavy for the one horse, or the possibility they might be attacked.

'Our beast is a thoroughbred, not like your poor animals, and no one would dare to attack our coach, for the emblem crest on its doors is known far and wide.'

The still dazed Sir Ralph was fastened in and surrounded with soft articles. The coach was stripped of all unnecessary weight, and Henry climbed up, haughtily taking the reins. Without a word of thanks or a backward glance, he whipped the horse into a gallop.

Davey was worried, knowing the roads were narrow and dangerous, the haunt of footpads and highwaymen. They all agreed they must follow the coach as fast as possible.

Breaking camp, they collected things removed from the coach to lighten the load; a chest with the lock intact, and another which had broken open, spilling sealed documents that Davey reckoned looked important. They were gathered in a sack and put on the cart with as much else as they could safely carry. The body of the coach driver, which Henry had refused to take, was tied across Beauty's back.

Davey hurried, leading Sian with one hand, and holding a pistol in the other. Phillip, running alongside the cart, held two loaded pistols. Robert brought up the rear, leading Beauty and holding Gabriel's unsheathed sword.

Will Turtle's primed musket was strapped across the dead man's back, together with a musket found in the coach along with two pistols that Robert had cleaned, oiled and offered to Henry, who had refused them. The pistols Robert now stuck in the belt around his waist.

Steadily for half an hour they progressed, descending one hill to arrive at the bottom of another.

The road curved to the right at the top of the hill, the way ahead obscured by trees covering the high banks on each side.

They arrived at the bend in the road at the top of the hill, almost colliding with Sir Ralph's stationary coach.

Up on the driver's seat, a figure pulled at the limp Henry's clothing and Davey took aim, firing a bullet that ripped through the robber's thigh.

Sir Ralph lay in the road, a ruffian standing astride him, holding a long knife to his throat.

Phillip rushed forward. Raising a pistol he fired at the man astride Sir Ralph, just as he threw himself to the left. The bullet narrowly missed him. The man lunged towards Phillip with his knife, the blade slashing through his breeches.

Phillip stooped to hold his leg. There was an explosion and a flash of light, as the ball from the smoking musket Robert held, whistled above him, striking his attacker as he raised his knife to slash at the boy again.

The still drunk and unsteady lord, appeared to have sustained no other injuries.

Sian again took it into her head to wander. Pulling the loaded cart behind her, she pushed her way forward, trotting up the road with Davey chasing after her. He caught up with her in a small hollow, very like the camp they had recently left.

As the robber was pulled down from the coach, he screamed he was bleeding to death. They bound him to his dead companion.

Gently, Henry's body was lowered and carried to the hollow. Robert placed his own jacket over him, to cover the horrible wound in his slashed throat.

The boys took it in turns to stand guard; two slept while one kept a look-out, pistols at the ready.

Davey insisted on taking first watch. Hearing a noise behind him, he knew attack from the rear was nigh impossible, as the hollow was a semi-circle backed by sheer rock, where a little waterfall tumbled down the face.

In the light of the lantern he saw the sound came from Phillip, as he turned uneasily in his sleep, the blood soaking his slashed breeches. He woke Robert, and between them they bathed and bound the deep gash on their friend's leg.

Sir Ralph held his head, moaning. His splints and bandages were still intact. The only new injuries he had suffered were a few extra bruises, but he declared there were little men with hammers banging in his head.

Laughing, Robert told him, 'It be the rum ye were given yesterday that causes that.'

Phillip said he knew of a cure, but needed a clove of garlic and an egg. He already had the other herbs in his pouch.

Davey asked if wild garlic would do, for it grew in those parts, and he knew there was some close by, as he had had a whiff of it during the night. But before he went to look for it, he wanted to discuss something with them.

Davey told them he knew they were but a few hours' ride from the town of Wells, and in his opinion, only two of them, himself and Robert, were fit to ride. One could go to Wells with a message from Sir Ralph, asking for help to fetch them.

This was thought to be an excellent idea with only one drawback. With his injured arm, Sir Ralph was unable to write.

'That's no problem, sir. Ye dictate, I will write but first I will go for the garlic.'

He was away for 15 minutes.

The pot was boiling and Robert was sizzling bacon in a pan. Phillip was in great discomfort from his wound, but he crushed a clove of garlic between two washed stones, scraping it into a tankard with a sprinkle of herbs from his pouch. He then cracked an egg into it, one of many that Maggie had carefully wrapped in straw, and gave it to Sir Ralph, instructing him to drink it straight down.

He swallowed the atrocity, as he called it, and belched loudly.

Sir Ralph thanked his rescuers and, after numerous belches, declared his headache was tolerably better. The herb tea made by Phillip he found most refreshing.

He was delighted to see the documents in the sack, having assumed they were lost. They were of great value to him, he said, having taken months of work to prepare, as they were briefs and case notes.

That was why he was in such a hurry. He was on his way to the assizes, to act as residing magistrate.

A letter was composed on paper from the intact chest, and wax melted for Sir Ralph to place on his seal. He had difficulty removing the crested ring from his finger, wanting to give it to the messenger as proof the letter was authentic. Its tight fit may have saved his life, however, as the robber had wasted minutes trying to remove the ring, instead of killing the wearer first.

When a little bacon grease was applied to the digit, the ring slid off, and was handed to Robert, who had been chosen to ride to Wells.

Sir Ralph told him to go straight to his friend, the Bishop, at his palace in Wells, for it would be easier and quicker than trying to find his residence.

The black gelding was skittish at being mounted by a stranger, and was still a little upset. Davey held the reins, asking Sir Ralph his name. He replied he was not sure, as both his horses were so alike they could be twins. It could be Mavro, the Greek word for 'black', or maybe it was Dancer.

Davey, trying Dancer, had no response. But he tried Mavro while blowing up into his nostrils, and the horse nuzzled him and became calm, happy to let Robert mount him.

33

Robert headed straight for the cathedral spire. He found the cathedral itself easily, it being well-signposted to help the many visiting pilgrims.

At the Bishop's palace, he showed the ring and letter, and explained the urgency.

After a few minutes, Robert was shown into the room of the Bishop's secretary, who issued orders for him to be fed, bathed and given fresh clothes.

A large coach with two drivers was supplied, one of them to drive Sir Ralph's coach, and two spare horses to pull it on the return journey. Four armed servants rode inside.

Robert asked to go with them, to show them the way, and was told the spot was well-known to them, it being Sir Ralph's usual route.

The Bishop sent for Robert, he standing before the cleric, speechless at the grandeur of the surroundings, and the other man's robes. But he was soon put at his ease by a gentle smile.

A ringed, gloved hand beckoned him to sit on a high-backed chair to the right of, what Robert could only describe as, a throne.

The Lord Bishop had been told the clothes Robert wore, when he arrived were those of a seaman.

'You have been to sea, sir, and have you journeyed far?'

Robert told him that he had recently come back from Egypt.

'You were with Lord Nelson at Alexandria?' The clergyman became quite excited, taking up a jewelled bell, which he shook rapidly.

Two footmen hurried into the room, ready to attack Robert.

Waving his hand to calm them, the Bishop gave them instructions then, gracefully rising, he asked Robert to follow him to another room.

The walls of the room were lined with books. Maps were spread on the table. Behind a screen, the Bishop was helped by a servant into simpler robes. Robert heard him instructing the servant to tell his secretary to cancel all appointments.

The secretary came and spoke briefly, begging leave to stay with his master. The Bishop acquiesced, knowing the man shared his interest in seafaring exploits, as they were both West Country men, born and bred in families steeped in centuries of maritime tradition.

They wanted to know all about Robert's journeys, and the smallest details of every battle he had participated in. Had he seen Lord Nelson? What was he really like?

Robert was quite taken aback at some of the questions they asked him, believing holy men should not know of such terrible happenings as war and battles.

In his innocence, he did not realize the Church and religion were the start, and cause, of many battles.

Time flew by, until word came that Sir Ralph Lifton and his party were in the cathedral gounds.

The Bishop greeted his friend, and was introduced to Davey and Phillip, whom he had heard about from Robert.

Sir Ralph was bathed, fed and seen by a medic, who declared that the setting of his fractures was a wonderful piece of doctoring. When told of the medicines given by Phillip, the doctor was keen to meet and converse with him, and was greatly surprised to learn it was the young lad he was also attending who had so much knowledge.

The three companions spent a restful night, each in an elaborate chamber, well-attended by servants.

Within minutes of waking, a large tray of food and beverages was set before them. Davey felt embarrassed, sitting eating and drinking in bed, never having done it before.

He asked could he first get dressed and sit at a table to eat his breakfast. The liveried servant servant went to a large wardrobe, withdrawing a quality jacket of grey serge, soft dark blue breeches and a fine white shirt and underwear, bringing them to Davey, who protested these were not his clothes.

The servant told him these garments were now his, presented with the compliments of his Lordship, at the request of Sir Ralph.

Robert received an apology that the clothes were not of a nautical nature for Phillip and himself, but some had been sent for from the town of Bristol. Perhaps he would not mind wearing ordinary clothes in the meantime.

Robert said he would be glad to wear such fine clothes until his own were returned, assuming they were away being washed.

Robert dressed and ate an excellent breakfast, then asked to be taken to his friends. He was escorted to the room next to his, where Davey was admiring his new apparel.

Both were then conducted down a corridor to a chamber where Phillip lay, pale through loss of blood. He begged them to assist him to get dressed.

A message came that the Bishop and Sir Ralph desired an audience with them as soon as it was convenient to themselves.

They were taken to see Sir Ralph, who sat up in bed, a tasselled nightcap perched on top of a bandage keeping cabbage leaves in place on his forehead. He laughed.

'The leaves your friend used are not to be found in these grounds.' He meant the soaked dock leaves Phillip had placed in his hat and on his head the previous day. 'So I had to have these.'

He wore a large nightshirt with the right sleeve cut away, revealing the original mud-stained cummerbund still in place. 'The doctor thinks ye fellows are marvellous. He wants to confer with ye.' The doctor had told him there was no need to disturb the professional job done on his wrist and arm, unless they bothered him, which they did not.

But his headache, he said, had returned, and the healing

effect of the leaves Phillip had used was so good, that half of the Bishop's staff had been out searching for them.

Sir Ralph told them he had travelled the road where he had been attacked many times before without incident, but his regular driver had been ill, and the new driver was very inexperienced.

Henry had driven the horse so hard for less than a quarter of a mile, it could barely get to the top of the hill. It had stopped at the top, giving the robbers a chance to leap out at them.

The Bishop's men returned without Sir Ralph's coach. As one wheel was badly damaged, a wheelwright would have to go to fit a replacement.

The doctor, accompanied by a colleague, came to ask Davey and Robert what medication had previously been given to the patient.

"Tis Master Phillip ye must ask. He has wondrous knowledge of herbs and the like,' said Robert.

The doctors went to see Phillip and examined his leg wound. It was badly inflamed. As they were debating what to use, Phillip asked them to pass him his personal kit bag.

Both looked on with interest as Phillip withdrew a book and turned to a page on the treatment of inflammation of wounds. Phillip then withdrew a wooden box containing small, labelled bottle and jars, each with a resin or oil in them.

Taking out one jar, he asked if the resin-like substance could be spread on some clean cloth to place on the swollen, discoloured gash.

The doctors asked what it was, and were told the resin was gabanum, from a herb of the fennel species.

The doctors were doubtful about using it, as neither had heard of it before, but Phillip told them all these remedies had been tried and tested, either by Doctor White, the ship's surgeon, or Fiona.

They then wanted to know who Fiona was, and who was T Cole, the name engraved on the box?

Phillip told them about Fiona, and how she used all manner of herbs and household vegetables, such as potato, for ointment and poultices, and as a soother for burns. This catalogue was really for her.

He expressed his hope that he would be able to continue his journey soon, for his beloved Fiona was ill and asking for him.

He explained about the name T Cole, the name by which he was known aboard ship, and how a badly wounded sailor, treated and cared for by himself, had in gratitude made the sandalwood box as a gift, carving the only name he knew Phillip by.

The doctors were fascinated by his catalogue and asked could they borrow it to copy down some of the cures and remedies.

Phillip was reluctant to let it out of his sight, and said that if paper, pens and crayons were given to him, he would copy some of the remedies of their choice, while he was there.

He was most upset to be advised that, on no account, in the doctor's opinion, should he travel for at least a week, with his wound. He made up his mind that as soon as the pain stopped, he would be on his way.

An argument arose between the Bishop and Sir Ralph, who wanted to move, taking his gallant rescuers, as he called them, to his own residence.

The Bishop, on the other hand, wanted them to stay at the palace near him, as he said they were like a breath of fresh, damp air blowing over the desert of dry, ecclesiastical affairs.

The Bishop won the argument, backed by the doctors, who said Sir Ralph and Phillip should take as much rest as possible, and a move, even of a short distance, would not do either a bit of good.

They were all sitting in a large, cheerful lounge where a fire crackled merrily. Sir Ralph, in a damask quilted dressing gown, had a page-boy at his side, who took out, one by one, the documents Davey had put in the sack, and which were now in a leather bag. He held them up for Sir Ralph to scrutinize them.

The two doctors, with Davey, and Phillip who had been

carried there, sat around a table, copying busily from the catalogue.

Phillip drew the diagrams and plants, passing the page to Davey who wrote the description and remedy in his beautiful handwriting on one loose page. Dr Lask and Dr Neeve did the same, on alternate pages, maybe not as well, but discernible, and delighting them both.

The two doctors declared they had not enjoyed themselves so much since nursery days, laughing as though their sides would burst at some diagrams; so much so, that the Bishop and Sir Ralph demanded to see them too.

The Bishop was deep in conversation with Robert as they pored over papers and maps. A man brought in more documents for Sir Ralph. After reading them, he became quite excited, almost shouting, 'I have news for ye, my bonny heroes. The two villains ye captured had a bounty on their heads of 50 guineas each, dead or alive. The murderous rascals were brothers, Asaph and Cabel Smith, who have evaded justice and been the curse of travellers for many years. As ye captured them, the reward of 100 guineas is yours.' He did not say that he was going to add an extra 50 guineas for saving his life and for the care they had given him.

They protested at being offered this reward, saying the hospitality they were receiving was more than enough payment.

Sir Ralph said the reward was little enough to be paid for getting rid of scum the likes of the brothers. There was also a strong belief the wounded man, Asaph Smith, was dying of his wound, so that would save the cost of bringing him to justice.

Sir Ralph looked at Davey's beautiful handwriting, and asked if he would consider taking a post with him as his personal secretary and clerk. Davey said he did not think he had the necessary experience to be capable of doing the job.

'Capable, with this fine hand? The chap that does the work now has writing so illegible, a few months ago I almost sentenced the accuser instead of the accused, through his abominable scribble.'

Both Robert and Phillip urged Davey to take the position offered, convinced there was no obstacle he could not overcome.

Sir Ralph presented them with horses for their journey.

The Bishop gave each a golden medal, telling them to show them at any religious place, and they would be granted shelter. He gave them, too, a list of places to which he had already sent couriers to arrange for their especial comfort.

At dawn, Phillip and Robert, helped by a couple of stalwart grooms, mounted two of the four saddled horses.

Waving goodbye, Davey promised he would return to Portsmouth, taking back the cart and two horses, Sian and Beauty.

By mid-morning they had arrived at Hereford.

At Runcorn Abbey, they took their supper. Robert helped Phillip to attend to his leg, applying the fresh dressing, supplied by the grateful doctors. The old dressing had stuck to the skin, for the deep wound had reopened.

The next night's stop was Penrith. All four were weary. And Robert and Phillip were not accustomed to long journeys on horseback. Phillip tried hard not to show his pain, so as not to slow down the journey.

They arrived at Peebles sooner than the couriers sent before them. They showed their medals and the monks let them in, although not forewarned of their arrival.

It was a very poor order, but the guests were given the pick of the meagre food by the monks in threadbare habits, who seemed to eat very little themselves. Phillip was taken by a barefoot monk to a narrow cell, and sank gratefully onto the pallet. He asked if he could have a bowl of water. This confused his young guide, who had seen him wash at the pump outside, but he returned with the bowl of water as requested.

He pulled the door behind him, but peering in at the grille, saw Phillip struggle with his breeches to remove them, and then unwind a wet and sticky bandage.

The young monk hurried away to bring an older man, and

knocking, they entered. Phillip was given a draught, then told to lie back while they bathed his wound. He felt drowsy as, carefully, the stitches were cut and plucked away, before they liberally applied ointment.

Phillip, asleep, was unaware of the two figures kneeling in prayer all through that night. It was late morning when he awoke, his mouth dry. He was given lime-water to drink and gently pushed to the pillow when he attempted to rise.

'It is late. Where are my friends?' he croaked.

His companion smiled, signalling with his hand for him to stay. He returned later with the older monk, who had attended Phillip the night before. They brought Robert with them, and he told Phillip his wound was infected. The monks were a silent order, and not allowed to speak.

They brought yet another dressing, and motioned that they would like to change the old one.

Strangely, Phillip felt no pain as they attended to him. They offered more prayers, and then left the two friends together.

Making sure they had really gone, Robert tipped out a pouch, and a shower of gold coins fell onto the bed.

'There be 50 guineas.'

The pouch Sir Ralph had given to Phillip contained the same amount. Although Phillip was desperate to move on, Robert persuaded him they should spend an extra night at Peebles.

Richard and John, the grooms, had gone in search of the couriers, finding them at an inn the worse for drink. They beat them, taking the little money the trollops out to rob them had been unable to find, and told them to make their own way south, if they dared, on foot.

Richard and John waited at the monastery gates, with the two extra horses taken from the couriers.

Phillip and Robert left, having thanked their hosts. They paused only to drop some coins into the charity box outside.

The monks prayed for their safety, giving thanks to the Lord for sending them travellers who could leave two golden guineas.

The grooms decided they would journey all the way. The four arrived at Phillip's home to a tumultuous welcome.

William, with tears in his eyes, hugged his son, thinking the boy was suddenly a man.

Aimee and young William were delirious.

Florrie, as usual, threw her apron over her head, and cried.

Alice collapsed onto the nearest chair.

Phillip introduced his friends, and was introduced to Matt and the others.

His father guessed he was afraid to ask after Fiona.

'First refresh yourself, then we will go up together to see Fiona, who has been waiting, and praying, for you to come.' Tears sprang to Phillip's eyes.

Evening was approaching, for it had been late afternoon when they arrived. Florrie held the lamp to light the way upstairs, as Phillip followed.

Florrie softly opened the door to the bedroom, and a weak voice came from the piled pillows, 'Be that ye, Florrie?'

Florrie answered, saying, 'I have bought someone tae see ye.'

'Hold up the light, my lass, for I tae see.'

Florrie held the lamp so that the light fell on Phillip's face. He leaned over the bed and said, "Tis I, your own boy, come back from the sea.'

The weak eyes searched his features, and spidery, transparent fingers touched his cheek, as she sobbed.

'It is my ain sweet laddie, growed. I would know ye anywhere. 'Tis dreaming that I be.'

'No, sweet mother, I am really here.' Phillip kissed the palm of her raised hand and reached for the other, that lay motionless on the bed cover.

Travel-stained as he was, Phillip stayed with her until Florrie returned with some chicken soup. Phillip spoon-fed her, one spoon for her, one for him. She told him this was the way she used to get him to eat when he was little, and he hushed her to stop tiring herself by talking.

When she had swallowed a little, she begged him not to

leave yet awhile, for her to have a little sleep, and asked, 'Did I hear ye right, did ye call me mother?'

'Aye little mother, for that is what you will always be to me. Rest now, as I shall not be far away for we have lots to talk about, and you have yet to meet my friend.'

'Stay and have a little prayer wi' me to thank the dear Lord, that he has let me see ye grown into a man, and tae be able tae tell thee that ye have been the light of my eyes, the very beat of my heart, from the day of your birth.'

Phillip held her hands until Florrie gently eased them free as Fiona slept.

Phillip had written to his father about Robert; how he had befriended him, and even taken a whipping on his account.

After they had refreshed themselves by washing, Phillip noticed that his wound seemed to have improved since the stitches had been removed by the monks.

William sat in the kitchen, where Phillip had asked for food to be put out for them, and shared with the Bishop's grooms, John and Richard.

They, hearing mention of Fiona, said it was strange, but that was the name of the lady who had been the benefactor of their parents, who had often told the story of her bounty to them. But then, Fiona was a common name in Scotland. It was too much of a coincidence.

Alice, Phillip's mother, however, had a recollection of Fiona saying she had travelled for a while with young newlyweds on her way back from France many years before, and that she had kept herself dirty and clothed in rags.

Richard became quite excited. 'It must be the same one. There cannot be two the like of her, for my ma often told how their Fiona did roll in a pigsty to cover herself with filth, to protect herself when they had to leave her company.'

He pleaded to be allowed to see Fiona, to pass on the blessings and regards of his parents, and to tell her they had given his sister the name Fiona, in her honour.

Tug and Matt came in, listening while William asked many questions. At last Alice put her foot down, declaring, 'Enough is enough! These lads must be dead on their feet.'

The three young ones, Aimee, Kate and young William, had already curled up together like kittens, fast asleep on a rug.

Florrie slept in Fiona's room, attending to her every need, constantly massaging her heels, buttocks and shoulders with alcohol, then oil, to keep away bed-sores.

Fiona smelt of lavender and rose-water as Phillip kissed her cheek. She told him that he being there was the best tonic she could have.

Phillip brought Robert to see her. She said she liked his looks, and made him promise always to be a friend to her lad, and look after him. Robert gave his solemn oath he would.

Robert had a long journey yet in front of him to the Northern Isles, in the hope that his mother and sisters had survived the hardships of their mean existence. They had begged him to leave them to make a life for himself and if he succeeded, to return to them.

With the reward money and his savings, he felt, for the first time, he had enough to go and take them away from the privations that had killed his father.

The groom, Richard, came to see Fiona. Seeing him, she said he had the likeness of someone she had met.

Richard asked her, did she recall a time when she had nursed a girl, giving her back her health, and providing her with the means to a happy marriage?

She did, for her memory was far from impaired. She was pleased to hear she had another namesake, and that the family prospered.

That evening, she asked William and Phillip if they would sit with her. She quietly thanked her employer for being such a good friend to her, asking him, could all the children, Tug and Alice come to her to say goodnight?

All came. Phillip held her hand, and Florrie sat quietly in the shadows, until Phillip called her softly, to say that Fiona had slipped into her last sleep.

Richard and John had said their thanks and goodbyes,

taking with them huge amounts of food, letters of thanks to Sir Ralph and the Bishop, and also letters to Portsmouth friends.

Phillip wrote to Davey with a footnote from Robert, wishing him the best of fortune, in the fervent hope that one day they would meet again.

Robert and Phillip stood at Fiona's graveside. They vowed, as together they threw in a little wooden cross, to keep the promise made to her, to be friends forever.

Robert asked Mr McCall, would he allow him to call and see him should he come that way again? William told him he would always be welcome.

Two weeks after Fiona's funeral, Phillip told his father he could not stay at home much longer, for the only life for him was on the sea.

Far from being disappointed, William was proud of the way his son had matured. But he asked him to wait until he had contacted Sir Francis Bayard, to see if he had any influence to get Phillip into a naval college.

A few years later, Phillip and Robert were side-by-side at Trafalgar.

William felt his dreams were now being fulfilled by his son.